JOSEPH

Titles available in this series

Yannis
Anna
Giovanni
Joseph

JOSEPH

Beryl Darby

Copyright © Beryl Darby 2009

ISBN 978-0-9554278-3-1

Printed and bound in Great Britain by
MPG Biddles Limited, King's Lynn, Norfolk

First published in the UK in 2009 by

JACH Publishing
92 Upper North Street, Brighton, East Sussex, England BN1 3FJ

website: www.beryldarby.co.uk

For Chantelle who gave unstintingly of her time
to show me every inch of Rhodes.
Without you I would not have had the information
for this book. Thank you for your help and support,
and thank you most of all for being my daughter.

Reviews for *Yannis* – the first title in the series

The Daily Mail (National Newspaper)

Yannis makes for a most interesting and enjoyable read.

Evening Argus (Local Newspaper)

Brighton based Beryl Darby is a compulsive writer and *Yannis* is the first of six novels she has written about the same Cretan family. Her saga is built around actual events in the island's history, although the characters are fictitious.

Essentially Worthing (Local Magazine)

A gripping read. You'll get hooked into the atmosphere of this exciting and sometimes harrowing tale, based on actual happenings at the leper colony of Spinalonga near Crete.

C.M.P.C.A (Local Area Magazine)

This is a chilling story, and even more disturbing because it all actually happened. But while everything certainly doesn't end happily ever after, you are not left sad. In fact, after living through the many triumphs and tragedies of these people for 700 odd pages, you are sorry to bid them farewell. Beryl has a comfortable style, an acute ear for dialogue, and total mastery of her subject. *Yannis* works on many levels: it tells a story too long untold, depicts a Greece few of us know at all – with human emotions at their most intense. I promise, once you've been drawn into this close Cretan community you'll be hooked.

Written by D. Shorley FCLIP Sussex University

Uckfield Lending Library (Michael Hollands)

I asked the library to buy *Yannis* and finished it at Easter. I thought it was absolutely wonderful how you got into the minds and situations of the characters and brought it all so vividly to life. There were moments that were really moving.

Ian Rees – Elektros Bookshop, Elounda

A remarkable read, I was unable to put the book down.

Readers' Reviews for Yannis

I started to read *Yannis* at 9.00 p.m. and when I lifted my eyes from it the time was 3.00 a.m.!!

* * *

Thank you so much for such a lovely story. I don't have a lot of time to read, but I couldn't put *Yannis* down.

* * *

Have only this morning closed *Yannis* with regret. There are moments in life when words seem so inadequate to the occasion – and this is another. A massive story – full of the keenest observation of the human condition and the compassion that strings us all together.

* * *

I just had to write to tell you how much I loved your book. It was compulsive reading and beautifully written – I read every single word! I found that whilst I was reading I was also seeing all the characters, places and situations in my mind and I think that is the sign of a great author. You are up there with the best of them and I can't wait to read *Anna* when it is published.

* * *

I just wanted to say how much I enjoyed the novel – if enjoy is the right word to use for such a tragic subject. I didn't realise leprosy was still a problem in this century, particularly the way the lepers were treated so thank you for opening my eyes to this subject. I kept imagining it as a film. It's got all the ingredients. Such a mixture of emotions and human conditions.

* * *

I have just finished reading *Yannis* and really enjoyed it.

* * *

I have read *Yannis* during my holiday and thoroughly enjoyed it. Wonderful! It made me cry.

Readers' Reviews for Anna

I couldn't put *ANNA* down and was trying to finish it with misty eyes when it all comes together at the end – that wonderful mixture of happiness, sadness and completion.

M. Hollands (Uckfield Library)

* * *

I have just finished reading *ANNA* wonderful. The end had me in tears.

S. Beard

* * *

I just had to tell you how much I enjoyed *ANNA*. I just could not put it down.

P. Jones

* * *

The characters are so real that I feel I know them.

D. Mason

* * *

I fell in love with Anna's nephew.

Y. Owens

* * *

I loved *YANNIS*. I thought *ANNA* was even better and I cannot wait to get my hands on *GIOVANNI*.

G. Newman

* * *

I become so involved in the plot of each book that I await the outcome as anxiously as if the fictitious characters were my own family.

G. King

* * *

Each time I finish a book by Beryl Darby I am eagerly anticipating the next. Please write many more about this family.

J. Wilson

Readers' Reviews for Giovanni

The plot widens out even more internationally and into the realms of crime. I think it is incredible the way you construct and move the plot forward, handle the dialogue and relationships, the scope and complexities of the places and situations. I put you up there with Maeve Binchy, Jeffrey Archer, and Colleen McCullough.
M. Hollands (Uckfield Library)

* * *

Thank you for giving me so much pleasure with your writing.
R. Shepherd

* * *

This series of books is the best I have read in thirty years.
C. Taylor

* * *

I absolutely love your books and cannot wait for *JOSEPH*.
S. Wood

* * *

These characters have become a part of our family. We talk about them as if they were real.
G. Hiscox

* * *

I so enjoyed reading *GIOVANNI* – this one had it all – love, loyalty, sex, intrigue, murder and of course "the family".
A. Warwick

Family Tree

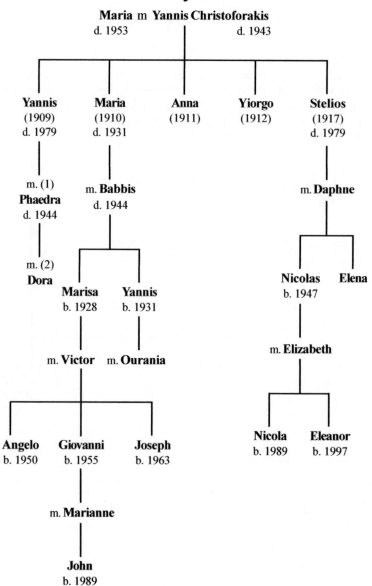

Family Tree

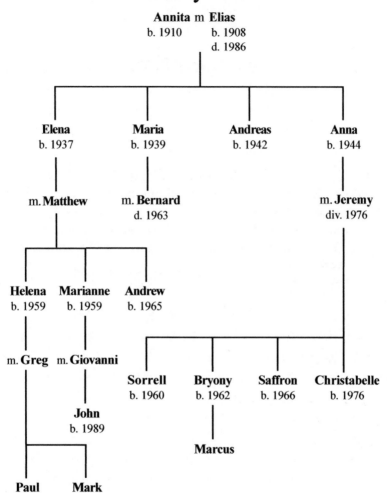

Annita m **Elias**
b. 1910   b. 1908
            d. 1986

Elena
b. 1937

Maria
b. 1939

Andreas
b. 1942

Anna
b. 1944

m. **Matthew**

m. **Bernard**
d. 1963

m. **Jeremy**
div. 1976

Helena
b. 1959

Marianne
b. 1959

Andrew
b. 1965

m. **Greg**

m. **Giovanni**

Sorrell
b. 1960

Bryony
b. 1962

Saffron
b. 1966

Christabelle
b. 1976

John
b. 1989

Marcus

Paul

Mark

Author's Note

All the characters in this novel are entirely fictitious. Any resemblance to actual persons, living or dead, is entirely coincidental.

Although the book is set in Rhodes and many of the locations can be found, all the criminal activity and people involved are entirely fictitious.

1990

Joseph gazed morosely at the occupants of the other tables. Many of them were local people, their dress and demeanour advertising they were taking a break from their work for quick refreshment before returning to their drudgery. Joseph's lip curled derisively. What fools they were, toiling each day for a pittance. He clenched his hands in anger. How could he have known the girl was a relative when she never revealed her true name? She should be languishing in jail for a considerable number of years and he should be living comfortably, instead of which she had been deported to America and he had no chance of repeating his idea now the hotels had been sold. At least that knowledge made him smile. He had revenged himself on his uncle and cousin for refusing to accept him as part of their small consortium. It was his father's fault. If he had not sent him into the army, his uncle would have accepted and helped him as he had done Giovanni. There was no justice in the world.

Now he waited. Whilst serving his prison sentence he had done a 'favour' for Dimitris. His payment had been the promise of help to make a new start when he was released. For three days he had sat at the same taverna and he was beginning to doubt if Dimitris intended to keep to the bargain.

A man slipped into the seat beside him, placing coffee in a plastic cup on the sticky metal table. He bent over the cup, as if to blow on the contents and spoke quietly to Joseph.

'Take the underground to Piraeus. Dimitris is in Zea Marina on the *'Aegean Pride.'*

Joseph did not reply. At last, this was the message he had been waiting for. He continued to sit in a sullen silence as the man lifted the cup to his mouth and grimaced as the heat burnt his lips. He bent his head over the cup again.

'I should get going if I were you. He won't wait all day.'

Joseph looked at his watch. It would take no more than fifteen minutes to reach Piraeus, but the Zea Marina was a considerably long walk up the hill and down the opposite side. No doubt he would be able to find the money for a taxi. He rose leisurely, strolling across the road towards the entrance to the underground station.

Without purchasing a ticket, he forced his way through the turnstile in the wake of a tourist and clattered down the stone steps to the platform. When the train arrived he entered the first carriage and pushed his way between the passengers, helping himself from their back pockets as he laid a hand on their arm or shoulder and requested they moved aside to allow him passage. Each time the train stopped he dismounted and entered the carriage lower down. One stop before Piraeus he jumped from the train, as the doors were about to close, and hurried into the toilets. He removed the cash and credit cards from each of the wallets he had purloined, placing the money in the pocket of his jacket and the cards into the back pocket of his jeans. He threw the empty wallets into the rubbish bin and returned to the platform to await the next train, which would arrive within a matter of minutes.

Piraeus was thronged with people and Joseph twisted and turned before he was able to reach the exit. He stood there for a few moments, gazing at the ships that were moored against the main road, and then turned swiftly to look behind. No one appeared to be taking the slightest notice of him. A small crowd had gathered around a police officer who was trying to understand the complaints of three men who had felt for their wallet and found it was missing when they had left the earlier train. He shrugged and smiled to himself. Tourists should take more care of their belongings, there were notices warning people of pickpockets on the underground.

The traffic was a steady stream on the road and he took his chance to weave amongst it until he reached the seaward side and was able to hail a taxi. At the beginning of Zea Marina he paid off the driver, lit a cigarette and began to look idly at the names of the ships. It occurred to him that the boat he was looking for could be at the other end of the large marina and quickened his step.

He was pleasantly surprised when he saw her. He had expected a small motorboat, but this was a cabin cruiser, gleaming white, her deck of polished wood clean and the ropes neatly coiled. As he stepped aboard the door to the saloon opened and a voice called to him to enter.

As his eyes became accustomed to the dark interior he could see Dimitris sitting at the far side of the table and an unknown man took up a stand behind him, blocking the doorway. Joseph extended his hand.

'It's good to see you again, Dimitris.'

Dimitris ignored the hand. 'Sit down Joseph. Drink?'

'I'll have a beer.'

A can was placed before him and Dimitris raised his glass. 'To profitable times.' The two large gold rings glinted on his fat fingers.

Joseph lifted his can. 'If this is yours, times must be very profitable.'

Dimitris shrugged. 'I promised you I would contact you when the time was right; give you a helping hand, so to speak, in return for the favour you did for me.'

Joseph nodded. He would really prefer to forget the unfortunate incident when he had lured Spiro to a corner of the prison yard and left him to his fate. Dimitris had kept his word when he had said that no suspicion would fall on Joseph and no one knew who had started a brawl, which had ended in Spiro hitting his head so hard on the concrete that he had never regained consciousness.

'It is essential that if you agree to work for me there must be no way of linking us. I am a respected businessman. I could not afford to have my name linked with a petty criminal.'

Joseph's face darkened. 'I was caught up in an unfortunate situation.'

'Quite so. We do not need to discuss that. Are you interested in a lucrative occupation, which requires very little effort on your part?'

Joseph nodded.

'Very well. Tonight you will take a ferry to Rhodes. I have your documents here. Once there you will visit Lakkis. He runs a taverna, *The Grapevine*, and I have booked a room for you. Thalia will meet you at the harbour and show you the way.'

Joseph opened his mouth to ask a question and Dimitris held up his hand again. 'I am not prepared to disclose the nature of the work he will offer you. Needless to say, your conversations with him will be entirely confidential and I shall know nothing about them. If you decide to refuse his offer there is nothing that will link you with me.'

The small black eyes, sunken in the rolls of fat that comprised Dimitris's face, bored into Joseph, who shivered despite the heat of the day.

'If you decide not to go to Rhodes you are free to go about your business, but I will not be prepared to offer to help you in the future. I am sure you know better than to accept passage to the island and not contact Lakkis upon your arrival, as I am equally sure that you would not be so foolish as to agree to work for Lakkis and then break your agreement.' Dimitris folded his hands and his mouth curved into a grim smile. 'It is an easy matter to shake off the Greek police if they decide to follow you. It is not so easy to escape the attentions of my men.'

'I wouldn't try to cross you, Dimitris,' Joseph licked his dry lips. 'If I decided not to work for Lakkis what would happen then?'

Dimitris shrugged. 'You could stay on Rhodes or return to Athens. The choice would be yours.'

Joseph swallowed the remainder of his beer. 'I've nothing to lose by visiting Rhodes and meeting Lakkis.' He tried to smile and appear relaxed, ignoring the knot of fear that was in his stomach.

Dimitris nodded and pushed an envelope across the table. 'The ferry leaves at six. You will find a ticket and your identity papers inside. I have enclosed a small amount for travelling expenses.'

Joseph nodded and pocketed the envelope. He rose from the seat and held out his hand to Dimitris. 'I'm grateful for your help.'

Dimitris nodded and shook Joseph's hand briefly. 'I suggest you return immediately to the city and make the necessary preparations for your departure.'

The large man standing by the door of the saloon moved to one side and Joseph returned to the bright sunshine. He crossed the short plank from the boat to the shore and began the return walk to the underground. He knew better than to ignore any instructions Dimitris had given him.

Dimitris watched Joseph's progress through the saloon window and as soon as he had been swallowed up amongst the throng of people, he spoke to the man still standing by the door.

'We can leave now, Anders.'

Joseph walked back to the Piraeus underground station, and again without a ticket, he boarded the train bound for Monasteriki station in the centre of Athens. Once more he removed wallets from unsuspecting passengers as he passed between them. He speculated on the possible occupation that was to be offered to him the following day, it was obviously illegal – anything that involved Dimitris was bound to be, although the man was clever enough never to have been prosecuted for anything more serious than traffic violations.

He strolled up the back streets of the Flea Market leading to the Plaka area. For some days now he had been formulating a plan and this would be an ideal opportunity as he was leaving the city that night. He slowed his step, looking into the windows of the shops as he went, checking the time and waiting to see the old man begin to close up his shop for the afternoon. Joseph hovered until the last shutter was in place, then he walked inside the shop.

The shutters in place made the interior dark and Nikos look in surprise at his customer. It was rare that the locals patronized him; he was there for the tourists to buy their souvenirs of nuts, fruits, honey and sweets before they returned to their homes.

'Just closing?' asked Joseph.

Nikos nodded. 'What can I get for you?'

Joseph pointed to a shelf behind the counter where a large box of assorted nuts, attractively packaged and adorned with a large red bow sat. 'I'd like that box of nuts, please.'

Nikos went behind the counter and reached up to take down the box. As he did so Joseph struck him on the back of his neck and Nikos fell forward, hitting his forehead on the shelf. Joseph grabbed the thin shoulders and slammed his head hard against the protruding shelf, pushing the old man to the ground as he collapsed with a groan. Wasting no time, Joseph placed the cardboard box that was used to store the daily takings from the shop onto the counter. He took a bunch of keys from Nikos's trouser pocket and as an afterthought drew the old man's wallet from his jacket pocket.

He stepped back to the other side of the counter, threw the money from the box into a carrier bag, the thick roll of notes from the wallet he placed in his jacket pocket, turned the notice on the door to read 'closed' before shutting the door and locking it carefully behind him. With luck it would be some time before the old man was discovered. The road was now nearly deserted; he hurried on his way, throwing the keys and wallet into a rubbish bin as he passed.

On returning to the room he had rented at the back of the market and near the railway station he removed the money from the bag and counted it carefully. He whistled with surprise and pleasure. The old man had been a fool to have so much money on the premises. It was a wonder he had not been hit over the head before. He added the money he had taken from the wallets on the metro and felt well pleased with himself.

Joseph flung himself on his bed, placed the pillows comfortably behind his head and opened the envelope from Dimitris carefully. He examined his new identity card and smiled with pleasure when he saw his name was still to be Joseph. Once or twice before he had nearly slipped up when he had forgotten to answer to his latest assumed name. Joseph Konstandides, born in Paleofalirion on the same date as himself. That would provide no problems at all.

Wrapped in a sheet of notepaper were his ferry ticket and some drachma, along with a brief message. '*Pay your bill before you leave*'. Joseph scowled; then smiled. It was not his money and Dimitris had said he would cover his expenses. He replaced the ferry ticket and identity card in the envelope and placed it on the table beside him. He would have a couple of hour's siesta before packing his belongings. That would still leave time for him to make a couple of quick trips on the metro to see if he could filch a few more drachmas from the unsuspecting public before he returned for his bags and left for the harbour.

'I guess we can only tell old Nikos what a lucky man he was. Nothing worse than cuts and bruises along with the concussion. He lost his week's takings, but his shop wasn't worked over or he could have lost a good deal more.'

'Maybe he'll take our advice and finally put his money in the bank each day. He's always been a fool to flash it around in front of his customers. He did it one time too many.'

'You think it was a tourist?'

Babbis shrugged. 'If it had been a local he would have recognised him.'

'He said the man spoke Greek.'

'Still doesn't mean he was a local. He could have been visiting from anywhere.'

Christos shook his head. 'Visitor, yes, but I think he could well have been in the area for quite a while. He timed his visit to coincide with the time Nikos was closing at midday. I presume there was no luck with fingerprints?'

'Hundreds, but superimposed and smudged. Most of them would probably be his.'

'And his wallet and the keys?'

'No sign of them. We've just got to call it quits on this one.'

Christos sighed. 'I don't like doing that. Do you think there'd be any point in putting out a call to other areas or the islands? See if there have been any other similar crimes?'

'You can, but personally I think it would be a waste of time.'

'You're probably right.' Christos flipped the slim folder closed and placed it in his tray for filing at a later date. 'Lunch?'

Joseph stood on the deck of the ferry and watched as they sailed into the commercial port. The massive walls of the medieval city wound their way along the waterfront and he regarded them dispassionately. He was not interested in history. During his years in Athens he had never bothered to visit the Acropolis or any other site of historical importance for pleasure. He was more interested in looking for the girl Dimitris had said would meet him, but unless she was the middle-aged woman sitting by the gate there was no sign of her. He picked up his bags and joined the straggling line of travellers waiting to disembark.

Once on the quayside he looked again for any sign of the girl he was supposed to meet. He lit a cigarette and cursed silently. He had no choice but to wait until she turned up, as there could be a hundred tavernas called *The Grapevine*, although he doubted a man called Lakkis would run them all. He drew the acrid smoke into his lungs greedily, leaning on the railing with his back to the imposing walls. He watched in appreciation as a tall, slim girl, wearing a dress that was so white it hurt his eyes, kissed a uniformed man on the cheek and walked away. He hoped she would come his way and he might be able to proposition her for some entertainment that evening.

To his surprise she drew level with him and smiled. 'Hello, Joseph. I'm Thalia.'

Joseph tossed his half-smoked cigarette to the ground. 'I'm pleased to meet you. I was beginning to wonder if I'd been stood up.' He grinned and raised his eyebrows. 'I was admiring you from a distance, but I must admit that the closer you come the better you look.'

A slight flush crept into Thalia's cheeks. 'I'm only here as your guide.'

Joseph smiled at her. 'That's a shame. Maybe another time? Do you want me to flag down a taxi?'

Thalia looked at Joseph with something like amusement lurking in her dark, luminous eyes. 'It will be easier to walk.'

Joseph picked up his bags and followed her, admiring the swing of her hips as she walked along the narrow pavement. He was so intent on watching her movement he nearly bumped into her when she stopped opposite an archway. She waited until there was a break in the traffic and told him to run when she did. He tried to follow her swiftly, the bags bumping against his legs, as he plunged after her. Thalia continued on her way through the arch without a backward glance to Joseph.

Once through the ancient gateway he stopped in surprise. Small shops already open for business, leaned against each other as if they received comfort and support from the proximity. Tourists were strolling leisurely, whilst locals went about their daily business. Rhodes was famous for its medieval city and he had always thought it was a collection of ruins with a few tavernas to serve the needs of the tourists, but instead it was a bustling town that met his eyes.

By the time he had recovered himself he could see the flash of Thalia's white dress disappearing into the distance and he hurried to catch her up.

'Hold on a minute. I nearly lost you.' He placed the bags on the ground.

Thalia looked at him impatiently, then at her tiny gold watch. She knew there was no immediate hurry to reach their destination, but it was amusing to see this self confident young man struggling. She waited until he had picked up the bags again and proceeded more slowly, immediately leading him away from the main thoroughfare and through a maze of streets, his expensive Italian shoes slipping on the cobbles as he was led left and right and across intersections until he was hopelessly lost.

'Are you sure you know the way?' he called anxiously.

Thalia turned and looked at him in derision. 'You can go on alone if you wish.'

'No, no, I didn't mean that. It just seems that we've been walking in circles.'

'This is the old town. You often have to walk in circles before you reach your destination. They didn't believe in town planning when this place was built. We're nearly there.'

She ducked through an archway on their right and led the way across a paved square to a small taverna on the corner. The raised patio had a selection of padded chairs around the tables and Joseph sank into one gratefully. A young man came forward and Joseph ordered a beer for himself and iced coffee for Thalia.

'Is that Lakkis?' he asked.

Thalia shook her head. 'He'll be here soon.'

Whilst Joseph drank his beer he took stock of the square before him. It appeared to be a thoroughfare, the road in front of the taverna entered into a short, narrow street that led to an intersection and directly opposite there were steps to the archway where they had entered. The centre of the square was dominated by three large trees, beneath which stood chairs and tables, taking advantage of the shade they offered.

People passed continually, but they appeared to be mostly locals, who did not even glance in his direction. An occasional tourist would give the place a cursory glance and continue on their way. Joseph wondered if he was going to be asked to run the taverna and grimaced at the idea. That could mean working hard – and any form of permanent, mundane occupation was an anathema to him. He called for another beer from the boy, who was using a long handled dustpan and brush to sweep around the tables, kicking the chairs out of the way with his foot and pushing them back with his hip.

The familiar noise of a scooter engine broke the stillness and he saw a middle-aged man arrive and lean the machine against the wall at the side. He seemed to take a long time fiddling around inside the seat and Joseph was certain it was to enable the man to take stock of him.

Finally the man stepped up into the courtyard of the taverna and went over to the boy at the bar. He was dressed in khaki shorts and a pale green shirt, the designer logos discreetly in evidence. He poured a beer for himself and joined Joseph and Thalia at the table.

'I understand you are looking for accommodation.'

'I believe it was booked from Athens for me. Joseph Konstandides.'

The man nodded. 'I'm Lakkis.'

'I was told you could have some work for me?'

'Maybe. We will talk about that later. Thank you, Thalia, for showing him the way.'

Thalia inclined her head briefly. 'It was no trouble.' She rose from her seat, kissed Lakkis on both cheeks, and in a swirl of white dress stepped down from the patio and began to walk down the road away from them.

'She is a good girl,' remarked Lakkis.

Joseph nodded. 'I would never have found my way here without her.'

Lakkis nodded. 'This time next week you will wonder why it was so difficult. Now, I will show you your room and we will talk.'

Lakkis led the way to an exterior stair next to a walkway between the house and the taverna, Joseph following, his bags bumping the wall and the railings alternately.

'I hope you have no objection to the annex.'

Joseph shook his head; he really had no choice where he stayed. Lakkis unlocked the door at the top of the stairs and handed him the key. He was pleasantly surprised and pleased when he stepped inside and saw the sparsely furnished room, with a curtained alcove serving as a bathroom. He smiled in approval.

'This is certainly better than some of the places I've had to stay.'

'You will only stay here for one week. At the end of that time I will decide whether you will be suitable for the job.'

Joseph sat down on the bed and Lakkis joined him. 'I thought the job was here, in the taverna.'

'Alecos is quite capable of taking care of the trade here. Your job would be at the warehouse.'

'What do I have to do?' This was beginning to sound like the arduous work that he abhorred and other people did to earn their money.

'Very little. It is necessary to be there each morning. You will receive telephone calls asking for a consignment, which you will prepare for collection. You will ensure the goods are paid for and a correct receipt given. You will bank the money each Monday afternoon. On a Saturday you will take the early morning ferry to Marmaris and return in the afternoon.'

Joseph's brow creased. 'Why on earth should I want to do that?'

'You have a young lady over there and you wish to see her.'

'I don't know anyone in Turkey!'

Lakkis did not reply. He eyed Joseph speculatively, his eyes the same pale green as his shirt, reminding Joseph of a cat. 'At the end of the week if I feel you are suitable for the job I will give you some more information.'

'Why not now?'

Lakkis's lips curved in a thin smile. 'It is better that you only know the briefest of details at this time. You are still in a position to decline the offer and go your own way.'

Joseph shook his head. 'I think it sounds a good offer. How much will I get paid?'

'Fifty thousand drachma a week, this includes your weekly travel expenses. You will live rent free, and in time, you may find you have other benefits.'

Joseph calculated rapidly. 'I can make more than that in Athens.'

Lakkis placed his fingertips together and looked up at the ceiling. 'You are free to return if you wish.' He pursed his lips. 'I did hear that a certain elderly gentleman in Plaka was robbed yesterday. Fortunately he was only knocked unconscious and was able to give the police a very good description of his assailant. It could mean there is a little more police activity around the area until someone has been arrested for the attack.'

The pale green eyes looked at Joseph and he shivered. He was trapped. Someone must have been watching his movements. If he declined the offer from Lakkis he could be fairly certain that on his return to Athens he would very soon be arrested. He cleared his throat. 'So what do I do with myself for this week until you decide on my suitability?'

Lakkis leant forward. 'You have to familiarise yourself with the town. As you said, you would never have found this taverna without the help of my niece. By this time next week you need to know every street, alley way, short cut, detour and landmark. If I ask you to visit anywhere in the old town you have to be able to do so without hesitation. You must be able to lose anyone who might think of following you and be capable of doubling back so you could follow them if necessary. The only way to learn this is to walk the streets, both by day and by night.'

Joseph frowned. 'Would Thalia be able to show me around for a day or two?'

'No. That is not the way to learn.' Lakkis fixed his eyes on Joseph. 'Besides, she is betrothed to my son. She is not for the likes of you.'

Joseph bristled at his words.

'There is one more thing; you do not draw attention to yourself in any way. You are just one of the many young men who come over here on a vacation and decide to stay.'

Joseph shrugged. 'Fine. How will I know if I have learnt my way about to your satisfaction?'

'We will talk again. You will be offered the job or a return ticket to Athens. I hope you will find your room comfortable.' Lakkis rose from the bed and in one swift movement had left the room and closed the door behind him.

Joseph dropped his head in his hands. He did not trust Lakkis. Someone, presumably an employee of Dimitris, had watched his every movement after he left their meeting in the Zea Marina. He thought he knew the Plaka area well enough to evade surveillance, but this was obviously not the case. He gave a deep sigh and stretched his arms above his head. Dimitris had said he could stay on Rhodes if he wished, so really there was no problem. He would make himself completely familiar with the area, then see what the rest of this job entailed. Lakkis had made it sound too simple to be true.

Stirring himself into action, Joseph unpacked his belongings. He looked ruefully at his expensive Italian shoes. They would be totally impractical on the slippery stones that were placed on edge to cobble the streets. He must find a shoe shop and purchase something flat with rubber soles. No doubt the boy in the taverna would be able to direct him to the nearest shop.

He showered, pleasantly surprised to find the showerhead was fully functional and gave more than a dribble of tepid water, and changed into a fresh shirt. He selected some drachmas from the roll and returned the remainder to a sock, pushing it to the back of the drawer.

The taverna was as deserted as it had been when he first arrived. Alecos was sitting behind the bar and hardly glanced at Joseph as he clattered down the stone stairway. Joseph eased himself onto a bar stool and Alecos dragged his eyes away unwillingly from the newspaper he was reading.

'Hi. I'm Joseph. I'm staying in Rhodes for a while and I thought you might be able to help me. I need some different shoes. I don't want to ruin my good leather ones on these stones. Where's the nearest place to buy some?'

'In the new town.'

'Where's that?'

'Go up the hill to the main gate,' Alecos waved his hand airily in the general direction. 'Turn right when you exit and cross a couple of roads. You'll be in the new town then.'

Joseph nodded. 'Thanks. I'll have a beer before I go.'

Alecos placed the bottle and a glass on the bar top.

'Do you fancy joining me?'

Alecos shook his head. 'I don't drink when I'm working.'

Joseph looked at the deserted bar. 'You don't look rushed off your feet. Do you ever have any customers here?'

'Of course. People drop in and out. Sometimes they just sit and chat with friends, other times they stay for a drink or a snack. It's early yet.'

Joseph looked at his watch. It was nearly twelve. 'I'd better be off. No doubt the shops close here the same as in Athens?'

'Not down here they don't, only in the new town.'

'Why not down here?'

'Tourists. They don't seem to worry about a siesta.' Alecos dropped his eyes back to the newspaper and Joseph drained his glass.

'I'll be off. I'll see you later.'

Alecos watched and smiled to himself as Joseph walked the short distance along the road to an archway where a cobbled road ran in both directions. He wondered how long it would take before the Athenian was completely lost.

At the intersection Joseph hesitated. The boy had said up the hill. He walked to the left and within a matter of minutes had reached another road running crosswise. A number of narrow lanes led off, some appearing to have an incline, others seeming level. He reasoned with himself as he tried to gain a sense of direction. He had come from the port and the taverna was slightly below him on the left. He would turn right and see how he fared.

It took Joseph almost an hour before he found himself on a wide road and he realised he had reached the top of the hill, although quite how he had done so he was not sure. He continued to walk until he passed through an archway and then to his surprise he found himself turning into another, which was more like a wide tunnel. As he emerged back into the sunlight he stopped. This was obviously a gate into the town. On each side of him there was a deep moat containing a few straggly trees struggling for life in the mud. The planking he had to cross to reach the road on the opposite side seemed firm and a motorbike passed him without hesitation. He followed in its wake and looked back.

There was no sign of the bustling activity he had been amongst only a short while ago. The high walls hid any sign of life and he could see no other obvious entrance or exit. He walked to the right and crossed a busy road. A short distance ahead he could see more traffic and assumed he was travelling in the right direction. Taking his chance to cross between the cars he realised he was in the new town. The difference was startling. The buildings were a confusing mixture of the old and the new. Modern, concrete shells of various shapes and sizes dominated, some using the ground floor as a shop and others giving over the whole building to apartments or offices, whilst between them were the older houses, wooden balconies jutting out over the street, low doorways and the windows tightly shuttered.

Joseph strode out purposefully. The sooner he found some trainers to change into the better. Not only were his shoes scratched, his feet were aching where the thin soles had done little to protect him from the rounded cobbles. He walked into the nearest shop and smiled pleasantly at the man behind the counter.

'Please, don't get up. I've only come to ask for directions. Can you tell me where I can find a shop that sells trainers? I'm staying in the old town and my footwear is quite unsuitable.'

Slowly the man removed his glasses and looked over the counter at Joseph's feet. He shook his head sadly at the state of Joseph's footwear. 'Go down the hill. You should find two or three places there that have what you're after.'

Joseph thanked him and hurried out. Once he had purchased a pair of trainers he would find a place to eat a snack and have another couple of beers. He was hot and sticky and not at all sure if he liked this island.

He bought two pairs of trainers, managing to pocket a pair of socks whilst they were being wrapped and swung out of the shop. This was more to his liking. A few easy pickings would make life a little more enjoyable and added spice to a boring day. He sat outside a bar eating gyros and drinking his beer until he decided he should delay his return to the old town no longer. The sooner he started to explore and find his way around the better.

The change of footwear made walking easier, but once he had left the main thoroughfare he was hopelessly lost. The town was thronged with tourists; stopping abruptly in front of him to consult their maps and deciding which direction they wanted. Twice he thought he caught sight of Thalia and hurried in that direction, hoping to persuade her to give him directions, only to find the girl had disappeared by the time he had forced his way through the people. Joseph was beginning to feel annoyed with both himself and the town generally. He returned to the main gate with the purpose of getting his bearings and remembering some landmarks.

For a further two hours he walked, crossing the streets in the small area, continually returning to his starting point until he felt confident he knew his way to both the main gate and two others on the seaward side. He sat and drank another beer, realising he did not actually know his way back to *The Grapevine* and he should have made that his priority. He debated the wisdom of asking for directions and decided against the idea.

Whilst he sipped his beer in the relative coolness of a taverna he tried to remember the layout of the town. He felt sure that if he could walk in a straight line from where he sat he would eventually find himself in the square where *The Grapevine* was situated. He needed a shower and a late siesta would help him to regain his equanimity. Stifling the desire to close his eyes where he sat, he left the drachmas for his drink and recommenced his walking.

He had been completely incorrect in his calculations to regain the taverna and within a short period of time found he had left the shops and tavernas behind him and was walking in a more residential area, with the unbroken city wall on his right. He dived down a winding side street, taking a turn to the left, and then stopping at the intersection in the hope of finding his bearings. He was sure he needed to go left again along the narrow cobbled street which seemed vaguely familiar, with houses on one side and a wall, too high to see over on the other. With a sigh of exasperation he continued, his efforts finally being rewarded as an archway appeared and through it he could see the square with the taverna on the far side. Somehow he had managed to find the entrance he had used with Thalia earlier in the day.

From his vantage point he could see Alecos moving around between the tables and he hoped Lakkis was not waiting for him. He wanted to retire to his room for a much-needed shower and sleep before he faced anyone. As he crossed the square he realised Alecos was serving customers and he drew a breath of relief, quickened his step, and only gave the young man a brief nod as he climbed the stairs to his room.

His room was hot and airless having been shut up for so long during the day and he threw open the window and switched on the fan. The noises from the taverna below drifted up to him whilst he towelled himself off after his shower and he closed the window firmly before he lay down on his bed and gave himself up to sleep. He slept longer than he had intended, finally dragging himself back to full consciousness from a dream where he was wandering through cobbled streets that continually ended in high, insurmountable walls. His head ached and his stomach was rumbling unpleasantly, reminding him that he had only eaten gyros since his breakfast on the ferry.

He doused his head under the cold tap and dressed in clean clothes. At least he should be able to get a meal at *The Grapevine* and not have to start his interminable wandering of the streets to find somewhere to eat. He was disappointed. Alecos offered snacks only, but he could recommend the eating-house across the square where he could get a meal.

Joseph sat beneath the trees and ordered stifado, eating hungrily when it arrived. There were more people around now than there had been during the morning, each table in *The Grapevine* was occupied and the sounds of laughter drifted across to where he sat. Behind him a German family was deciphering the menu and at other tables people were already eating. A few children were playing catch around a deserted fountain and groups of youths lounged against the wall, sniggering and making lewd remarks about the young girls who strolled through the square looking for evening entertainment. The sight lifted Joseph's spirits. Maybe this old city was not so different from Plaka after all.

For the remainder of the week Joseph walked the streets until he realised the truth of Lakkis's words. It was really very simple to find *The Grapevine* as it was just off one of the main thoroughfares. The tangle of small roads, medieval stone arches holding the walls apart, sunless courtyards and garish tourist shops made the whole area confusing. Now he knew the shortcut that took him up to the main gate in the minimum amount of time, and how to traverse the city without spending hours walking in small circles. He was still astounded at the difference that took place each day. Early mornings saw the town languid and sleepy, as if recovering slowly from a night of debauchery. By mid morning tourists had invaded everywhere, and stayed, waiting for the evening when the town came to life in a different and exciting way.

The narrow streets were dimly lit, but buildings that had spent the day closed and shuttered were opened with bright lights and throbbing music, being patronised by both tourists and locals. Once confident of his ability to find his way in daylight it had taken Joseph very little time to convert that knowledge to encompass the hours of darkness, and it was during his wandering in the early hours of the morning that he had discovered the less reputable area of the town.

Situated near to an exit from the furthest point of the city, on a route not frequented by tourists after dark, were half a dozen small roads where the houses huddled cheek by jowl. No lights illuminated the streets, but above each doorway was a subdued red glow, the name of the girl who occupied the building scrawled in red crayon or paint on the doorpost. Joseph had smiled in appreciation at the discovery, certain that when he had discovered a girl to his liking he would be able to charm her to give him a special rate as a regular customer. He resisted the urge to become a patron that week. He did not want the information to get back to Lakkis, and even more important, he did not want Thalia to learn of his promiscuity. She excited him. Despite her obvious disinterest in him during their first meeting, she now represented a challenge, and he was determined to seduce her as soon as the opportunity arose. Whatever the job Lakkis was offering entailed he had decided to accept it. This could be an island of rich pickings.

To Joseph's surprise and delight Thalia was sitting at a table at *The Grapevine* when he returned from a short shopping expedition to purchase cigarettes. Dressed in jeans and a bright red blouse she looked even more attractive to him than she had at their first meeting. He sat beside her and smiled.

'This is a pleasant surprise.'

Thalia regarded him coolly. 'My uncle wants to see you. I'm to take you to him.'

Joseph lit a cigarette, blowing the smoke from the side of his mouth. 'Have I got time for a beer?'

'I would rather leave now.'

Joseph shrugged and rose to his feet. 'Very well. Lead the way.'

Thalia shook her head. 'You are leading the way.'

Joseph raised his eyebrows. 'That should be no problem. Where are we headed?'

'Aghios Athanasiou Gate.'

'That's not a very good area for a girl like you to walk in.'

'I'm quite safe during the day.' She began to walk towards the cross road and Joseph caught her elbow.

'It's quicker this way.' He steered her across the square, keeping his hand on her elbow as they walked. 'Where have you been all week? I've looked for you.'

'Working,' she replied briefly.

'And where do you work?'

'In a travel office.'

'That must be interesting.'

Thalia shrugged. 'No different from working in any other office.' She stopped to allow Joseph to take the lead through the narrow streets, effectively curtailing any further conversation.

He walked on in silence until they emerged onto the main road leading to the gate, where he dropped back beside her.

'I was wondering if you would consider having dinner with me one evening?'

Thalia shook her head. 'I am busy during the evenings.'

'That's a shame. I was hoping you might be able to introduce me to some of your friends. It's pretty lonely over here on my own.'

'I'm sure you will make friends very quickly.' Thalia stopped before the last building in the road and opened the door. 'We're here, uncle Lakkis.'

Lakkis came forward and Joseph blinked to get his eyes accustomed to the dim light.

'Thank you, Thalia. I presume Joseph knew his way?'

'Perfectly.'

'That's good.' He eyed Joseph speculatively. 'We will go upstairs and talk.'

Lakkis led the way through to a second room where a wooden staircase led the way to an upper floor. As Joseph followed him he heard the sound of the door closing, the latch snapping into place to prevent anyone else from entering. In the semi-darkness Joseph could make out the irregular shape of furniture and stopped before he bumped into anything. Confidently Lakkis walked over to the wall and pressed a switch, illuminating the room. He waved his hand indicating Joseph should take a seat at the table.

Lakkis removed the caps from two bottles of beer and handed one to Joseph. 'I understand that you have familiarised yourself with the old town as I requested.'

Joseph nodded.

'And have you decided to accept my offer of a job?'

'I'd like to know a bit more about it. What am I selling from the warehouse and why do I need to go over to Turkey each week?'

Lakkis studied the young man across the table from him. He did not like him and he certainly did not trust him, but Dimitris had recommended him as both suitable and expendable if necessary.

'This conversation is confidential. It would not be wise for you to repeat it to any of your friends.'

'Naturally, but I have no friends over here.'

'No doubt that will change.' Lakkis took a mouthful of beer. 'This is where you will live. It is not luxurious, but quite adequate.'

Joseph looked around the large room and nodded. There was a bed, sofa, bookcase, two chests, a table and two chairs. The alcoves on either side of an old fireplace had been utilised, one with shelves and the other with doors. On a shelf were a number of books with pens and pencils beside them. The far wall had two closed doors, which he presumed led to a kitchen and bathroom.

'We discussed before,' continued Lakkis, 'the nature of your employment. You must not leave the premises during the morning, as that is when you will receive telephone orders. As soon as you have taken an order you will go downstairs where the goods are stored and box up the number of packets required. You will make out a receipt for the correct amount and fill in the recipient's name when they come to collect the goods.'

Joseph nodded. 'What do these goods comprise of? What are you selling?'

Lakkis sat back with a smile. 'Organic flour.'

'Organic flour!' Joseph could not believe that he had heard correctly.

'It is the latest craze amongst many of the bakers here. We also stock cartons of cigarettes.' Lakkis leant forward confidentially. 'Sometimes you will be asked for something extra. You will be told the number of packets required. For these extra items you will make out a separate receipt and keep the money separate also. Each Monday afternoon you will take the money for the flour and the cigarettes to the bank. Each Saturday you will be on the ferry to go for your weekly visit to Turkey. You will take to Marmaris the money you have received for the other packets you have sold and discreetly hand it over to your girlfriend.' Lakkis paused and fixed Joseph with his pale green eyes. 'Do you understand?'

Joseph nodded slowly. 'I get the picture. I assume the other packets contain drugs?'

Lakkis looked at him steadily. 'I have no idea. I deal only in organic flour and cigarettes.'

A slow smile curled Joseph's lips. 'I see. If I am picked up you deny all knowledge of the operation.'

'Exactly. I have simply employed you to look after the warehouse. How should I know what else you do?'

'And where do these other supplies come from?'

'Each Tuesday a consignment of flour will arrive. You will receive an additional delivery of goods on a Wednesday and be expected to sign a receipt. The shipper is very particular that the receipts match with the money deposited in Turkey, so do not get any ideas about falsifying the accounts.'

'I wouldn't dream of it,' Joseph assured him, and for once he meant what he said. He knew how drug cartels worked, and you obeyed instructions to the letter if you valued your life.

'You will keep the additional delivery in the bottom of the trunk under the window.' Lakkis waved his hand. 'When you examine it you will see it has a false bottom. I suggest you store some of your clothes there. Now, I will explain the financial arrangements to you.'

Lakkis went over to the shelves in the alcove and returned with an assortment of books. He placed them on the table. 'This is your receipt book and bank book for the flour and this one is for the cigarettes. The blue book is for other commodities. When you travel to Turkey it will be necessary for you to take the copies of the receipts. You take over only notes, so sometimes there is a small discrepancy. Keep a record of the difference and carry it forward to include in the following week.'

'That sounds simple enough. How will I know this 'girl friend' of mine when I reach Marmaris?'

'She will make herself known to you when you disembark. She will also tell you when to hand over the money. You will be paid in cash each Friday, and your ferry ticket will be included in the envelope. If there is no ticket you can assume that the trip to Turkey will not take place.' Lakkis delved into his pocket. 'When you have a request for another commodity you remove some cigarettes from the packets and replace them with the amount requested. Return the packets to the carton and reseal it before you hand it over. You will always obtain a receipt before you hand over a special carton. The amount in each packet is exact to the last grain and I will expect it to remain that way.'

Joseph nodded. 'Where do I get further supplies of cigarettes?'

'Let Alecos know what you want. You can collect them from him and sign a receipt.'

'Fine. If I have any problems how can I contact you?'

'It should not be necessary, but if you go to Alecos he will know where to find me.' Lakkis leant towards him. 'Remember, you are to do nothing to attract attention to yourself. Now, you return to *The Grapevine*, collect your belongings and make yourself at home here. Make sure the doors are double locked and the shutters barred whenever you leave. You will receive your first delivery tomorrow.' Lakkis stood up. 'Remember your instructions and there should be no problems.'

Joseph nodded. 'What am I supposed to do in my spare time?'

Lakkis shrugged. 'You can do whatever you wish, but you do not bring anyone back here.' He placed two keys on the table. 'These are for the door downstairs.'

After Lakkis had left Joseph opened the shutters and turned off the light. Across the street from him two women sat outside their house gossiping. At the sound of his shutters opening they had both looked up and he gave them a smile and a wave. It would probably be as well to be on friendly terms with the neighbours.

He took stock of the room again and went over and bounced on the bed, pleased to find it was well sprung, checked out the small kitchen and adequate bathroom and turned his attention back to the main room again. The cupboard had a rail fixed where he could hang his clothes, although he frowned when he saw the wall was roughly plastered, leaving small nibs and projections that could snag his expensive Italian shirts. On the bookcase in the other alcove stood a small television set which he plugged in and checked it was in working order. He went over to the fridge for another beer and found it was empty. Joseph slammed the door in disgust. He would obviously have to make some purchases if he was going to make the place habitable. It was fortunate he had the money he had obtained from the old shopkeeper in Athens or he would have had a miserable week.

He would go to *The Grapevine* to have a beer, then collect his belongings. There would be time enough later to stock up his fridge. He picked up his jacket, placing the keys to the building in his pocket. He was about to leave when he remembered Lakkis's instructions about closing the shutters. There was nothing in the building at present and it really did seem an unnecessary chore. He hesitated; the two women were still sitting opposite. Maybe they would report back to Lakkis that he had disobeyed his instructions within the first hour of his arrival. With a sigh he slammed the shutters and clattered down the stairs to the lower floor that was to serve as the warehouse. He would abide by the rules just as long as it suited him.

Yannis sat with Marianne and Giovanni at the table. Spread out before them were the plans Giovanni had drawn up for the proposed self catering apartments. The first sheet had a rough outline of the land and he had drawn four small oblongs bordering the road. Behind them he had drawn three more rows and behind those again were some larger oblongs. He had coloured them from yellow to red, and the larger oblongs were in green and blue. The old farmhouse stood out in purple.

The second sheet had the design of an apartment with measurements carefully worked out. The door opened directly into a small hallway and the bathroom led off at a right angle. Opposite was a bedroom and at the end of the hallway an 'L' shaped area, the width of the property.

Giovanni pointed with his finger. 'Obviously the bedroom is larger than the bathroom, so I thought it would be practical to make a small kitchenette there and leave the remainder of the area as a lounge. There will be patio doors that can be opened and a small terrace outside where people can sit with a drink or eat their meal. What do you think?'

Marianne smiled in delight. 'You are clever, Giovanni.'

'The plans will still have to be passed. These are just my ideas.'

Yannis nodded. 'Have you any idea of the cost of each unit?'

Giovanni shook his head. 'Not yet. I need to speak to an architect and get his approval. Once I have done that I can approach various builders and see what they quote. When we have their quotes we can work out how much each unit will cost and how much we will need to charge visitors to cover our expenses. It's really only at that stage that we'll know if this is a viable proposition.'

Yannis smiled. 'You're being very cautious suddenly. Usually you persuade me to go ahead without any regard for the cost involved.'

Giovanni grinned at him. 'It was easy before. At the hotels we knew we would have bookings and would recoup our expenditure. This is a bit different. We will be lucky to break even in the first season, maybe a little profit to show for the second. I know it will work once we are up and running, but we will need more than four units for the whole to be a success. I don't want us to be borrowing so much from the bank that we pay all our profit back to them and can't use it for expansion. I'm working on a ten year project.'

'Ten years!'

Giovanni pulled the sheet with the coloured oblongs towards his uncle. 'This is why I've coloured it in. It's obviously practical to build closest to the road at first, the yellow blocks. As we can afford it we gradually build more behind the first row and so on. I've got other plans, too.'

Yannis raised his eyebrows. As usual, his nephew was full of ideas. 'Tell me.'

'We turn the farmhouse into a taverna. Nothing grand, just snacks and drinks, and incorporating a little general store.'

Yannis held up his hand. 'What do we need a general store for? There's no one living there.'

'If you're on holiday and catering for yourself you don't want to have to spend half the day going shopping for food. We won't stock anything fancy. Bread, butter, cheese, milk, coffee and tea, salad, olives, fruit juice, beer, wine, ice cream, toothpaste, sun glasses, sun tan lotion, aspirins, camera film. Just basic supplies. Maybe a few postcards.'

'A pity Ourania's mother is no longer around. She would have been in her element!'

'There's more, Uncle. We'll have to build a toilet block on the side of the taverna. You can't serve food and drink without having the facilities available. I've drawn up the plans for those as well.'

Yannis looked with interest as Giovanni produced another sheet of paper.

'This is how I envisage it will look when it's converted. The whole of the ground floor knocked out, the general store taking up most of the space. The other side will be the kitchen. There will be a low dividing wall with a counter where the food can be placed before it is taken out to the customers or where they can place their purchases whilst they pay for them. Outside we'll pave an area and have tables and chairs where the people can sit. We'll put a door on at the bottom of the stairs and the upper floor will have to wait.'

'What about staff? The units will need to be cleaned and also the public toilets. Someone will have to work in the store and also do the cooking. There will be bedding to wash. You and Marianne can't manage all that on your own.'

'We've talked it over. The shop and taverna can be open from seven thirty until ten. If people are too lazy to get their own breakfast they can have it there or buy something to make up for a picnic. Marianne can manage that and do the cleaning between ten and twelve. The visitors should all be out by then. The shop and taverna can be open again between one and six.'

'And what are you going to be doing whilst Marianne is working her fingers to the bone?' asked Yannis.

'I shall do any of the odd jobs that crop up, be responsible for the laundry, clean the public toilets and the outside areas, keep the shop stocked and remove all the rubbish. I will run the taverna and shop between one and six so Marianne has the afternoon free to look after John.'

'What happens to John in the morning?'

For the first time Giovanni looked a little apprehensive. 'I thought, maybe, Aunt Ourania would look after him for a couple of hours, before she goes into Aghios Nikolaos. I'll take Marianne out to the taverna and check whatever needs to be done. As soon as I've finished there I'll be back to look after him. He can always come out in the car with me when I have to go into town.'

'As usual you have it all worked out.' Yannis sighed. 'I'm still not convinced that people will want to come and stay out here. There's nothing for them to do.'

'They can visit Spinalonga. Most people hire a car whilst they are away so they can go off on their own exploring. That's my next idea.' Giovanni pointed to the larger shapes that he had coloured blue and green. 'I know we can't start on this yet, but I thought if we made a tennis court and a crazy golf at the back of the complex it could be an added attraction.'

'People would probably prefer a swimming pool.'

'That's for the future again. In the meantime they have the beach. We'll have to do some negotiation with the Prefecture, probably pay them a license fee to make an area private, and provide some loungers and umbrellas.'

Yannis turned to Marianne. 'You've not said a word. How do you feel about all Giovanni's grand plans?'

Marianne smiled happily. 'I think it will work. I just wish we could start today.'

Giovanni rolled up the plans. 'No reason why we shouldn't. We'll make an appointment with the architect in Aghios Nikolaos. Whilst we're there we can have a look at the prices of kitchen equipment and work out the quantity we will need.'

Yannis held up his hand. 'Not quite so fast. What do you expect to get out of this project?'

'A living. The land and the buildings belong to you, Aunt Anna and Uncle Yiorgo. I'm just an employee, the same as I was when I first started working for you.'

Yannis shook his head. 'No, you are the manager. This is your idea. You have virtually a free hand, with one proviso – you do not go over the budget I set. I won't have any reserves to draw on if things get out of hand.'

'I promise, Uncle Yannis. I'll consult you whenever I have an idea that will cost more money.'

Sorrell had sat in the hostel room for a week, desperate to leave, but not daring to approach her grandparents lest they knew of her deportation from Greece. She had finally made a telephone call to them, pretending to be her sister's ex-employer and asking for Bryony's current address. She assured them there was no problem, just a query that had arisen. Her grandmother had been anxious to help, giving the address without hesitation, and Sorrell had smiled contentedly. She would pay her a visit. Her sister's apartment had to be better than the hostel and whilst she was there she would be able to think and come up with a plan.

Her story ready, she had waited until she saw her sister enter the building and after a reasonable amount of time she had taken the elevator and knocked on the door. Bryony had been reluctant to let her stay at all, but after she had pleaded that she was temporarily homeless, having had her apartment flooded with water from a burst tank from the floor above, and it would only be for a few days whilst the necessary repairs were carried out, she had finally relented.

'I really don't know why I should,' Bryony grumbled. 'No one hears a word from you for years, but the moment you want a favour you are on my doorstep. What have you been up to?'

'Travelling.' Sorrell waved her hand airily. 'My job takes me to all parts of the world. It makes it difficult to stay in touch.'

Bryony eyed her sister sceptically. 'What kind of a job is that?'

'I'm in advertising. Freelance. I have to be able to go at a moment's notice wherever they need a bit of advice.' She smiled easily. 'I could easily get you onto their books. You could make a fortune, the same as I am,' she lied.

Bryony shook her head. 'I don't want to be rushing off anywhere. I've got a steady job and I'm getting married in a month.'

'Who's the lucky man?'

Bryony picked up a framed photograph. 'Marcus.'

Sorrell raised her eyebrows. 'Marcus? Why not plain Mark?'

'It happens to be his name.' Bryony took back the photograph.

'Where did you meet him?'

'Do you remember my friend Sabena when we were at school?'

'What – Beanbag? The little fat spotty girl with glasses?' Sorrell smiled at the memory of the taunting she had given to the unfortunate teenager.

'She's no longer fat and spotty. I used to visit occasionally at weekends and I met Marcus there. He's her brother.'

'What does he do for a living?'

'Sells insurance.'

'How exciting!' murmured Sorrell.

'It's a job that pays well. He's saved enough to furnish the apartment. It's in a new development and grandma was able to negotiate a good price. She wasn't able to buy it outright for us, but it will give us a good start. We're very grateful to her. I've saved enough to equip the kitchen out and we have the rest of the furnishings planned.'

Sorrell raised her eyebrows. 'I would have thought grandma would have been willing to set you up completely.'

Bryony shook her head. 'I wouldn't dream of asking her after all the years that she gave me a home and paid for me to go on to college. She's already done more for me than she did for Helena and Greg. She only provided them with their carpets and a bedroom suite.'

Sorrell frowned. Maybe she should visit her grandmother at some point and tell her she was getting married and see what she could extricate from her bank account. She looked at her sister critically. 'Are you planning to lose any weight before your wedding day?'

Bryony flushed miserably. 'I keep trying, but it just doesn't seem to work for me.'

Sorrell smiled maliciously. 'Rather like your school reports "must try harder". So fill me in with what else has been happening to the family whilst I've been away.' Sorrell settled herself back in the chair. 'You haven't got a drink, by any chance?'

'Fruit juice or coffee?'

Sorrell looked at her sister in amazement. 'I meant a proper drink.'

Bryony shook her head. 'We don't. Marcus is teetotal.'

'God, what a bore!'

Bryony compressed her lips and refused to allow the older girl annoy her. 'Grandpa died three years ago, but I expect you know that.'

Sorrell shook her head. 'I didn't know. Did he leave us anything in his will?'

'Of course not,' Bryony smiled. 'He left everything to grandma.'

'So she's a very wealthy old lady?'

'I've no idea. It's not my business. Grandma has arthritis and it makes it a bit difficult for her to get around, but apart from that she's fine. Aunt Maria is still in Brazil, aunt Elena still hasn't forgiven Marianne for staying in Crete with Giovanni, Helena and Greg…'

Sorrell held up her hand. 'Wait a minute, you're going too fast for me. What's this about Marianne?'

Bryony tucked her legs up beneath her. 'You wouldn't have heard, of course. There was a quite a scandal about it. She went over there to visit her friend who'd married some distant cousin of ours. She met up with another relative, don't ask me for details of the family tree, although grandma did explain at the time, and when she returned to America she was pregnant.'

'Why did she come back?'

'It was when her father had his heart attack. She rushed back to see him. It was just as well she was here. Aunt Elena fell to pieces, and Helena was useless. All she could think about was the fact that her boys had lost their grandfather and the emotional effect it could have on them.'

Sorrell snorted. 'Load of rubbish.'

'Anyway, everyone had thought Marianne would marry that man she had kept in touch with whilst she was in England studying, but he went off to Atlanta. I don't know why, but I guess it could be to do with Marianne being pregnant. She had a little boy. The next thing we knew she was flying out to Athens as her friend's husband had been shot. There was some robbery or something at the hotel where he worked. When she got there she found this Giovanni had also been shot and that was when it all came out that he was John's father. They got married and she stayed out there.'

'And?'

Bryony shrugged. 'That's all I know. Grandma could probably tell you more if you wanted to ask her. Uncle Andreas has become very successful. He's just had one of his plays turned into a film. I've never heard a word from Jeremy or Saffron, and mother and Christabelle are still in Florida as far as I know.'

Sorrell was no longer listening. Obviously the details of the shooting at the Athens hotel were not known by Bryony, and she wondered if her grandmother knew the full facts. She yawned.

'I've had a pretty tiring day, Bryony. I wouldn't mind an early night. Where am I sleeping?'

'Well, I've only got the sofa to offer you, but I'm going out to meet Marcus. You can bed down when you please.'

'Thanks. I really appreciate this, Bryony. I'll have to give you a special wedding present.'

Bryony smiled. Maybe her sister was not as uncaring as she had thought. It was her job taking her away so much that had made communication difficult. She could imagine how pleased her grandmother would be when she told them at the weekend that Sorrell had been staying with her. Maybe Sorrell would even come with her for a visit. She was about to suggest the idea when she saw Sorrell's eyes were closed.

Quietly Bryony rose from her chair and went to freshen up before her date with Marcus and leave a pillow and blanket for her sister. Sorrell stayed where she was, feigning sleep, until she heard the door close and the whine of the elevator as it arrived on the fourth floor.

Sorrell stayed on the sofa for a further ten minutes. She wanted to be certain that her sister did not return for something she may have forgotten. Slowly she stretched and rose from the chair, her eyes sweeping round the room. She would have a quick look round whilst Bryony was out. It could help her to formulate a plan.

The apartment was sparsely furnished, and Sorrell guessed that everything came as a package deal in with the rent. She crossed to the shelves. A couple of imitation silver candlesticks, two white china cats and a bunch of artificial flowers adorned the top shelf, and the lower ones held a miscellaneous collection of books, videos and cassettes. Pushed in at one corner was a cheque book and the month's utility bills, each one marked with the date it had been paid.

She turned her attention to the kitchenette, finding only the usual paraphernalia associated with cooking and serving. The bathroom cabinet yielded only cosmetics, a spare toilet roll and tube of toothpaste. Sorrell entered the bedroom. If Bryony had been saving hard to furnish a new apartment she must have a bank book somewhere, or the money hidden in cash.

Sorrell collected a tea towel from one of the drawers in the kitchen. Carefully she pulled open each cupboard door and drawer in turn and examined the contents. Underwear, neatly folded, a new packet of tights, nightdress, pyjamas, jumpers, exactly what one would expect to find. In the wardrobe Sorrell felt every article of clothing, there was nothing stitched into a seam, the pockets were empty. Shoeboxes, neatly arranged, held nothing but the shoes they were designed for. The photograph of Marcus, which stood on the table next to Bryony's bed, seemed to be mocking her and she had a distinct longing to knock it to the ground.

She returned to the chair and pressed the remote control for the television, pushing the buttons until she found a news channel followed by the weather forecast. It would be turning colder and wetter. She shuddered. She had not wintered in the States for a considerable number of years; the sooner she returned to the balmier climate of the Mediterranean the better she would be pleased. She picked up the photograph of Marcus that Bryony had shown her. There was nothing distinguished or good looking about him. In Sorrell's eyes he looked rather intense and definitely boring. She was about to replace it when she felt the slight bulge beneath the cardboard backing. She traced the outline with her fingers. It was the right size and shape for a bank book, definitely worth investigating.

She pried back the clasps holding the backing into position and slid the piece of cardboard out. There, nestling in the back, was a bank book. With a pleased smile Sorrell opened it and gasped at the amount she saw in there. Very carefully she returned it to its previous hiding place and replaced the picture where Bryony had left it. All she needed now was a signature.

Sorrell crossed to the shelves where she had seen the cheque book. She pulled it out and held a blank cheque up to the light, just able to make out the indentations made by a signature. She frowned. It could take some time before she was able to make a passable copy from such a faint imprint. The photograph of Marcus was grinning at her mockingly again and she remembered the one in the bedroom. That one could be worth investigating also.

This time the photograph was larger and the frame heavier, the backing being made from a rigid sheet of plastic, but still fastened with the small clips. Sorrell pulled back the clasps and removed the plastic.

'Bingo!' she murmured to herself. There was Bryony's passport and also five hundred dollars in notes. Sorrell removed the passport and opened it where there was a picture of her sister. She studied it carefully. They were not unalike, approximately the same colouring, although Bryony was shorter and plumper, but neither had any distinguishing marks. The passport had been issued two months earlier, no doubt in readiness for a honeymoon somewhere outside of the State. Even better was the fact that Bryony had not yet signed it. Smiling happily, Sorrell replaced the picture exactly as she had found it, resisted the urge to use her sister's bed instead of the sofa, and went to run herself a long, hot bath. She needed to relax and think.

Joseph was beginning to feel at home. His fridge was well stocked and he worked out a system that both sped up and simplified his preparation of the orders. He opened a quantity of cigarette packets and removed ten from each for his own use. In the space left he would pack twenty of the small packets of white powder and glue the flap closed. These packets he stored behind the cartons of two hundred and it was a simple matter of exchanging packets when he needed to complete an order. The work was undemanding and left him plenty of time to do as he wished. The real test was coming this Saturday when he had to visit Marmaris.

He rose early and dressed with care, checked that the money agreed with the receipts, folded them together and placed them in a small leather pouch. He hung the pouch over his shoulder where it fitted snugly into his armpit. Once he had adjusted the strap and donned his jacket it was completely invisible.

The ferry to Marmaris left only twenty minutes late and Joseph was prepared for a boring journey. He noted that most of the passengers were tourists, no doubt carrying all their money in their back pockets, assuming that a button kept it safe. He took up a position at the small bar and sat back and watched whilst he sipped at his beer.

Harassed parents tried to keep their children occupied during the journey with crisps, drinks and games. He doubted that the pickings would be very great there. A few couples were holding hands or had their arms entwined about each other and he watched them carefully as they approached the bar. His attention was finally attracted to four men who bought steadily and were gradually becoming more inebriated as the journey continued. Their voices rose as they discussed the benefits of visiting Turkey to purchase watches, perfume and jewellery.

Joseph waited until the ferry was nosing her way into the harbour and finished his drink. He followed the men to the upper deck where they took up a stance on the rails, watching the deckhands throwing out the mooring lines. He removed two wallets, one in each hand, and put them into his jacket pocket, repeating the action as he passed behind them. He hurried back down to the bar and into the toilet. As usual he removed the money and deposited the wallets into the waste bin. As he exited the men returned to the bar, red in the face and desperately looking for their wallets. He waited for them to pass him, which they did without a second glance, and returned to the upper deck ready to disembark with the other travellers.

Once ashore he walked slowly to the end of the jetty, ignoring the importunate cries of the vendors, and hoped he would soon be met. The language around him was totally alien to his ears and he doubted his ability to make even the most mundane request understood.

A diminutive girl detached herself from a group of youths with bicycles as he approached. 'It's Joseph, isn't it?'

Joseph stopped. 'How did you know?'

'You fitted the description I was given.' She linked her arm in his. 'Come and meet my brother.'

He allowed himself to be led towards the group of youths and be introduced. He had no idea whether she told him their names, but if she did they were unrecognisable by him.

'Where are we going?' he asked her.

'I will show you Marmaris and we will talk and get to know each other. I am Nimet and this is my brother, Kadir.'

'Well, you know who I am.'

'Smile, Joseph. You are happy to see me. I am your girl friend, remember.'

'Should I kiss you?'

'That is not necessary at this moment. I will tell you when you should do so.'

Joseph strolled along, Nimet on one side and her brother on the other. They turned into a side road and reached the first of many shopping arcades. Joseph found the multitude of arcades, with shops all selling like products, as confusing as he had Rhodes town when he had first arrived and he followed where Nimet led. Kadir darted from side to side of them, sometimes chattering to Nimet in Turkish.

'Does your brother speak Greek?' asked Joseph.

'He has no need,' she answered. 'He speaks the English language.'

'Do you?'

'Of course.'

'Then why don't we all speak in English? That way we could at least hold a proper conversation.'

Nimet inclined her head. 'If you wish. It will be good for us to practise.'

Joseph smiled grimly. 'Well, the first thing, Kadir, stop darting from side to side of us. You're making me feel ill.'

Kadir grinned at him. 'Okay.' He walked sedately at Nimet's side. 'Where are we going for lunch?'

'That depends what Joseph would like. We are not going to eat beef burgers with you and your friends.'

Kadir's face fell. 'There's nothing wrong with beef burgers.'

'We will go for kebab, if Joseph is happy with that. You can have a beef burger there if you wish.'

Kadir pulled a face. 'It would be more fun with my friends.'

'Why don't you go off with your friends and leave us alone?' suggested Joseph.

'I can't do that. I have to chaperone Nimet.'

'You still have chaperones over here?' Joseph looked at her in surprise.

'Of course. You do not think my father would let me go out alone with a young man, do you? What would happen to my reputation?'

'I am sure your reputation would be quite safe with me.'

Nimet glanced at him from beneath her dark lashes and did not reply.

Joseph found the day monotonous and dull. They had lingered over a mid-day meal; then wandered along the waterfront until it was time for him to return to the ferry. As they approached the quay Nimet pulled him into the shelter of a doorway.

'Now I will kiss you. Whilst I do so I shall relieve you of the burden you have been carrying all day.' She turned up her face towards him and as Joseph bent to kiss her she slipped her hands beneath his jacket. He could feel her hand as it unclipped the pouch from the strap and withdrew it from under his armpit. She stood back from him and smiled.

'I am so sorry to have to bid farewell to my boyfriend. I shall count the hours until he returns next week.'

Dark, soulful eyes looked into Joseph's and he could almost believe she meant it.

Sorrell waited until her sister had finished in the bathroom before she rose from the sofa.

'Did you have a good evening?'

'Fine. I told Marcus about you turning up and he would like to meet you. I said I would cook a meal this evening.'

Sorrell yawned. She was not interested in meeting this young man. 'What time?'

'Probably about eight. Marcus will want to go home and freshen up after work and I'll be home about six to start the cooking. What are you doing today?'

'Finding out when I can return to my apartment. I don't want to spend too many nights cramped up on your sofa or I shall be a hunchback.'

Bryony looked guilty. 'I'm sorry. You can have my bed tonight.'

'Thanks. I'll see how things are progressing. I can cope with another night if necessary.' Sorrell flopped back on the sofa. 'I think I'll sleep in for a while. There's no point in going round too early.'

'I'm looking forward to hearing about your foreign travels over dinner tonight. Marcus and I are going to New York for a week after the wedding. Have you been there?'

Sorrell shook her head. She had no intention of participating in the impending conversation. 'I've passed through on my way to Europe.'

'We decided we would spend the money on our home instead of going to England as so many people do. Besides, we only have a couple of weeks before Marcus has to be back at work, so it isn't really long enough to go very far. I'll see you later.' Bryony picked up her purse. 'By the way, I've left a spare key on my dressing table for you.'

Sorrell nodded. 'Thanks,' she called as Bryony closed the door.

As soon as she was certain Bryony would not return Sorrell rose from the sofa. In truth she had slept well and she knew exactly how she planned to spend her day. From her over-night bag she selected a pair of evening shoes and began to remove two of the stones that decorated the heel. The time had come to turn them into ready cash.

She raided Bryony's drawers for a large pair of jeans and an old, baggy jumper. Over her panties she placed a large pair of elastic legged knickers, pulling them up to just below her bra. With her hair scraped back into a ponytail and the minimum of makeup she looked like any other young woman who worked in the poorer areas of the town. Tucking the key of the apartment into the pocket of her jacket, she drank a second cup of coffee and left the apartment, the dirty cup sitting beside the rumpled sofa. If everything went as she planned, she would not have to spend the evening inventing boring stories about her travels in Europe.

A shopping bag on her arm she made her way to the nearest multiple store and mingled with the customers, pretending to examine the prices of the fruit and vegetables on display. It took her only a matter of minutes to spot a purse gaping open and she slipped her hand inside. The contents transferred to her pocket she picked up a lettuce and walked towards the longest checkout queue. Before she reached her turn, she gave a deep sigh, abandoned her basket and hurried from the shop as if having run out of time.

Once round the corner she counted the dollars in her pocket. There was enough for a subway fare and lunch. She left the subway five stops down the line and emerged into a district that she would not dream of entering at night. Her head down, she tried to walk casually past the grim tenements, not wishing to draw attention to herself. Ragged children played improvised games of ball or chase, oblivious to the addicts or drunks that lounged in the doorways and cursed them.

Sorrell turned into an alley festooned with rusty fire escapes. Half way down, almost hidden, was a door, the paint peeling and the knocker worn thin by continual use. She walked to the end of the alley and was relieved to see a cheap coffee house on the opposite side of the road. She retraced her steps until she reached the door and knocked. The sound of a bolt being withdrawn made her take a deep breath.

'Can I come in?' The door opened wider to admit her, being bolted again after her entry. She followed the Puerto Rican into a small room.

'What can I do for you?'

'I have something to sell.'

He nodded and held out his hand. From her purse Sorrell took a screw of paper and placed it in his hand. He opened the paper carefully and squinted at the stones.

'Why should I be interested in these?'

'They're good ones.'

The man shrugged. 'They're uncut.'

'I know.'

'Where did you get them?'

54

'I've had them for years. Present from an old friend.'

He raised his eyebrows in disbelief.

'They're untraceable,' Sorrell assured him.

'How much are you asking?'

Sorrell hesitated. Should she use the story she had ready about being a single parent, using drugs and desperate for ready cash, or ask an extortionate amount and be prepared to go elsewhere if he refused. She decided on the latter.

'I know their value. In their uncut state they're worth at least five hundred thousand dollars. When you've worked on them they'll be worth double.'

He shook his head. 'I'd have to pay for expert cutting. That work does not come cheap. Three hundred thousand is the most I could offer.'

Sorrell shook her head and held out her hand. 'I'll go elsewhere.'

'You'll not get a better offer.' He continued to turn a stone between his fingers. 'Three fifty.'

'Four. In cash. Now.' She knew the risk she was taking by trying to bargain.

The Puerto Rican looked at them again. 'Are you sure they're untraceable?'

'Certain.'

'Three seventy five. I'll go no higher.'

'Cash?'

'Wait outside. I'll call you.'

'How do I know you'll keep your side of the bargain?'

'You can take the stones with you.'

Reluctantly Sorrell walked out into the dark hallway, the waiting seemed an eternity before he called to her. On the table sat a pile of high denomination notes. With shaking hands she counted the dollars until she was satisfied it was the full amount, whilst he watched, his eyes unblinking. He held out his hand and she placed a diamond in his palm.

'The second one.' He slid a knife from his pocket and with a flick exposed the blade.

'I'll give it to you when I've put this away.' Brazenly she stared him out and began to place the notes inside the shopping bag and closing the zipper before placing the second gem in his outstretched hand.

Without another word he escorted her to the door and once outside Sorrell took to her heels and ran to the end of the alley, taking advantage of a break in the traffic to sprint across the road and into the coffee house.

'Do you have a rest room?' She gasped as she entered.

The woman behind the counter jerked her thumb towards the rear and Sorrell hurried through.

Once in the cubicle she unzipped her jeans, placing the dollar bills inside the voluminous knickers, padding herself evenly at the sides and ensuring there was a bulge at the front. She helped herself to two toilet rolls and flushed the toilet. She held each roll beneath the tap at the grimy basin until they had absorbed enough water to increase their weight and placed them in her shopping bag. Satisfied she pulled her jumper down as far as she could and returned to the coffee room.

She sat down at the first table and placed her head in her hands. The woman from behind the counter walked over.

'You all right?'

'Yeah – bloody kids. Never would've kept it if I'd known I'd keep throwin' up.' Sorrell patted her stomach.

The woman nodded sympathetically. 'What can I get you?'

'Just a glass of water or I'll be back in there. Can't keep nothin' down.'

Sorrell forced herself to drink half the water, thanked the woman and left, assuring her that she felt considerably better. She walked confidently along the sidewalk of the undesirable area towards the subway, knowing she was being followed. As she waited to cross an intersection her bag was snatched from her hand and a youth ran down the street, passing it to another on a bicycle, who rode past her with a broad grin on his face.

'Hey, thief!' A man standing next to her put a steadying hand on her elbow. 'I saw that. Are you going to report it?'

Sorrell shook her head. 'What would be the point? It was so fast I couldn't give a description, besides, there were only a couple of toilet rolls in there.'

He smiled at her. 'Are you feeling okay? I mean, bit of a shock in your condition.'

Sorrell smiled back. 'I guess so.'

'Where are you making for? I'll walk along with you. They might come back for your purse when they find they've only got a couple of toilet rolls for their trouble.'

'I'm making for the subway.'

He walked beside her until they reached the entrance.

'Thanks for your company.'

'My pleasure.' He raised his hand and Sorrell hurried to get a ticket. The sooner she was back at her sister's apartment the sooner she could put into action the next part of her plan.

Sorrell threw herself onto the sofa. She was elated. She had done it! She had known it would be risky, and she had not been so frightened since she had stood in the dock in Athens on a trumped up murder charge. She had even outwitted the fence by transferring the money to her jeans. He must have considered her a novice if he thought she would carry the money in her shopping bag. She laughed aloud at the thought of his face when he found the two wet toilet rolls.

Whilst she waited for the coffee to percolate she removed the jeans and jumper, folded them carefully and replaced them in Bryony's drawer. She removed the money from the knickers and placed it in the over-night bag she had brought with her, along with the evening shoes. It was time to leave.

An hour later she was smartly dressed in a cantaloupe linen

suit that she had borrowed from Bryony's wardrobe and tightly belted to make it fit. With her hair piled on top of her head, her makeup immaculate and her over-night bag in her hand, Sorrell closed the door of the apartment. She waved down a taxi and directed the driver to a branch of the bank that Bryony used for her savings, walking in confidently and requested the closure of the savings account. She explained it was the money she had been saving for her wedding and the wonderful day was drawing close, necessitating the payment for her dress and the reception. She explained that she was unable to go to her usual branch due to her mother being terminally ill. She wiped away a fictitious tear, as she added that it was highly unlikely that her mother would live to attend her wedding.

The young teller, full of sympathy and envious of the fortunate man who was to marry the beautiful young woman, hardly glanced at the passport confirming her identity and signature. He pushed the money across the counter to her, glowing under her effusive thanks and watched longingly as she glided towards the exit.

The photographic studio she needed was the other side of the town and she hoped Jimmy was still working there. If he had moved it could take her a considerable amount of time to find another contact with his capabilities. She refused to let her mind dwell on the possibility as she entered and asked for him by name from the assistant at the counter.

'He's gone to lunch.'

'What time will he be back?'

The man glanced at the clock. ''Bout an hour.'

'I'll be back.'

He nodded. If she were a model wanting a portfolio she would have to wait her turn.

Sorrell retired to a fashionable restaurant and ate a leisurely meal, timing her return to the studio for when she was certain Jimmy would be there. He greeted her cautiously and invited her into his office.

'It's been a while. What can I do for you?'

'One of your specials, but fast.'

Jimmy raised his eyebrows. 'What have you been up to?'

Sorrell gazed at him innocently. 'I need to get to Europe as quickly as possible. Affairs of the heart.'

'How many?'

'Only one. It must be watertight. I don't want to be picked up on a technicality.'

Jimmy nodded. 'It will cost, rush job.'

'How much?'

'A thousand'

'A thousand!' Sorrell frowned. 'It was half that for three before.'

'You want it fast. If you can wait a week I can lower the price.'

'No. I want it this afternoon.'

'Cash.'

'Of course.'

'Half now and the rest when you pick it up.'

Sorrell nodded and peeled off the notes. She looked at her watch. 'I'll be back at three thirty.'

Jimmy nodded. He picked up his camera and focused it on her. 'Three thirty will be fine.'

Sorrell returned to the hostel and began to sort her meagre possessions. She really did need a new wardrobe. She packed her underwear, two blouses and a skirt into her overnight bag before deciding she would leave the remainder of the clothes. It was also unlikely the hostel would realise that she had left if they saw clothes hanging in the closet. Unconcerned she locked her door, leaving the key sitting in the lock, and sauntered out past the reception desk. A block away she hailed a taxi and asked for the bus station, where she studied the timetable for the various destinations. There was a bus that would take her to Charleston at five thirty. By the time Bryony returned to her apartment she would be well on her way and with luck she would even be out of the country before her sister needed her bankbook or passport. Everything was going very smoothly.

Her new passport safely in her purse Sorrell boarded the bus. She would be able to catch a few hours sleep; then when she reached the town it should be a fairly simple matter of finding an unlocked and unattended car that she could borrow to take her further into her journey. She would do as Joseph had done when they had driven across Europe. Abandon the car and take a short journey by bus or train before picking up another. That way the trail continually went cold and the theft was attributed to youngsters' joy riding. No doubt she would also be able to find an unattended wallet and begin to replenish her wardrobe. She smiled grimly to herself.

'You taught me a lot of useful tricks, Joseph.'

Bryony entered her apartment. She was later than she had intended, having been held up at the supermarket. She froze with annoyance when she saw the rumpled bedding on the sofa and the dirty cups. Sorrell might at least have cleared up; she knew Marcus was coming round for supper. Dumping her bags on the table, Bryony placed the two dirty cups in the sink, folded the blanket and pushed it back on the top shelf of her wardrobe along with the pillow. As she stepped back she caught sight of her key and the scrap of paper on her dressing table. It had the word '*thanks*' scrawled across it.

She sat down on her bed. Sorrell hadn't changed a bit. She had been taken in by her, as she had been when they were younger, when she had lent a favourite dress, only to have it returned in a heap on her bedroom floor with stains that would not come out, pocket money borrowed and never repaid, jewellery damaged beyond repair. Each time she had vowed that she would never let her sister touch any of her possessions again, only to be cajoled and persuaded, and always to her cost. It had happened again.

Wearily she rose; the strength seemed to have drained from her. At least Marcus was coming for dinner. She had overspent in an attempt to impress her sister, but she could always freeze some and it would make a meal the following week. Suddenly she was pleased that Sorrell would not be there, at least she would not be able to charm Marcus away from her.

She returned to the living room and picked up his framed photograph intending to place it where she could see it as she worked in the kitchen. Very soon she would be Mrs Mannerheim. Her fingers slid down the backing of the picture and her heart seemed to miss a beat. Frantically she pulled back the clips and removed the cardboard. Her bankbook was missing. Surely not – it couldn't be possible – her sister wouldn't … Desperately she tore at the photograph in her bedroom, removing the plastic. Her passport had gone also.

The colour drained from her face. What would Marcus say? She was such a fool! She had no idea where Sorrell lived and had accepted her story of a water-damaged apartment at face value. In fact she had accepted everything she had been told – what a gullible fool she was. Tears filled her eyes and ran down her cheeks. All their dreams for furnishing the new kitchen and their honeymoon in New York – now there was nothing.

She returned to the living room and dialled Marcus's phone number. She was just about to replace the receiver when he answered.

'Sorry,' he said when he heard her voice. 'I was in the shower, didn't hear it ringing at first.'

'Marcus, can you come now, right now. Something terrible has happened.'

'What? Tell me? Are you all right?'

Bryony passed a shaking hand over her forehead. 'Yes, I'm fine. Just get here as soon as you can, please, Marcus.'

'Is it your sister?'

'I can't tell you over the phone. Just come now.' Bryony replaced the receiver. She needed to be held in his arms when she told him the news. She knew he would not be cross with her; he never let anything she did or said upset him, but she could imagine how hurt he would be on her behalf.

Joseph arrived back in Rhodes and was surprised to see Thalia at the dock waiting for him.

'Lakkis is at *The Grapevine*. He wants to see you.'

Joseph shrugged. 'Fine. I could do with a decent beer.' Thalia turned away and Joseph caught her arm. 'Wait a moment.'

'What for?'

'I'd just like to hold a conversation with you. I'd like us to be friends.'

'I'm betrothed to Lakkis's son.'

'That doesn't stop you from having friends, does it?'

'No, I suppose not.'

'Good.' Joseph searched wildly for a reason to meet her again. 'You told me you are in the travel business. I'd like to get to know the island better. I thought if we could meet for coffee you could tell me the best places to visit.'

'Anyone can tell you that.'

'They will tell me which ones are best for tourists to visit. I want to know where the local people go when they have time off, those beauty spots that are off the beaten track. Please,' persisted Joseph. 'I'd be grateful and I don't know anyone else to ask.'

Thalia hesitated. Other girls met friends in coffee shops during their lunch hour or after work. There was no reason why she should not give him directions. 'I'll be at Spiro's coffee shop on Mandraki Harbour at two on Monday.'

'Really? That's great. I'll see you there.'

Thalia hurried off and Joseph looked after her in appreciation. It was a start. Whistling cheerfully he set off towards *The Grapevine*.

Lakkis placed a beer in front of him as he sat down. 'No problems?'

'None at all.'

Lakkis regarded him with his cold, cat-like eyes. 'And Nimet?'

'She's terrific. I could really fall for her,' lied Joseph. 'It's a shame that brother of hers tags along all the time.'

'It is probably fortunate for her that he does! Still, it is good that you like her. It adds credibility to your story. It will soon be noticed that you go over on a regular basis. Did you bring anything back?'

Joseph looked at him in horror. 'Was I supposed to?'

'No. You are free to bring back small items for your own use. I do not suggest that you bring back enough to make the customs officers think you are in business.'

Joseph looked around; they were the only occupants of the taverna. He lowered his voice. 'Can I ask you something?' Lakkis frowned and Joseph continued. 'Would it be all right if I purchased a bike and went out of town during my time off?'

'I assume you have a driving licence?'

'Of course.'

Lakkis shrugged. 'Then there is no reason why you should not.' He finished his beer and pushed a small black pouch across the table, a replica of the one Nimet had taken earlier. 'You will need this next week. Stay and have another. I will see you again.'

Joseph signalled to Alecos. Lakkis had made it sound more like an order than an invitation.

Joseph was looking forward to his meeting with Thalia. He planned to gain her confidence by talking generally to her; he would say nothing that would put her on her guard against him. He dressed carefully, wearing an open-necked shirt instead of a vest and cotton trousers took the place of his jeans. He debated on the wisdom of wearing a pair of his smart Italian shoes and decided the occasion warranted them. It also meant he walked the long way round the outer walls of the old town to avoid the cobbled streets.

He paid in the money at the bank, grateful that he had not had to stand in the queue for too long, finally arriving early at the coffee house and bought a newspaper. He must not seem too eager. He opened it on the table in front of him and pretended to read, whilst watching for her approach. As she entered he rose, indicated the seat opposite and signalled to the waiter.

'What would you like?'

'Just coffee please. I can't stay long. I'm in my lunch hour.'

'Then you must eat. I insist. If you have given up your lunch hour it is only fair.'

Thalia shook her head. 'I have a sandwich back at the office.'

With a resigned shrug Joseph ordered for both of them, whilst Thalia delved into her bag and brought out a map of the island.

'I thought you might find this useful. You can buy them anywhere, but I've marked the places that might interest you.'

Joseph smiled at her. 'I'm really grateful to you. I've met a couple of young men up in the town, but they seemed to think it was a bit odd that I wanted to go anywhere else.'

'Why do you?'

'I'm used to travelling around. I've worked in Spain and Italy as well as Greece. I lived in Italy when I was a child.'

'Did you?'

Joseph realised he had caught her interest and he began to tell her about his life in Turin, making her laugh with exaggerated tales of his childish misdeeds. 'What about you?' he asked finally.

'I was born here and I've lived here all my life.'

'Don't you want to travel?'

'One day, maybe, when I'm married.'

'When will that be?'

'In a couple of years. Manolis must finish his army service first.'

'How long have you been betrothed?'

'Since we were children.'

'I thought that practice had died out?'

A guarded look came over Thalia's face. 'Not in Rhodes.'

'Are you happy to marry Manolis?'

'Of course.'

'When do you get to see him if he's in the army?'

'He returns to the town when he has leave. We spend time together then.' Thalia looked at her watch. 'I have to go, Joseph. I must get back to work.'

'May I walk with you?'

'It would be better not. My uncle might see us and he would not approve.'

'Will you meet me again – next Monday, for coffee? I can tell you where I've visited.'

Thalia hesitated. 'Very well.'

Joseph watched as she left the café, a pleased smile on his face. He had definitely made progress there! He wondered how many weeks he would have to meet her for coffee before he would be able to persuade her to meet him elsewhere.

Impatient as she was to reach Greece, Sorrell was determined not to draw attention to herself. She had no illusions. In the States she was of no importance, just a petty criminal who made her living as a pickpocket and small time thief, but once she reached Europe she was suspected of a diamond theft and murder. She had no way of knowing if she would be able to find Joseph, but she was determined to try. She wanted revenge for the months she had spent in the Greek jail. She had no doubt that whatever activity he was engaged in would be illegal and if she could inform the police and ensure he was convicted she would certainly pay him a visit in prison and gloat over his predicament.

She had used buses, trains and 'borrowed' cars during the week it had taken her to cross three States, a flight had taken her to Heathrow in England and a day later she had arrived in Athens. Apart from some discreet pick pocketing at train stations and in the airport she had kept a very low profile. She had used two stolen credit cards at Heathrow to withdraw money, making sure she did so just before the last call for her flight, disposing of both cards afterwards in an empty cigarette carton, tossed carelessly into a rubbish bin.

Now she sat in a small hotel room and considered how best she could go about her task to track down Joseph. She recalled all he had ever told her about himself. He was half Italian, but hated his father, so it was unlikely that he would have returned to his parent's home. He bore a grudge against his uncle who had the Athenia hotel, but that could be a starting point to discover his whereabouts. She just had to concoct a good cover story for her enquiries.

She showered and dressed carefully, choosing jeans, white blouse and trainers; she wanted to look much the same as other tourists. Her hair she left loose, sunglasses hid her eyes and she wore no jewellery. She wandered through the Plaka area, looking into the shop windows, mingling with the tourists, until she reached the Athenia De Luxe hotel. She strolled inside, treating the desk clerk with a dazzling smile.

'I am sorry to trouble you, but I was wondering if you would be able to help me.'

He smiled in return. 'My pleasure.'

'I am trying to find someone, a distant relative, and I was told I would probably find him here.'

'He is a guest?'

'No, I believe he works here.'

'Not all our staff are here, the shift system, you know, but if you would like to give me his name I can look at the work roster for you.'

'Yannis Andronicatis.'

The young man frowned. 'There is no one of that name here.'

'Are you sure?'

'Maybe he has moved elsewhere. Wait a moment and I'll ask for you.' The clerk picked up the telephone and held a quick conversation with someone.

The door to the manager's office opened and Sorrell's heart missed a beat. She had a horrible feeling that Giovanni would walk out and she was sure he would recognise her. Poised for instant flight she drew a sigh of relief when an unknown man approached her.

'Can I help you? I believe you are looking for Yannis Andronicatis, the former owner of this hotel?'

'I didn't realise he was the owner!' lied Sorrell. 'I thought he just worked here, as a manager or something.'

'I am the manager. The hotel is under new management. Mr Andronicatis decided to retire. He lives in Crete. I think he was finding the travelling very tiring.'

Sorrell bit at her lip. 'You wouldn't have an address or telephone number for him by any chance?'

The manager shook his head. 'I'm sorry. Once all the papers were signed there was no need to keep in touch with Mr Andronicatis.'

Sorrell appeared to consider. 'I suppose you wouldn't know if his nephew is still in Athens? I was told he worked at this hotel also.'

'You mean Mr Giovanni. I understand that he also returned to Crete when he was well enough.'

'I thought he also had another nephew.'

'You are probably thinking of Mr Nicolas who ran the night club. I have no idea of his whereabouts.'

Sorrell frowned. 'I didn't think that was his name.'

'Maybe he has other nephews. I do not know. I am sorry, madam, I am quite unable to help you.'

'Oh, well,' Sorrell shrugged. 'I'm not prepared to go to Crete to look for him. I shall just continue to enjoy my holiday here.'

'Can I offer you some refreshment?'

'Thank you, no.' Sorrell extended her hand. 'I have already taken up too much of your time.'

The manager watched her leave and returned to his office, dismissing her from his mind.

Sorrell frowned in annoyance as she walked down the narrow street. She would have to fall back on her second line of enquiry. If she sat down at the taverna by the entrance to the flea market and the underground there was just a chance that Joseph might be there if he was still living in the city. It had been there that she had first met him, and they had used the area as a rich source of income for some months. She would do that for a while and hope she could find him. She sighed in exasperation. It was such a waste of the time that she could have spent improving her financial situation.

Sorrell haunted the taverna for three days, interspersing the boring hours of waiting with trips on the underground to keep herself supplied with ready cash. The waiters began to greet her as an old friend and she decided to take a chance.

'You haven't seen Joseph around, I suppose? He said he'd meet me here this week, but so far he hasn't shown up.'

The waiter shook his head. 'He's not been around for a few weeks now.'

'Any idea where else he might be?'

'No, but I could ask around.'

'I'd be grateful. I'm fed up with sitting here each day waiting for him.'

The waiter grinned. Joseph should consider himself a lucky man to have a beautiful young woman looking for him, and then a thought crossed his mind. Maybe she was about to saddle him with a child. That would not be so fortunate. Joseph should be warned so he could keep his distance.

'I'll do my best,' he promised. 'It could take a day or two.' Yiorgo disappeared into the interior of the taverna and lifted the telephone. 'I need to speak to Dimitris. Ask him to call me.'

Sorrell returned to the taverna the next day in a fever of anticipation only to find the waiter she had spoken to was not in evidence.

'Where's Yiorgo?' she asked.

'His day off,' the man replied gruffly. He had worked at the taverna for the last five years and was used to the girls asking after the waiters.

Sorrell clicked her tongue in annoyance. She was tired of waiting.

Dimitris pursed his lips. Who was this girl who was enquiring after Joseph? He decided he would have her watched. If she were working for the police he would leave her alone. Joseph had disappeared from the Athenian scene and, whilst he was useful, Dimitris was prepared to protect his anonymity.

Stelios telephoned the following morning and his report intrigued Dimitris further. The girl had travelled several times on the underground during the day, just up and down between stations and he thought he had seen her take a wallet, but could not be sure. He had followed her back to the hotel where she was staying. Her name was Suzanna Hirsch, and her passport showed she was an American citizen. She had eaten in her hotel and retired alone to her room at eleven.

A few drachmas to the chambermaid had given him the freedom to search her room and he had found nothing more suspicious than thousands of American dollars and Greek drachmas in a travelling bag.

Dimitris tapped his tobacco stained teeth with a gold pen. There was just a remote possibility… he would take a chance. If he was wrong she could very swiftly be disposed of.

'Anders,' he called. 'Get clearance to leave the harbour. We're going to Zea Marina.'

Sorrell resisted the urge to be at the taverna as it opened. She managed to curtail her impatience until almost mid-day. There was no sign of Yiorgo or the waiter she had spoken to the previous day.

'Where's Yiorgo today?' she tried to make the enquiry sound light and unimportant.

'His wife called in to say he was sick. Something he'd eaten.'

Sorrell pulled a face. 'I hope he recovers quickly. He didn't leave a message for me, I suppose?'

The waiter shook his head. If Yiorgo were seeing this girl he would hardly give his wife a message for her!

Sighing with frustration and annoyance Sorrell left. She had acquired a credit card earlier that morning and it could be worth her while to visit the shopping centre and see if she could pick up a bargain. Some smart trousers and a cashmere jumper would be a welcome addition to her wardrobe for when the weather turned cooler.

Dimitris sat in the cabin of *Aegean Pride*. He considered his investment in the high-powered cruiser had been a stroke of genius on his part. It made travelling easy and comfortable between the islands, no long delays at airports or checking in or out of hotels. He had all he needed aboard; Anders was an excellent navigator and his Norwegian wife a superb cook and adequate housekeeper. Whenever he fancied a companion he was always able to find a suitable girl for the night or a few days. He poured a generous measure of ouzo and wondered how long he would have to wait before Stelios persuaded the girl to visit him.

Stelios sat at a table by the entrance to the taverna, a beer, hardly touched before him. Sorrell wandered down the road, appeared to hesitate and then sat at a table. The waiter touched Stelios on the shoulder as he made his way over to her to take her order.

Sorrell regarded Stelios with suspicion as he slipped into the seat next to her and began to explain his errand. 'Who is this Dimitris who wants to see me?'

'Dimitris is a very important man. You have been asking about Joseph and Dimitris knows where he is.'

'So why didn't he give you his address for me?'

'The situation is delicate. Dimitris would prefer to speak to you in person. He has asked me to invite you to have lunch with him.' He pushed a piece of paper across the table to her. 'That is the name of his boat. If you wish you can check with the harbour master. He will confirm that the boat is registered in Dimitris's name and is in Zea Marina. You can leave word at your hotel of your proposed destination if you are concerned.'

Sorrell considered the invitation. There had been no sign of Yiorgo at the taverna and she could think of no other line of enquiry. 'Very well, but I need to be back in Athens by five. I have an appointment.'

'That will be no problem,' smiled Stelios. 'I have a car at my disposal.'

Sorrell shook her head. 'I will make my own way.'

'As you please. I will telephone Dimitris to expect you.'

Stelios stayed at the taverna as Sorrell walked away. He had no need to telephone; he would simply drive back to Piraeus and inform Dimitris that she was on her way.

It was an hour later when Sorrell strolled along the waterfront to the Zea Marina. From her hotel she had checked with the harbour master and verified the information Stelios had given her. Dimitris Stephanotis was a millionaire businessman. She need have no qualms about visiting him on his cabin cruiser, which was currently moored in the harbour.

Tentatively she crossed the walkway and stepped on board. The door leading to the interior apartments was open and she looked inside cautiously. A large, middle-aged man, dressed in white shirt and slacks rose to greet her. He held out his hand and helped her down the shallow steps.

'Please, Miss Hirsch, take a seat. Can I offer you a drink before our lunch is served?'

'Orange juice, please.' Sorrell wanted to keep a clear head and she could smell the ouzo on his breath.

'With ice?'

Sorrell nodded, taking in her surroundings whilst she waited for the tall glass to be placed before her. The saloon was neat and tidy, spotlessly clean and furnished in impeccable taste. The burgundy carpet set off the mahogany, polished chrome and sparkling glass fitments to perfection.

Dimitris lifted his glass of ouzo and she followed suite with her orange juice.

'I am so pleased you accepted my invitation.' He took in the details of the girl before him. She was beautiful. Stelios had not told him that. It could make all the difference to his plans. 'It is not every day that I am fortunate enough to have such a charming young lady to dine with me.'

'It is not every day I am invited to have lunch with a millionaire.'

Dimitris raised his eyebrows. She had done some checking up on him. That was to her credit. They could exchange small talk before lunch and talk business afterwards.

'You have travelled from America, I believe?'

Sorrell nodded and sipped at her drink. How had he found out?

'It is a long way to come for a holiday. Regrettably I have never visited the country. I would be interested in hearing about your life over there.'

'I would have thought a man in your position would have holidayed all over the world.'

'My commitments keep me mainly in Greece.' A smile played on his lips. It was going to be a sparring game. That suited him. 'And how do you make your living, Miss Hirsch – unless you also are a millionaire?'

'I have a modelling agency. I am over here to find suitable locations to model our latest range of beachwear.'

'I would not expect you to find a very suitable location in Athens.'

'Oh, you never know what appeals. Skimpy bikinis with a backdrop of the Parthenon can be ideal for some of our clients.'

'Would it not be easier to use a little trick photography rather than go to the expense of bringing models to the Parthenon?'

'I was only using that as an example,' smiled Sorrell. 'Personally I think beachwear is better displayed in secluded, rocky coves; or on vast tracts of sand with the sea shimmering in the background. Nothing is a substitute for reality.'

'My sentiments entirely.' Dimitris poured himself another glass of ouzo. 'Maybe we could work together on your project. It is easier to discover hidden coves when travelling by sea.'

'What an excellent idea.' Sorrell was not sure if he was propositioning her. 'We could even use your boat in some of the shots.'

'I thought you were selling clothing, not shipping.' He raised his eyebrows quizzically.

'Our range is more extensive than swimming costumes. Casual clothes, very suitable for relaxing on a boat after a day on the beach, or evening dress for that special invitation to dinner with a millionaire.' Sorrell raised her glass, the light of challenge in her eyes. She could lead him on for hours if this was the game he wanted to play.

'And do you have one of these evening dresses in your wardrobe should that special invitation be extended to you?'

'Of course.'

'Then maybe this evening you would do me the honour of wearing it.'

Sorrell frowned. 'I have an appointment in Athens at five.'

Dimitris shrugged. 'That is no problem. You can return in time to keep your appointment. I will send a car for you at eight. Finish your drink, my dear. There will be wine with our lunch and Frida will be serving us within a matter of minutes.'

The meal was excellent and Sorrell was beginning to enjoy herself. It had been amusing, telling this seemingly gullible man about a fictitious modelling agency. She found she quite liked him, despite him being overweight and smelling so strongly of ouzo.

When she returned to Athens she would visit one of the most exclusive shops and purchase an evening gown. It could be quite a good investment.

Frida cleared the dishes and placed a pot of coffee on the table, closing the saloon door behind her as she left. Dimitris searched his pockets and drew forth a cigar. 'You have no objection, my dear?'

'Of course not. I enjoy the smell of a good cigar.'

He clipped the end and sucked on it appreciatively, the smoke curling upwards. He eyed Sorrell speculatively.

'Shall we now discuss the business that brought you here in the first place?' He smiled disarmingly at her. 'You were enquiring about a certain young man, I believe.'

Sorrell was about to open her mouth and spin him the tissue of lies she had concocted about being his sister and the family wanting him back in their bosom, all past misdeeds forgotten, when she remembered that Dimitris knew she was an American.

'Joseph and I had a big thing going a while back. I wanted to meet up with him again.'

Dimitris raised his eyebrows. 'It must have been a very big thing indeed for you to come half way across the world in pursuit of him.'

'There had been some misunderstandings between us. I wanted to put the record straight, see if we could start again.'

'Suppose I contacted Joseph on your behalf? See how he feels about a reunion.'

'No.' Sorrell shook her head. 'I want to surprise him.'

'And what is it that you wish to surprise him with, my dear? The gun he so conveniently left with you?'

The blood drained from Sorrell's face. Dimitris knew who she was. 'Off course not,' she tried to smile. 'I want to talk to him. To tell him I understand and have no hard feelings against him.'

'Really?' Dimitris drew on his cigar again. It could be amusing being the cat playing with two mice.

Sorrell nodded her head vigorously.

Dimitris leaned across the table towards her. 'I am not prepared to tell you where Joseph is at the moment. At present his services are useful to me.' He stroked her hand gently with one fat finger. 'Maybe we could come to some arrangement, and at a mutually convenient time I could put you in touch with Joseph again?'

Sorrell swallowed. 'What do you mean?'

'From time to time I require the services of a beautiful young woman to accompany me on social engagements. I need to have a young lady on my arm that does credit to my reputation as a connoisseur. This can be difficult to arrange at short notice if I am moving from island to island. It would be useful to me to have such a person with me on my travels.'

'What are you suggesting?'

'I am suggesting that you stop playing games with me. You are nothing to do with a modelling agency. You have come to Greece with the idea of revenge on the man who betrayed you and very nearly destroyed you.' Dimitris held up his hand to stop Sorrell from interrupting. 'I am the only person who can tell you where he is. The choice is yours. You can stay on this boat as my companion until I tire of you and leave you with Joseph, or you can leave for your appointment in Athens and not return for dinner tonight. I would appreciate your answer before you depart as Frida will need to know how many people she is to cater for.'

Sorrell bit at her lip in indecision. If she left now she knew she would never find Joseph, but if she stayed she would certainly be living in luxury for a while. Dimitris appeared to be a large and gentle giant but if she found him too obnoxious she would simply find some excuse to leave. It was even possible that some of his associates knew where Joseph was living and she might be able to worm the information out of them.

'Very well,' she murmured. 'I accept your offer.'

'A very sensible decision, if I may say so. The name you are using at the moment is Suzanna, is it not?'

Sorrell nodded.

'Then I suggest, Suzanna, that you bring your luggage when you come to dinner tonight. I plan to sail tomorrow morning and it will save any delay. I will show you your cabin.' Dimitris led the way and opened a door on the right. 'This cabin will be yours. My own is opposite. Frida and Anders sleep below, opposite the galley.'

'Very convenient,' murmured Sorrell. The cabin looked more like a hotel room, having a tiny bathroom hidden just inside the door, powder blue carpet covering the wooden floor and fitted cupboards of bleached pine.

'I am sure you will be very comfortable. If there is anything you need you will only have to ask Frida. She speaks very good Greek, despite being Norwegian.'

'Why are you doing this, Dimitris?'

Dimitris shrugged. 'You have a fertile imagination. I am sure you will be able to keep me entertained. Also I do not want anyone to interfere with the work that Joseph is doing at present. When the time is right he will be at your disposal. Trust me. I will not go back on my word.'

Stelios drove Sorrell back to the centre of Athens, assuring her he would return at eight. As he departed he handed Sorrell an envelope and she opened it curiously. *'Pay your hotel bill before you leave'* was written on a single sheet of paper that was wrapped around a quantity of drachma notes. She smiled. How had he known she had planned to leave by the fire exit?

Hurriedly she showered and made her way to the most exclusive shopping area in Athens. She walked through the departments selecting three evening dresses and two bikinis. She wished she had a credit card to charge the purchases. She would have to use some of her capital this time.

She examined herself in the evening dresses critically, finally settling for a black, off the shoulder sheath. The splits at the sides reached almost to the top of her thighs and had a discreet decorative edging of silver flowers. Both the bikinis fitted and she left one on beneath her clothes, buying the cheaper of the two. When she returned to her hotel she still had an hour before Stelios would arrive and she packed carefully. She decided against wearing the evening dress and settled for a beige safari dress with a wide belt. If Dimitris was serious she could always change on the boat.

Dimitris frowned in annoyance as he saw her dress. He was wearing black trousers, an evening shirt and black bow tie. 'I was expecting something a little more glamorous,' he remarked.

Sorrell smiled confidently. 'You will not be disappointed. I did not want to crush it.' She indicated the large bag bearing the name of the famous shop. 'It will take me only a moment to change.'

'You have five minutes before Frida serves.'

'I'll be ready.'

Swiftly Sorrell removed her beige dress and underwear. She wriggled herself into the dress and pulled up the long zip, smoothed her hands over the length of her body, checked her reflection in the mirror and returned to the saloon.

Dimitris literally licked his lips. 'You look exquisite, my dear.' He took her hand and kissed it. 'I am quite looking forward to the devastating effect you will have on some of my acquaintances. Come, Frida is ready.'

The meal was more sumptuous than the lunch had been, with five courses. Sorrell ate slowly and drank the wine sparingly.

'Do you eat like this every night?' she asked.

'Why do you ask?'

'I shall have to buy a new wardrobe a size larger,' she smiled. 'This amount of food would keep me for a week.'

'Tonight was to be a special occasion. I do not always expect Frida to prepare so much.' Dimitris regarded her gravely. 'I think now would be a good time to explain the rules.'

'Rules?' Sorrell looked at him puzzled.

'The rules that you will abide by whilst you are with me. If these are not agreeable to you, please say so now. Whilst you are aboard you can be friendly with Frida and Anders. They are not treated as servants, but you never discuss anything of a personal nature with them. They will not ask about your background and you will not volunteer any information about yourself.'

Sorrell nodded. 'That's fine.'

'When we dock you will ask my permission before you go ashore. I will have good reason if I refuse you. If you do go ashore you are free to do as you please, but you are always to be back on board by eight, unless I am accompanying you. You do nothing, I repeat, nothing that draws attention to yourself. I am a respectable businessman and I cannot afford to have my name linked with any criminal activity, however minor. Should you be indiscreet enough to let anything of that nature happen I shall say I picked you up the night before and know nothing of your background. You will have only the clothes you are wearing at the time and will be entirely at the mercy of the local judiciary. Mentioning my name will not help you.'

'Dimitris!' Sorrell gave him a sorrowful stare. 'I wouldn't dream of it. The only reason I've been – devious – before, was because I wanted a lifestyle like this. I would be a fool to do anything stupid and jeopardise this opportunity that you've given me.'

'So long as you know, and remember, it will not last for ever. Don't have any foolish illusions about me falling in love with you.'

'I understand. It's a business arrangement for as long as it suits us both.'

'Exactly.' Dimitris almost laughed aloud at her naiveté. The arrangement would only last as long as it suited him. 'Now, we will talk of more pleasant things. Tomorrow we will sail for Paros. Have you ever visited the island?'

Sorrell shook her head and throughout the remainder of the meal Dimitris described the island to her. This, decided Sorrell, was going to be enjoyable.

Their meal finished, Frida cleared away and Anders folded down the table. Soft music from hidden speakers filled the cabin and the lights lowered to a romantic glow.

'You would like to dance?'

Sorrell nodded, expecting to have to suffer her feet being trodden on repeatedly, but to her surprise Dimitris was an excellent dancer. The music slowed and he pulled her closer to him, his hands caressing her sides until they reached the splits in her skirt when they slid beneath.

'Not only a beautiful dress, but one that is extremely practical,' he breathed. He buried his face in her neck and began an exploration with his hands that continually aroused her to a pitch of unimaginable intensity, before bringing her gently down again. She moaned deep in her throat and Dimitris chuckled softly as he steered her gently towards her cabin.

When Sorrell awoke she was alone. The motion and gentle throbbing told her they were at sea. She lay there, luxuriating in a sense of well-being, and realised she was enjoying the aftermath of her night with Dimitris. A little thrill went through her body. Dimitris had been so tender and considerate. Reluctantly Sorrell rose from the comfortable bed and showered leisurely. Her luggage still sat untouched on the floor and she breathed a sigh of relief. A gentle knock sounded on the door and Frida entered.

'Mr Dimitris thought you might like some coffee in your cabin.'

'How kind of him. Thank you.'

'Would you like me to unpack your bags for you?'

Sorrell shook her head. 'I prefer to do that for myself, thank you. Where are we?'

'On the way to Paros. The weather forecast is good, so it should be a pleasant trip.'

'How long will it take?'

Frida shrugged. 'We will arrive about mid-day and dock in the evening. There is breakfast in the galley when you are ready.'

Sorrell dressed carefully. Frida had been wearing shorts and a T-shirt and she emulated her, exchanging the T-shirt for a short-sleeved blouse. She wore her bikini beneath, but felt she should check with Dimitris before she exposed her body to the sun.

Dimitris shrugged. 'When we are at sea you can sunbathe naked if you wish. When you are on a public beach you will always cover the more delicate parts of your body.'

'Do you often sail between the islands?' she asked.

'Frequently. My business makes it necessary. Now, you must excuse me. I have work that I need to do. You are free until dinner to do as you please. There is no need to dress tonight.'

Sorrell felt that she had been dismissed. She lay on deck and soaked up the sun until she felt she could take no more, then retired to her cabin, showered and ate a snack, before sleeping away the afternoon.

She had another shower and washed her hair, wondering what she should wear at dinner that night, finally deciding on a crimson silk dress. The look of approval she received from Dimitris let her know that she had made the right choice.

Over dinner she tried to draw out of him the reason why they had sailed for Paros. Dimitris looked at her speculatively. 'It is a pleasant island. You will be able to go ashore tomorrow and see for yourself. I always prefer to be in a harbour at night. It can be very unpleasant if you are at sea and a storm blows up.'

'I would have thought you were a match for any storm.' Sorrell raised her eyebrows at him. 'I begin to feel one brewing in myself, maybe you would like to quell it?'

Dimitris shook his head. 'Tonight you will have to amuse yourself. When we have finished dinner I have work to be done ready for tomorrow.'

Sorrell pouted prettily. 'You have had all day to do your work.'

Dimitris regarded her steadily. 'I am in charge of this cruiser. I work when I wish to work and those on board do as I say. Do you understand?'

Sorrell dropped her eyes. 'Yes, Dimitris.'

'Then please remember that I am not one of your casual pick-ups to be seduced by small talk and sultry looks.'

Sorrell's eyes flashed. 'I have never picked anyone up.'

'Really? I seem to have heard about a jeweller in Holland. Naturally it turned out to his disadvantage.'

Sorrell flushed and looked down at her plate. 'He was just a fool,' she muttered.

'Quite so, but I am not.' Dimitris rose from the table. 'I will ask Frida to serve you coffee and petit fours here. I shall have mine in my cabin whilst I work.'

Sorrell shrugged. 'As you wish, Dimitris.'

Despite having slept for some hours during the afternoon Sorrell had no difficulty falling asleep that night and she awoke to the sounds of the busy waterfront of Paros. Curiously she drew back her curtain and looked out. Her view was the boat moored next to them. She remembered Dimitris's instructions regarding her clothing and selected white shorts with a pale blue sleeveless blouse. The sandals presented more of a problem, she chose a pair that had a heel no higher than an inch and hoped he would be satisfied.

At seven she helped herself to breakfast from the galley and walked through to the cabin where Dimitris already sat. He gave a nod of approval.

'You have your swimming costume?' he asked.

Sorrell nodded. 'I'm wearing a bikini. Should I take some underwear with me?'

Dimitris shrugged. 'That is up to you.' He rose from the table. 'I will see you at eight.'

Sorrell looked after him, a puzzled frown creasing her forehead. After their previous intimacy he was now treating her as a virtual stranger. Had she offended him, or did he treat every woman he had in this way? Thinking of him made her body crave the erotic lovemaking she had experienced with him and a small shiver went through her. Maybe after their dinner tonight he would want to dance with her again and they would retire to her cabin.

'I must stop this,' she told herself firmly. 'This is a business arrangement for both of us.'

She collected some underwear and a towel, emerging from her cabin at the same time as Dimitris. She followed him out onto the deck and he handed her ashore. As she stood beside him on the quay she realised why he had told her to wear flat sandals, he was no taller than she was, something she had not been aware of previously. She smiled to herself – the vanity of men.

'Now I will show you the town,' he said. 'I would not want you to get lost.'

Obediently she walked beside him as they wandered the streets. To her surprise it was a small place, no more than a few roads between the waterfront and the main square. Patiently he allowed her to gaze her fill at the shops, stopping for coffee at eleven, and asking if she would like an early lunch.

'Whatever you please, Dimitris. I'm in your hands,' she murmured.

He nodded slowly. 'In that case I think we will go to swim now and eat later.'

He hailed a taxi and they drove slowly towards the outskirts of the town, finally drawing up outside a lavish hotel. He stood and inspected the outside critically, before leading the way up the driveway and down to the sandy beach. He chose a shady spot beneath a tree.

'You will wait for me here. I have some business to attend to. We will swim when I return.'

Sorrell removed her clothes and stretched herself out on the sun-bed. This was her kind of life. Joseph could wait awhile.

Dimitris was gone over an hour and by the time he returned she was hot and desperately needing to cool herself in the turquoise sea that was lapping at the sand only a few feet away from her. To her relief Dimitris immediately removed his shirt and trousers.

'Now we will swim.'

He followed her down to the water's edge, then strode ahead of her, plunging into the water and swimming strongly out to sea. Sorrell followed at a distance. There was no way she could match his power and she had no great desire to swim too far from the shore. He returned to her side, cleaving the water cleanly with his hands, and trod water at her side.

'You are enjoying yourself?' he asked.

'Very much,' answered Sorrell truthfully.

'I, too, plan to enjoy myself.'

He reached out his hand and held her firmly, his other hand exploring her body as he had before, probing, exploring, caressing. She felt faint with longing. She stretched her hand towards him.

'Shall I …?'

He brushed her hand away. 'No, I am enjoying myself.'

He continued to arouse her, until she was shivering with anticipation and frustration.

'You are feeling cold,' he announced. 'Go back into the sunshine or you will catch a chill.'

Sorrell looked at him in disbelief. He dropped his hands from her and began to swim back out to sea, whilst Sorrell trod water and tried to regain possession of her senses. Slowly she swam back to the shore and returned to the sun-bed, her mind in turmoil. She was the one who had the power to torment a man with longing, but here the position was reversed. Dimitris seemed to be completely in command of himself and totally in control of her.

She was almost asleep when Dimitris returned to lie beside her. 'It was a good swim,' he announced. 'When we are dry we will go for lunch.'

They lunched at the hotel, Dimitris commanding excellent service, and Sorrell was forced to comment.

'They seem to know you well here.'

Dimitris shrugged. 'Whenever I visit Paros I dine here. Do you want more coffee, or are you ready to return to town?'

Sorrell looked at her watch. 'Provided I have time to shower and wash my hair before dinner this evening I can do whatever you wish.'

'Then we will return. That will also give you time for a short siesta.'

They stayed for two days at Paros, returning each day to the hotel where they lounged on the beach and swam. To Sorrell's consternation Dimitris made no advances to her, either during the day or after their dinner each night. She wondered if she had offended him, or whether, in reality, he had little sexual energy and he had expended it on her first night aboard.

From Paros they sailed to Samos, where Dimitris declared they would stay for a week.

The second day they were there Anders gently nosed the cruiser out of the harbour and they sailed leisurely round to one of the numerous bays, where a hotel stood in a prime position. Whilst Sorrell swam from the boat or sun-bathed on deck, Dimitris sat with high-powered binoculars trained on the shore. Overcome with curiosity Sorrell finally asked him what he was watching.

'I am looking at my hotel. I like to see what is going on outside as well as inside.'

'Do you own many hotels?'

'Hotels are part of my business. The islands are popular with tourists and they need somewhere to stay. Tonight the manager and his wife will come to dinner. You will act as my hostess.'

Sorrell nodded. 'I am sure I shall enjoy meeting them.'

'You will be very circumspect. You told me a garbled story about having a modelling agency. If you are asked you will tell the same story. You are travelling with me because I may be making an investment in, what you call, the rag trade.'

Sorrell nodded. 'Whatever you say, Dimitris.'

'Exactly.' He consulted his expensive gold watch. 'We will return to the harbour. Our visitors will arrive at seven thirty.'

Just before seven thirty Sorrell joined Dimitris and waited for Makkis and Constantina to arrive. Sorrell looked at Constantina curiously. Her hair was unnaturally blonde, contrasting oddly with her olive skin; the fuchsia dress she wore accentuated her plumpness and she reached only to Dimitris' shoulder. Sorrell was feeling nervous, continually reminding herself that she was acting as Dimitris's hostess and she must be careful to please him. Makkis, having greeted her, began a conversation almost exclusively with Dimitris, whilst Constantina engaged Sorrell immediately in a discussion on fashion.

At her ease, Sorrell talked glibly of fashion houses and designs. Constantina added anecdotes of her own, describing the difficulties of finding fashionable clothes that would fit her, amusing Sorrell with her droll descriptions of her shopping expeditions. The evening passed swiftly and Sorrell had to admit that she had enjoyed herself, although she had been relieved that Makkis had paid her very little personal attention and Dimitris had not felt that soft music and dancing were necessary. When Dimitris bade her a courteous goodnight at three in the morning, she retired to her cabin, thankful that he had not demanded her to be ready to go ashore the next morning.

The days they spent in the harbour she would leave the boat and wander around the town, have a swim from one of the beaches during the afternoon and return in good time to be ready to greet Dimitris at dinner. On two further occasions he told her they would be having visitors and she began to look forward to entertaining, although Dimitris remained an enigma to her.

Some evenings he would exchange hardly a word during their meal, on other occasions he was charming and entertaining. Finally he ordered her to wear her black evening dress and she felt a thrill of excitement. Dimitris, she knew, could be most inventive; delaying the exquisite moment of satisfying her until she felt she could no longer bear the delicious torment that was racking her body, but at all times he was in command of her.

From Samos they sailed to Patmos and Dimitris had insisted that she stayed aboard whilst he went ashore.

'Don't you want me with you?' she had pouted prettily at him.

'You would be very bored at business meetings. Frida will keep you company until I return.'

During the afternoon, whilst they sunbathed, Sorrell tried to draw their proposed itinerary from Frida.

Frida rolled over lazily onto her back. 'I don't know. We shall probably stay here for a day or two and eventually sail on to Kos. It seems to be Dimitris's favourite island. I just do as I'm told.'

Dimitris did not return to the cruiser for a meal that night and Sorrell dined alone. She ate sparingly, fear nagging at her that maybe Dimitris had found a girl ashore whom he preferred and she would be asked to leave.

Sleep did not come easily to her until the early hours of the morning, but when she entered the saloon Dimitris was eating breakfast and smiled warmly at her.

'Today we sail to Kalymnos,' he informed her.

'Will I be able to go ashore?'

'Certainly. I will escort you and show you the shopping area.'

'I would enjoy that, provided it fits in with your plans,' she added hurriedly.

'If it did not I would not have made the offer,' he answered coldly.

'Thank you, Dimitris,' she murmured.

Dimitris escorted her round the shops on Kalymnos, but he resisted any veiled suggestions from her that he should purchase anything on her behalf. She admired dresses and jewellery, but for all the response she received she may as well have been discussing vegetables in the local market.

They ate at a waterfront restaurant where Dimitris recommended the fish, which had been caught locally. Throughout the meal Dimitris was attentive and charming, and Sorrell thought she might well be requested to don her evening dress when they returned to the cruiser.

She was destined to disappointment as Dimitris wished her goodnight and retired to his cabin. She lay in her bed and assessed her situation. She was certainly not unhappy, travelling from one sun-drenched island to another, and although she did not pretend to understand Dimitris, she enjoyed his company when he favoured her during the day and particularly at night.

To her surprise, when she joined him for breakfast, he asked if she wished to go ashore again at Kalymnos or if she would prefer to travel on to Kos that morning.

'I am happy to do whatever you would prefer, Dimitris.'

'Very well. We will sail for Kos and you can spend the afternoon ashore. I suggest you take some money with you if you wish to purchase clothes or jewellery.'

Sorrell was about to say that she had no money, when she realised that Dimitris had probably searched her luggage and knew exactly how much she was carrying with her.

'Are you coming with me?' she asked.

'What difference does that make?'

'I could ask you to carry my money for me. I don't like to carry large sums on my person.'

Dimitris raised his eyebrows mockingly. 'I shall not be coming ashore. I regret you will have to carry your own burdens.'

Kos was something of a disappointment to Sorrell. The shops seemed to be predominately for the tourists and she returned to the cruiser with no more than two pairs of shorts and a blouse.

Dimitris laughed at her when she complained. 'You obviously only found the tourist area. Further into the town centre they have some fashionable shops and also some good jewellers. We will be staying here for most of the summer I expect, so you will also be able to visit Turkey. You will have plenty of time to enlarge your wardrobe.'

Sorrell looked at him in surprise. 'I thought you continually moved around.'

'I find Kos a useful base. I move to various islands as my business dictates. As I had business in Piraeus I decided it was only practical to make inspections of my properties as I returned.'

'What do you do in the winter?' asked Sorrell curiously.

Dimitris shrugged. 'I usually travel down to Cyprus and when the weather becomes inclement I cross over to Egypt.'

'Do you have businesses there also?'

'What is this sudden interest?'

'No particular reason. I just wondered how long it would be before you put me in touch with Joseph.'

Dimitris regarded her steadily. 'I will put you in touch with Joseph when it suits me to do so. If you are tired of our arrangement you are free to leave.'

Sorrell squeezed his arm. 'I love being with you. I was hoping you would take me to Egypt with you. Joseph can wait.'

'My sentiments entirely. Maybe you should wear your special evening dress tonight. I have been neglecting you recently.' He smiled and Sorrell felt a thrill of anticipation go through her.

Sorrell began to enjoy Kos. As Dimitris had said, the town, although small, had a fashionable area and she spent hours each morning wandering from shop to shop until she finally decided on a purchase. During the afternoon she would sunbathe on board or swim from the boat. Each evening when she had showered she would show the latest additions to her wardrobe to Dimitris and he would demand that she modelled them for him. He would spend time admiring and criticising, often telling her what she was to wear the next time he went ashore with her or when he planned to entertain on board.

Giovanni looked at the finished buildings with pride. He placed his arm round Marianne's shoulders. 'We've done it.'

'You've done it, you mean. I'm so proud of you, Giovanni.'

Giovanni's eyes were moist. 'I have a feeling of accomplishment that I've never experienced before. It must be akin to the way old uncle Yannis felt when he was building on Spinalonga; to suddenly see a dream take shape.' He grinned sheepishly at her. 'I'll go and get Yannis and Ourania. You stay here and have coffee and biscuits ready for us in our taverna.' He kissed her quickly. 'Thank you, Marianne. I couldn't have done it without you.'

Marianne took Giovanni's hands and held them between her own. 'I want to ask you something,' she said.

Giovanni smiled. 'No, you want something. You always hold my hands like this when you want something from me.'

Marianne gave a little laugh. 'I hadn't realised.'

'Well, what is it?'

'The taverna, farm house, shop – we continually call it something different. Why don't we give it a name?'

Giovanni frowned. 'How do you mean?'

'If we called it *'ANNA'S'* that is how people would know it.'

'ANNA'S. Why *'ANNA'S'*? Why not *'MARIANNE'S'*?

Marianne shook her head. 'It was Aunt Anna's home for most of her life – and there's something else.'

Giovanni raised his eyebrows.

'I'd like to enlarge the photograph of Anna that I took on Spinalonga and mount it on the wall. It's symbolic somehow.'

Giovanni grinned. 'I'm supposed to be the one who has ideas! We will call the place *'ANNA'S'* after Aunt Anna and little Anna from the island. I'm sure Aunt Anna will be honoured.'

Giovanni stood with his aunt and uncle outside the four small self-catering bungalows.

'Do you want to see inside?' he asked after he felt they had stood long enough to admire the small paved area with a potted olive tree beneath the window. He pushed open the door. 'Well, what do you think?'

Yannis inspected the building critically, running his hands along the woodwork, opening the cupboard doors, inspecting the china and cooking utensils that were in there and finally turning on the taps in the bathroom. Eventually he nodded and turned to Giovanni. 'You've done a good job here. Why haven't you put down any carpet in the lounge or bedroom?'

'This is a summer holiday resort only; not an all year round hotel. People will come in wet from the beach or muddy from the hills and carpets would be ruined in no time. It will be hot whilst they are here, they don't need carpet.'

Yannis looked at the bedroom again. 'There are only two beds. Suppose they bring children with them?'

Giovanni pointed to the corner. 'There's a spare bed that will accommodate a child. The rooms are not really big enough for more than three people, but we could squeeze another bed in if necessary.'

'Suppose they have a baby?'

'We have John's old cot. They could use that.'

Yannis nodded. He could think of nothing else to criticise.

'What do you think, Aunt Ourania?'

'You've worked very hard, Giovanni. I would be happy to stay here for a week. Are they all the same?'

'Exactly.' Giovanni grinned. 'Would you like to see the taverna?'

Marianne was waiting for them with coffee brewing and a selection of pastries. Giovanni pointed out the name above the doorway. 'That was Marianne's idea,' he announced proudly.

As he entered Yannis drew in his breath. 'I would never have believed it! There's so much space.'

'No more than before. We've just rearranged it and put in the patio windows down that wall. We'll have them wide open in the summer so the guests can wander in as they please. Out there we shall have the tables and umbrellas. We've got them stored in the other bungalow at the moment until the weather settles.'

'Have you any bookings?'

Giovanni's enthusiasm left him for a moment. 'We have one for next week and about a dozen during the rest of the season.'

'Is that all?'

'That's a start. We missed the beginning of the season, remember. I've paid for advertising in the brochures. Once the hotels are filled people will be looking to see where else is available. When they realise how much cheaper it is to stay here than in a hotel they'll tell their friends. I'm sure that by next season all the bungalows will be booked and we'll be turning customers away.' Giovanni spoke more confidently than he felt.

'Do you think Aunt Anna and Uncle Yiorgo would like to come and see what we've done?' asked Marianne, sensing Giovanni's discomfort.

'I'm sure they would, but I'm not sure they'll know where they are.'

'We'll bring them out tomorrow. Now whilst we have our coffee I'll get you to look over the questionnaires I've prepared. See if I've missed off anything.'

'Questionnaires?'

'For the guests to fill in,' explained Giovanni. 'I want them to tell us if they were comfortable, was there anything missing from their bungalow, you know, not enough tea spoons or cups, was the water hot enough in the shower, are there any improvements we could make, also where they visited whilst they stayed here. By next season I want to have a little brochure in each bungalow with recommendations from the guests, where to visit, where to swim, where to eat, where to buy your souvenirs.' Giovanni grinned. 'I shall obviously recommend Ourania's shop and have copies of old Uncle Yannis's book here.'

'So I should hope!'

'Marianne and I are going to keep a list of the most popular goods that we sell from the shop. That way we'll know what stock to increase and what we need not bother with.'

Yannis smiled. 'I wondered why there weren't any of your famous notices up anywhere. Now I know; you've been too busy making questionnaires!'

Anna looked at the old farmhouse. It no longer resembled the house where she had spent most of her life. 'It looks different, Yannis. What have you done?'

'Giovanni has made some alterations. Come inside and I'll show you.'

Bewildered, Anna looked around. 'You've brought me to the wrong place. This isn't my farmhouse. I can't live here. I don't know where anything is.'

'No one is going to ask you to live here. You live with us, remember? Giovanni and Marianne are going to use the farmhouse as a taverna and a general store. They have knocked down a wall and put in some new windows.'

Anna shook her head. 'Why does Giovanni want a taverna? He has a night club.'

'He doesn't have the night club any longer. We sold the hotel in Athens. This is where he's going to work now. Visitors are going to come and stay in the bungalows and they will be able to come here and buy groceries to make a meal or ask Marianne to cook for them.'

Anna shrugged. 'Well, if that's what they want. Do you think Marianne would like me to come up here and do the cooking?'

Yannis placed his arms around her frail shoulders. 'I wouldn't dream of letting you come up here to work. Think of all the years you spent looking after us. Now it is our turn to look after you. You and Yiorgo gave us your savings and your land so we wanted to bring you out to see what has been done. Giovanni has named the taverna after you.'

Slowly Anna nodded. 'After me? Why did he do that?'

'It was your home, Aunt Anna. He wanted everyone to know that.'

'Can I sit here for a while?'

'Of course.' Yannis drew out a chair from under the table on the patio, but Anna shook her head.

'Not there, over here.'

Yannis followed her and placed the chair where she indicated. He watched as she looked down at the paved area, then up to the hills, rising and moving the chair a few inches to the left. 'That's better.'

'I'll go and see what uncle Yiorgo thinks.' Yannis was puzzled by his aunt's behaviour. He looked back at her as he re-entered the taverna and stopped in surprise. The chair was placed in exactly the same spot as she had always sat when preparing vegetables.

Sorrell watched as the ferry docked at the port of Bodrum. Both Frida and Anders had visited the town earlier in the week, returning loaded with parcels and two large melons, but Dimitris had refused to allow Sorrell to accompany them. Finally he suggested she and Frida went to Turkey for the day and when she had agreed readily he had proceeded to give her instructions. There was a shoemaker's close to the quay and she was to make sure she knew the location. They were free to enjoy themselves and make any purchases they wished until half an hour before they were due back for the ferry. She was then to visit the shoemaker and collect a box from him. He had placed an order for a pair of shoes to be made some weeks ago and he had been advised they were ready. It seemed a very simple request from him and she had no qualms about carrying it out. He had given her a final warning.

'Just remember to keep the receipts for anything you purchase. Turkish jails are even more unpleasant than those in Greece.'

The journey had taken no more than twenty minutes and now they waited with the rest of the visitors to go ashore. The port was attractive, a castle on the right and the arc of the marina to the left, with cafes and eating-places.

Sorrell smiled at Frida. 'I think we should be able to enjoy ourselves.'

They strolled leisurely, entering the small, attractive shops and Sorrell purchased whatever she fancied until she had numerous bags and parcels. Hot and exhausted they drank fresh lemon juice before Frida announced that she needed to buy some fruit.

Sorrell walked over to the nearest stall, but Frida shook her head. 'I have a regular supplier. Mr Dimitris insists that I always use him.' Sorrell trailed after her as they turned away from the main thoroughfare and Frida finally stopped before a stall where the vegetables were wilting visibly under the sun.

Without asking what she required the owner placed two large melons into a bag and added some oranges and lemons. Sorrell looked at them in surprise. Anders had brought melons back only the day before and Frida had not served melon before or after a meal. Sorrell opened her mouth to query the purchase with Frida, who frowned and shook her head. Sorrell shrugged. Maybe Dimitris ate them alone in his cabin.

'Why do you need to buy fruit over here? It's just as good if not better on Kos.'

Frida looked at her steadily. 'I do as Mr Dimitris says. If he wants the fruit from Bodrum then that is where I buy it.'

It was obviously another little foible on the part of the Greek. Having returned to the quay to await the ferry Sorrell left her purchases with Frida and walked over to the shoemaker. She handed him the scrap of paper Dimitris had given her and the shoemaker passed her a large box, the lid taped down. She wondered if she should check the contents and began to slide her fingernail beneath the tape. The shopkeeper snatched the box back and pressed the tape back into place. He glared at her and shook his head as he handed it back and Sorrell left the shop hurriedly.

As they walked down the quay Frida placed her bag of fruit on the ground and rubbed her arm. 'If I take some of your parcels could you carry that for me? It's heavier than I realised and my arm really hurts.'

Sorrell handed over her purchases and lifted the bag of fruit. It was nowhere near as heavy as she had expected. With the shoebox in one bag and the fruit in the other she followed Frida on to the ferry.

Dimitris was waiting for them in the lounge of the cabin cruiser and relieved Sorrell of the shoebox immediately whilst Frida retired to the galley with the bag of fruit, her arm no longer seeming to trouble her.

'I assume you had an enjoyable day?'

'I'm exhausted.' smiled Sorrell. 'I've tried on so many clothes! It was difficult to make a choice, everything was so cheap. You should have come, Dimitris.'

Dimitris shook his head. 'I do not like Turkey.'

It became a regular weekly event for Frida and Sorrell to visit Bodrum. Each time Dimitris would give her instructions how to find a particular shop and collect some goods he had ordered whilst Frida would visit the greengrocer. She was always to complete the errand shortly before the ferry was due to leave. Sorrell complied happily; it was a small service she could render as a way of thanking Dimitris. The same evening Dimitris would always announce that he had a predilection for night fishing and she would enjoy feeling the movement of the cruiser as they left the harbour, anchoring off-shore whilst they ate their evening meal.

As darkness fell the cruiser would begin to move again and Sorrell would watch the lights of Kos as they receded into the darkness. 'Where do you go to fish?' she asked innocently.

Dimitris shrugged. 'Wherever it takes my fancy to stop.'

'Do you ever catch anything? I've never seen any freshly caught fish on board.'

'Sometimes. If they are small we return them to the sea. If I consider they will make a meal I hand them over in the morning to Frida and she prepares them for the freezer. Why are you so interested, my dear?'

Sorrell shrugged. 'I'm not really. I have never understood why people fish for pleasure.'

'I have never understood why grown men wish to kick a ball up and down on a patch of grass. You will go to bed as Frida does and leave us men to amuse ourselves.' Despite Dimitris's casual sounding words Sorrell realised he had given her an order.

Joseph caressed the girl beside him. For a prostitute she was remarkably good looking. He had visited all the girls in the area in turn and Nadia was certainly the most attractive to look at and inventive in bed. He begrudged having to pay for his pleasure. He had managed to persuade some of the girls who were on holiday to meet him during the evening and taken them to secluded areas, even persuading a couple to take him back to their hotel room, but he dared not invite them back to his room.

'A beautiful girl like you shouldn't have to do this for a living,' he remarked.

'Why not? I make good money and it gives me a roof over my head.'

'What about your pimp? What kind of a percentage does he take from you?'

'Sixty per cent.'

'Sixty per cent!' echoed Joseph. 'That's robbery.'

'It's the usual rate. All the girls pay it.'

'Do they all have the same pimp?'

'No, and we call them protectors, not pimps.'

'What's the difference?'

'The pimp is the big man, in overall charge. He owns the rooms and allows our protectors to rent them.'

'So how would I go about becoming your protector?'

Nadia giggled. 'Don't be silly, Joseph. You couldn't afford to pay into the syndicate, and besides I don't think my brother would be willing to sell me.'

'He could always find another girl. Suppose I found one for him?'

'Where would you find a suitable girl?' Nadia raised herself up on her elbow. 'Time to go, Joseph. I have another appointment in half an hour.'

Nadia repeated the conversation to her brother when he called for his money and he raised his eyebrows.

'That young man sounds ambitious. See if you can find out who he has in mind.'

Nadia frowned. 'You wouldn't seriously think about replacing me, would you, Alecos?'

He patted her hand comfortingly. 'You're doing a good job, but you know as well as I do that the day will come eventually. It could be as well to have someone else ready the next time a room becomes free. I don't think Melissa will be wanted much longer.'

Alecos telephoned Lakkis from *The Grapevine* and suggested he called in for a drink the next time he was passing, knowing he would arrive the next morning before any customers were likely to be about.

'What's the problem?' he asked immediately.

'No problem,' Alecos assured him. 'I just thought you should be aware that Joseph is getting ideas.'

Lakkis raised his eyebrows. 'Tell me.'

'He suggested to Nadia that he would like to become a protector.' Alecos grinned. 'What he really means is that he doesn't want to have to pay for her.'

Lakkis smiled grimly. 'He's greedy. I'll let the big man know.'

Joseph sat astride his motor scooter, driving slowly across the cobbles and out of the gate. He had a routine now. Every Sunday he would go to Lindos. It was almost the end of the tourist season, but there were still plenty of visitors wandering around the old town. The streets were narrow and crowded, much the same as the medieval city where he lived, and it was a simple matter to remove the contents from an unguarded back pocket.

He would spend a couple of hours wandering and improving his finances before having a meal. Depending how the day went he might then ride a bit further down the island and return by a different route.

In the afternoons, when he was free, he would drive until he reached one of the villages that were frequented by a coach load of tourists. He would mingle with them and, as yet, had never returned empty handed.

When the coaches left he would return to one of the beaches and sit with the pair of binoculars that he had been forced to purchase, as the shopkeeper had them chained, and watch the girls who sunbathed topless. It gave him a feeling of power to know that he could see their every move and they had no knowledge that they were being watched.

Whilst he rode he considered how he could break into the syndicate and become a protector for Nadia. It would be a good return on his money. After the initial outlay, he would cream off the sixty per cent and no longer have to pay for Nadia. She should have at least ten more useful working years and by then he should have managed to buy out some of the other men, putting in younger girls of his own. It was an attractive scheme and he felt confident that he could make it work.

In the meantime he would continue working for Lakkis. It was undemanding. During the height of the tourist season he had been busier, often having as many as twenty telephone calls in a morning. The thing he really disliked was the monotonous trip to Turkey and meeting Nimet each Saturday. He was not attracted to the girl, had run out of small talk, and found her brother a perfect nuisance.

He would have preferred to spend his day at Lindos or sitting in *The Grapevine*. During the late afternoon and evening the taverna was a meeting place for the youths who worked on the tourist boats during the season and also the drifters who picked up work wherever they could find it. They were of all nationalities, but English seemed to be the common language, understood and spoken by all of them with varying degrees of ability.

Joseph would sit and listen whilst they recounted the stories of their life and the events of the day whilst they drank steadily. During the summer their numbers had fluctuated, but now they were diminishing each week and he had asked the reason of Alecos.

'The season is finishing. The tourists go home, so those who came to work over here during the summer go home also.'

Joseph considered the information. Without the tourists his income would be seriously affected. There was nowhere on the island where the townsfolk crowded together as they did in Athens on the underground or in the flea market. He really did need the additional income that would be his if he were able to set Nadia up for himself. The more he thought about the idea the more appealing it became and he wondered if she would be willing to arrange a meeting for him with her protector so that he could meet the pimp.

Lakkis telephoned the hotel on Kos and left a message for Dimitris asking him to return his call. Dimitris frowned when he received the request and telephoned Lakkis at his home and held a guarded conversation.

'You wanted to speak to me,' said Dimitris.

'Is there any chance you could come over? I have heard of an idea and I'd like to share it with you.'

'I could be there by tomorrow. Tell our friend to arrange a fishing trip for tonight.'

'That would be convenient.'

Dimitris replaced the receiver. Obviously the problem was not urgent or Lakkis would have told him a crack had appeared in the swimming pool at the hotel, their agreed code should there be an emergency.

Dimitris returned to the cruiser and spoke to Anders, requesting that he advised the port authorities that they would be sailing that evening for Rhodes. Anders nodded. He knew the procedure by now and did not question the decision. He was used to Dimitris's sudden change of plans. He loved the cruiser, which was fast and easy to manage, and would have happily sailed anywhere in the world at a moment's notice.

Sorrell made no comment when Dimitris informed her. She would be sorry to leave Kos, but provided Rhodes had a shopping centre where she could spend her time she was not unduly concerned which island the cruiser visited.

'We shall stop at some point during the night,' Dimitris advised her. 'Anders and I wish to do a little fishing. You will stay in your cabin once we have finished dinner. Our fishing would hold no interest for you.'

Sorrell shrugged. She was used to their evening fishing trips and smelly fish held no attraction for her..

Dimitris retired to his cabin and continued checking the receipts against the money that he had received and entering the figures into his private ledger. All seemed to be in order. He unscrewed the rail inside his wardrobe and placed the money inside the hollow aluminium tube. It was safer there than in the bank. It avoided any awkward questions when he had to file his tax return. There was more than enough to pay his harbour fees, purchase the diesel for the cruiser, pay Frida and Anders for their services and keep him in luxury.

As they sailed into Rhodes harbour, Sorrell was intrigued by the imposing walls and impressed by the attractiveness of the waterfront. She had seen no evidence of any fish the men might have caught during the night, although she had awakened briefly when the engines had been silenced. Dimitris called her to him as Anders moored and to her disappointment ordered her to stay aboard the cruiser.

'Tomorrow you can go ashore. You will find the old town quite impressive. We will be having guests for dinner tonight. The dress you bought on Kos would be most suitable.'

Sorrell shrugged and turned away. She had a feeling that if she tried to disobey Dimitris's orders, Anders would pick her up bodily and deposit her back on board. 'I'll read my book and wash my hair,' she said nonchalantly.

Dimitris visited the office of the harbour master and was greeted as an old friend by Nikos, who produced a battle of ouzo and glasses. He accepted the invitation for him and Thalia to dine on board with alacrity and then asked what had brought Dimitris to Rhodes.

'Lakkis contacted me. Said he wanted to talk to me.'

'I've not heard of any problem.' Nikos frowned. 'I make sure the patrol avoids that area each Wednesday.'

'I don't think it has anything to do with you. If there was a problem with the patrols he would have spoken to you first.'

Nikos nodded sombrely and refilled their glasses. He shifted uneasily in his chair. Everything had seemed to be running so smoothly.

Dimitris drained his glass and pushed his chair back. He placed a bundle of notes on the table. 'This is yours. Anders will be along shortly to complete the paperwork and pay the harbour fees.'

'Thank you, Dimitris.' Nikos relaxed visibly. Dimitris would not have paid him if he considered he was not fulfilling his side of the agreement. 'We will see you at eight.'

Dimitris left the office. He strolled across the road and found his way easily to *The Grapevine* where Lakkis was waiting for him.

'I've just seen Nikos,' Dimitris announced. 'There's been no problem with the patrols.'

Lakkis shook his head. 'It's nothing to do with that business. Nikos has made sure that everything his end runs very smoothly.'

Dimitris frowned. 'So what did you want to see me about?'

'Joseph.'

'What's he done? Has he been picked up by the police?'

Lakkis held up his hand. 'Nothing like that. He's bought a scooter and is going out of town to supplement his wages. I'm sure of that, but he's being discreet and not drawing any attention to himself so I've ignored it. This is to do with our other interests. He wants to run a girl of his own.'

Dimitris threw back his head and laughed. 'Where did he get that idea from?'

'He's been seeing Nadia. He suggested to her that she worked for him and he found another girl to take her place.'

Dimitris frowned. 'Where is he going to find another girl?'

'He watches the girls on the beach and he's picked up one or two. Maybe he's found one that he thinks would be willing.' Lakkis spread his hands. 'It's probably just talk on his part. Nadia spoke to Alecos when he collected the percentage and he passed the information on to me.'

'So why did you telephone me? Just tell him he's out of his league. Remind him to get on with his job or he can return to Athens.'

Lakkis looked doubtful. 'The thing is, once the tourists have left he's not going to find any easy pickings. He could decide to try to sell some goods on the side.'

Dimitris face darkened, and then he smiled grimly. 'Remind him about old Nikos in Plaka. Tell him the police are still looking for him.'

'You don't think he's fulfilled his usefulness?'

Dimitris considered. 'No, he's doing a good job. We'll be expanding next summer and I'd rather have someone experienced in place.' Dimitris rested his chin on his hands. 'Leave things as they are for the present. Now, I've got Nikos and Thalia coming to dinner tonight. Would you and Maria like to come tomorrow?'

Lakkis nodded. 'I'll tell her. Talking of Thalia, I know she has been seeing Joseph.' Lakkis held up his hand as Dimitris was about to interrupt him. 'She's been meeting him sometimes in her lunch hour.'

'That sounds innocent enough.'

'I don't like it. She's betrothed to my son.'

'Is that the only time they meet?'

Lakkis nodded.

'Then I suggest you ignore it. If you let him know you disapprove he will probably try to see her more often.' Dimitris placed a roll of notes on the table and Lakkis covered them quickly with his hand. 'That should cover expenses. The rest is yours.'

'Thank you, Dimitris,' said Lakkis humbly. He knew he would have been dealt with fairly. 'How long are you planning to stay?'

'Two or three days. I thought I might sail down and anchor off Faliraki. I should be able to watch the business action from the boat.'

Dimitris returned to the cruiser and retired to his cabin. He needed to think. Was it time to dispose of Joseph's services? He could always tell the girl he was on Rhodes, even give her his address. The girl! Of course! He threw back his head and laughed. What a perfect solution!

Nikos and Thalia arrived promptly and Sorrell was impressed by the girl's natural beauty. Nikos seemed a little uneasy when he first came aboard, but after Dimitris had spoken to him quietly he relaxed visibly. He had a droll sense of humour and Sorrell found herself liking the man.

At first Thalia had been very quiet, but Sorrell had gradually drawn her out and before the evening had ended she knew the girl was betrothed to her cousin, but no date had been set for her wedding. The talk had moved on to clothes and Sorrell had asked Dimitris's permission to take Thalia to her cabin and show off her wardrobe. Thalia had gasped at the array of expensive dresses and suits, touching the silks, satins and cottons gently between her fingers and Sorrell had revelled in her admiration, finally throwing a dress on the bed and offering it to Thalia.

'Do you mean it?' Thalia stroked the silk lovingly.

'If it fits you're welcome. I picked it up in a hurry one day, but I've only worn it once. I don't feel comfortable in it.'

'May I try it on?'

'Of course.'

Thalia looked at herself in the long mirror. The flame red dress enhanced her dark hair and skin, the silk clung to her body and the wide belt accentuated her slim waist, the skirt scalloped in such a way as to be ankle length at the back and knee length at the front. She was enthralled by the vision that stared back at her.

'May I show Pappa?'

'Certainly.'

Nikos raised his eyebrows at the sight of his daughter, then frowned. 'It is a beautiful dress and it suits you very well, but when would you wear it?'

'I thought I could save it for my engagement party,' suggested Thalia.

Nikos smiled indulgently at her. 'That is a good idea. I would not want to think you wore it as a day dress. It's not designed for casual wear.'

Thalia returned to the cabin to change back into the pale pink cotton dress she had worn when she had arrived and Nikos turned to Dimitris.

'I'll not refuse to let her accept the gift this time, but I don't want it to become a habit.'

'I'll speak to Suzanna,' Dimitris assured him. 'I imagine it was a sudden whim on her part.'

Nikos shifted uncomfortable in his chair. 'I don't wish to offend, Dimitris, but I would rather Thalia did not become friendly with Suzanna.'

Dimitris laughed. 'You have no need to worry. We have a business arrangement and she will only stay as long as it suits me. I have a use for her at present.' He refilled Nikos's glass. 'I know her background and I agree that she would not be suitable as a friend for Thalia.'

Sorrell was ready to go ashore at eight and she was surprised when Dimitris said Frida was to accompany her, rather than himself, and delayed them for almost half an hour whilst he spoke to Frida.

'You will stay with Frida at all times,' he told Sorrell. 'She knows her way and will show you the old town. It is not a place to wander in alone or you will be hopelessly lost.'

Sorrell looked at him with amusement. She had an uncanny sense of direction and had demonstrated this when in Bodrum and Frida had seemed uncertain which way to walk to regain the waterfront. She and Frida had struck up a friendship and it would be pleasant to spend the day with her again and indulge their mutual passion for shopping.

Frida led the way along the waterfront until they reached a large arched entrance. 'We will go in here,' she said. 'This is the main area for the tourists. There are three streets for shopping. Most of them sell souvenirs, but sometimes you can see something attractive. When you've looked your fill we can go into the new town. That is where you will find the better shops.'

Sorrell wandered from shop to shop. Frida had been correct in her assessment that they were for the tourists, with the exception of the jewellers. An amazing array of attractive earrings, necklaces, bracelets and rings were on show and she began to compare the prices, one shop with another.

'Don't buy anything yet,' Frida warned her. 'There are more jewellers in the other roads, and the ones in the town are probably better quality. You know that gold is cheaper in Turkey and when we return to Kos we can visit Bodrum again.'

They spent over two hours investigating the shops on both sides of the wide street, entering the enticing side streets and returning again to the main road.

'I don't see why Dimitris thought I might get lost,' remarked Sorrell.

Frida smiled. 'You would have no problem provided you did not leave this area. Once you start walking down any of the side roads they twist and turn so you lose your sense of direction. Sometimes you end back almost where you started and others are dead ends, they just lead to someone's house or yard.'

'People actually live here!' Sorrell was surprised.

'Of course. This is a town in its own right. It's hard to imagine when all the goods are displayed outside, but some people live above their shops and the other part of the town is almost entirely residential.'

'Can we wander through and have a look?' asked Sorrell.

'There would be no point. There is nothing of interest. The only shops are tiny general stores. Why don't we have lunch? We could go into the new town and then walk around up here again afterwards.' Frida was desperate to distract Sorrell's attention from the residential side of the town.

They sat outside at a café and Sorrell watched the visitors milling around with a sense of frustration. If only she were alone. The opportunity to help herself from pockets and bags was everywhere. She consoled herself with the thought that she would probably be able to come ashore the next day and she would assure Dimitris that she would not get lost.

When Lakkis and Maria visited for dinner that night Sorrell was bored. Dimitris and Lakkis had spent some time closeted in Dimitris's cabin, whilst Maria sat in the saloon with Sorrell. Maria seemed nervous and ill at ease and spoke hardly a word, despite all Sorrell's attempts at conversation. Lakkis made her feel distinctly uneasy. His pale green eyes, which he turned frequently on her, sent a chill down her spine, and she was relieved when the evening ended early.

Sorrell had been disappointed when she learned they were to spend the next day at sea. She had hoped to be able to go ashore alone, to wander amongst the tourists, helping herself to their belongings as she pleased. She had spent liberally from her cache of money and would have liked the opportunity to replenish her stock of drachmas.

'You and Frida can go ashore again on Friday. I have some business to attend to, and we shall return to Kos the following day.'

Joseph sat on his bike at the top of the beach at Faliraki, his binoculars held to his eyes. The beach was less crowded and the tourists were less interested in swimming than soaking up the sun, knowing the water would have a chill to it. The newcomers were easy to spot, their white limbs very noticeable amongst those who had already spent a week at the resort. Joseph's attention was caught by a tall, slim blonde. Her green bikini bottom was so small as to be almost indecent; the rest of her body tanned a golden bronze.

He followed her progress down to the water's edge, where she bent and splashed her arms, before straightening and striding into the blue water. He guessed by her looks that she was Scandinavian, but he really did not care what her nationality was. He would like to entice her into his bed and remove that green bikini. As if in answer to his thoughts she waved the skimpy costume in the air. A young man, as blonde as her, raced down to the water and plunged in. By the time he reached her she was waving bare hands at him and he laughingly took her in his arms and kissed her.

Joseph turned away. Obviously there was no point in trying to ingratiate himself with her. He swept the area of the beach, and then looked out to sea. He trained his binoculars on the cabin cruiser that was anchored off shore. Girls often sunbathed naked if they were out on a boat, thinking they were safe from prying eyes. He could see no one on board and he continued to admire the craft.

He wished he could afford to buy a boat. It should be easy enough to entice a girl on board, and it would not be so easy for her to refuse his advances out at sea. If he could only get Nadia to work for him he might even be able to have a boat by next season. He smiled to himself. The idea appealed to him.

A tourist boat made its ponderous way across the bay, making small waves, which rocked the cruiser, and it turned on its mooring rope. *Aegean Pride*, he could just make out the name before it settled back into its original position. It was Dimitris's boat. The knowledge that Dimitris was in the vicinity sent a shiver down Joseph's spine. He continued to keep his binoculars trained on the vessel. Two girls rose from the prow and pulled their towels around them in readiness to go below. Joseph caught his breath. Surely, that was Madeleine, or whatever she had called herself when she had worked with him in Athens. Even as he looked she bent her head, so he could not see her face, and the other girl moved in front of her blocking his view completely.

The wash from a second passing boat rocked the cruiser gently, swinging it round again, the prow pointing towards the shore. As Joseph watched the girls made their way towards the stern and disappeared below. He lowered his binoculars. He must have been mistaken. The girl had been deported to America. She could not possibly be in Rhodes.

Lakkis sat in *The Grapevine* with Alecos, who was sulky and unhappy.

'I don't want to give up Nadia. She's my sister and I set her up. I look after her, besides, she's my income.'

'You have nothing to lose, Alecos. I talked to Dimitris yesterday. You will still receive your percentage and he has promised that by this time next year you will have Nadia back.'

'I don't understand. Why should he take my girl away and still pay me?'

'He has a plan,' Lakkis explained patiently. 'It will be to your advantage.'

Alecos shrugged. 'What guarantee do I have that he will give Nadia back to me?'

'You can trust Dimitris.'

Alecos gave Lakkis a scathing look. 'It's to do with Joseph, isn't it? He wants Nadia for himself.'

Lakkis spread his hands. 'Joseph wants to become part of the syndicate. Dimitris is agreeable, but only until next summer.' Lakkis lowered his voice further. 'I probably should not tell you this, but when you take control of Nadia again she will be entirely yours. No percentage to the syndicate.'

'Nadia should be completely mine now, after all, she is my sister.' he said mutinously.

Lakkis sighed. 'Alecos, I do not have time to play games with you. I have to meet with Dimitris tomorrow and tell him that you are agreeable.'

'And if I'm not?'

'That would not be a wise decision.' Lakkis regarded the young man steadily with his green eyes. 'I would not want to refuse Dimitris.'

Alecos shivered. The veiled threat was not lost on him. He shrugged. 'Tell him I agree, but only until next summer.'

Joseph rode back to Rhodes town deep in thought. If Dimitris were there it would be as well if he kept a low profile. He would take a stroll along the harbour that evening to see if the *Aegean Pride* was berthed in the port. He would know where to avoid if that were the case. He wished he knew if Dimitris's visit had anything to do with him. He had carried out his instructions assiduously, obeying them to the letter. Surely the few misdemeanours he had committed amongst the tourists had not attracted attention. He had been so careful.

Lakkis waited until mid-day before visiting Dimitris to report on his conversation with Alecos.

'He was unwilling, despite your generous offer. I had to tell him he would not have to pay a percentage next year,' Lakkis spoke hesitantly, hoping Dimitris would not be annoyed by his disclosure.

Dimitris shrugged. 'If I had not wanted him to know I would not have told you.'

'When should I tell Joseph?'

Dimitris smiled slowly. 'Whenever you wish. Tell him he can have Nadia when he can afford to buy into the syndicate. Five hundred thousand drachmas is the asking price.'

Lakkis looked at Dimitris in surprise. 'Do you think he can afford that much?'

'I would imagine so. He has old Nikos's money and whatever else he has picked up along with his wages. No bargains. That is the asking price. I will collect it from you the next time I visit.'

'When will that be?'

Dimitris shrugged. 'A couple of weeks. I return to Kos tomorrow. Supplies need to be replenished.'

Marianne looked at the figures before her and smiled. They had covered their running costs for the first season and made a small profit. She would have to discuss with Giovanni whether they should save it towards another bungalow or spend it on building a storage unit.

'What would you like to do with it?' asked Giovanni.

'Build a storage unit, a larger freezer maybe, and some of it should go on more bedding.'

'What is most essential?'

'The storage facilities. It's all very well using the upper floor of the taverna at the moment, but if we plan to put in a shower and changing room we shall lose most of the space. We need to keep the stock for the shop close by.'

Giovanni nodded. 'I'll have a word with the bank manager on that. I have some other plans for our profit. Do you want to hear them?'

Marianne waited, expecting her husband to begin to outline grandiose plans for the extension of their self catering holiday business.

'I would like to ask your mother to visit us. You haven't seen her for almost two years. She must think I'm keeping you a prisoner.'

'I speak to her every week on the telephone,' smiled Marianne.

'That is not the same and I am sure she would like to see John.' He leant forward seriously. 'I can't afford to take you over to America to see your mother, but I thought we could invite her to stay here and maybe ask my parents to visit at the same time. That way the families will get to know each other.'

'I'm not sure she would feel safe staying in a self-catering bungalow,' frowned Marianne.

'She would not have to. We can move John into our room and she could use his bedroom.'

'What about your parents?'

'They would be happy to stay in a bungalow. My mother lived here until she went to Italy, remember, and my father will be with her.'

'What about the storage unit?'

Giovanni shrugged. 'I am sure I can persuade the builder to wait awhile for his money. He knows we plan to build more bungalows and will employ him to do the work. There will be no problem there. You telephone your mother and see when she will be able to come. When you tell me the date I will 'phone my parents.'

Marianne rose from the table and placed her arms around her husband. 'I do love you, Giovanni.'

Marianne hugged her mother. 'It's been such a long time since I saw you. You look so well. Giovanni is waiting for us in the car.' She eyed the amount of luggage her mother had with her and mentally calculated if it would fit in their car.

Elena scrutinized her daughter. 'You seem to have lost a lot of weight,' she observed.

'I'm on the go most of the time. What with the bungalows and John I never seem to stop.' She took the luggage trolley from her mother and led her out through the doors and across to where their car was parked.

Giovanni saw them coming and climbed out of the car, approaching his mother-in-law a little hesitantly. 'I am so pleased to meet you at last. Welcome to Crete.' He took the trolley from Marianne and proceeded to place the cases into the boot, relieved to find that he was able to close it.

'Get in, Mamma. We'll both sit in the back so you can tell me all your news. Giovanni will take the trolley back; then we'll be off.'

'You didn't bring John with you?'

'Aunt Ourania is looking after him. I've told him his grandmother is coming for a visit, but I don't think he will remember you. I know I've sent you photographs, but you'll be amazed at the change in him. He's no baby any more. He's running around everywhere and getting into all sorts of mischief.' Marianne smiled fondly. 'I say he takes after his father.'

Marianne sat on the patio with her mother. 'When you've had breakfast I'll show you around. We'll have John with us as Aunt Ourania has to go into the shop and Uncle Yannis and Giovanni are going to the airport to collect Marisa and Victor.' Marianne rose and picked John up from where he was digging in a plant pot. 'I've told you that is a naughty thing to do,' she scolded him. 'You will hurt the poor plant. You dig in your sand pit.'

John wriggled from her arms and made his way determinedly back towards the potted plants.

'John.' Marianne spoke sternly and he turned and looked at her with large dark eyes before picking up a handful of earth and throwing it on the ground defiantly. Marianne sighed and scooped him up in her arms again. 'I really will have to ask Uncle Yannis if he can move the pots somewhere else. John won't leave them alone.'

'He doesn't seem as obedient as Helena's boys,' observed Elena.

Marianne flushed. 'He's not really naughty. He just wants to investigate everything. You have to remember that Helena's boys are that bit older. They've been through this stage.' John's face began to redden and he opened his mouth to let out a piercing cry as he struggled frantically in his mother's arms.

'No, John. You are not getting your own way.' Marianne rose with the wriggling child in her arms. 'I'll take him inside and let you finish your breakfast in peace. Give me a call when you're ready.'

Elena nodded. She would never have believed that her academic daughter would have such an unruly child. No doubt it was due to the fact that she was for ever running about and leaving him in the care of his aunt and uncle.

'It's quite a long walk, Mamma; so we'll go in the car.' Marianne looked at her mother's high heeled sandals and tight skirt. 'Would you be comfortable in something less formal? Did you bring a summer skirt and sandals with you?'

'I'll be fine,' Elena assured her daughter. 'Will John have a screaming fit whilst we are in the car?'

'I doubt it, besides it's no more than a fifteen minute drive. I'll strap him in, so you won't have to deal with him if he gets restless.'

Marianne drove slowly along the road towards Plaka. 'You have a view of the island the whole way along,' she slowed to a halt. 'You see that little inlet down there? Giovanni plans to turn it into a scuba diving area eventually. We shall need permission, of course, and have to make a walk way down the cliff, but he thinks the more attractions we have close to home the more money we shall make.'

Elena craned her neck and could just catch a glimpse of the sea between the bushes. 'Are you making any money?'

Marianne smiled complacently as she drove on. 'We made a little profit this season and we had only expected to cover our expenses. As we expand we should find it more profitable.'

'I'm not sure I'd want to stay this far out in one of these bungalows,' observed Elena as Marianne drew to a halt. 'It's very deserted.'

'It's deserted now because it's the end of the season and we've closed down. During the summer there were people around and they used to hire a car to go off exploring. Would you like to see inside?' Marianne took a key from her purse and her mother followed her up to the bungalow.

'Are you leaving John in the car?'

'We'll only be a few minutes. He's quite safe. I'll take him out when we get to *'ANNA'S'*.'

Elena was pleasantly surprised when she saw the interior of the bungalow. 'It looks quite comfortable.'

'It is. We haven't had any complaints from anyone who has stayed here. Marisa and Victor are going to stay in this one, so we haven't removed the bedding or anything. The others are quite bare and we've turned the water off and closed the shutters. We'll check them after it rains to make sure they are watertight, but that is how they'll stay now until March. Just before the season starts we'll air them and Giovanni will do any little jobs that are needed.'

Elena nodded. 'So what are you going to do with yourselves during the winter?'

'We have plans for a couple more bungalows and we want to make a shower and changing room on the upper floor of the taverna.'

'Whatever for?'

'If we expand as we hope we shall need to employ people. We can't expect anyone to work as a chambermaid for a couple of hours and then go to cook food without a proper wash and change of clothes. It's for our benefit too. Sometimes Giovanni is up here most of the day and often doing hot and dirty jobs. It would be so nice to have a cool shower.'

Elena took in the small shop. The shelves were bare, umbrellas and tables were stacked in one corner and John had immediately made his way over to them and was attempting to climb to the top of the unsteady pile. The remainder of the space was taken up with boxes.

'Do people actually buy things here?'

'They certainly do.' Marianne lifted John back down to the floor so he could start his climb again. 'This was a brilliant idea. You'd be amazed how many people forget their toothbrush, or need sun tan lotion. They can also buy everything they need here to make a basic picnic, and when they return they can come here for a drink and pastry before getting ready to go out in the evening. Again, if they don't want to go out they can buy food here to make a meal in their bungalow. We plan to stock a few guide books to the local area next season and see whether that pays.' She lifted John back down to the floor for a second time.

Elena shook her head sadly. 'What a waste of your education.'

'It is not!' replied Marianne defiantly. 'I'm able to deal with all the legal formalities for permission to build and draw up the contracts for our builders and suppliers. If we had to employ a lawyer it would cost a fortune.'

'And you are actually happy living like this? Working as a chambermaid and shop assistant.'

'I'm very happy,' Marianne reassured her mother. 'I love Giovanni and John and I also love my life out here. I couldn't imagine being back in the States, possibly cooped up in an office all day and returning to a small apartment each night. The mere thought makes me shudder.'

Elena shrugged. 'Well, if you say you're happy I have to believe you. Is there anything else to see or shall we go back?'

'Only the toilet block.' Marianne grinned mischievously. 'I can show you where it is if you need it.'

'I think I can give that a miss. No doubt the water has been turned off for the winter.'

'We'll put it back on when there's work going on up here. Come on, John, climbing is over for today. We'll go back home in the car and you can play in your sand pit. How does that sound? Good? Pappa and Uncle Yannis will be back soon and they'll have your other grandma and grandpa with them. They haven't seen you since you were a tiny baby. You'll be able to show them what a naughty boy you are and how loudly you can scream.'

John seemed to be listening intently to his mother and before he could protest in his usual fashion he was strapped back into his seat in the car.

'I'll take you for a drive up the hill so you can see the view, then we'll go back. I'll have to make sure Aunt Anna and Uncle Yiorgo are presentable for when Marisa and Victor arrive so I'll ask you to keep an eye on John for me for five minutes.'

Elena nodded. She looked after Helena's two boys frequently, but the thought of looking after John for a short while filled her with dread.

Marisa sat with her aunt. She was saddened to see how shrunken and old she appeared to be. 'You're looking very well, Aunt Anna. I'm so pleased you're living her with Yannis. I would worry about you if you still lived out on the farm.'

'It doesn't look like my home any more.'

'Does that make you sad?'

Anna shook her head. 'No, not now. When I first saw what Yannis and Giovanni had done I couldn't believe it. I thought they had taken me to somewhere I had never been before. I asked Yannis to put a chair where I used to sit and prepare the vegetables, and I could still see the carob trees and the hills, so then I knew I was at home. Yannis is such a good man. Your mother would have been so proud of him.'

'I don't remember her now, Aunt Anna. You were my mother.'

Anna smiled. In truth she could hardly remember her older sister. 'Yannis is happy with Ourania. Are you still happy with Victor?'

'Very happy,' Marisa assured her. 'My only regret is that I live so far away from you.'

'You don't have to worry about me. I'm well looked after. I just hope I'm not too much of a trial to Ourania and Marianne.'

'They both love you dearly. You're not a trial to them.'

'I'm old and useless.'

'You are certainly not useless. You never will be. Marianne said you were the only one who could calm John when he was teething badly and you knew exactly what medicine to make up when he had a nasty cold.'

'I wish I could still walk up on the hills, as I did when you were a child. I miss searching for the wild herbs.'

'You have your herb garden here. You showed it to me yesterday.'

'It's not the same. I know where everything is. I don't have to look for it, and some things prefer to grow out on the hills.' Anna sighed.

Marisa patted her aunt's hand. 'I probably shouldn't tell you this, but I know Marianne has had an idea. She wants to make up some packets of herbs to sell up at the shop. She doesn't know how long some of them have to be dried before they can be packaged or how long she can keep them before they become stale and unusable. The knowledge you have is invaluable and she is going to ask you to help her.'

A slow smile crept across Anna's face. 'Do you think she'd let me go up there so I can tell people how to use them?'

Marisa considered her answer carefully. 'I'm sure she'd appreciate your help sometimes. When people ask her about herbs and she doesn't know the answer she could arrange to take you up the following day to meet them.'

'Marianne is a good girl. She works hard. Giovanni made a good choice there. What about your other boys? What are they doing and when are they going to visit me?'

'Angelo has said he would like to come over the next time we visit. He has to arrange his holiday dates well in advance and he'd used up his allocation for this year.'

'Is he married?'

Marisa shook her head. 'No, but I hope he will be able to eventually. He's been with the same girl for the last five years, but she's Catholic.'

'What difference does that make?'

'She's already married. Catholics don't believe in divorce.'

Anna sniffed. 'Better to have a divorce and be happy with someone else.' A spasm of pain crossed Anna's face. 'Michael....' her voice tailed away.

Marisa made no comment. Her brother had told her about the visit from Michael and the subsequent one made by Michael's daughter a few years ago. 'Joseph is for ever moving around,' she said quickly. 'We're never sure where he is or where he'll turn up.' She looked at her watch. 'I must go. I promised to help Marianne to prepare our evening meal. There are quite a few of us around to cater for at present.' She needed an excuse to talk to Marianne about the proposal she had made to her aunt about the herbs and hoped her daughter in law would approve and not consider her interfering.

Anna did not appear to hear her. Her eyes were on the framed photograph of Michael and his daughter that she kept on the table beside her during the day, and moved into her bedroom each night.

Marisa repeated her idea regarding the herbs to Marianne whilst they prepared the evening meal together.

'I think it's an excellent idea. It would certainly make Aunt Anna think she was being useful. She's always led such an active life that it must be frustrating for her to sit and do nothing for most of the day. I'll discuss it with her tomorrow and let her think it was her idea.'

Marisa smiled. 'You know just how to keep her happy.'

Marianne sighed. 'I just wish Uncle Yiorgo was as easy.'

Christos and Babbis sat in their office in the central police station in Athens. They were examining the files that were sent to them from each of the Greek islands at the end of the season.

'Crime seems to be increasing,' remarked Babbis as he threw the folder relating to Corfu onto the pile for filing.

'More tourists, more crime,' remarked Christos.

'Personally I don't see what the point is of sending all the paper work to us. Most of it has already been dealt with by the local police.'

'It's just a formality.' Christos balanced the slim file for Hydra on top of the others.

'It's just an excuse to clutter up our filing system. It's all shop lifting or pick pocketing, and that's the tourists,' grumbled Babbis. 'They spend their money on drink and find they haven't got enough for the hotel bill, so they steal a friend's wallet. They make me sick.'

'Better to have pick pockets than murderers.'

'Mark my words, it will come. Look at the way crime has escalated in the States. You're not safe to walk down the road over there.'

Christos smiled. He heard the same comments from Babbis every year. 'You watch too many American films. I'll do one more file; then I'm off for lunch.' He picked up the one marked 'SAMOS' and began to turn the pages. Long experience had taught him that it was not necessary to read every report in its entirety. He frowned and turned back to check the previous pages before passing the file across to Babbis. 'Take a look through that and tell me if anything strikes you.'

Babbis scanned the pages. The file was in date order, five or six reports for each day. They were for minor accidents, shoplifting, details of lost money and passports, drunks who had become a nuisance and arrests for being in possession of drugs. The further he delved into the file the more the drug related incidences increased, often necessitating ten or more reports.

'Drugs?' he asked.

Christos nodded. 'There are always a few, but this year it seems to be the major offence.' He looked at the map pinned up on the wall. 'Close to Turkey. Could be coming over from there.'

'What about the other islands in that area?'

'I haven't looked at any others yet. Maybe we should concentrate on those this afternoon? See if there's any sort of pattern.'

'Or leave them until last,' suggested Babbis.

Joseph was feeling very satisfied with life. His weekly journey to Marmaris had been changed to once a fortnight now the summer season was drawing to a close, and Nadia was going to be working exclusively for him.

Lakkis had sent for him and explained the terms of the syndicate. Joseph had demurred at the prospect of handing over five hundred thousand drachmas, but Lakkis was adamant. It was the full amount in cash immediately or the deal would be off. Joseph stalled and promised to meet Lakkis the next day with his answer.

Joseph returned to his room and removed the money he had hidden in the false bottom of the chest. He counted it out carefully. He would be left with just under two hundred thousand drachmas. It would be sufficient, with his wages and the percentage from Nadia, to see him through the winter months.

Sorrell was disappointed when Dimitris told her they would be sailing for Kos the next day. She had been ashore, again accompanied by Frida. They had stopped for coffee at a café at Mandraki harbour and watched the pedestrians and traffic that flowed past them. It had been a mistake to stop there. The road was being repaired and the traffic was being held up continually, spewing fumes into the air.

Sorrell coughed and wrinkled her nose. 'Are you ready? I don't think I can stand the smell of petrol much longer. I'm beginning to feel sick.'

Frida nodded agreement and delved into her purse. Sorrell bent to retrieve her parcels and as she rose she drew in her breath sharply. Surely that was Joseph sitting astride a scooter. As she looked a taxi drew up beside him, obscuring her view.

'What's wrong?' asked Frida. 'You've gone quite pale.'

'Nothing.' Sorrell shook her head. 'I'll be fine when we've found some clean air to breathe.'

'Would you rather go back to the boat?'

'No, I'm all right, really.' Sorrell was feeling quite light-headed. Was it Joseph she had seen or just someone who resembled him?

She spent the remainder of the afternoon looking at the rider each time a scooter passed them, and could not concentrate on either Frida's conversation or the goods in the shops they visited.

As always, on their return to the cruiser, Frida reported on their day to Dimitris. Usually this took no more than a few minutes, but on this occasion she felt she should make him aware of Sorrell's distraction throughout the afternoon.

'She said she was feeling sick from the traffic fumes. She did turn pale for a few moments, but her behaviour was different, somehow. She seemed to be looking at everyone and thinking of something other than shopping.'

'Thank you, Frida. I'm sure it was nothing more than the smell upsetting her. I'll see how she's feeling now.'

Dimitris knocked gently on Sorrell's cabin door. 'May I come in?'

'Of course.' Sorrell had removed her shorts and blouse and was lying on her bed. 'I was just about to have a short siesta before I showered.'

'That is a good idea. Frida told me you felt unwell.'

Sorrell laughed shakily. 'It was only for a short while. We chose the wrong place to sit and have coffee.'

Dimitris nodded understandingly. 'You are sure you feel perfectly well now?'

'I really am fine now.'

'Then maybe you should wear your black evening dress tonight.' He ran a finger between her breasts, feeling the immediate response from her body.

'If you wish, Dimitris.'

'I think it could be a good idea. Enjoy your siesta.'

A month later Christos and Babbis had completed their examination of the files relating to the Greek islands. All but three had been stamped 'closed'. Those three remained on their desks.

'Time to pass these over to narcotics, I think,' said Christos. Babbis shrugged. 'They'll be pleased!'

Yiorgo looked at the three files that had been delivered to his office. He and Takkis had read through the files as requested and they were forced to agree that there appeared to have been a problem with drugs entering the islands during the summer season.

'I think we should go through these again together, see if we can find any sort of pattern. I'll read and you take the notes,' ordered Yiorgo.

Takkis sighed. It would be monotonous work and there was probably little point to the exercise. He drew a pad of paper towards him and picked up his pen.

'March tenth – local picked up drunk – in possession – heroin. March fifteenth – local picked up drunk – in possession – heroin. March sixteenth …'

'Do you think we should make a note of their names?' asked Takkis.

'Good idea.'

Takkis drew another column on his sheet of paper.

It took three weeks for the two men to extract the information from the file and a further two days to collate it. Yiorgo tapped his pen against his teeth as he looked at the sheets of paper in his hand.

'According to this, there were a few cases in March and April. Nothing remarkable there, but when we go into the summer months they multiply alarmingly. Admittedly they seem to be the foreign tourists, but they must have been supplied locally. It has to be coming in from Turkey and I would say it was organised. Let's move on to the 'KOS' file, see how that compares.'

Yiorgo looked at the figures before him. There was definitely a drug problem on the three islands. It could not be coincidence that so many of the arrests that had been made and the admissions to the local hospitals had been attributed to drug taking. He clicked his worry beads between his fingers. Takkis sat quietly. If Yiorgo was playing with his beads it meant that he was thinking deeply. Finally he slipped them back into his pocket and looked at Takkis.

'Any ideas?'

Takkis shook his head.

'Let's go through the files again. Maybe there's something we've missed.'

'Do you want to do the lists again?'

'No, we'll just check them. You call the details to me this time.'

With a sigh Takkis opened the first file and began to recite the list. Half an hour later he looked at his colleague. 'A number of these people seem to have been staying at the same hotel.'

Yiorgo looked at him eagerly. 'That was something we didn't think to look at.' He drew a further column on the sheets of paper. 'Let's start again.'

Joseph studied the map that Thalia had given him some months previously. During the summer season he had restricted his movements to the haunts of the tourists. Now the time had come to move further afield and see what the island had to offer during the winter. He had ridden through the quiet towns of Kremasti, Paradisi, and Fanes. There were a couple of larger towns further down and he decided he might as well continue. It was unlikely that he would find a way to supplement his income from this side of the island, but it could be to his advantage to know the area.

With this thought in mind, Joseph continued on his way, passing farmland and occasional clusters of poor looking houses until he reached Kamiros. He examined the ancient site and decided it was far too open and vast for his purposes, however many tourists were there visiting. He remounted his bike and rode through two sizeable villages, beginning to climb higher into the mountainous terrain until he could look down at the sea and small fishing boats were in evidence. Judging by the number he could see there could be a sizeable village on the coast, probably boasting a taverna where he would be able to have a beer and maybe some lunch.

He swung off onto a well-made side road and began to weave his way from the heights down to sea level. Each bend of the road showed either a view of the sea or a vista of terraced farmland, interspersed with tiny stone buildings that were obviously deserted. He began to regret his decision, the road, winding and twisting, not bringing him any nearer to a fishing village. He assumed that when he reached the coast the road would continue round the headland and the fishing village would be situated in the next bay.

Almost as the thought entered his mind the road levelled out and the sea was in front of him, the road leading only to a beach and a substantial concrete building. Metal gates covered in strong wire mesh guarded the entrance to a piece of waste ground and drawn up before the building was a van that was definitely familiar to him. Joseph smiled. He should be able to get a beer, if nothing else.

He parked the bike beside the van and sauntered towards the building. Before he reached the door it was opened and Christos looked at him in surprise.

'What brings you down here?'

'I was just out riding. I thought there would be a village down here where I could get a beer.'

Christos opened the door wider. 'You're welcome.'

Joseph entered the building and looked round curiously. The large room was sparsely furnished and Christos had disappeared into the adjoining kitchen, returning moments later with a beer for both of them.

Joseph drank gratefully, whilst Christos only took a mouthful before putting his aside. 'I'll be back in a moment. Something cooking,' he mumbled and returned to the kitchen.

Joseph followed him to the door. 'I don't mind sitting in the kitchen if you're busy.' His eyes swivelled from the empty stove to the table, taking in the pair of small scales, foil wraps, plastic bags and large jar of brown powder. 'Well, well, and I thought you were just the delivery boy!'

Christos gave him a venomous look. 'I'll bring you another beer.'

Joseph nodded and returned to his seat in the living room. This was interesting, and already his fertile mind was thinking of ways in which he could exploit his discovery.

Christos sat opposite him, obviously ill at ease. Joseph smiled and took a mouthful of his second beer.

'So what's the story?' he asked.

'None of your business,' growled Christos.

Joseph raised his eyebrows. 'I think it could be. Lakkis would be – distressed – if he thought you were short-changing him.'

'I'm not short-changing anyone.'

'So tell me. I know how to keep my mouth shut – if it's worth my while,' he added.

'There's nothing to tell. I just make up the packets before I deliver them to you.'

Joseph nodded slowly. 'And where do you get it from?'

'I enjoy a spot of fishing.'

'Bit risky, isn't it? What about the patrols?'

'They never patrol this area on Wednesday nights.'

'Never?' Joseph was surprised. 'How come?'

'A little arrangement with the harbour master.'

'Clever.' Joseph raised his bottle in salutation.

'I just pack it and deliver to you.'

'How much do you keep for your own use?'

Christos looked at Joseph indignantly. 'None.'

Joseph smiled slowly. 'I don't believe you. No one would notice a couple of grains from each pack. It could add up quite nicely over a period of time.'

Christos did not answer and Joseph knew he had guessed correctly.

'Lakkis wouldn't be very happy about that, would he?' Joseph continued. 'Not that he needs to know, of course. For a small favour, we could forget I've ever visited.'

'What do you mean?'

Joseph sat forward on his chair. 'I'm not a user, but I want to know what it's like. How do you feel? What effect does it have on you afterwards?'

'Why?'

'Call it curiosity.'

'Within a few seconds you feel fantastic. You can do anything; you're invincible, super man. The world's a different place; everything takes on a different dimension.'

'How long does it last?'

Christos shrugged. 'It depends. The first time is usually the best and can last about half an hour. After that you want to keep repeating the experience. The trouble is you begin to need more to get to that level and after a while you never want to leave it, never want to return to reality.'

'How often do you use it?'

'I don't. I'm clean now.'

'I don't believe you.'

'It's true. I haven't touched it for years. I had enough sense to realise it was destroying me. It was hard, but I managed it.'

'So how did you get this job? I would have thought it would have been temptation all the way.'

'I was a school teacher. I got involved with someone, had a lot of stress, and a friend suggested I used it to relax. Within a few weeks I was totally dependent. I couldn't walk into a classroom unless I was on a high. The trouble is, it doesn't last. I needed more and more to get me through each day. I thought it was making me a better teacher, when my class failed their grades, the education authorities thought otherwise. I was out. No job, no money, no more highs. By the end of a week I was desperate. I started pilfering, but it wasn't enough, so I tried a filling station, and that was when I was caught. There was no treatment in jail, you just sweated it out.'

Christos emptied his beer bottle. 'I did five years. When I came out I was determined to stay clean. I couldn't ever go through that again. I bummed around, doing odd jobs, couldn't ever get a job as a teacher again. Somehow Lakkis got to hear of me and reckoned I'd be the right man for the job.'

'So if you don't use it what do you do with the amount you cream off? Sell it on the side?'

Christos lowered his eyes. 'I give it to my wife.'

Joseph was startled. 'Your wife!'

'It helps her pain. Helps her to sleep. I've never given her enough to make her dependent.'

'What's wrong with her?'

'We got married whilst I was a teacher. She stuck by me, trusted me throughout everything. We were managing to have a good life together. She thought I was just a van driver, but that didn't matter to her. I had a job. She went swimming one day and there was an accident with a motorboat. It ploughed right into her, she didn't stand a chance. She lost an arm.' Christos suddenly looked sad and careworn. 'Some of the time she's fine, then she gets hit by a bout of depression and the pain starts. When someone screams in agony all night you have to do something. I was desperate, so I tried a few grains. It was the answer.'

Joseph nodded; he felt sympathy for the man, an emotion unusual for him. 'I'll not tell Lakkis.'

A silence fell between them and Joseph wondered how he could best approach the favour he had mentioned earlier.

'I'd best be going. Thanks for the beer.' He stood and walked towards the kitchen. 'I suppose you couldn't let me have a packet?'

Christos eyes opened wide. 'A packet! You're joking. There's enough for a hundred shots in a packet. I could never cover that up.'

Joseph shrugged. 'Shows my ignorance. I just want enough to persuade a certain young lady to be nice to me. She's resisted all my charms so far and I'm getting desperate. Once she realises what she's been missing I'll have no problem with her in the future.'

Christos smiled. 'You don't need much for that.' He pushed past Joseph and placed a measured quantity in a screw of paper. 'Be careful, Joseph,' he warned.

'I will, and thanks, Christos.' Joseph placed the packet in the inside pocket of his jacket. 'I'll let you get back to work now.'

He raised his hand to Christos, who watched him mount his bike and begin the ride back up the steep and winding hill. He felt uneasy and wished Joseph had never found the road down to the secluded bay.

Dimitris returned to Kos as he had planned. The sea had been choppy and Sorrell had retired to her cabin, leaving him to sit and think carefully about the operation he was running. It amused him to think of himself as the spider, spinning a web and entrapping everyone else in the sticky, silken threads.

He was able to deliver the supplies he received from Bodrum on a regular basis to each of the three islands, the harbour masters in each case ensuring the patrols were elsewhere at the critical times. He knew the packers would not dare to steal more than a few grains from each consignment. Each man had been hand picked. Manolis, on Samos, had begged for his help after the unfortunate rape of an Italian diplomat's fourteen-year-old daughter had been traced back to him. Lukas, on Kos certainly did not want it to become common knowledge that he was the one who had robbed his father's shop, hitting him over the head with such violence that he had lost his sight. Christos, on Rhodes, who had been at the wheel of the speedboat the day his wife had suffered the unfortunate accident. All of them had too much to lose to double cross him.

He had set up an intricate network; a warehouse storing and supplying something innocuous and innocent, those collecting the cigarette packets had no knowledge of their contents and passed them on to a further contact as they had been instructed. It was worth their while not to enquire about the contents, or they could find they had to answer some very awkward questions about petty crimes that had occurred some years before.

The recipients of the cigarette packets would sell a few packs to 'the boys', as he called them. They would tout on the beaches and in the nightclubs and pubs for likely users amongst the tourists. Fifty per cent of the money from their sales was theirs to keep. If they wished to continue as a pusher the money for further supplies had to be paid in full when they collected their quota. He felt confident that if one of 'the boys' was arrested they could only name their supplier, and he would have disappeared by the time the police tried to interview him.

He had spent some years working out the exact procedure, ensuring that no suspicion should fall on him. His only involvement was keeping control of the accounts. He had even been cautious there, ensuring the money was taken over to Turkey and by a series of couriers eventually reached Bodrum where he would again send a courier to collect it for him and bring the money back into Greece where he banked it as money from the hotels or hid it safely on the cruiser. This was his province. He knew how much would have been deducted to pay his suppliers and couriers in Turkey, and he regulated the cost of the drugs down as far as 'the boys', ensuring that not only were his expenses covered, but he also made a small fortune. His investments in the hotels providing a perfect cover for his excessive income.

Now, with the winter approaching, the operation would be run down, catering only for the needs of the local inhabitants, until the following summer, when the tourists once again flooded the islands. He would send the girl to Turkey one last time to pick up the money that had been delivered there from each of the islands, then it would be time to sail to Cyprus, for the last of the winter sunshine, before moving on to Egypt.

Egypt would probably be the ideal place to begin his preparations with the girl. When he judged she was ready he would lend her to some of his acquaintances. Dimitris smiled to himself. It would be good practice for her. Thinking of his plans for the girl in the next cabin amused him. He would see if she was really feeling seasick. If not, he could spend an hour or two playing with her body, teasing her into a frenzy of frustration that would be unfulfilled.

'Well,' said Yiorgo, 'have we got anything to go on?'

Takkis shook his head. 'I'm not sure. There were arrests from most of the hotels, but on Samos the majority was from the *'Aegean Pearl'*, on Kos the *'Aegean Jewel'* is predominant and most of the Rhodes arrests were from the *'Aegean Gem'*.

'How big are those hotels?'

'I've no idea. We should be able to find out from the travel agencies.'

'It could be they're the largest, so would naturally have the most trouble makers, hence the largest number of arrests. On the other hand, there could be an employee who's a pusher,' mused Yiorgo. 'Who owns them?'

'Dimitris Stephanotis.'

'I've heard the name. Do we know anything about him?'

'Nothing detrimental. So where do we go from here?' asked Takkis.

'I think we've reached a dead end for the time being. The season's finished. It's too late to get a lead now.' Yiorgo tapped his teeth with his pen. 'I'd like to find out how it's getting into the country. Maybe we should look at the harbour reports.'

'What? You mean look at the movement of all the boats in and out? That would take for ever.'

'No,' Yiorgo shook his head, 'we'd be looking for a pattern. We could ignore the ferries for the time being, although it could be an employee. I'd be more inclined to look for an individual who made regular trips across.'

'Why don't we ask the harbour masters? They've usually a pretty good idea what's going on.'

'Not at this point, they could inadvertently tip someone off. It's better we do it ourselves and check with them later.'

Sorrell was becoming bored. The novelty of stepping ashore on the islands from the cabin cruiser and having all eyes turn to look at her had worn off. The towns, particularly now they were closing for the end of the season, seemed to shrink daily, and she knew the entire stock of most of the shops. Sorrell had suggested she accompanied Dimitris when he went ashore, but on most occasions he had refused her offer.

'I am sitting at the hotel and going through the accounts for the season. I have appointments with builders and decorators as there is work to be done and I want to ensure it is completed before we re-open. Do you really think you would want to discuss cracks in a ceiling or roof repairs?' He shook his head. 'It is far better that you stay here. Amuse yourself with Frida. I shall be back for dinner and next week, when I have finished my business on Rhodes we will sail for Cyprus.'

Sorrell was frustrated. Whenever she had left the cruiser on Rhodes Frida accompanied her and she found she was always steered away from the old, walled town and into the newer area. She was convinced Joseph was on Rhodes; probably living somewhere in the old town, and this was the reason for Frida's close companionship. Wherever they walked she looked for him, unsure what she would do if they came face to face, but wanting the knowledge. She had tried to draw Dimitris on the subject, but he had only smiled in amusement.

'I have asked you to be patient. Next season I will arrange for you to meet Joseph. In the meantime enjoy yourself. It is unlikely you will have the opportunity to live like this in the future.'

Sorrell had considered his last remark, and then dismissed it from her mind. She could always find someone else. There were plenty of lonely millionaires in the world. Maybe she would go to the Caribbean and sail around those islands once she had revenged herself on Joseph. She had vague ideas about exposing him as a thief to the local police force, but as yet she had not formulated any clear plan.

1991

January – April

Marianne closed the account books. 'You see,' she said to Giovanni, 'I was right about building those other two bungalows. We've made a small profit.'

Giovanni smiled at her. 'Did I ever disagree with you?'

'You argued for so long it was a wonder they were ready by August. Shall we aim at building a couple more for next season?'

Giovanni shook his head and laughed as he saw the disappointed look on his wife's face. 'I thought we'd aim at four, and then try to expand the beach area.'

Marianne looked at him in disbelief. 'Do you mean that? Can we really afford it?'

'That depends upon you. I never take you anywhere or buy you clothes. Maybe you'd like to go to America this year and visit your family. You deserve a treat after the way you worked last season.'

'If we went to America we couldn't build the bungalows or work on the beach area, could we?'

'We might manage one bungalow.'

'Then we don't go to America,' Marianne said firmly. 'It was wonderful to see my mother last year and we can give my sister and her family an invitation to visit us here. Maybe my grandmother could come? I love my family memories of them from when I was a child, and if my father was still alive I expect it would be different, but we've all grown apart. My life is over here. This is where I'm at home.'

Giovanni took her hand. 'Do you mean that?'

'You know I do. Provided I have you and John I'm happy.'

He squeezed her fingers. 'We'll build four bungalows and I'll ask Thanassis if he'll rent that stretch of coast line he owns to me. If we have any money left over we could have a weekend in Aghios Nikolaos!'

Marianne shook her head. 'There are two problems. The first is staff. I won't be able to clean eight bungalows in two hours. It was as much as I could do to cope with four.'

'We'll employ a girl. Someone who would like to make some pocket money during their holiday from University. What's your other problem?'

'John. He's not going to be as easy as last year. He wants to be on the go the whole time now. I can't expect Aunt Ourania to look after him for any longer during the day and he's too much for Aunt Anna on her own.'

'Would you consider sending him to a nursery school? Just for a couple of mornings to start with? It would be good for him. He rarely meets other children and he ought to know how to behave with them before he goes to school. If he settled now by the time the season starts he'd probably be ready to go every morning.'

Marianne felt her heart constrict. It was one thing leaving their son to be cared for by relatives, but how would she feel about leaving him with strangers? 'I'm not sure he'd be happy.'

Giovanni shook his head. 'He would probably be happy enough. It's you who wouldn't be happy.'

Marianne tried to smile at her husband. 'We can give it a try. If he's unhappy we will have to think again. Once he starts going off to a nursery school he'll no longer be my baby.'

'Good thing too. You don't want him to stay a baby all his life.'

Sorrell had enjoyed their stay in Cyprus immensely. The island, having had so much influence from the British, was a delight to her. The pattern of her life shifted. She slept late each day, spent a leisurely afternoon ashore, and was ready to play the hostess during the evening and early hours of each morning. Dimitris appeared more attentive, both during the day and the evenings they spent together. He would accompany her on shopping expeditions, sitting patiently whilst she tried various items of clothing and would give his opinion on their suitability. Twice he had selected evening dresses for her and then insisted Frida alter them to make them more revealing and evocative.

'These are for my pleasure,' he smiled. 'I shall enjoy gazing at your attractive body whilst we have dinner. I shall be able to savour the delights in store for me later. Besides, I am sure you are tired of wearing the black one.'

Sorrell did not object. She now knew Dimitris's mood if he told her to wear her black dress at dinner each night and by the time he gave her his full attention she was taut with expectation and desire. She had purchased one without his knowledge and asked Frida to remove the lining. Now she looked at herself in the cream lace and smiled in anticipation. She might as well be naked!

As she entered the saloon for dinner Dimitris looked at her in surprise. If he had not requested a particular dress she usually wore a conventional silk or satin creation, always attractive, but not suggestive in any way.

'Do you like it?' she asked.

'Very much. It exhibits your charms to perfection. I could not have chosen better myself.' It amused Dimitris that she was so willing to debase herself before him. It was obviously the right time to start grooming her for her future role.

Joseph disliked the winter months. There was little call for supplies of organic flour and even less for the other commodity he dealt in. He would spend most of the morning lying on his bed watching the television. During the afternoon he would make his way to

The Grapevine and sit with other young men who only worked during the season and play cards and drink, often staying into the early hours of the morning before staggering away to see if Nadia had a free hour.

That arrangement was working well. Business was brisker now the local people had more time on their hands. The summer was a time for work, and the winter a time to play. He called on her each day to discuss the number of clients she had entertained the previous night, keeping a tally to ensure that his percentage would be correct at the end of each week.

He dreaded opening his envelope of money on a Friday and finding a ticket for Marmaris for the following day. His visits had been reduced to one a month now, but even that was too many for him. Three times he had experienced miserable journeys, the sea being rough and the day ashore spent in pouring rain, being forced to sit in a café and make small talk to Nimet. Now the weather was cold and wet he did not even have the inclination to ride about the island on his bike, the deserted beaches were depressing, and he could always find an excuse to lie on his bed for longer.

He would lay and calculate the amount of money he had earned from Nadia to date and how long it would be before he had managed to recoup the money he had paid to join the syndicate and save enough to buy another girl. Any girl would do, provided she had plenty of regular customers. He decided by the end of the next summer he should have enough. On that reckoning he would be able to have at least six, if not seven girls in five years time. That would put him in control of the majority of the business. He would be able to leave the warehouse job and live a life of complete luxury. He had been foolish not to try to break into the lucrative market of prostitution before.

Dimitris was unsure how a small dose of heroin would affect Sorrell. He had heard reports of people suffering so badly from depression afterwards that they committed suicide, or they became violent and attacked anyone in sight. He did not want to be involved in either scenario, but he needed to ensure that she became dependent on a regular supply.

He bought a large box of handmade chocolates, stipulating that they must all have a soft centre. It had been a simple matter to insert a minute amount of heroin into each one, and tonight he would make his first experiment.

He suggested Sorrell wore her cream lace dress when they dined at the usual time, and he was complimentary when she took her seat opposite him and kept her entertained throughout their meal. She was surprised when he offered her a chocolate after their coffee and at first refused.

'I bought them especially for you. I thought you would like them.' He looked sad at the rejection of his gift.

'I love chocolates, but I never eat them. Can you imagine how much weight I would put on if I ate chocolates as well as these delicious meals that Frida prepares?'

'I am sure one will not add to your weight. Please, just one and I will put them away. They can be a treat after dinner each night.'

Sorrell relented. For months now she had resisted buying any chocolate, telling herself that the sauces and sweet desserts she was eating more than made up for confectionary. She bit into it delicately, and then had to pop the whole chocolate into her mouth as the liquid inside began to run out.

'You should have warned me they were liqueurs,' she said reproachfully.

Dimitris closed the box and smiled. 'Did you enjoy it?'

'It was delicious. May I have another?'

Dimitris shook his head. 'No. We agreed. One after dinner each night as a treat.'

Sorrell threw back her head and laughed. 'You are so strict with me!' She felt very slightly drunk, yet she had only consumed two glasses of wine. 'Let's dance, Dimitris.'

'Frida has not yet cleared the table.'

'I don't care!' Sorrell almost shouted. 'I want to dance now.'

'If you insist.' Dimitris took her in his arms. She wriggled herself against him.

'I want to go to my cabin now,' she whispered in his ear.

'It is too soon. The time is not right.'

'Of course it is,' Sorrell flashed back at him. 'It is always the right time. All day every day it is the right time.'

Sorrell could not believe the words that were coming from her mouth.

'It is unfortunate that I am not capable of satisfying your desire.'

Sorrell nuzzled against him. 'I'm sure you can satisfy me,' she murmured docilely. 'I just feel so ready now. I don't want to waste the moment.'

'Very well.' Dimitris led her to her cabin and Sorrell immediately removed her dress.

'Be quick, Dimitris. I feel so alive, so desperately alive tonight.' Her fingers were frantically undoing the buttons on his shirt and he took her hands in his.

'I regret I have to disappoint you. I have just remembered I have some work to complete.' He began to re-button his shirt.

An agonized look crossed Sorrell's face. 'You can't! Not now! Work later – please, Dimitris.'

Dimitris stroked her naked thigh, feeling her tremble beneath his caress. 'Would you like me to call Anders? He would be able to satisfy your immediate needs.'

'Anders! What about Frida?'

'You could have Frida also if that is what you wish.'

Sorrell shook her head. 'I want you, Dimitris. I'm desperate, please.'

A small smile curved Dimitris's lips as he continued to stroke Sorrell's bare leg, feeling her body tensing in anticipation, her eyes closed she moaned deep in her throat. He reached across and pressed the bell set into the bed-head. Within moments the

139

cabin door opened silently and Anders entered. Dimitris nodded to him, and without a word Anders began to strip off his clothes.

Dimitris stood up and Sorrell opened her eyes. 'Please,' she begged.

By way of reply Dimitris patted her cheek. 'Enjoy yourself.' He moved to the armchair and sat to watch as Anders pushed Sorrell gently down onto the bed. She was about to protest, but her body betrayed her and she found she was welcoming Anders's attentions with pleasure.

Sorrell lay in her cabin. She tried to analyse her feelings from the night before, but her memories were hazy and indistinct. She remembered feeling wonderful, absolutely ecstatically happy, but she could not recall why. Now she felt tense, her body exhausted and bruised. She would have a shower, and then see if Dimitris was planning to go ashore with her. As she thought about going ashore she realised the boat was moving and she felt unreasonably annoyed that they should be leaving Cyprus and Dimitris had not told her of his plans.

She dressed, helped herself to coffee from the galley and went to find him in the saloon.

'Why didn't you tell me we were leaving Cyprus?' she demanded.

Dimitris regarded her carefully. Should he antagonise her or be placatory? He decided it would be easier to explain his reasons calmly.

'Anders brought me the long range weather forecast. Windy conditions are expected, so I decided it would be better to leave early this morning. I do not appreciate being at sea during a storm. It is not a pleasant experience.'

Sorrell bit at her lips. It really made no difference to her where they were; she shrugged and sat down, placing her head in her hands.

'Are you not feeling well?' asked Dimitris.

'I'm fine, no, I feel odd. I have a headache.'

'Maybe some more coffee?' suggested Dimitris. 'You were feeling quite well last night.'

'Last night! I felt wonderful last night.'

'I'm pleased to hear it. I know Anders appreciated the experience.'

'Anders?' Sorrell's head shot up.

'Don't you remember? I had some work to complete and Anders was happy to oblige you.'

Sorrell paled. 'Why can't I remember?'

Dimitris shrugged. 'One man is much the same as another.'

'Does Frida know?'

'I expect he told her.'

'What will she say?'

'Anders and Frida take their orders from me. It is not up to her to say anything.'

'You mean you ordered Anders to come to me?'

'Naturally. He was not averse to the order, I might add.'

'But why?'

'You are an attractive woman.'

'No,' Sorrell shook her head. 'Why did you give him that order?'

'You were very insistent, I could even say desperate.' Dimitris leant forward and patted her hand. 'You were very happy with the arrangement at the time. Just remember, if you need company Anders is available.'

Sorrell hung her head. She felt disgusted with herself. She needed to think, although her head felt stuffed with cotton wool. 'I'll take my coffee to my cabin.'

'As you wish.'

Dimitris watched with a smile on his lips as she returned unsteadily to her cabin. He appeared to have the dosage correct. She would soon be craving for more to combat the adverse effects.

By the time Sorrell joined Dimitris for dinner she felt considerably better. She had spent most of the day lying on her bed, alternating between a feeling of nausea that was accompanied by a throbbing headache and a lassitude that drained her of energy, but would not let her sleep. They had docked a short time earlier in Port Said and she gazed at the myriad lights on the shore, wondering what the town would look like in daylight.

Dimitris was solicitous, enquiring after her health, complimenting her appearance and describing the town as she would see it the next day.

'How long are we staying?' she asked.

Dimitris shrugged. 'We will stay a week, maybe two. Then we can sail on to Alexandria. Maybe take a short trip down the Nile. I am like a migrating bird during the winter months. I follow the sunshine. I think you will enjoy Egypt. It is very different from the European countries.'

Sorrell nodded. 'I won't understand a word they say.' She finished her second glass of wine.

'That is of no great importance. Many people speak English, and I speak a little Arabic. No doubt you will have learnt a little by the time we leave.'

Sorrell shrugged. She really did not care if she spoke Arabic, then she changed her mind and thought it could be an asset to her. She shook herself irritably. If she made an effort to learn the language it could pass the time for her whilst Dimitris left her to her own devices and could be of help when she went shopping.

'A chocolate, my dear.' Dimitris offered the box to her and she accepted unhesitatingly, remembering how the liqueur had dribbled out the night before and placing the whole sweet into her mouth.

Within a short while she realised she felt so much better. Maybe she had been hungry; she had not had much appetite during the day. Her energy was returning, she looked at Dimitris and smiled happily.

'Shall we dance?' she suggested.

'Later,' he demurred. 'I need to check with Anders that all is in order for our stay here.' He picked up the box of chocolates. 'I will get Frida to put these in the fridge.'

As he passed her she stretched out her hand and caught at his leg. 'Hurry back. I'm on fire for you.'

Dimitris delayed his return to the cabin lounge and there was no sign of Sorrell. He nodded to Anders who opened her cabin door. She was lying naked on her bed and stretched her arms out to him. 'I am so ready for you,' she murmured.

Dimitris smiled as he sat down in the armchair to watch. As he had told her, one man was the same as another.

Sorrell was puzzled and ashamed by her behaviour. She rose each morning lacking energy, a continual headache hovering behind her eyes, wishing she could feel as she had the previous night when everything had seemed so extraordinarily exciting, colours brighter and her touch and feeling so sensitive, her body desperately craving the attention of a man. If only she could feel like that all the time. Even when she went ashore with Dimitris she felt apathetic and disinterested in the bazaars, often cold and shivering despite the warmth, the crowded streets seeming to close in on her. He finally produced a small jar of smelling salts and allowed her to sniff them briefly after which she began to feel considerably better, but wished they had not made her nose drip.

It seemed she only truly became alive each night after dinner and finally put her condition down to the heat of the day and the contrasting coolness of the night. She went ashore each morning at Dimitris's insistence and tried to make conversation with the many people he would introduce to her. He had agreed she could return to the cruiser at mid-day to rest and she would spend the afternoon tossing and turning on her bed, before finally forcing herself to her feet to shower and dress for dinner. Each evening there were guests for dinner. Dimitris had begun to allow her a chocolate before they arrived and she found herself playing the charming hostess and most evenings ended with Anders in her cabin. It was only when she was alone that she began to feel cold and nauseous, depression creeping up on her.

Dimitris appeared to show concern for her daily lethargy, but she had shrugged his solicitous enquiries aside. 'I'm fine during the evening. It's probably this unrelenting sunshine, it seems to drain me.'

He considered her carefully. The time was right.

'I think maybe I have the answer. It is my fault. I should not have encouraged you to spoil yourself.'

'What do you mean?' frowned Sorrell.

'I think your body is craving chocolate. Having abstained for so long, one in the evening is not enough to keep your sugar levels balanced.'

'Don't be silly,' she snapped back at him.

'At least indulge me by trying an experiment. Have a chocolate now. If you feel no better, then I am wrong in my assumption.'

To humour him she had accepted and to her surprise she immediately felt so much better. She showered and dressed, entering the cabin lounge with a delighted smile on her face.

'You were obviously right, Dimitris. My sugar levels were out of balance. I feel wonderful. Are we going ashore? I feel I've been missing so much.' She fingered the material of her dress. 'This feels so soft and cool against my body. Maybe I can find another in the same material. Do you think a gold chain would look right with it?'

'If you want a gold chain I will take you to a good place to buy one. Decide how much you want to spend.'

Sorrell shrugged. 'It really doesn't matter provided I get what I want. I've decided I am not going to worry about mundane things any more.'

'A very good philosophy, my dear.' Dimitris smiled to himself.

'So how many do we have that are worth looking at a second time?' asked Yiorgo.

'Thirty seven craft were moving around the area pretty regularly last year. We could wait and see if they do the same in the coming season.'

'I'd rather have narrowed it down to just a few and concentrate on their movements. We'll have a closer look at those and see if we can find any sort of pattern. Did any of them visit Turkey regularly?'

Takkis looked at his notes. 'Seven of them visited Turkey more than once.'

'Right then, we'll start with those.'

At the end of the morning Yiorgo pushed his notes to one side in disgust. 'Another dead end! They all check out as legitimate tourists taking advantage of the cheap shopping over there.'

'That leaves the other thirty.'

Yiorgo pursed his lips. 'They none of them went to Turkey.' He sat deep in thought for some moments. 'Maybe we're approaching this from the wrong side. We're looking for someone going from Greece to Turkey, suppose they're coming the other way?'

'We checked that against the harbour master's reports and drew a blank.'

'I know the answer's there, staring us in the face. Give me the lists again.'

Takkis handed them over. 'I think we should start looking for an employee on the ferries.'

'No, that would be like looking for an even smaller needle in a haystack.' Yiorgo frowned at the list before him. 'Suppose it isn't going directly to those islands. Suppose they're taking it to one of the others and it's being collected from there.'

'If they're doing that we don't stand a chance of finding them.'

Yiorgo sat and brooded. 'We've got some discrepancies here,' he said finally. 'All these boats stopped at the three islands we've been concentrating on, but where were they in the meantime? They logged their proposed destination when they left, but what time did they arrive at that island? The time of their arrival in port could be crucial. If they sail out in the morning and dock elsewhere late at night they could have been up to anything under cover of darkness. We'll have to get the records for those islands.'

Takkis sighed deeply. 'They could have spent their day fishing.'

'Very true, but most fishermen return to the same port. Boat owners who are keen fishermen very rarely sail between the islands. What's the point? Fish are fish.'

'Divers?'

Yiorgo nodded. 'That's possible, but the same thing applies. You wouldn't go that far off shore if you wanted to look at the marine life.'

'But if you were moving on to another island you could stop somewhere interesting on the way and go into port later.'

'Very true; but I think times of departure and arrival are worth looking at.'

Takkis made a note. 'You don't think it might be worth our while to make some investigations on shore? However the stuff gets there it has to be distributed. Maybe one of the locals who was picked up as a user is also a pusher, or could give us a lead on one?'

'That's an idea. What about those hotels that seemed to have the greatest problem? Have we heard back from the travel agents regarding their capacity?'

'They're not the largest, but they were full all season.'

'What was their staff turnover like? Was anyone sacked for pilfering or slackness?'

'How does that equate?' Takkis frowned.

'If they were pilfering they could have needed money to buy, and if they were lax in their duties it could mean they were using. Check them out.'

'Do we tell them why we want the information?'

'No, say we're checking on illegal immigration. Visitors who are working without permits. Just a formality.'

Takkis nodded. He would have preferred to wait until the season got under way and then take a closer look at the problem. It was proving to be such a waste of time, making and looking at never ending lists.

Dimitris decided the time was right to increase the dosage he inserted into the chocolates. Sorrell's euphoria was wearing off more quickly and her periods of withdrawal were increasing in length. It could also be the right time to introduce her to some more acquaintances.

Anders had complained that her incessant demands on him were becoming tiring and Dimitris was no longer interested in her. He would be relieved when he could leave her on Rhodes with Lakkis.

For a week he invited different business acquaintances to dine on board with them and left Sorrell with no illusions how they would expect to be entertained. The first evening Sorrell had refused. Dimitris waited. They finished their meal and the chocolate box was not produced. He could see that Sorrell was becoming restless and unhappy.

'Is there a problem, my dear?'

'I was looking for my chocolates.'

Dimitris shook his head. 'Chocolates are not given to girls who do not do as they are told.'

'What do you mean?'

'I have asked you to entertain our guest and you have refused. I refuse to give you a chocolate until you change your mind.'

Sorrell sat sullenly at the table whilst the two men conversed in Arabic. Her skin was burning, maybe she had sunstroke. As the thought crossed her mind she began to shiver, then she felt sick. Dimitris eyes continually flicked across her.

'I'm sorry,' she said. 'Would you excuse me? I am feeling really ill. I think I have had too much sun.'

Dimitris shook his head. 'You are the hostess. You will stay at the table until our guest leaves.'

'Dimitris, I can't.'

'Of course, if you had a chocolate you would probably feel considerably better.'

'Let me have one, please.'

Dimitris shook his head.

'Please, Dimitris. I'll do anything to feel better,' she begged.

'Anything?' Dimitris raised his eyebrows enquiringly. 'Are you willing to entertain our guest? If so I will give you a chocolate.'

'I'll do as you say,' she muttered.

Sorrell looked at the man across the table from her. The lights that seemed to be flashing before her eyes distorted him and disorientated her. She shivered again and felt the beginning of a pounding headache as she stretched out her hand to select a chocolate from the box Dimitris held.

Sorrell looked at Port Said with new eyes, enjoying the sights and sounds that on some of her previous trips ashore she had hardly noticed. As she dressed for dinner she recalled the time they had spent ashore that day. She had accompanied Dimitris as he took her to a number of different locations and introduced her as his companion. On two occasions he had made some excuse and left her alone in the office.

The first man had risen from his desk and stood in front of her, taking her chin in his hands and tilting her head from left to right. He had run his fingers down her neck, then returned to his seat.

When Dimitris returned he smiled broadly and the two men conversed in Arabic, Dimitris opened his diary and made an entry whilst a large quantity of notes were pushed across the desk to him. He pocketed them swiftly, shook hands with the man and left.

On their second visit the man shook his head. Dimitris had obviously been surprised by his refusal and by his tone of voice Sorrell guessed he was trying to be persuasive, but to no avail. After only a short while Dimitris had taken her arm, said a polite farewell and steered her back down the stairwell.

The third visit had been to the office of a shipping company. Four men had joined them and they had sat politely drinking mint tea and she had nibbled on a sweet biscuit. Dimitris had excused himself again, and she had been left to continue sipping her tea. Immediately Dimitris left, the man nearest to her had stretched out his hand and stroked her breast. Inadvertently she had pulled away from him.

'No,' she shook her head; wishing Dimitris had not left her.

'Yes,' he smiled, showing gold teeth. He slipped his hand inside her blouse and squeezed her breast hard, beckoning to the other men who stood there smiling. A second man took up a stance on the other side of her, pushing his hand up her skirt and stroking her leg. Sorrell closed her eyes. This could not be happening. If only Dimitris would return.

He licked his lips and said something indistinguishable to his companions. They laughed together and one began to unbutton her blouse. He touched her breasts, stroking them, cupping them, caressing them and making comments to his companions.

Sorrell shivered. She was seriously frightened. She had heard of girls who had been raped and murdered and had no desire to join their number. Hands ran up and down her body, accompanied by a continual dialogue and laughter between the men.

'Please stop,' she whispered. 'Please, please leave me alone.'

The men seemed to find her pleas amusing and totally ignored her request.

By the time Dimitris returned the men were sitting behind their desks and she had rearranged her disordered clothing. The instigator of the assault on her body spoke a few words in Arabic to Dimitris, who smiled and answered in the same language before accepting a thick envelope that was pushed across the desk to him.

'I have thanked my friends for looking after you in my absence. They said they found your company delightful and are looking forward to getting to know you better this evening.' Dimitris smiled mockingly at her. 'Are you ready to leave now, my dear? You wished to do some more shopping before we left the town, I believe.'

Sorrell was unable to answer him. Her mouth was dry and she felt cold and sick. Dimitris helped her to her feet and she leaned gratefully on his arm.

She told Dimitris of her experience whilst he left her in the office and he was amused. 'Why are you making such a fuss about a couple of men touching you?'

'They all touched me, Dimitris. They held me so I couldn't move. They assaulted me. One of them really hurt me.'

'I'm sure no one meant to hurt you.'

'I thought they were going to rape me and kill me.'

Dimitris threw back his head and laughed. 'You have a very vivid imagination, my dear. These people like to inspect their purchases. I'm sure after you have spent this evening with them you will realise that you misconstrued the situation.'

Dimitris had made her parade before him, insisting she modelled all her evening dresses, before finally deciding the cream lace would be the most suitable.

'Every time they look at you they will be able to see the promise in store for them,' he had murmured as he left her cabin, leaving Sorrell with no illusions about how she would be expected to entertain their guests.

The four men went ashore as dawn was bringing a blush to the sky. Dimitris had offered them an evening of unparalleled pleasure and he had been as good as his word. It had been worth every piastre of the extortionate price he had asked. The girl had been incredible, continually demanding more and exciting them to new efforts each time they had thought themselves finally spent.

Sorrell lay on her bed, reliving what she could remember of the night. She was not sure if they had eaten dinner, and if they did she had no recollection of the meal. They had all retired to her cabin and she had undressed the visitors, her hands lingering against their skin, entwining the wiry hair of the Egyptians between her fingers, exploring their bodies intimately, although they had needed no encouragement to become aroused. After that everything became a blur, a tangle of bodies, grunting, groaning and exquisite relief time and time again. The only tangible memory she had was of Dimitris sitting in the chair watching her with a smile on his face and occasionally holding the bottle of smelling salts beneath her nose.

Reluctantly she dragged her bruised and aching body from the bed. Before she showered and dressed she would beg Dimitris for a chocolate.

'I want reports from those three islands every week during the season,' said Yiorgo. 'There's just a chance that if the incidents increase we can link them with the movement of one of the boats.'

Takkis nodded and picked up the telephone. He knew the police on each of the islands would be annoyed by the request, as it would mean considerably more work for them.

'It might help if we knew what they had been up to during the winter months. Were they put in moth balls or did they move away?'

'Are you thinking aloud or do you want me to find that out?' asked Takkis.

'Both.'

Two hours later Takkis had the required information and he presented it to Yiorgo.

'Five went to the States, ten haven't left their home ports, one went to the Caribbean and is still there, five went to Spain, three to Italy, three to the south of France, two are in shipyards for maintenance and one went to Egypt.'

Yiorgo nodded, satisfied. 'Make sure we are advised when any of them make a move into our waters.'

'Some of the ones that stayed in the harbours have been taken out for short spells and then returned. The one that went to Egypt is now in Cyprus.'

'Which one is that?'

"*Aegean Pride.*"

"*Aegean Pride*"? Why does that ring a bell with me?'

Takkis shrugged. 'It's registered in Piraeus, owned by Dimitris Stephanotis, hotelier by trade.'

'That's it! That's what rang a bell for me. What were the names of those hotels, the ones where most of the arrests were made?'

Takkis consulted the collated information. "*Aegean Pearl*', '*Aegean Gem*' and '*Aegean Jewel*'. If those belong to him it's logical that he should call his boat '*Aegean Pride*'.'

'Logical, yes, but could it be a link?' Yiorgo took out his worry beads, running them through his fingers as he sat back in his chair. Finally he leant forward. 'Let's have another look at his activities last season.'

The two men sat together, charting the many sailings that Dimitris had made between the islands. Yiorgo finally threw his pen aside in disgust.

'On the face of it there's nothing to connect him. He has hotels on various islands, so he visits them periodically. All his departure and arrival times are logged, but I notice that he often takes a considerable time to travel between the closest of islands.'

'Maybe he takes a romantic moonlight cruise!' remarked Takkis.

'That's possible,' Yiorgo nodded. 'A man in his position usually has the pick of the available talent. Dig up what you can on his background. How did he start in the hotel business? Where did he get the money for the initial investment? I'm probably clutching at straws, but I feel there's a connection here somewhere.'

Takkis shrugged. He thought it unlikely they would find anything suspicious relating to the millionaire.

Joseph was pleased the season was underway again. He had been annoyed when he discovered that half the sixty percent he collected from Nadia each week had to be passed over to Lakkis.

'It's the rental for the rooms,' Alecos explained smugly. 'He owns the property. He keeps it in good repair.'

Joseph had handed over the money grudgingly. This altered his calculations for buying another girl the following year unless he had a very good season pilfering from the tourists.Even so it was unlikely that he would recoup five hundred thousand drachmas in six months. He also fretted over Thalia. He was no nearer to seducing her than he had been a year ago. She still met him occasionally for coffee, but continually refused his overtures. He had the grains of heroin carefully concealed in his room, but he had no idea how he was to administer it to her.

Dimitris regarded Sorrell covertly. Since her experiences she had entertained other acquaintances on board without demur, allowing Dimitris to select the dress she was to wear and instruct her on her behaviour before they arrived. Only once had he forbidden her to make any overtures to their guest, the harbour master in Cyprus, threatening to withdraw her supply of chocolates if she disobeyed him. Sulkily she looked at him.

'I can buy my own chocolates,' she muttered.

'Of course you can, my dear. I don't think you would find them quite as satisfying as those I give you.'

Sorrell glowered at him and retired to her cabin. She felt completely out of sorts, but could not put a name to her feelings.

She knew her behaviour with the friends that Dimitris brought on board was completely out of character for her. She had been very careful whom she fraternised with in the past. Her longest relationship had been with Joseph, and in retrospect that had been a matter of convenience for him. She very much suspected that her relationship with Dimitris was the same, but she felt trapped and dependent upon him.

During the evening she was charming to the harbour master, behaving impeccably throughout their meal and whilst they sat around the table drinking and chatting afterwards. By midnight she was wishing the man would leave. Her hands were shaking visibly whenever she raised her glass and a feeling of nausea washed over her at intervals. She closed her eyes, but the feeling of sickness persisted, finally she excused herself and retired to her cabin.

She lay on her bed feeling thoroughly wretched. Maybe if she asked Dimitris for a chocolate she would feel better. He had refused to let her have one since the Cypriot harbour master had arrived and she needed the beneficial effect it always had on her. She dared not return to the saloon whilst the man was still there, as she would be expected to stay. She laid on her bed, her hands clenched and her body twitching spasmodically.

From Cyprus, Dimitris sailed to Rhodes to check with Lakkis that all was in readiness for the season.

'We're ready for the start, but we'll need another consignment as soon as possible if we're to keep pace with demand.'

'And how was it out of season?'

'Quiet. We have some regulars and no doubt their numbers will increase each year. The orders for the flour were low, but as most of the island is closed down it's not surprising.'

Dimitris assimilated the information. 'How are the workers?'

'There have been no changes in the chain. I expect there will be some new 'boys' but that never presents any problem.'

'We need more beach cover,' said Dimitris. 'It's the best place to pass it and if people are picked up there's far less chance of tracing it back to source.'

'I'll spread the word,' promised Lakkis.

'Is Joseph behaving himself?'

Lakkis nodded. 'He seems to be. He visited Christos once.'

Dimitris frowned. 'How did he know where to find him?'

'I think it was chance. He was just out on his bike and happened to take the turn down to the bay. He recognised Christos's van and reckoned he lived there.'

'What does Christos say about it?'

'He said he was surprised, they had a beer and Joseph left.'

'That was all?'

Lakkis nodded. 'Christos swore he didn't enter the kitchen.'

'I hope he's telling the truth. The less that young man knows about anything the better. By the way, is he happy with Nadia?'

Lakkis grinned. 'He wasn't very happy when Alecos told him that half his percentage would go in rent.'

Dimitris laughed. 'Who did he think paid the rent? Father Christmas?'

'Alecos is still agitating to have her back.'

'He'll have her in a few weeks. When I return to Rhodes you and Maria must come to dinner. You will be surprised in the change to your hostess.'

Lakkis raised his eyebrows. 'What have you done to her?'

'Merely introduced her to a little something. She is quite uninhibited. You would never have believed Port Said.' Dimitris leaned forward and began to describe in detail the nights of debauchery he had organised and witnessed.

Lakkis laughed with him. 'Do I have to bring Maria?'

Dimitris shook his head. 'It could be a wise precaution! When the time is right I'll send her ashore to you. What you do before you hand her over to Joseph is entirely up to you.'

'What's your timetable?'

155

Dimitris shrugged. 'Much the same as usual. Nikos is coming to dinner tonight and I'll sail for Kos tomorrow and check there, after that I'll go to Samos. Provided all is in order Anders will visit Bodrum and we'll commence distribution. I shall use Kos as my base. It's a useful halfway point between the islands.'

Lakkis frowned. 'Will you be coming to Thalia's wedding?'

'Am I invited?'

'Of course. The date is set for October twentieth.'

Dimitris entered the date in his diary. 'I'll not miss it. Is she still meeting Joseph?'

'Occasionally, and always in a public place. She's always back at work on time,' Lakkis shrugged. 'I've turned a blind eye there. He knows she's not available.'

'I must give her a wedding present. Is there anything they want or would it be more acceptable if I gave them some money?'

Lakkis spread his hands. 'They will be grateful for anything you wish to give them.'

Dimitris nodded. He would give them an envelope. It would save him having to think of a suitable present.

Sorrell was disappointed. She had hoped Dimitris would have taken her to meet Joseph when they arrived back in Rhodes, but he had forbidden her to go ashore. He had patted her hand and spoken much as one would to a small, truculent child.

'You mustn't fret, my dear. Nikos is coming to dinner with us tonight. He will not have Thalia with him, so it will be up to you to entertain him, but discreetly, no overtures. We shall then sail for Kos tomorrow and you will be able to go ashore there.'

A spark of interest showed in her dull eyes. 'I would enjoy that, Dimitris. What do you wish me to wear tonight?'

'Your navy blue silk. He is, after all, a respectable widower.'

'What have you unearthed so far?' asked Yiorgo.

'Nothing. The fact that I can't find anything about his origins worries me. Where did he get the money to build his first hotel?'

'The lottery maybe?'

'Maybe, but I can't find out anything about him at all. He just suddenly appeared on the scene.'

'Where from?'

'I don't know.' Takkis lit a cigarette. 'His passport shows his name as Dimitris Stephanotis, born on Karpathos. I checked with records there and that is correct. According to Karpathos the family left for Santorini when he was fifteen, but he never arrived.'

'What do you mean? Never arrived?'

'Their records show a couple arriving from Karpathos; they set up a small general store and have lived there ever since. I made a few discreet enquiries. There has never been any mention of a son, there's no photograph, nothing. It's as though he didn't exist.'

Yiorgo frowned. 'Maybe he was sent somewhere for his education?'

'That's quite possible, but why isn't there a photograph of him? Every family has photographs of its children.'

'Maybe something happened to him, maybe he died.'

Takkis shook his head. 'If he were dead they would have his photograph everywhere, besides, how does that account for him turning up again as a hotel owner?'

'There must be two men named Dimitris Stephanotis, pure coincidence that they were both born on Karpathos. Records found the first one and they didn't bother to look any further.'

'I thought of that,' Takkis spoke smugly. 'I got back to them and asked them to look for another man of the same name. Nothing.'

Yiorgo pulled his worry beads from his pocket. 'Something is not adding up here. How can anyone disappear for years and turn up again as a wealthy hotelier? If he'd made such a success of his life he would be the talk of the village. His parents would never stop boasting about him.'

'Unless he went to Leros.'

'Leros! How do you work that one out? If you get sent to Leros that's where you stay.'

Takkis shook his head. 'It's the only thing I can think of that could explain his disappearance and his parents disowning him. For some reason it was decided that he would go to Leros. Rather than face the shame they decided to uproot and move to Santorini to start a new life.'

Yiorgo looked at the map of the Greek islands. 'It's possible, I suppose. Those islands are in the same general area. Have you approached Leros?'

Takkis shook his head. 'I wanted to see what you thought first?'

'I think we'll both be sent to Leros if the authorities hear we've been making enquiries about Dimitris Stephanotis on that island!'

'So do you want me to forget it?'

'No,' Yiorgo smiled. 'You've got me curious now. I doubt if you'll turn up anything over there, but we will be able to say that we tried every avenue.'

'Maybe we could approach Karpathos first. See if any of the villagers there remember the family; maybe the boy was simple, in which case they'd remember him.'

Yiorgo nodded. 'They would, but that doesn't quite fit in with the idea of a hotel magnate.'

Nikos was charmed anew by Sorrell, she was attentive to his conversation and laughed at his little jokes, but Dimitris noticed both her eyes and Nikos's continually strayed towards the box of chocolates that were sitting on the side. He would allow her to have one when Nikos had left.

There was a loud bang and the boat rocked alarmingly, spilling the contents of Sorrell's coffee cup down the front of her dress.

Both she and Dimitris jumped up in alarm. Dimitris rushed to find Anders and the cause of the disruption and Sorrell excused herself and went to change her dress.

Nikos stayed where he was, his eyes on the box of chocolates. He loved chocolates. Dimitris would not begrudge him a few. He opened the box and selected six from the bottom layer, wrapped them in a serviette and placed them in his jacket pocket. He would enjoy those before he went to bed tonight.

Dimitris returned to the cabin, thoroughly disgruntled. 'Some idiot went straight into us when he was mooring. Anders doesn't think there's any damage apart from scraped paintwork. I'll check it out in the morning before we sail.'

'Let me know the details and the cost of repairs. I'll not let him leave until he's paid you,' promised Nikos. 'If I'm not there just leave a note on the desk or give it to Vassilis.' He looked at his watch. 'It's late for anyone coming in, and I should be going. Thalia will wonder what has kept me.'

'Lakkis tells me the marriage date has been set.'

Nikos smiled happily. 'It will be a big day. Will you be there?'

'I have the date in my diary.'

Nikos shrugged himself into his jacket, touching his pocket to ensure the chocolates were still there. He was going to enjoy those so much.

When he arrived home Thalia had retired to bed. He smiled fondly as he looked at her sleeping form. He was going to miss her. She had been such a comfort to him since her mother died. He took the chocolates out of his pocket. He would leave her one for the morning. That way he would not feel quite so guilty about indulging himself.

Dimitris sailed into the harbour on Kos at mid-day and was immediately greeted by a sombre-faced harbour master.

'There is an urgent message for you from Lakkis on Rhodes. You're to telephone him immediately?'

Dimitris frowned. 'What's wrong? I only saw him yesterday. He didn't mention any problems to me.'

Manolis shrugged. 'He didn't say, but I think he feels he should give you the sad news himself.'

'What news?'

'Nikos died last night.'

'Nikos? Nikos! You mean Nikos the harbour master of Rhodes?'

Manolis nodded. 'I expect that is what Lakkis wishes to tell you. He will give you the details.'

'May I use your telephone?' asked Dimitris.

'Certainly. Take as long as you like. I'll be outside when you've finished.'

Dimitris telephoned Lakkis at his home, only to be told that he had been out since the news of Nikos's death had been brought to him. Annoyed that Lakkis was not readily available Dimitris telephoned *The Grapevine* and Alecos answered immediately.

'He's not here. I think he's with Thalia. Leave me your number and I'll find him and get him to 'phone you back.'

Dimitris sat at Manolis's desk for almost an hour until Lakkis telephoned him.

'I'm sorry, Dimitris. It took Alecos a while to find me.'

'Tell me the details,' ordered Dimitris.

'There doesn't seem anything to tell. Thalia found him dead in his bed this morning. There has to be an autopsy, but the doctor is almost sure he had a heart attack.'

'So why are they going to carry out an autopsy?'

'He has no history of heart problems. Thalia said he had not complained of feeling ill at any time to her.'

'How is the girl?'

'Very shocked, of course. I have taken her to be with Maria.'

'Naturally. Should I come back?'

'Why? There is nothing you can do.'

'The funeral?'

'It will not be for at least a week, because of the autopsy.'

'Let me know when the date is set. I should like to attend.'
Dimitris shook his head. 'We had dinner last night and he seemed
quite well when he left.'

Yiorgo swung his worry beads between his fingers. 'Well that's
a twist I didn't expect. Have you finished reading the report?'

Takkis lifted his eyes from the last page. 'He died from an
overdose of heroin. Do you think he was a user?'

Yiorgo shrugged. 'Maybe.' He shut his eyes and leaned back
in his chair. 'Maybe all the time we've been looking at the activity
of small boats in the area he's been letting it in through the harbour.
Signing for it as part of a legitimate consignment and creaming
off a supply for himself as payment for turning a blind eye.'

'It's possible,' agreed Takkis.

'He also had dinner with Dimitris Stephanotis on his boat the
night he died.'

'So he could, in fact, have been the courier we were looking
for all along. He receives a consignment, openly goes to dinner
on the boat and collects the goods. The boat sails off, with the
blessing of the harbour master, to make a delivery to the next
island. Where is this boat now? Still at Rhodes?'

Yiorgo shook his head. 'It sailed the next morning for Kos.'

'Knowing that the man was dead?'

Yiorgo shrugged. 'Who knows? Departure details had been
filed the previous day.' Yiorgo pushed his beads back into his
pocket. 'I've instructed them to keep the report confidential and
not release the body for burial. I think the time has come for us to
go over to Rhodes and take a closer look. We might even manage
to find out how this Dimitris Stephanotis did his disappearing trick
when he was fifteen.'

Joseph heard the news dispassionately. He had never met the

man, but he did know he was Thalia's father. Maybe if he presented himself as a sympathetic friend she would begin to regard him in a more favourable light. He smiled. That was the answer. He would meet her for coffee and offer her comfort and support, then suggest that he took her for dinner one night so that she did not have to sit at home and brood. It should be quite simple then to persuade her to return to his house for him to administer some additional comfort.

1991

May – June

Yiorgo and Takkis booked into a small hotel on Rhodes close to both the harbour and the police station.

'So how do we approach this?' asked Takkis.

Yiorgo scratched his ear. 'Cautiously, I think. We don't want to put them on their guard. Let them think we are just investigating the harbour master's death. Appear to be concentrating just on him, the usual rubbish, enemies, revenge killing, that sort of thing. No mention of drugs. We can make it an excuse to look more closely at his associates, particularly Mr Stephanotis.'

'Is he still on Kos?' asked Takkis.

'I don't know. Once we've had a look at the autopsy report we can use that as an excuse to visit him, see what he says they ate that night and see whether that equates with the stomach contents.'

'So first call the police station?'

Yiorgo nodded. 'Introduce ourselves and see what they can tell us, officially and unofficially about the man. We can impound the harbour reports at the same time on the excuse that we're looking for illegal workers over here.'

'You don't think it might be better to tell them what we're looking for?' suggested Takkis. 'They might have some information that would help.'

'Not at this stage. We don't want anyone tipped off. No, we're just over here to investigate the death of Nikos Pavlides and taking advantage of being on the spot to look at the other reports.'

Takkis shrugged. Yiorgo was in charge of the investigation as his superior officer, but he disagreed with his tactics. It could save them a lot of time and trouble if they enlisted the help of the local police force.

'So,' Yiorgo addressed the chief of police, 'tell me all you know about Nikos Pavlides.'

Lambros spread his hands. 'It is in the report.'

Yiorgo shook his head. 'The report gives me the facts. What was he like as a person?'

'Pleasant. I always had a good relationship with him.'

'Go on.'

'What more do you want?'

'Everything. What about his family? How did he spend his leisure time? Who were his friends? Any financial worries?'

Lambros frowned. 'We were never close friends. Our paths didn't cross outside work. He has – had – a daughter. His wife died some years ago.'

'Where is this daughter now?'

'Staying with her uncle and his wife. She's devastated. She was close to her father.'

Yiorgo nodded. 'Can you give me their address? I'll need to speak to her. In view of this report,' Yiorgo tapped the folder before him, 'did you ever notice anything that would have made you think Nikos was using drugs?'

Lambros shook his head. 'Not whenever I met up with him. He always seemed – normal.'

'You say his wife died some years ago. How did she die?'

'Cancer, I believe.'

'Did you know him then?'

'I knew who he was if I saw him out, and on a couple of occasions I had to go to the port. I saw him more often after I gained my promotion. He'd bring his reports up to the office once a month. Sometimes we'd have a drink together, but he never stayed long.'

'When you had this drink together what did you talk about?'

Lambros shrugged. 'Nothing particular that I can recall. The last time he came he told me the date had been set for his daughter's wedding.'

Yiorgo nodded. 'Who is she marrying?'

'Her cousin, I don't know his name.'

'Did Nikos say it was going to be a big wedding?'

'Not that I remember.' Lambros frowned. 'He didn't stop very long, said he had to get home to change as he was going out to dinner.'

'When was this?'

'The night he died. Said he was going to dinner on the '*Aegean Pride*', but you know that, it's in the report.'

Yiorgo placed his fingertips together and sat back in his chair. 'Why didn't you tell us before that you had seen him that night?'

'I didn't think it was relevant.'

'Everything is relevant. How did he appear to you?'

'The same as he always did.'

'Did he appear to be nervous about going out to dinner?'

'No. Why should he?'

Yiorgo did not answer the question. 'Did he have anything with him? A present for his host, maybe?'

'No.' Lambros shook his head, bewildered. 'He just brought the reports.'

Yiorgo smiled. 'If you do remember anything that you think might be useful you know where to find us. If you would just write down the address where we can find his daughter, then we'll be off.'

Takkis waited until they were walking along Mandraki harbour before he spoke. 'Where now?'

'Lakkis Pavlides next. See what he has to say about his brother. If the girl is there we could speak to her about her father. We'll take a taxi.' Yiorgo headed off across the road.

The two policemen looked at the well-kept house. The garden was grassed over, a small border containing hibiscus plants by the wall and the traditional black and white design on the path leading to the front door. The house had recently been painted a cream colour with the shutters picked out in green.

The door was opened at their ring by a young girl, her face pale and dark rings beneath her eyes. 'Yes?'

'Miss Pavlides?'

She nodded.

'I'm so sorry to trouble you, but we would like to speak to Mr Lakkis Pavlides.'

Thalia frowned. 'He's not here at the moment.'

'You are Miss Thalia Pavlides? Maybe we could come inside and talk to you?'

'Who are you?'

'We've one or two questions we'd like to ask about your father.' Yiorgo produced his police identity for her.

Thalia's face paled even more and she stepped aside. 'You'd better come in. My aunt is here.'

She led the way through to a pleasant sitting room and offered them a seat on the cream settee. 'Would you like some refreshment? A coffee, perhaps?' She remembered her manners, despite her evident distress.

Yiorgo smiled at her. 'That would be very welcome.'

During her absence Yiorgo looked around the room. It was expensively furnished, but not ostentatious. He guessed that the silver he saw was real and the crystal glass sparkled. There were photographs of family members on the sideboard and walls, one of them showing a young man and the girl who had just left the room. Yiorgo picked it up and studied it.

'Presumably the fiancée.' He replaced it as Thalia returned, Maria in her wake.

'This is my aunt,' she said as she placed cups of coffee and water before each man.

Yiorgo and Takkis rose and introduced themselves.

'I'm so sorry to have to intrude upon you at this time.' Yiorgo spoke sincerely. 'Please accept our condolences; unfortunately we have to make some enquiries.'

'What kind of enquiries?'

'We are trying to find out the reason behind your father's heart attack. As far as we know he had no previous history of heart trouble. It is possible that something caused it. You were at home the night your father died?'

Thalia nodded.

'He went out to dinner, I understand. How did he seem when he returned?'

'I don't know.' Thalia's eyes filled with tears. 'I had gone to bed and was asleep when he came back.'

'Did you see him before he left for his dinner engagement?'

'Yes.'

'How did he seem to you then?'

Thalia shrugged. 'Just as he usually seemed. Pleased to be home after a day's work, looking forward to going out to dinner.'

'You didn't notice anything out of the ordinary? He didn't complain of feeling ill at all?'

'No. He came home and showered and changed as usual. He told me not to wait up as he didn't know what time he would return.'

'Did he often go out to dinner with friends?'

'What do you call often? We usually spent Sunday over here and stayed to dinner.'

'I understand your father was dining on board one of the boats that night.'

'With Mr Dimitris.'

'Did he regularly dine with him?'

'When Mr Dimitris was in port he used to be invited occasionally.'

'What do you call occasionally? Once a week?'

'Oh, no.' Thalia shook her head. 'Mr Dimitris usually only stayed a few days.'

'Why was that?'

'I think he probably just called in to see that everything was in order at his hotel.'

'And where is his hotel?'

'At Faliraki.'

'Did you ever accompany your father when he went to dinner with Mr Dimitris?'

'Once.'

'Only once?'

Thalia nodded. 'Mr Dimitris had a friend with him. I think he thought I would be company for her whilst he and Pappa talked.'

'And what did your father and Mr Dimitris talk about?'

Thalia shrugged. 'Nothing in particular. What do people talk about at dinner parties?'

'Did your father take a gift on board for Mr Dimitris?'

'No. Why should he?'

'Visitors will often take a bottle of wine, flowers for the hostess, that kind of thing.'

A ghost of a smile played on Thalia's lips. 'It would be insulting to take Mr Dimitris a bottle of wine, besides, Pappa could not afford the kind of wine he drinks.'

'Why do you say that?'

'Mr Dimitris is a very wealthy man.'

'And your father was not?'

Thalia shook her head. 'Certainly not wealthy.'

'Was he worried about money?'

'He never said so.'

'I believe you are to be married shortly. Would your father have had a problem finding the money for such an occasion?'

'He had been saving since I was a child. It was not going to be a very lavish affair. Just family and a few friends.'

'Going back to the evening that your father spent with Mr Dimitris, was anyone else going to be present?'

'I have no idea. You would have to ask Mr Dimitris.'

Yiorgo nodded. 'You have been so helpful. There is just one more thing I need to ask. May I visit your house?'

'Visit my house?' Thalia looked puzzled. 'Why?'

'I would like to see if your father had any medication that he was taking for his heart. Maybe he had kept his condition concealed from you.'

'I'm sure he wasn't, but you can look.'

'Would it be convenient if we went there now? Maybe Mr Pavlides will have returned by the time we have finished.'

'If it's really necessary.'

Yiorgo nodded. 'I understand you are staying here with your relatives. Do you wish to accompany us or would it be too painful for you at this moment?'

Thalia looked at her aunt, who had sat silently throughout. 'I'll come with you. I'll telephone my uncle and tell him you want to see him.'

'Where is your uncle?'

'At work. He is the manager of the Faliraki hotel for Mr Dimitris.'

Maria spoke for the first time. 'I could telephone my husband and ask him to return.'

'Thank you. How long would the journey take him?'

'Half an hour, probably, maybe a little longer, depending upon the traffic.'

Yiorgo nodded. 'Then we would be able to visit your house and by the time we returned your uncle should be here. I will ask Takkis to find a taxi.'

'It will be quicker to walk. By the time you have found a taxi we would be half way there.'

Thalia led the way up the hill and for a while they followed the road beside the medieval walls of the town before she branched into a side road, finally stopping before a low building. She inserted her key in the lock and bent to collect the mail before admitting them. Yiorgo noticed her hands were shaking and he led her to a chair.

169

'Please believe me when I say how distressed I am to have to ask you these questions at such a time. Can you just tell me where your father's bedroom is?'

Thalia spoke dully without looking up. 'The first door on the left is the kitchen, the second is the bathroom. Opposite the kitchen is my father's room. The other room is mine.'

Takkis sat down beside the distressed girl. 'It must have been terrible for you when you found your father.'

'I thought he'd overslept.'

'Did you usually see him in the mornings?'

Thalia nodded. 'He usually left about ten minutes before me. I used to ask him if there was any shopping he wanted.'

'What kind of shopping? For your evening meal?'

'No. I always bought that. I would ask if he wanted shaving cream or toothpaste. Something he had forgotten to put on my weekend shopping list.'

'Tell me, I'm sorry to have to go back to this, but when you thought he'd overslept and went in to wake him did you notice anything unusual at all?'

'What kind of thing?'

'Anything that would indicate that he had been feeling unwell when he returned home. Had he put his clothes away, set his alarm clock, the usual things one does before finally putting out the light.'

'The light was on.'

'Was that usual? Some people prefer to sleep with the light on.'

Thalia dropped her head into her hands. 'He had hung up his suit and his underclothes were on the chair. I think he had sat in bed reading and eating some chocolates.'

'Some chocolates?'

'I expect Mr Dimitris gave them to him.'

'Why would Mr Dimitris give your father chocolates?'

'Pappa loved chocolates.' Thalia's voice broke. 'He had left one on the side. I think he meant to give it to me in the morning.'

Takkis patted her on the shoulder. 'It's always the little things that hurt so much,' he said as he pushed his handkerchief into her hand. 'I'll see if my colleague is nearly finished.'

Yiorgo was just leaving the bathroom as Takkis entered the hall and nodded towards the door of Nikos's bedroom. On the bedside table sat a chocolate on a napkin.

'Take the chocolate and the napkin,' said Takkis quietly. 'Are you nearly finished, Yiorgo?' he asked in normal tone.

'Give me five minutes,' replied Yiorgo as he carefully placed the napkin containing the chocolate inside his handkerchief. He opened the drawers and cupboards, giving a cursory glance to their contents, and returned to the living room.

'Did you find any medication?' asked Thalia.

'Only some headache tablets,' replied Yiorgo honestly.

Lakkis was waiting for them when they arrived back at his house. 'How dare you come here and browbeat my niece and search my brother's house.'

Yiorgo raised his eyebrows. 'I can assure you, Mr Pavlides, that we did not browbeat your niece, as you put it. Your wife was present the whole time and I am sure she would not consider that we badgered Miss Pavlides.'

'So why did you search my brother's house?'

'They didn't search it, uncle. They were looking for medicine.'

'Medicine?'

'As I explained, Mr Pavlides was not known to have a heart condition. It is possible that he knew he was a sick man, but had told no one. In that case we would have expected to find an appropriate medication, probably in his bedroom.'

'And did you find anything?'

'No. May I ask you some questions now, Mr Pavlides?'

Lakkis nodded, his green eyes wary.

'When did you last see your brother?'

'Last Sunday, when he and Thalia came over for the day.'

'And he seemed quite well to you?'

'Yes, perfectly well.'

'He did not complain of indigestion, heart-burn, chest pains? Nothing?'

Lakkis shook his head.

'Do you know if anything was worrying him?'

Again Lakkis shook his head. 'Where's all this leading?'

Yiorgo spread his hands. 'I wish I could tell you. We are simply trying to find the reason why a normally healthy man should suffer a heart attack. I understand he went to dinner with a Mr Dimitris on board his boat that night. Could anything have happened on board to upset him enough to give him a heart attack?'

'How would I know? I wasn't there. Dimitris was only staying in port the one night and said he would invite Maria and myself to dinner when he returned.'

'Why did he come to Rhodes?'

'As you know, he has a hotel on the island. I am his manager. He came to check that all was in order for the start of the season.'

'Is that normal?'

'Quite normal.' Lakkis spoke firmly. 'He usually bases himself on Kos. He has a hotel there and another on Samos. He was returning from Egypt, again as usual after the winter, and called on me. He planned to leave for Kos the next morning and then travel on to Samos.'

'And has he done so?'

'No. I telephoned the hotel on Kos and left a message asking him to contact me. I had to break the news of my brother's death to him. He said he would stay on Kos and then return for the funeral.'

'Why did he not return here immediately?'

'For what reason?'

Yiorgo shrugged. 'As far as we can ascertain he was the last person to see Mr Pavlides alive. We will need to speak to him, ask if he noticed anything untoward about his behaviour.'

'You will be able to do that when he comes for the funeral.'

'Exactly.' Yiorgo nodded. 'Thank you very much for giving up your time to speak to us. I am sorry we had to intrude upon your privacy. If you do happen to think of anything please leave a message for me with Lambros at the police station. It will be no trouble to call on you again.'

Lakkis watched the two men as they walked down the path from his house. He had been distressed when he had heard his brother had died, but he could not fathom out the reason for police involvement. He would have to telephone Dimitris again.

Yiorgo and Takkis strolled back down the road and walked over to a seat, conveniently placed to give a view of the medieval town walls.

'I'd like to have a look at that town,' admitted Yiorgo. 'I've heard there's nowhere else quite like it in the world.'

'We could ask Lambros if there's anywhere decent to eat in there. I presume it's open in the evening?'

'I think so, but we can check with him. Now, tell me, why did you want me to take that chocolate?'

'I was talking to the girl whilst you were doing your snooping. She thinks, only thinks, mind you, that Dimitris may have given her father some chocolates to bring home. She also thinks he may have sat in bed eating them and left one on the side ready to give to her the following day. According to the autopsy the contents of the stomach contained chocolate.'

'It would have done if he had eaten them in bed!'

Takkis nodded. 'He died in bed – yes? The last thing he ate, we think, was some chocolate. Could the chocolates be laced with heroin, hence the overdose that killed him?'

Yiorgo sat and considered the theory. 'I suppose so. It sounds logical, although I don't know why the chocolates should be contaminated, or by what we've heard so far, anyone would want to do away with him.'

'I thought it could be worth while having that chocolate analysed.'

'I agree. It's a good job you got that information out of the girl. I wouldn't have taken any notice of a stray chocolate.'

'I just asked her if she'd noticed anything unusual about her father's room when she found him. She said the light was still on in the morning, and then said she thought he had been sitting in bed eating chocolates.'

'Was he in the habit of doing that?'

Takkis frowned. 'I didn't ask her that. She thought Dimitris had given them to him.'

'Why should Dimitris give him a box of chocolates to bring home?'

Takkis shrugged. 'How should I know? Was there any sign of a box in the rubbish? Maybe he just gave him some to bring home for the girl.'

Yiorgo stretched his legs out in front of him and then stood up. 'If this theory of yours about the chocolate is to be put to the test we'd better get back quickly to the station before it melts in my pocket.'

Lakkis telephoned the '*Aegean Jewel*' and Dimitris returned the call.

'Is there a problem?' he asked.

'I'm not sure. Nikos's body will be released for burial tomorrow, but I had a visit from the police. They made Thalia take them to the house. They said they were looking for medication.'

'What kind of medication?'

'They are trying to find out why a healthy man had a heart attack. Thought maybe he had the condition and was keeping quiet about it.'

'Did they find anything?'

'No. Now they're wondering if something upset him enough to cause it. They want to talk to you when you return to Rhodes as you seem to be the last person to see him alive.'

Dimitris shrugged. 'That's no problem. I'll talk to them. Nikos was fine when he left me. I'll sail tonight, do some fishing, and arrive tomorrow.'

Dimitris replaced the receiver thoughtfully. He was as puzzled as everyone else why Nikos should have suffered a heart attack.

Yiorgo and Takkis returned to the police station and Yiorgo withdrew a sticky handkerchief from his pocket.

'Have you got a fridge we can put this in? I want to have it analysed.'

Lambros raised his eyebrows in surprise. 'What is it?'

'A chocolate.'

'It's too late now to send it off.' Lambros produced a box and the disintegrating sweet was placed inside. 'Where did you get it?'

'Nikos's house. It's just a hunch we have.'

Lambros was too professional to question them further and set the box on a shelf in the fridge, placing a note on top declaring it was evidence and not to be touched.

'Is it safe there?' asked Takkis.

'Perfectly,' Lambros assured him. 'We only use the fridge for our beer. What are your plans now, gentlemen?'

'Tomorrow we'll start having a look at the port records. We may as well do that whilst we're waiting for Dimitris Stephanotis to return to Rhodes. Mr Pavlides said he plans to attend the funeral. We thought we'd like to have a look at this medieval town you have. Is it open in the evening?'

'Of course,' Lambros smiled at their ignorance. 'It is a town. People live there.'

Yiorgo nodded and brushed the information aside. 'Then we will see you tomorrow. I trust you will remember to send the chocolate for analysis first thing in the morning.'

'It will be at the laboratory by eight thirty.' Lambros turned reproachful eyes on them. 'Enjoy your evening.'

Yiorgo and Takkis crossed from the police station to the entrance of the old town and began to walk through the arches towards the main streets. Yiorgo let out his breath.

'I never imagined it would be like this. It really is a town.'

'What were you expecting?' asked Takkis.

'I'm not sure. Something ruined, I suppose, like Mycenae or Delphi perhaps.'

The men wandered back and forth between the streets, removing their ties and carrying their jackets over their arms. 'I could do with a beer,' announced Takkis. 'It's twice as hot here.'

Yiorgo agreed with him. 'The next place we see.'

They had detoured from the main tourist streets and there seemed to be only small general stores and houses. They twisted and turned, finally Yiorgo grinned at Takkis.

'Do we admit we're lost and ask for directions?'

'No way,' replied Takkis. 'We have to end up somewhere soon, even if it's only the perimeter wall.' He stood and tried to get his bearings. 'I think if we go that way we'll end up on the waterfront eventually.'

They continued to slip and slide over the cobbles, taking turns that appeared to lead down towards the harbour, they passed a church and peered through an archway into a paved courtyard. Beneath shady trees they could see tables and chairs set out. Both men turned simultaneously into the square. To their disappointment there was no one in attendance at the tables, but a chalk notice advertised that the taverna would be open during the evening for meals. Resigned to having to find an exit from the town they across the square and as they reached the corner they realised there was a small taverna, a young man in attendance.

'Are you open?' called Takkis.

Alecos nodded.

'Two beers, please.'

Both men sank gratefully into the chairs and Yiorgo searched for his handkerchief to mop his brow, then remembered it was in the fridge at the police station, and used the sleeve of his shirt instead.

'This is very pleasant,' he remarked, as he looked around. 'I could happily sit here for an afternoon.'

Joseph entered the square on his way to *The Grapevine* and saw the two men. A tingle of apprehension went down his spine. He was certain they were police and if so he wanted nothing to do with them. He sauntered past the entrance to the taverna, raised his hand to Alecos, and continued on his way. Alecos shook his fist at Joseph's back.

Yiorgo and Takkis spent the morning studying the harbour reports, every craft, large or small, commercial or private that entered and left the harbour had been logged under their appropriate headings. The patrol ship for the waters was logged separately and Yiorgo began to turn the pages.

The ship would depart on a Monday, sail to the perimeter of the Greek waters and swing back from Turkey on the Tuesday morning, continuing down the east coast until it reached Prassonissi. Tuesday night it would sail up the west coast of the island and return to the port, ready to repeat the procedure on the Wednesday. The route never varied and at no time had the patrol reported any incidents in the last month.

Yiorgo took out his worry beads and began to play with them. One boat to patrol that extent of water was impractical and as the route and times were never varied it would be a simple matter for anyone to avoid being seen. He stood up and studied the large map pinned to the wall of the police station.

'Lambros,' he called. 'Can you help me out here?'

Lambros rose from his desk and came and stood before the map with Yiorgo. 'What's your problem?'

'Tell me about the island. Where are the best beaches?'

'On the east side. Beautiful sandy beaches, wonderful swimming. It's where most of the tourists head for.'

'And on the west?'

'Not so commercial. Rocky bays, not a lot of good for swimming or boating, but the scenery is magnificent in parts. If you drive from Kamiros to Kritina the view of the islands is spectacular.'

'What's on those islands?'

'Nothing. There's a small town on Alimia, but the others are just rocks.'

Yiorgo nodded thoughtfully. 'So if I had a motor boat how long would it take me from Mandraki harbour to get to Alimia?'

Lambros shrugged. 'I don't know. Someone down at the harbour could probably tell you. Why?'

'I just wondered if I would have the time to make the trip,' smiled Yiorgo.

Lambros gave him a sceptical look and returned to his desk. Yiorgo followed him and perched on the corner.

'Tell me, Lambros, what do you know about Lakkis Pavlides?'

Lambros shook his head. 'Nothing much. He's the manager of the *'Aegean Gem'* at Faliraki and has a taverna in the old town.'

'Has he? How does he manage to run both of them?'

'He's got a youngster running *The Grapevine*. He probably kept it as an investment for his old age. When he can't run the hotel any more he'll potter around at the taverna, or maybe he plans to give it to his son.'

'That's the young man who's marrying Nikos's daughter, I understand.'

Lambros raised his eyebrows, then shook his head. 'They're first cousins.'

'That doesn't mean they can't marry each other.'

'It's not good. They're too closely related. The children …' He spread his hands expressively.

'That's their problem, nothing to do with us. Whereabouts in the old town is this taverna? I'd like to take a look at it out of curiosity.'

Lambros took a map showing the old town and ringed a small area. 'It's not hard to find.'

'Thanks. We might take a walk up there tonight.'

Lambros nodded, not really interested, and answered his telephone that had started to ring. 'I'll tell him,' he said into the mouthpiece. He turned back to Yiorgo. 'Dimitris Stephanotis has just docked.'

Yiorgo picked up his jacket. 'Then we'll stroll along and see him now. Maybe you'll have the results of the chocolate analysis by the time we return,' he suggested.

Lambros nodded. He would telephone the laboratory and remind them that he had told them to give it priority.

Dimitris greeted Yiorgo and Takkis amicably, offering them ouzo, beer or coffee.

'We ought to stick to coffee,' smiled Takkis. 'We're supposed to be on duty, although it feels more as if we were on holiday over here.'

'Rhodes is a beautiful island on which to spend a holiday,' observed Dimitris.

'Quite so, but I understand you spend most of your time on Kos.'

Dimitris smiled. 'Naturally. I have hotels on Samos, Kos and Rhodes. Kos lies between the two other islands so it is practical for me to be based between them.'

'How many hotels do you have?'

'Four. I have one on Ikaria also that I am in the process of selling.'

'Why is that?'

'It is old and needs a considerable amount of money spent on it to bring it up to standard. Ikaria is one of the less popular islands. I would do better to invest in another property on Kos or Rhodes.'

'You sail frequently between the islands, I believe,' said Yiorgo.

'As the need arises. I had planned to visit Samos, then I heard of poor Nikos's death and I decided it would be more practical to

179

stay at Kos until I knew when his funeral would take place. It takes only a morning to sail from there, whereas from Samos it takes a whole day.'

'I understand that Nikos Pavlides spent the evening prior to his death with you.'

Dimitris nodded sadly. 'It was most unfortunate. He appeared perfectly well when he left here.'

'Nothing happened to disturb him? I don't mean to sound rude Mr Stephanotis, but did you upset him in any way?'

Dimitris shook his head. 'No, not at all. We had a very pleasant evening. It was only marred when a stupid Englishman who obviously did not know how to steer a boat ran into me.'

Yiorgo raised his eyebrows. 'It probably has no relevance, but I'd be grateful if you would tell us about it.'

'We were just having coffee. There was a bang and the boat lurched. I went to find Anders, my captain, and my companion went to change her dress as her coffee had spilled down it. Nikos said I was to let him know when I had inspected the damage in daylight and he would not let the man leave Mandraki without paying for repairs. Luckily there was no real damage, just a scrape of paint.'

'Who was your companion who had to change her dress?'

'A young lady who has been travelling with me.'

'She is on board now?' asked Takkis.

'I believe so. She is probably talking to Frida, my cook, and discussing what to wear when they go ashore.'

'Would it be possible to have a quick word with her? Maybe she noticed something untoward about Mr Pavlides,' suggested Yiorgo.

Dimitris frowned. 'I doubt if she would know him well enough. She has only met him a few times.'

'It could still be helpful,' persisted Yiorgo.

'Very well. I will call her.'

'You say you have a cook on board, Frida? Is that right?'

Dimitris nodded.

'Did she prepare the meal you shared with Mr Pavlides and your friend?'

'Of course. She is an excellent cook.'

'With your permission I should like to speak to her and ask her exactly what she prepared. There is just a chance that she used something that disagreed with Mr Pavlides.'

'You mean poisoned him?' Dimitris's neck and face began to take on a purplish hue.

Yiorgo shook his head. 'Not poisoned, no, no. Something that Mr Pavlides was allergic to that brought on his heart condition.'

The redness began to disappear from Dimitris's face. 'I have never known Nikos to have an allergy.'

'Sometimes these things go unnoticed for years; then flare up suddenly. He may have eaten something for lunch and then again with you at dinner, his body unable to deal with a double dose of something he had a mild allergy to. Who knows? These things happen.' Yiorgo shrugged and immediately dropped the subject. 'What is the name of the young lady travelling with you?'

Dimitris was taken unawares by the swift change. 'Miss Hirsch, Suzanna Hirsch,' he stuttered.

Takkis made a note. 'If I went and spoke to the cook whilst you spoke to Miss Hirsch we could save delaying Mr Stephanotis further. Where will I find her?'

'I will find both ladies.' Dimitris rose from his seat and opened a door at the side of the steps that led into the saloon from the deck. 'Frida, Suzanna, you are wanted.'

Sorrell entered the saloon fearfully. Were the police here looking for her? She smiled timidly at them and sat down beside Dimitris.

'There's nothing to worry about, my dear. The police want to ask you about poor Nikos and the night he came to dinner.'

Sorrell nodded. 'It was very sad. He seemed to be a nice man.'

Yiorgo smiled at her. What a fantastic looking girl! 'Miss Hirsch, did you notice anything about Mr Pavlides' behaviour that night that might have made you think he was unwell?'

'No, nothing. We had a very enjoyable evening.'

'How many times have you met Mr Pavlides?'

'I'm not sure. Dimitris entertains a good deal. Two, three times, maybe.'

'And you noticed nothing different about his behaviour on this occasion?'

Sorrell shook her head.

'I understand there was an incident towards the end of the evening when a boat had a slight accident whilst mooring?'

Sorrell frowned. 'Was there? I don't remember?'

Yiorgo looked at her curiously. If she was unable to remember the incident with the boat it was unlikely she would know if Nikos Pavlides had acted out of character at any time.

'I understand from Mr Stephanotis that whilst you were drinking coffee a boat that was mooring bumped into you. You had to go and change your dress.'

'Oh, yes, that,' Sorrell replied in a flat voice. 'I'd forgotten that.'

'Did anything else happen that you may have forgotten?' asked Yiorgo gently. 'What was Mr Pavlides reaction to the incident?'

'He said he was sorry my dress was spoiled.'

'That was all?'

'All I can remember. He left shortly afterwards.'

'What did you have to eat that night?'

Sorrell shrugged. 'I've no idea. Frida would be able to tell you. She does all the cooking.'

'Was there anything that Mr Pavlides had requested because he was particularly fond of it?'

Sorrell shrugged again. 'I don't know what he liked.'

'And he ate everything he was given?'

'Ask Frida. She would have cleared the table and washed up. She would know if he had left anything.' Sorrell lifted her eyes to the detective for the first time and he was surprised at the dull, vacuous look.

'I'm sorry to have had to trouble you, Miss Hirsch. Have a good day ashore.'

Takkis had effectively blocked Frida's way into the saloon and asked her to take him to the kitchen.

Frida smiled at his ignorance. 'On a boat it is called a galley.'

'My mistake,' he smiled back at her. 'I shouldn't have to keep you very long.' He looked around the spotless galley with approval. 'Even I might consider cooking here. It's incredible, so much packed into such a small space.' He opened a door and found a dish washer, the next cupboard held a freezer and the third a fridge. Sitting on the shelf was a box of chocolates. He lifted them out and raised the lid. 'These look good. Did you make them?'

Frida shook her head. 'They are the chocolates Mr Dimitris buys for Miss Suzanna.'

Takkis lifted one out. 'He wouldn't mind if I took one, would he? I love chocolates.' He looked behind him. 'I'll pop it into my pocket. It wouldn't look good if he caught me in here with a mouth full of chocolate.' He wrapped it in his handkerchief and slipped it into his pocket, replacing the box in the fridge and closing the door.

Frida smiled, amused at his childish behaviour. 'What did you want to ask me?'

'Can you remember what you served the night Mr Pavlides died?'

'Of course I can. We started with asparagus soup, followed by toast and pate, tiger prawns and avocado, chicken fillet stuffed with mushrooms and wild herbs, salad and chipped potatoes and we finished with strawberry cheesecake.'

Takkis wrote down the list. 'You're making my mouth water. Did everyone eat the same?'

'Yes. I cooked for the five of us.'

'Five?'

'Anders and myself. We always eat the same food as Mr Dimitris, but we eat it down here.'

Takkis nodded understandingly. 'And there was coffee and chocolates to follow, yes?'

'Just coffee. It was then that the boat was bumped. I had just served our meal and Anders ran up on deck to see what had happened. Mr Dimitris followed him.'

'So you didn't hand round any of those delicious chocolates?'

Frida shook her head. 'Miss Suzanna has one after her meals. They are hers.'

'Suppose Mr Pavlides had asked for one? Would she have given it to him?'

'I expect so. Why don't you ask her?'

'I will,' smiled Takkis. 'Thank you. I doubt if I shall have to bother you again.' He turned to leave from the galley. 'I've just thought of a couple of things. Did Mr Pavlides eat everything?'

Frida nodded. 'Mr Pavlides always enjoyed his food.'

'He never said that there was anything he should not eat?'

'Not to me.'

Takkis snapped his notebook closed. 'You've been a great help.'

Takkis and Yiorgo walked along the harbour arm past the windmills. 'Well?' asked Yiorgo.

'We need to go back to the police station. I've got a chocolate in my pocket.'

'What!'

Takkis smiled. 'There happened to be a box in the fridge, so I took one. They look the same as the one I found at Nikos Pavlides' house.'

'What did you think of that girl who's travelling with Dimitris Stephanotis?'

'A good looker. Apart from that I didn't take much notice of her.'

'She's a user. You could see by her eyes.'

'Yes? That could explain a few things. According to the cook the chocolates belong to her and she has one after a meal.'

Yiorgo looked at his colleague. 'Nikos's daughter said he loved chocolates. Suppose he took a couple. Ate one and left the other for his daughter?'

Takkis shook his head. 'It would be unlikely that one would kill him. Probably make him wonder what planet he was on, and he'd feel pretty rough when the effects wore off. Besides, we don't know yet that the chocolates are the source.'

'True,' admitted Yiorgo. 'If they are, the question is why. If the girl's a user why bother to put it inside a chocolate?'

Takkis shrugged. 'I can't answer that. Just a peculiarity on her part, I imagine.'

'The funeral is tomorrow, right?'

Takkis nodded.

'We should get the result from this chocolate by tomorrow. If it's positive I suggest we return to the '*Aegean Pride*' and remove the rest of the box. Put a ban on the boat leaving the harbour until we have the result. If it's positive Mr Stephanotis and Miss Hirsch could have some awkward questions to answer.'

'And what do we do whilst we're waiting?' asked Takkis.

'A visit to *The Grapevine*, I think. I'd like to find out a bit more about Mr Lakkis Pavlides.'

'You think he's involved in some way?'

'Takkis, to tell you the truth, I am completely confused by the whole situation. The harbour master dies from an overdose of heroin; we find some suspect chocolates, and a woman who's a user. We know we have drugs coming into the island; the problem appears to be predominantly at the hotel where the harbour master's brother is the manager. Is it all coincidence or is this a far bigger operation than we ever suspected?'

The report confirmed that the chocolate they had sent for analysis contained heroin, but the quantity was not enough to kill. Lambros had raised his eyebrows when a second chocolate was given to him with a request that it was again analysed as quickly as possible.

'Where did you find this one?'

'In the fridge on Mr Stephanotis's cabin cruiser,' said Takkis, 'but that's just between ourselves.'

'Do you think that's where the other one came from?'

'I think it very likely, but I can't prove it. Even if this one comes back positive we can't prove it came from the same box.'

'Why should anyone want to put heroin inside chocolates anyway? I thought it was either sniffed or injected.'

'The cook said the chocolates were bought by Mr Stephanotis for the girl who's travelling with him. Maybe she doesn't want him to know she's a user and hides her supply in there.'

Yiorgo looked sceptical, then pointed a finger at Takkis. 'It's just possible you have something there. Suppose Mr Stephanotis is doctoring the chocolates?'

'Why would he want to do that?'

'Maybe to get the girl hooked without her knowledge.'

'What would be the point of that?'

Yiorgo shook his head. 'I don't know,' he admitted. 'It doesn't make a lot of sense whichever way you look at it. Shall we see if *The Grapevine* is open? Maybe we could get some lunch there whilst we try to find out a bit more about Mr Lakkis Pavlides.'

'We've got to find the place first!'

With the help of the map Lambros had given them Takkis and Yiorgo wandered through the streets of the old town. Their journey took them a considerable amount of time as they continually stopped and looked into the shops they passed and admired ancient buildings, some in a ruinous state and others that were open for the tourists to enter. To their surprise they finally ended up in the square where they had sat and drank their beer the previous day.

'Well we were pretty stupid,' remarked Yiorgo.

Half hidden by the trailing grapevine was the name of the

taverna and written below was the name of the owner, Mr Lakkis Pavlides. Two young men were sitting at a table playing backgammon, whilst a tourist, his map spread before him, sat drinking his beer with a puzzled frown on his face. Yiorgo and Takkis took a seat and signalled to Alecos that they would like a beer each.

'Do you serve food here?' asked Yiorgo.

Alecos shook his head. 'I can do you a snack, toasted sandwich, if you want.'

Takkis nodded. 'That will do me. Two sandwiches, please.'

Alecos retired behind the counter and the two men waited until he returned. 'My friend and I are visitors here. I wondered if you could recommend anywhere for a good meal.'

Alecos shrugged. 'Plenty of places will be open in the evening.'

'It's a shame this place doesn't do food. This is one of the most pleasant squares I've seen. Maybe you could suggest it to the owner.'

'I doubt if Mr Pavlides would take any notice of any suggestions from me.'

'Why's that? You work here so you would know what the customers want.'

'I just do as Mr Pavlides tells me. He's the boss.'

'I still think you should suggest it to him,' persisted Yiorgo.

'I don't expect to be here much longer.'

'Why's that? Aren't you happy here?'

'Mr Pavlides has promised me another job. I don't want to work in a taverna.'

'What do you want to do?'

'I'd rather work in the warehouse. That's what he said I would be doing originally.'

Yiorgo took a bite of his sandwich and spoke with his mouth full. 'Given the choice I think I'd rather work here. You're out in the air and you meet people.'

'If I worked in the warehouse I'd have the afternoons free.'

'You wouldn't earn as much, though.'

Alecos gave a short laugh. 'I'd earn as much as I do here.' He placed their bill on the table and walked back to the bar.

Yiorgo raised his eyebrows at Takkis. 'Not a happy man,' he observed.

They finished their sandwich and Takkis raised his hand for another beer. When it arrived Yiorgo spoke to Alecos again.

'If you leave here who will run this taverna? The owner?'

Alecos shook his head. 'He's too busy with his hotel.'

Yiorgo raised his eyebrows. 'I'm intrigued by this man. You say he has a hotel, a taverna and a warehouse. What else does he do?'

'How should I know?'

'You work for him.'

Alecos shrugged and Yiorgo tried again.

'Why did he go back on his word about your warehouse job?'

'Mr Dimitris brought in someone else.'

'I thought it was Mr Pavlides's warehouse?'

'He runs it, but it belongs to Mr Dimitris.'

'I see,' said Yiorgo. 'And that's where you want to work?'

'Yes. Why are you interested anyway?'

'Just making conversation,' smiled Yiorgo. 'What does the warehouse store?'

'Organic flour.'

'Organic flour!'

Alecos nodded. 'The hotels and bakers use it. They phone in the quantity they want in the morning and you get it ready for them to collect. Easy. Then you have the afternoon and evening to yourself.'

'Sounds a good job. I wouldn't mind something like that myself.'

'What do you do?' asked Alecos.

'In the travel business,' answered Yiorgo quickly. 'That's why we're over here. Seeing the potential market for tourists.'

Alecos picked up their empty bottles and plates. 'How long are you here?'

Yiorgo shrugged. 'A week, maybe more.'

A young man walked towards the taverna and swerved across towards the side road, raising his hand to Alecos as he passed. Alecos shook his fist at the man's back.

'That's the man from the warehouse,' he said.

'Not your friend, obviously.'

'He took my girl,' growled Alecos, turned on his heel and returned to the bar.

'No wonder he dislikes the man if he took both his job and his girl,' observed Takkis. 'Shall we wander or is there anything we can do back at the station?'

'May as well take advantage of an afternoon off. We need to find out the chemist's report before we can move.'

Dimitris sent for Frida and quizzed her thoroughly about the visit Takkis had paid to the galley.

'He wanted to know exactly what food I'd served the night Mr Pavlides died. That was all.'

Dimitris frowned. 'Nothing else?'

Frida shook her head. 'He admired the galley and the fitments. Oh, and he took a chocolate from Miss Suzanna's box.'

'He did what!'

'He took a chocolate.' Frida giggled. 'He was like a little boy. He said he would eat it later in case you caught him with it in his mouth.'

Dimitris's fist crashed down on the table. 'How dare he.'

'He only took a chocolate,' protested Frida.

'You should not have let him. I made it quite clear to you that those chocolates were for Miss Suzanna only.'

Dimitris ran his hand through his hair. 'I should not have let him go to the galley. I should have insisted you spoke to him in here, in front of me.'

Frida turned puzzled eyes on her employer. 'I'm sorry, Mr Dimitris. I didn't think it would matter.'

Dimitris shook his head. 'I'll have to think about this.'

Dimitris sat with his head in his hands. He must get rid of the girl. He could not hand her over to Joseph after the funeral and sail for Kos as he had planned. She would easily be found in the old town. He did not want her questioned by the police. She would say anything to obtain a shot to alleviate the painful and unpleasant withdrawal symptoms she would experience if she were in jail.

He sat and thought for a further five minutes. Lakkis would have to help him. He rose and knocked on Sorrell's cabin door. She was lying on her bed and blinked at him owlishly.

'I want you to be ready to go ashore in half an hour,' he said.

'What are we doing?'

'I think it would be a good idea if you stayed ashore for a short while. I have to attend Nikos's funeral this afternoon. As you know the police have been making enquiries regarding his unfortunate death. I am sure you would not want them to start enquiring into your background, would you?'

Sorrell paled and threw back the sheet. 'Why should they do that?'

Dimitris spread his hands. 'Who knows? Once the police start to make enquiries they often spread their net very wide. I will arrange for you to stay at my hotel in Faliraki for a few days. There is no need for you to pack. I will get Frida to send some clothing and your toiletries down for you.' Dimitris closed the door and hurried away to speak to Anders.

After his conversation with Anders, Dimitris headed for the pay phone at the end of the harbour arm. He telephoned Lakkis and explained the situation to him briefly, following with explicit instructions. Lakkis replaced the receiver looking very thoughtful.

Dimitris returned to the cruiser and found Sorrell dressed and ready to go ashore.

'I've packed a small case,' she smiled.

'You will not need to take it with you,' said Dimitris. 'I will send it down to you later.' He studied her carefully. 'You will place a scarf over your head and wear your sun glasses. Anders will go with you in a taxi.'

Sorrell looked at him suspiciously. 'What's going on, Dimitris?'

'If you are seen leaving the boat with a suitcase it will be obvious that you do not plan to return today. I will ensure it is sent on to you this afternoon. Trust me, my dear. I am merely thinking of your welfare.'

Sorrell sat in the taxi with Anders. He made no attempt at conversation with her and after she had asked him twice where they were going and he had not replied she gave up, watching the scenery from her window in sulky silence. Half an hour later they drew up outside a large hotel and Sorrell smiled for the first time. This looked like her kind of place. Anders helped her out and paid the driver, waiting for him to depart before escorting Sorrell into the hotel.

Lakkis met her, his hands outstretched. 'This is a pleasure. I will show you to your room myself.' He opened the door of the lift and ushered her in, pressing the button for the top floor. They walked the length of a corridor and he opened the door to the room at the end.

'I am sorry that you have to be up here, but the hotel is virtually full. It is still one of our best rooms.'

Sorrell nodded and took in her surroundings. The room was tastefully furnished, a lounge with patio doors opening onto a balcony, an arch leading through to a bedroom with en suite facilities.

'I shan't know what to do with all this space after living on the boat for so long,' she smiled.

'Rest assured, I shall do everything in my power to make your stay here as memorable as possible.' Lakkis smiled back at her. 'I have to return to town, for my brother's funeral, you understand, but I will bring some refreshment up for you before I leave.' As he spoke he opened the door, closing it firmly behind him, and Sorrell heard the key turn in the lock.

She stared at the door; then tried the handle. She was locked in! She shook her head in disbelief and looked around the lounge for a key. Finding none she entered the bedroom, but again her search was fruitless. She kicked off her sandals and padded back to the lounge barefoot. Because she had not checked in at reception in the conventional manner Lakkis must have forgotten she did not have her own key. She padded back into the bedroom and lifted the receiver of the telephone beside the bed. She would call down to reception and tell them her dilemma. To her surprise the telephone was dead. She shrugged. Lakkis had said he would return, she would just have to wait and explain the situation to him. He would no doubt rectify it immediately.

The time began to drag. Sorrell looked at her watch. It was just after twelve. Lakkis must have been gone at least ten minutes. She had no idea when he would return. In the meantime she would sit out on the balcony in the sun. However hard she pulled at the patio doors they would not open and the horrendous truth suddenly dawned on her. She was a prisoner.

Dimitris returned from Nikos's funeral in a sombre mood. Everything had been running so well. Now he would have to ingratiate himself with a new harbour master and it might not be so easy this time. Paying all the bills for Nikos's wife when she was ill had made the man beholden to him. He sighed. Then there was the problem of the girl. Once the police gave him permission to leave Rhodes, which he was sure they would do once he had convinced them that the doctoring of the chocolates was nothing to do with him, he would leave her with Joseph. He would visit the warehouse in the morning and have a little talk with him.

As he had promised, he packed all Sorrell's possessions into three large suitcases. He removed the money from her overnight bag and placed it in his pocket. He noted that it was considerably less than when she had first come aboard. Her jewellery he placed in a separate bag; then wrote a short note addressed to Lakkis and attached it to the outside.

He called Anders to him and instructed him to hire a taxi for the airport. Whilst he was awaiting its arrival he was to take two cases to the end of the jetty and return for the bag and remaining suitcase. Having reached the airport he was to wait inside for half an hour, then catch another taxi to the house of Lakkis Pavlides where he was to leave the baggage. From Lakkis's house he was to walk back to the boat, taking a circuitous route through the old town.

Anders nodded and repeated his instructions. This was not the first time Mr Dimitris had discarded a travelling companion. Usually the young lady had a taxi directly from whichever harbour they happened to be in to a hotel of her choice. He was puzzled by his strange instructions, but no doubt he would be paid well.

Dimitris returned to his own cabin and took the syringe and a supply of heroin from its hiding place. He smiled to himself as he placed the items in the drawer beside the bed and covered them with a handkerchief.

Sorrell was sulky and bad tempered and she felt ill. Her skin crawled and she trembled intermittently. She had spent the day locked in the hotel room.

Lakkis had returned briefly, bringing her a tray laden with cold meat, fish, salad, bread, and fresh fruit. The fridge inside her room had an array of alcoholic and soft drinks, or she could make herself coffee or tea, but the fact remained that she was a prisoner.

It was gone seven when Lakkis finally unlocked the door to her room and entered with a smile.

193

'Good evening. I trust you are well and have not found the day too boring?'

'What do you think?' she snapped back at him.

'I think you are in a most unfortunate situation. Believe me, Mr Dimitris and I will do all we can to help you.' Lakkis sat down on the settee. 'I have your luggage with me as Mr Dimitris requested. I regret I was unable to bring it to you earlier, but the funeral, you understand.'

Sorrell nodded dully. 'Did you bring my chocolates?'

Lakkis cleared his throat. 'Mr Dimitris thought it better if the chocolates stayed where they were.'

Sorrell sprang to her feet. 'I need my chocolates. My sugar levels are low.'

Lakkis held out his hand. 'Calm down, my dear. I have brought you something else to take their place. You see, the chocolates that you were eating had a little addition in them. I can give you that. You don't need the chocolates.'

'What do you mean?' Sorrell felt confused and angry.

Lakkis smiled. 'A small quantity of heroin. To take the place of the chocolates.'

'No, oh, no. I don't use drugs.' Sorrell folded her arms.

'Really? In that case we will forget about it. Your telephone has been connected directly to my office. You can call me if you change your mind.'

Sorrell threw her shoe at his retreating form and flung herself down on the bed. She wanted a chocolate. She wrapped her arms around herself and drew up her legs into a foetal position. Her stomach was cramping and she was shivering violently. She moaned softly to herself. The withdrawal symptoms persisted and began to worsen, almost involuntarily Sorrell reached out for the telephone.

Lakkis let it ring a number of times before he answered. 'You are feeling ready now? I will come up right away and bring your luggage with me.'

He unlocked the door and smiled at the curled figure, shivering and clutching at the sheet. He pushed her cases inside the room and locked the door behind him. 'This won't take a moment.' From his pocket Lakkis withdrew a small syringe. He removed the cap and squirted a small amount into the air to disperse any air bubbles. 'Very soon you will be able to do this for yourself without a second thought. Alternatively you can always sniff some of the powder.'

He took her hand and stretched her arm out straight, rubbing a vein to bring it to the surface. Whilst she watched, bemused, he inserted the needle and depressed the plunger. 'There you are. You will find that even more effective than the chocolates.'

Sorrell dropped her head into her hands. 'You're wicked. I've never taken drugs.'

'Oh, but you have, my dear. For the last six months you have been enjoying the beneficial effects. Think how good you have felt after you have consumed a chocolate, just because there was a little addition to the filling. Remember those wonderful evenings when you were asked to entertain? You have been having the most wonderful experiences of your life. You want that to continue, don't you?'

Sorrell lifted her eyes to his. 'Why have you done this to me?'

Lakkis shrugged. 'I have done nothing, merely carried out Dimitris's instructions. You are beginning to feel better now?'

Sorrell nodded as the drug began to take effect. She sat up straighter on the bed. 'So why am I a prisoner here?'

Lakkis shook his head. 'You are not a prisoner. It was unfortunate that you arrived today and I was unable to spend time with you to explain the arrangements.' His green cat-like eyes flickered over her. 'I understand from Dimitris that the police have visited him regarding the sad death of my brother. They also spoke to you. Something – unfortunate – occurred during their visit and Dimitris realised it could have repercussions on you. I believe there could be a problem regarding your passport?'

He raised his eyebrows quizzically. 'He thought it would be better if you were not available if the police returned. You had a sudden whim to sail off to one of the other islands. They can look for you on Santorini or Crete, but, of course, they will not find you as you are sitting happily in Faliraki.'

'How long am I supposed to stay here?'

'A few days; maybe a week. Just until the police have finished their enquiries and lost interest in you.'

'I'm free to go out?'

'You are free to make use of the hotel's facilities. It would not be wise of you to leave the hotel complex, of course. I would also prefer that you did not talk to the other guests. I have arranged for a companion for you, so that you will not be lonely during the day. Thalia needs a little time to come to terms with the death of her father. She will come down each day with me and you can spend your time by the pool or on the beach, whichever you prefer.'

'And what am I supposed to do with myself in the evenings?'

'I am sure I can arrange some entertainment for you. I have brought your bags and I suggest you unpack and make yourself at home. Your jewellery and money have been placed in my personal safe at my house at Dimitris's request. I will return in, say, an hour? That should give you time to wash and change before I escort you down to dinner. Afterwards, well, we will see.'

Sorrell tossed her head. 'I would rather eat in my room.'

'Whatever you prefer, my dear.'

Dimitris was just about to leave the cruiser to call on Joseph when Takkis and Yiorgo arrived on board.

'Good morning, Mr Stephanotis. I apologise for arriving so early, but we wanted to speak to you before you went ashore.'

Dimitris frowned in annoyance, but stepped aside and ushered the two men below.

'My colleague would like to have a quick word with your cook. She is aboard, is she not?' asked Yiorgo.

Dimitris nodded. 'She'll be in the galley.'

Yiorgo sat down and looked around the cabin admiringly whilst Takkis made his way to the galley. He popped his head round the door and smiled at Frida who was replacing the breakfast dishes into the cupboard.

'I'm sorry to trouble you so early; I won't keep you more than a few minutes.' Takkis opened the fridge and took out the box of chocolates. 'These belong to the young lady who is travelling with Mr Stephanotis, I believe?'

Frida nodded. 'I told you they were hers. Did you enjoy the one you took?'

'Very much,' smiled Takkis. 'It was just what I needed. Do you ever eat these?'

Frida shook her head. 'Mr Stephanotis said they were for her and we were not to touch them.'

'Have you never had a sneaky one?'

Frida shook her head. 'I do as I'm told. I can always buy myself a box of chocolates if I want.'

Takkis picked up the box. 'You don't mind if I borrow these for a short while?'

Frida shrugged. 'You must ask Mr Stephanotis.'

Takkis returned to the saloon and placed the box of chocolates on the table. He opened the box. Most of the top layer had been eaten. He lifted the packaging and was surprised to find there were six chocolates missing from the lower layer. He replaced the paper quickly.

'Mr Stephanotis, I understand you purchase these chocolates for the young lady who is travelling with you.'

Dimitris nodded.

'Where do you usually purchase them?'

Dimitris shrugged. 'It depends where we are berthed. When I am in Rhodes I usually get them from the shop that specialises in chocolates at the end of Mandraki harbour.'

'Did you buy these chocolates there?'

'No, I would have bought those when we visited Cyprus.'

'And from the same sort of shop, I presume.'

'Of course.'

'Does anyone else eat these chocolates?'

'No. They are exclusively for Miss Suzanna.'

'And they are always kept in the fridge?'

'Of course, they would melt otherwise.'

'So who would have access to these chocolates, apart from your cook?'

'Anyone who went to the fridge.'

'Are you familiar with the contents of these chocolates?'

'Some sort of cream and liqueur filling. Suzanna prefers a soft centre.'

Takkis sat forward, covering the box of chocolates with his arms. 'I took one of these chocolates yesterday. I also sent it for analysis. Do you know what we found inside?'

Dimitris shrugged. 'Whatever it says the contents are on the box I presume.'

Takkis shook his head slowly. 'We found all those ingredients, but a little something has been added. We found heroin in them.'

'Heroin?' Dimitris managed to look shocked.

Takkis nodded solemnly.

'You see,' said Yiorgo, his eyes boring into Dimitris, 'it is obvious that your companion is a user. The puzzling thing is; why should she put it into her chocolates?'

'I had no idea she took anything.'

'Please, Mr Stephanotis, you can hardly expect us to believe that! You are a well-travelled man. I am sure you are well aware of the signs of drug abuse.'

Dimitris spread his hands. 'It had never occurred to me. Of course, now you say, it is obvious. How very foolish of me.'

'Have you any idea where she would have purchased the drug?'

'No idea at all. She could have bought it anywhere when we were in Egypt.'

'Why Egypt? Why not Cyprus?' asked Takkis.

'I am saying Egypt because now you have brought it to my attention that is when her behaviour began to change.'

'In what way did it change?'

'She became very lethargic. Often she did not want to go ashore. She said the heat was troubling her, or she had a headache. Then her mood would change and she would be full of energy.'

'How many of these 'chocolates' did she usually consume during the course of the day?' asked Takkis.

'She usually had one after meals.'

'And you bought this box in Cyprus?'

'Yes. I bought it the day before we left.'

'And when was that exactly?'

Dimitris removed a diary from his pocket. 'I can tell you exactly.' He flipped over the pages. 'Eight days ago.'

Takkis began to count the chocolates. 'The box would have contained fifty chocolates. Twenty-five on each layer. By my reckoning the bottom layer should be intact and there should be two or more left of the first layer.'

Dimitris nodded. 'I don't remember when Suzanna opened this box.'

'But you agree that my calculations should be near enough correct, making allowances for the one I took yesterday?'

Dimitris nodded again.

'So how do you account for six chocolates that are missing from the lower level?'

Dimitris looked into the box as Takkis opened it. He lifted the paper and was genuinely surprised when he saw the spaces where the chocolates had rested.

'I don't know. Maybe Suzanna has eaten more than I thought.'

'Why should she take them from the lower layer? They were her chocolates. You would, presumably buy her another box when this one was finished. She had no need to hide the fact that she had eaten them?'

Dimitris shook his head. 'I have no answer to your question. You would have to ask her.'

Takkis nodded slowly. 'I don't think your companion ate these. Cast your mind back to the night that Mr Pavlides came to dinner. Where was the box of chocolates?'

Dimitris frowned. 'I don't know. Probably on the table over there. That's where Frida usually puts them when she takes them out of the fridge.'

'And you told us that there was a slight incident whilst you were drinking coffee. You went to find your captain and the young lady went to change her soiled dress.'

Dimitris nodded.

'Did you know that Mr Pavlides was passionately fond of chocolates?'

Dimitris face paled beneath his suntan

'You see,' Yiorgo sat forward confidentially, 'when the autopsy was carried out on Mr Pavlides the contents of his stomach were analysed. The analysis showed the ingredients of the meal he had eaten with you, including chocolate. Unfortunately he had also consumed a quantity of heroin. When we spoke to Mr Pavlides's daughter she said he loved chocolates. She thought he had sat in bed and eaten some, leaving one to give to her the next morning. Under the circumstances she had thought no more about it and the chocolate was still sitting there. My colleague decided to take it for analysis and it was found to be contaminated.'

Yiorgo looked at Dimitris who was following his reasoning carefully.

'We thought we should check where Mr Pavlides obtained the chocolates. When my colleague saw a box of chocolates in your fridge he took one, obviously to eliminate them from suspicion. Unfortunately that chocolate was also contaminated. Now we need to take the remainder with us. If they also turn out to be laced with heroin, as I suspect they will, we will need to speak to you further and also to the young lady. Obviously we shall contact the shop where they were purchased and request further checks are made on their remaining stock. It would be most unfortunate if other boxes were found to be contaminated also. That would mean withdrawing all supplies from the market and investigating the factory also. It could ruin them.'

Yiorgo stood up. 'We will not detain you any longer, Mr Stephanotis. I need hardly tell you that you must remain in this harbour until our investigations are completed.'

Dimitris nodded. He passed a trembling hand over his forehead. 'Poor Nikos,' he managed to murmur.

The box of chocolates in a bag, Takkis and Yiorgo left the cruiser and made their way towards the police station.

'What now?' asked Takkis.

'Analysis and apply for a search warrant for that cruiser.'

'Do you think he knew the girl was using?'

'Of course,' answered Yiorgo scornfully, 'but I do think he was genuinely surprised when we told him Nikos Pavlides died from an overdose of heroin.'

'Do you think he'll try to leave?'

'No. He would know the consequences. It's my guess that he's going to plead ignorance all the way along and blame the girl.'

'Maybe we should have spoken to her whilst we were there,' suggested Takkis.

'I doubt if we'd have got much out of her. She would just have denied everything. How do we prove that she put the stuff inside the chocolates?'

'Maybe she didn't.'

'What do you mean?'

Takkis frowned. 'I'm not sure. Suppose someone wanted her to become an addict. They could have tampered with the chocolates.'

Yiorgo gave him a sceptical look. 'Why would they want to do that? Easier to get her drunk one night and give her a shot.'

'That can be dangerous, besides, she may not drink.'

'It's all maybe. We need some direct evidence.'

Joseph answered the knock on his door and was amazed when he saw Dimitris standing there.

'What have I done?' he asked anxiously. 'Is there a problem?'

Dimitris smiled reassuringly. 'No problem with you. May I come in?'

Joseph opened the door wider and Dimitris stepped inside the warehouse, noting the sacks of flour neatly stacked over most of the floor area.

'Business is good?'

Joseph nodded. 'You'd better come upstairs to my room.' He wished he had made his bed and washed his dirty dishes that morning. He led the way and indicated a chair to Dimitris. 'Can I get you anything? I have coffee or beer.'

Dimitris shook his head. 'Thank you, no. Our business will not take very long.'

Joseph shifted uncomfortably in his chair and lit a cigarette.

'I am bringing you a companion.'

'I don't need a companion. I'm quite happy on my own.'

'With the services of Nadia for when you are lonely,' added Dimitris. 'I have promised Alecos that he will have Nadia back this season. It is only fair I replace her for you.'

Joseph frowned. 'I bought into the syndicate. You can't just take her away from me.'

'I can do whatever I wish,' replied Dimitris coldly. 'Nadia will return to Alecos. You will have Suzanna, or whatever her name is, to replace her. I have been gradually conditioning her over the winter months. She had some very – interesting – experiences, when we were in Egypt. She has entertained regularly since then, whenever I have requested that she did so.'

'What makes you think she will be happy working for me?'

Dimitris placed his fingertips together. 'Unfortunately she has developed a bad habit. She has become a user. Provided you supply her regularly you should have no problems. If she is difficult you simply refuse to feed her habit. I can assure you that within a very short time she will be only too happy to do your bidding. She does not appreciate the unpleasant side effects of withdrawal.'

Joseph regarded Dimitris suspiciously. 'Why are you doing this?'

Dimitris spread his hands. 'A young American lady was looking for you in Athens. She claimed to be an old acquaintance of yours. I decided she could be useful to me for a while.' Dimitris sat forward. 'Then you became greedy. You were not content with what you had. You had to buy into the syndicate. That was when I had the idea of – grooming – this young lady for your use. It really is to your advantage. Had she found you herself it is very likely that you would regret it. She had a little problem in an Athens prison, I believe.' Dimitris stood up. 'There is no need to see me out.'

Joseph stood, speechless, as Dimitris clattered down the wooden steps and he heard the door close behind him.

Thalia was puzzled by her uncle's request. 'I have to go back to work. I've already had a week off.'

Lakkis patted her hand. 'I have spoken to your employer. He understands that you need a little more time.'

'But I hardly know this girl. I've only met her once.'

'You can get to know her. All I ask is that you spend the days with her, beside the pool or on the beach, anywhere you please within the hotel complex. If she leaves the *'Aegean Gem'* you are to notify me immediately. She has a little problem with her memory. If she wandered into town she would get hopelessly lost and then she would panic. It will only be for a few days, my dear.'

'What about the evenings?'

'That is no problem. She prefers to spend the evening in her room. You will have a taxi back to town at six each day.'

Thalia pretended to consider the proposal. She knew she had to do as her uncle had requested, and it would also be a relief to get away from the house and the cloying affection of her aunt. 'Very well,' she sighed. 'What time do I have to be ready in the morning?'

Lakkis left his niece in his office whilst he went to Sorrell's room. She was still lying in the soiled and rumpled bed. He ran his hand down her arm and she opened her eyes and shook her head.

'No. Please, no. Not again.'

Lakkis smiled. 'No, my dear, not until this evening. We will be able to enjoy ourselves again then.'

Sorrell shook her head more vigorously, remembering the indignities she had suffered at his hands the previous night. 'I don't want to.'

'You don't want to? After all Dimitris has told me about you I would have thought you would be only too willing and eager to repeat the experiences we shared.'

'I didn't enjoy it.'

'That is a great pity because I did, and I intend to enjoy myself again. Unfortunately I have to work this morning or we could start now.' His eyes raked over her nakedness and he wished he could stay. He had thought up some other little experiments that he would take a delight in executing with her. 'I think it is time you prepared yourself for the day. Thalia is here and looking forward to spending time with you.'

'I don't want to get up.'

'That is unfortunate, as I am going to insist that you do so. My niece has taken time from work to be a companion for you. It would be very churlish of you to stay in bed all day and deprive her of a day beside the pool or on the beach.'

'I don't feel well enough.'

'I understand. You need a little boost to your system to give you some energy. I have brought it with me.'

'I don't want it.'

'Really? I seem to remember you said the same thing to me yesterday evening. Within half an hour you were begging me to return. I regret I shall be far too busy to return before this afternoon to assist you.'

Sorrell looked at him with hatred in her eyes. 'You're wicked, you and Dimitris.'

'Not at all, my dear. Now, if you will just stretch out your arm.'

Yiorgo and Takkis had to wait until mid-day before they had the results of the analysis of the box of chocolates and also a warrant to search the '*Aegean Pride*'. They boarded the craft and explained to Dimitris that they wished to interview Miss Hirsch and also search the entire boat.

Dimitris spread his hands apologetically. 'I have no problem with you searching my boat. I know you will find nothing incriminating. As for Miss Hirsh, I regret I cannot help you. She decided to leave.'

Yiorgo sat down opposite Dimitris and looked at him gravely. 'Mr Stephanotis, instructions were given that you and your boat were not to leave the harbour. I would have thought that would have been obvious to you that also meant anyone who was living on the boat with you at this time.'

'What can I say? I went ashore yesterday and when I returned Miss Hirsch had packed her cases and departed. I have no idea where she is.'

'Did you speak to Miss Hirsch after we left yesterday?'

Dimitris shook his head. 'She appeared to be asleep when I left.'

Yiorgo nodded. 'I see. Do you know if she spoke to either of your crew before she left?'

'Anders did not see her, but Frida said she planned to take a ferry for Turkey.'

'Had you informed your crew that you were being detained here whilst we completed our enquiries?'

'There was no need. They sail when I say.'

'I see. I would like to speak to both your crewmembers. If you would be good enough to ask your cook to come up.'

Dimitris nodded and went to the head of the stairs leading to the lower level. Within minutes Frida appeared and sat opposite Yiorgo and Takkis.

Takkis smiled at her. 'I'm sorry to have to trouble you again. I believe you saw Miss Hirsch yesterday, before she left the boat.'

Frida nodded, her hands were clenched in her lap, the knuckles showing white.

'Did she say anything to you before she left?'

'She said she was tired of being here and was going to take a ferry to Turkey.'

'That was all she said?'

Frida nodded again.

'And where were you when this conversation took place?'

'I – I – I was in the galley.'

'So she made a point of coming to tell you that she was leaving? Did she ask for any help with her luggage?'

'No.'

'I imagine she would have a considerable amount, more than she could carry easily.'

'I don't know.'

'Did she ask your husband for help?'

'No.'

'How can you be so sure?'

'He would have told me.'

'Of course.' Takkis nodded. 'There's just one more thing. Would you have any objection to your cabin being searched?'

Frida frowned. 'Yes. It would be an invasion of my privacy.'

Takkis spread his hands. 'Unfortunately we are required to do so as part of our duties.'

Frida shrugged. 'I have nothing to hide.'

Takkis smiled at her. 'I'm sure you haven't. Would you ask your husband to come up now, please?'

Frida left them and Anders took her place.

Yiorgo smiled at him, but Anders would not meet his eyes.

'Can you tell me where you were when Miss Hirsch left the boat yesterday?' asked Yiorgo.

Anders shrugged. 'Probably below, checking the engine.'

'Why would you be checking the engine if you were not sailing that day?'

'I check the engine every day. Mr Dimitris might want to sail and I like to know everything is in readiness.'

'So you would not have known that Miss Hirsch had left?'

Anders shook his head, still not meeting Yiorgo's eyes.

Yiorgo sighed. 'Thank you. I have to tell you that we have a warrant to search the boat. That will obviously include your quarters and the engine room.'

Anders shrugged. 'Whatever.'

Yiorgo escorted Anders below to the small area that housed the engine. He could hear footsteps above him and he looked at Anders speculatively.

'You did not hear Miss Hirsch moving her luggage onto the deck?'

Anders shook his head. 'I may have done, but I would not have taken any notice.'

'Why would that be?'

'I would think it was Frida, cleaning the cabins.'

'Of course.'

Yiorgo turned his attention to the array of paraphernalia stowed methodically in the small space. There was nothing obvious worthy of more than a glance. Yiorgo smiled at him. 'I can see you are a good captain. How long have you been with Mr Stephanotis?'

Anders shrugged. 'Some years now.'

'What did you do before?'

'I was in the navy.'

'That gave you good training, no doubt. Where did you sail?'

'The world.'

'What kind of ships were you on?'

'Everything. Wherever I could get work.'

Yiorgo raised his eyebrows in surprise. 'I would not have thought getting work for an experienced sailor was difficult.'

'It wasn't,' answered Anders shortly and folded his arms.

'Well, there's obviously nothing down here. I believe my colleague is with your wife in the cabin. Shall we join them?'

Takkis methodically opened drawers and cupboards, checked beneath the mattress of the bed and ensured the carpet was firmly fixed to the floor in all places. As Yiorgo entered he shook his head.

'There's nothing here.'

'I did not expect there to be,' smiled Yiorgo. 'Mr Stephanotis, if we could visit your cabin next, whilst my colleague has a quick look in the galley.'

Dimitris's cabin yielded nothing and Yiorgo crossed to the cabin Sorrell had occupied. There was nothing to show that the cabin had been used only the day before. The cupboards and drawers were empty of clothes and Yiorgo felt frustrated until he opened the drawer beside the bed. Beneath a handkerchief lay a syringe and a packet containing a few grains of powder. From his pocket Yiorgo took a polythene bag and a pair of tweezers, carefully he picked up the items and placed them inside the bag, sealing it firmly.

Dimitris stood impassively watching him. Yiorgo raised his eyebrows enquiringly.

'I find it strange that Miss Hirsch should have left a syringe and some powder in her cabin when she obviously took everything else.'

Dimitris shrugged. 'I expect she has others.'

'Very likely,' answered Yiorgo noncommittally. 'I would just like to have another word with Frida, if I may.'

Frida sat before him, she still appeared ill at ease and nervous, clenching and unclenching her hands.

Yiorgo smiled, noticing her unease. 'I understand that you clean the cabins.'

Frida nodded. 'Every day.'

'What exactly do you do?'

Frida frowned. 'Make the beds, clean the bathrooms, dust, vacuum the carpets. The usual things.'

'And empty the rubbish?'

'Of course.'

'Did you at any time find any needles or syringes in Miss Hirsch's rubbish?'

'I don't examine people's rubbish.'

'No, of course not. I just thought you might have seen one in the waste bin.'

Frida shook her head. 'I've never seen anything except cotton wool and tissues.'

'And did you clean Miss Hirsch's cabin yesterday?'

'Of course.'

'Did you check the drawers and wardrobe to ensure that they were clean and she had not left anything behind?

'Naturally.'

Yiorgo shrugged his shoulders and stood up. 'Thank you all for your time and co-operation. We will be in touch Mr Stephanotis.'

Dimitris frowned. 'You mean I cannot sail yet?'

Yiorgo shook his head. 'In view of the find in Miss Hirsch's cabin and her subsequent disappearance I would like you to stay here a little longer. If Miss Hirsch should contact you I would appreciate you passing that information on to us.'

Dimitris nodded and scowled at the backs of Yiorgo and Takkis. He had thought the planting of the syringe in Sorrell's cabin would have cleared him of any suspicion and he would have been free to leave.

Joseph went to the coffee house on Mandraki harbour, hoping to find Thalia there during her lunch hour. He was desperate to relay his condolences to her and persuade her to spend some time with him alone. To his annoyance she did not put in an appearance and after waiting an extra half an hour in case she had been delayed, he walked through the new part of the town to her office.

He entered and looked around. Three girls sat at desks, a fourth was empty. 'Is Thalia here?' he asked.

One of the girls shook her head. 'She's having some time off. Her father died, you know.'

Joseph nodded. 'I've been out of town and only just heard. I just wanted to tell her how sorry I was.'

He backed out of the office and the girl bent her head back to her work.

Joseph walked slowly down the road, thinking hard. If Thalia was not at work it was most likely she was at her uncle's or her own home. He knew where she lived having followed her surreptitiously one day and now he made his way there. He knocked on the door and when there was no answer he shrugged and walked away. Wherever she was she would return at some time, if only to collect a change of clothing. He would just wait for his opportunity.

Yiorgo and Takkis closeted themselves in a small room at the police station. The syringe had been sent for fingerprinting and then on for analysis along with the powder.

'So what do you think?' asked Yiorgo.

'I think everyone is lying through their teeth. The woman was obviously frightened and the man was equally unhelpful. I'm sure they both know far more than they're telling us.'

'What about the syringe?'

'Planted,' replied Takkis firmly. 'No user is going to leave that behind. She would have been more likely to have left her clothes.'

Yiorgo nodded. 'Exactly. I think we should get some checks done on those two crew members. We can always go back and take fingerprints. Tell them it's to eliminate them from handling the syringe.'

'Suppose there are no prints on it?'

'They're not going to know that,' smiled Yiorgo.

'Where do you think the girl is?'

'Somewhere on the island. I don't believe the story that she packed up and left for one minute.' Yiorgo tapped his teeth with his pen. 'We can check the airlines, of course, and ferry entry to Turkey, but if she really has gone to one of the other islands we're not going to be able to find her. Maybe a taxi driver would remember her. She's pretty striking to look at and would have had a considerable amount of luggage with her.'

'It's worth a try, I suppose.'

'You don't sound very enthusiastic.'

'Like you, I think she's still on the island. We'll be wasting our time checking the airport and ferries.'

Yiorgo threw the pen aside. 'Lunch. We can't do anything more today until we get those results back.'

Thalia waited for over an hour before Sorrell lifted the telephone and advised Lakkis that she was showered and dressed. He smiled with relief and immediately went up to her room.

'You look delightful, my dear.' He took her elbow, gripping it tightly. 'Thalia is here, but it would be inadvisable for you to try to leave the hotel complex. I have told her that you have been unwell. The medication you are on has caused unfortunate memory lapses and delusions. It is quite possible you would become lost in the town. I have told her to notify me immediately in the interest of your safety. Besides, if you did go wandering off on your own, what would you do when the effects wore off? Where would you get some more? As you know the withdrawal symptoms are both unpleasant and painful. I assure you, the longer you go without the worse they become.'

Sorrell pulled her arm free. She shot Lakkis a look of pure venom. 'Maybe I should tell your niece just what kind of a man you are.'

'She would never believe you. Remember, I have explained any strange behaviour on your part as unfortunate side effects of your medicine; and do not forget, you are dependent upon my good nature to give you that medicine each day. If you behave yourself I will bring you a little present at lunch time. It would not be wise to make an enemy of me.'

Sorrell picked up her towel. She really did not care. She was feeling good. A day beside the pool would be very enjoyable.

Thalia enjoyed her day. Sorrell was amusing and good company, lifting her from the depression she had felt over the death of her father. They had talked and laughed together, criticised the other guests and the clothes they were wearing, swum and sun bathed. Thalia had told Sorrell about her impending wedding to Manolis and Sorrell had shown an interest in the arrangements.

'You will still go ahead with it, although your father died recently?'

Thalia looked downcast. 'My uncle says I have to. If I waited another year as I should he says people will laugh at Manolis and say I don't want to marry him.'

'Do you want to marry him?'

Thalia smiled. 'I think so. I have known since I was ten that we were to be married. He is a good man, very clever. He is just finishing his army service, but uncle Lakkis has a job waiting for him. We will run *The Grapevine* together.'

'Haven't you ever been out with anyone else?'

Thalia shook her head. 'Of course not. I wasn't even sure if I should meet Joseph for coffee in my lunch hour, but I asked my friends and they said there was no reason why I shouldn't have a cup of coffee with anyone.'

'Joseph?' Sorrell honed in on the name.

'He works for uncle Lakkis at the warehouse.'

'I thought your uncle was the manager of this hotel?'

'He is, but he also has a taverna and a warehouse.'

'What does he keep in the warehouse?'

'Organic flour. It's become very popular over here with people. They think it's better for them because it hasn't any chemicals in it.'

Sorrell nodded absently. 'Where is this warehouse? Down at the harbour?'

'No, in the old town.'

'And Joseph runs it?'

Thalia nodded. 'I didn't like him much when I first met him, but he's quite nice when you get to know him. He's half Italian and tells such amusing stories about himself and his brothers when they were small.'

'I'm sure he does!' Sorrell spoke through gritted teeth. 'I can't wait to meet him.'

'Why should you want to meet him?'

Sorrell hesitated. Should she take Thalia into her confidence? She thought better of it. Thalia would probably go straight to her uncle. 'He sounds an interesting character.' She yawned. 'I think I'll have a nap. I didn't sleep very well last night.'

'Weren't you comfortable?' asked Thalia solicitously.

Sorrell shrugged. 'The bed was comfortable enough. I've become used to the slight motion that you have on board a boat. I probably missed it.'

Sorrell did not want to go into the reason for her lack of sleep. She adjusted her eyeshade and closed her eyes. She wanted to think about this piece of information that Thalia had given her. How could she get into the old town and find Joseph? She smiled to herself. She had been correct when she thought she had seen him on the motorbike. No wonder she had not been allowed to wander around the old town as she wished, she could so easily have bumped into him.

Takkis looked at Yiorgo and raised his eyebrows. 'What now? The syringe has definitely held heroin and they managed to lift some prints from it.'

'Good. Another visit to our friend Mr Stephanotis, I think. We'll want prints from everyone. If anyone tries to stall say we need them for elimination purposes. We say we are convinced they belong to the girl.'

'Do you think they are hers?'

'Not for a minute, but at this stage we can't prove they're not.'

'We could see if there are any prints in the cabin,' suggested Takkis.

'Highly unlikely. No doubt the industrious Frida has cleaned and polished thoroughly.'

Dimitris was annoyed when he saw the two narcotics officers approaching. He greeted them with a forced smile. 'Good morning, gentlemen. No doubt you have come to tell me that I may sail. You did not need to come in person; you could have sent a message to the harbour.'

Yiorgo shook his head. 'I regret that we have to ask you to remain here a little longer. We have found some fingerprints on the syringe. They will naturally belong to the girl, but it is necessary to eliminate yourself and your crew.'

'Surely not. It was found in her cabin and she has disappeared.' Dimitris frowned. He had not expected the men to be so thorough.

'Exactly, she has disappeared. If she were here it would be a simple matter of just checking her prints. As it is,' Yiorgo shrugged eloquently, 'we have to inconvenience all of you. It will only take a matter of moments.'

'Surely her prints must be on the furniture of the cabin. You could take some samples from there.'

'Do you have a problem with having your prints taken, Mr Stephanotis?' asked Takkis.

'No, no, not at all. I am just thinking of my crew.'

'Why should they be perturbed?'

Dimitris looked uncomfortable. 'I trust this will go no further.' He looked at Yiorgo and Takkis anxiously and both men nodded. 'You see, both Anders and Frida have had a little problem in the past. I decided I would give them the chance to make a new start. They are grateful for the opportunity and would do nothing to jeopardise their future with me. I would rather they were not asked to give their prints, it would be distressing for them.'

'We are not looking into old crimes,' Yiorgo assured him. 'We only wish to eliminate their prints from those found on the syringe.'

'And if I refuse on their behalf?'

'That would not be very sensible, would it? We would simply return with a warrant for their arrest and take their prints at the station. I'm sure they would prefer to give them here in privacy.' Yiorgo smiled disarmingly. 'If we could just go below, we will only detain you for a few minutes.'

Dimitris scowled. There as no way he was going to be able to avoid having his fingerprints taken.

Yiorgo smiled happily and slapped Takkis on the back. 'We've got him! The only prints on that syringe are his.'

'Are you certain?'

'Absolutely. Look for yourself.'

Takkis compared the papers and agreed with Yiorgo. 'There's only one problem,' he demurred. 'We can prove that he handled the syringe, but we can't prove he put the heroin inside or laced the chocolates.'

Yiorgo sighed. 'I know. If we pull him in, he'll simply say he found it in the drawer and picked it up. We need that girl. See what she has to say about the situation.'

'Maybe if we ran a check on his prints we could find out a bit more about his background. There could be something there that we could use to twist his arm a bit.'

'It's worth a try, but somehow I don't think we'll find anything. I'll contact Athens and get them to run them through. What about Anders and Frida, shall we do those at the same time?'

'Might as well. See what it is they're hiding.'

1991
July

Joseph waited across the road from the travel agency each day when it was time for Thalia to leave for lunch, but there was no sign of her. Each evening he would ride his bike to the road where she had lived with her father and park at the corner in the hope that she would return to the house. No lights showed and he had returned to the warehouse annoyed and frustrated until Thursday. He had been waiting no more than half an hour when he saw Lakkis draw up and she climbed out of the car.

'Telephone me when you're ready,' called Lakkis after her and she nodded and waved her hand.

Joseph immediately revved his motorcycle and drove off. He did not want Lakkis to see him hanging around Thalia's house. He drove round in a circle, finally returning to the road and could see no sign of Lakkis. Prudently he parked the motorcycle on the opposite side of the road and walked openly up to her door.

Thalia opened at his knock and smiled when she saw her visitor. Joseph stood hesitantly on the doorstep.

'I wanted to come and say how sorry I was to hear about your father.'

Thalia's eyes' filled with tears. 'Thank you,' she said.

'I didn't mean to upset you.' Joseph pushed the door open wider and stepped inside, closing it behind him. 'I went to the travel shop and they said you were having some time off or I would not have troubled you at home.'

'How did you know where I lived?'

Joseph shrugged. 'Pure chance. I happened to be passing one day as you were opening your door.'

'I'm staying with my aunt and uncle at present. I've only come this evening to check on the house and collect some clean clothes.'

'That was lucky for me, then. I was passing and saw your light was on. I thought I would take a chance that you were in.'

Thalia stood in the hallway hesitantly. Should she offer Joseph a beer or ask him to leave? Joseph sensed her indecision.

'Maybe I could stay for a few minutes and have a beer?'

'Of course.' Thalia led the way into the kitchen and opened the fridge, handing him a bottle of beer whilst she searched for an opener.

Joseph walked back into the living room and sat down in an easy chair, whilst Thalia sat opposite on the sofa. He regarded her cautiously. He must be careful and gain her complete confidence.

'Is there anything I could do to help you?' he asked. 'You know, the kind of jobs your father used to do, clean the windows, sweep the yard, odd jobs.'

Thalia smiled at him. 'That's so kind of you to offer, but everything is fine at the moment.'

'Will you continue to live here – alone?'

Thalia nodded. 'I have to. I could not possibly live with my aunt and uncle until I get married. My aunt means so well, but she stifles me with affection and care.'

'What about your uncle?'

'He's very good to me. He has insisted I spend some time down at his hotel in Faliraki.' She gave a little laugh. 'It isn't just for a holiday; he wants me to be a companion to a girl who's staying there.'

Joseph frowned. 'If she needs a companion why did she come on holiday alone?'

'She didn't. She came on Mr Dimitris's boat. Uncle Lakkis has taken her down to the hotel to stay as she hasn't been well. The medicine she has to take gives her a problem with her memory. My uncle is worried that she might wander off and get lost.'

'So you are her keeper?'

'Not really. We just spend the day at the pool or on the beach. I walk round the shops with her at the hotel. I just have to make sure she doesn't start wandering off into the town.'

'What is she like?'

'Very beautiful. She's American and great fun to be with. I met her before when I went on board for dinner – with my father.' Thalia's voice broke.

Joseph moved over and sat beside her on the sofa, placing his arm round her shoulders and giving her a little squeeze. 'I wish there was something I could do to help.'

Thalia looked at him with moist eyes. 'I shall get over it in time. It was just so unexpected.'

'Maybe this is why your uncle has asked this American woman to stay at the hotel. I don't expect she has a memory problem at all; it is to help you relax and feel better. What's her name?'

'Suzanna.'

Joseph raised his eyebrows and made no comment. He would take a little ride down to Faliraki and see what he could find out. He squeezed Thalia's shoulders again.

'Maybe you would like to come out to dinner with me one night?'

Thalia shook her head. 'Thank you, Joseph, but I can't.'

'Why not?'

'I am getting married in October. I can't go out to dinner with a young man unescorted.'

Joseph scowled. 'You are sitting here with me. You are quite safe and there is no one around. There's no reason why you shouldn't come out to dinner with me.'

Thalia shook her head again.

'Please,' begged Joseph. 'Think about it. We can go to a restaurant in town and I will see you safely home afterwards.' He could sense that Thalia was wavering. 'If there's nothing I can do for you, I'll go now. I'll call in on Saturday evening and we can discuss that dinner date again.'

He squeezed her shoulders again and placed a light kiss on her cheek. The blood rushed to Thalia's face and she stood up hurriedly.

'It was very good of you to call, Joseph.'

'It was no trouble. I'll see you on Saturday.'

Thalia watched him as he left the house. He was so kind and thoughtful. Maybe she would ask Suzanna if she should go out to dinner with him.

'Any advance on the fingerprints?' asked Yiorgo.

Takkis nodded. 'We have the background on Frida and Anders. Frida has served time for blackmail. The usual sort of thing, pay me and I won't tell your wife you've been sleeping with me. Anders's never had a conviction, but he left the navy rather abruptly after a brawl that resulted in the death of a seaman. All the signs were that he was the culprit, but nothing could be proved.'

'And Dimitris Stephanotis?'

'They're still working on that. Nothing found at the moment.'

'Why am I surprised!' remarked Yiorgo.

'I still wish we could find that girl.'

Yiorgo shrugged. 'I don't honestly think she had anything to do with Nikos's death. If he hadn't had a craving for chocolate he would still be alive now.' He placed his fingertips together. 'Whatever the reason for having heroin in the chocolates I'm sure it was not meant for him. Why not send him a box? I'm convinced that he saw them and couldn't resist the temptation.'

'So what do we do whilst we're waiting for Athens to come up with anything on the fingerprint front?'

'We have a choice. We can sit down at Mandraki and drink coffee all day whilst we watch for any sign of suspicious activity on board the *'Aegean Pride'*, which I personally think would be a waste of time. Alternatively we could take a little boat trip round the island and see what the possibilities are of secluded bays where drugs could be off loaded.'

Takkis frowned. 'There are probably hundreds of them.'

Yiorgo nodded. 'Very likely. What we will be looking for is somewhere that is accessible for a small fishing boat, has some convenient storage facility and a reasonable road for transporting them on to their intended destination.'

'It's a better option that sitting at the harbour,' agreed Takkis.

Lambros offered to arrange the police motor launch, but Yiorgo refused. 'We don't want to advertise that we're around. We need someone who knows the area, but with an unmarked boat. We want to look like tourists.'

Lambros nodded. 'Whatever you say. I'll speak to Alexis and see if he can be relieved of his duties.'

'Who is Alexis?'

'He works on the patrol boat and has a boat of his own.'

'Provided he can keep his mouth shut, he sounds ideal.'

'He can,' Lambros assured him.

An hour later the three men motored out of the harbour and began to cruise down the west side of the island. Yiorgo and Takkis held binoculars to their eyes. The shoreline between the small towns was flat and deserted. Twice Yiorgo asked Alexis to take them in closer, but as they neared the shore it became obvious that no boat, however small could land due to the submerged rocks that effectively blocked their passage.

Further down the coastline became more rugged. Cliffs dropped down into small, secluded bays that were totally inaccessible from the shore. In two of them a boat was moored and holidaymakers were swimming. Takkis made a note of the names of the craft for them to check out their authenticity when they returned to the town.

Small islands, hardly more than rocks, loomed up and Yiorgo consulted his map. The largest island, Alimia, boasted a small town. Alexis headed in that direction, but Yiorgo shook his head.

'An ideal place possibly for dropping anything off, but you still have to get them to the mainland.'

'I think we're going too far down,' demurred Takkis. 'If a Turkish boat came this far down into Greek waters he would be noticed and challenged.'

'Not if he was flying a Greek flag.'

Alexis entered the conversation. 'If we saw a Turkish boat flying a Greek flag in our waters we would immediately stop it and demand an explanation. A few metres inside our area would be a genuine mistake, but if they came this far it would mean they were up to no good.'

'Suppose they came in at night? Maybe with the name covered over?'

'The patrol would spot them.'

'But the patrol is not in this area every night.'

Alexis pursed his lips. It was true. The patrol could not be everywhere. 'Do you want me to continue or turn back?'

'We'll go on for another hour; then I'm inclined to agree with Takkis. It would be too far down the island to be feasible.'

Alexis nodded. He was quite happy to be out on the water. It was a beautiful day and he was avoiding his monotonous daytime duties.

For a further half an hour they motored down the coast, until Yiorgo held up his hand. 'I'd like to go in closer here, Alexis.'

Alexis slowed the engine and they cruised slowly into the bay. The two men surveyed the scene, taking in the few isolated buildings and the boats pulled up on the narrow strip of beach, glimpses of a road could be seen, winding its way through cultivated land.

'Where are we, Alexis?'

Alexis placed a finger on the map before him. 'It's a farming area.'

Yiorgo nodded slowly. 'This is the first place I've seen that fits what we've been looking for. I think we could stay and do a bit of fishing, Takkis.' He picked up a rod and balanced it against the side of the boat. 'We'll move on in about half an hour when we haven't caught anything.' Yiorgo trained his binoculars on the land. 'What's that building?'

Alexis looked at the white concrete building, the perimeter walls topped with wire netting. There were no windows visible. He shrugged 'A storage area I presume.'

'A very secure one, by the look of it,' commented Yiorgo.

Takkis continued to monitor the coastline and fields through the binoculars. There was little sign of activity that he could see. A three-wheeled vehicle wound its way slowly up the mountainous road, turning off into a field where two figures could be seen picking crops. 'All very quiet and innocent,' he remarked.

Yiorgo nodded. 'Depending on local developments we could take a little motor trip tomorrow. Do a bit of exploring and end up lost down here. We might have to ask whoever we can find around for directions, maybe for a bit of hospitality if there isn't a taverna.' He grinned. 'I have a feel about this place.'

Thalia told Sorrell about the visit she had received from Joseph. She stressed how kind he had been to her and asked Sorrell whether she should accept his invitation to dinner.

Sorrell smiled to herself. Unless Joseph had changed drastically since she had last seen him she had no doubt what plan he had in mind for Thalia. It could be an ideal way to get her revenge on both Joseph and the girl's uncle, whom Sorrell both feared and hated. Once Lakkis found out what Joseph had done to his niece he would be after Joseph's blood, quite literally.

'There's no harm in going out to dinner with him. You've been meeting him for coffee. It simply means you will be spending a little longer in his company,' Sorrell assured her.

Thalia considered. 'You don't think Manolis would mind?'

'Don't tell him,' answered Sorrell immediately. 'Have you told him you've been going for coffee?'

Thalia shook her head. 'It didn't seem important.'

'And neither is going to dinner. Just because you're betrothed to someone doesn't mean you have to tell him everything. Do you want to borrow a dress of mine to wear?'

'Thank you, but no. I have something suitable.'

'I shall look forward to hearing about it afterwards.'

Thalia's face fell. 'I doubt if I shall be seeing you. I return to work on Monday. I can't have any more time off, whatever Uncle Lakkis says.'

'You mean I shall be on my own down here?' Sorrell was truly alarmed at the prospect.

'I don't know. Maybe you will go back to the boat if you're feeling better.'

'Feeling better? There's nothing wrong with me.'

Thalia bit at her lip. 'Uncle Lakkis said that you have been ill and have memory lapses and suffer from delusions.'

Sorrell snorted. 'There are some things I would prefer to forget,' she murmured.

Yiorgo and Takkis returned to the police station to make arrangements to borrow a car the following day. Lambros handed them a message that had been sent from Athens and Yiorgo read it eagerly before handing it to Takkis.

'What does that mean? They cannot find any trace of fingerprints on record for Dimitris Stephanotis. The fingerprints we sent belong to Christos Drakonisis.'

Takkis scratched his ear and shrugged. 'Maybe the girl we think we are looking for is a man?'

Yiorgo snorted in disgust. 'That girl we interviewed was no man! I know they do sex change operations in America, but I can't believe she was the result of one. No,' Yiorgo shook his head. 'There's a good deal more to this than we originally thought.'

Takkis drove whilst Yiorgo read the map and crossed off each town and village as they passed through. They stopped briefly at Kamiros for coffee, then proceeded to climb up the mountain road, marvelling at the view they had across the sea.

'There are those islands,' said Yiorgo and lifted the binoculars to his eyes. The small village could be seen on Alimia and he studied it carefully. 'Maybe we should go over there and have a look around.'

Takkis shrugged and concentrated on negotiating the curves and bends of the road. 'Personally I think everyone would know if anything underhand was going on. It would be too risky.'

'What do you mean?'

'Everyone would know each other. If you fell out with your neighbour and he suspected you were up to something illegal he'd tell the police out of spite.'

Yiorgo nodded slowly. 'You've got a point there. Slow down a bit, there should be a turning soon down to that bay.'

Takkis obeyed and swung the car to the right. The road twisted and turned, giving views of cultivated fields and ruined buildings, with occasional glimpses of the sea far below.

'I think we ought to have a look and see what's in these buildings.'

Takkis drew to a halt, parking the car as close to the ditch as he dared. Together they edged their way round the field and peered into the stone building. A selection of farming implements was stacked against the wall and Yiorgo shrugged.

'I don't fancy going through all this. There must be a dozen such buildings. It would take all day, besides which, we have no search warrant. The locals would be up in arms.'

Takkis nodded. He had no wish to spend his time sifting through tools in the dark interior. He had a nasty suspicion that rats could be lurking in the dark corners and he had a horror of the vermin.

They returned to the car and slowly continued their descent, until the road suddenly gave them a choice of direction.

'Which way?' asked Takkis.

'Right,' said Yiorgo decisively. 'There's that building along there. We'll stop and see if there's anyone around. We can always ask for directions and see if we can get the occupant to chat.'

Takkis followed his directions. The gate was open leading into a small courtyard. On one side was an area with a makeshift roof where a quantity of small boxes were stored and opposite was a low building that looked like a house and they drew up outside Christos's door. He looked out from his window suspiciously. The car clearly displayed the name of a rental company. They must be tourists.

Yiorgo climbed out and stretched. Both men walked over to where two heavy wooden gates shut off the steps that led down to a rocky beach. Yiorgo pushed at the gates that were chained and padlocked and through the crack he made he could see the beach. The stones were like small boulders and a narrow path had been cleared to give access to the sea.

'I wouldn't fancy swimming here,' remarked Takkis. 'Far too many rocks; your legs could be ripped to bits.'

Yiorgo leant against the tree that shaded the patch of dirt in front of the building. He gazed around, noting the sheer cliffs that ringed the bay and the few buildings on the level ground that appeared to be occupied.

'A pretty isolated place to live. Shall we knock and see if there's anyone at home?'

Christos saw them coming and sighed. He hated being interrupted when he was busy weighing heroin for the packets. He covered his scales with a cloth and went to answer their knock at the door.

'Can I help you?'

Yiorgo smiled easily. 'I hope so. We've driven down from the town and thought we'd be able to have a swim down here. It was so hot at Kamiros.'

Christos frowned. 'This isn't a good place for a swim. You need to go back to the main road and drive further down.'

'Yes, we've realised that. I suppose you haven't got a beer you would sell us? I'm parched and stupidly we didn't bring any water with us. We didn't expect to be driving through such deserted countryside.'

Christos nodded and opened the door wider. 'Go through and I'll bring you one.'

Yiorgo and Takkis entered the small living room and each took a seat. Christos reappeared with three cold beers from the fridge and uncapped them. At the rate he gave out beers each week to tourists who lost their way he really should open a bar down there.

The three men raised their bottles, Yiorgo and Takkis taking a long draught.

'Pretty isolated isn't it, living down here?' said Yiorgo.

Christos shrugged. 'I'm used to it.'

'What do you do with yourself?'

'I drive the produce up to the town.'

'What about the other people who live round here? What do they do?'

'They farm the land. Considering how rocky it is and close to the sea the land is good for farming.'

Takkis nodded. 'We noticed on the way down. What are all those little buildings for?'

'They keep their tools in them. You don't want to have to keep hauling your tools around with you each time you go to work.'

'Practical,' agreed Takkis.

Christos nodded. He was tired of their small talk and wished they would go so he could continue with his weighing and packing.

'How many people live and work here?' asked Yiorgo.

'No one actually lives down here. They only come down during the summer.'

'Really? Why's that?'

'You can't do much in the fields when it rains in the winter. There's nothing else to do round here so why should they stay.'

'Do they stay down here during the summer?'

'Occasionally. Usually they go back to their families at the end of the day.

'I see. There isn't even a general store. Do you do the same?'

Christos nodded. 'There would be no point in staying here at night.' He drained his bottle and placed it deliberately on the table, hoping the two men would take the hint.

Yiorgo followed suit. 'Could I use your toilet before we leave, do you think?'

Christos nodded and led the way out of the door towards the lean to at the back of the house. In a trice Takkis was on his feet and in the kitchen looking around swiftly. The furnishings were sparse. A double-ringed gas burner stood on a worktop next to the sink and on the shelves above stood a couple of saucepans and some plates. Stuck into an empty jar was the cutlery. The table on the other side of the room had something covered over and he lifted the edge of the cloth quickly. Hiding underneath was a small pair of scales, small packets and a scoop. He dropped the cloth back into place and was standing at the kitchen door as Christos returned.

'I'll make use of your facilities also,' he smiled. 'How much do we owe you?'

'Nothing. I often get travellers dropping by and they are always in need of a drink.'

'Why don't you open a taverna,' suggested Takkis.

'I've thought of it, but I doubt it would be worth it.'

'Wouldn't the farmers come in the evening?'

'Maybe, but why should they pay extra to sit and drink here when they can do so in their own homes.'

'Very true.'

Takkis made good his escape to the toilet, whilst Yiorgo thanked Christos for his hospitality and also offered to pay for the beer they had consumed.

They drove away, waving cheerfully and commenced the long drive back to the main road.

'Well?' asked Yiorgo impatiently as soon as they had rounded the first bend.

'He's our man. I saw the scales in the kitchen. He was obviously busy weighing up when we arrived.'

Yiorgo smiled delightedly. 'We're actually getting somewhere at last.'

'We need to know where he delivers.'

Yiorgo nodded. 'That shouldn't be too difficult.'

Joseph planned carefully for his dinner with Thalia. He booked a table for Monday evening at a small taverna in the old town, knowing that it was one popular with tourists and would be crowded. Late in the afternoon he purchased a bouquet of flowers, choosing ones that were naturally highly scented and placed them in his sink to keep them fresh. Next to them he laid the packet containing a small dose of heroin. He just hoped his experiment would work.

At eight thirty he knocked on Thalia's door, complimented her on her appearance, and told her where he planned for them to eat.

'That's an expensive place, Joseph.'

'If you were my girl nowhere would be too expensive for you,' he smiled and held up his hand as she was about to remind him that she was betrothed. 'I know; you're not my girl. I just want to pretend for one evening.'

Thalia laughed with him. Sorrell had convinced her there was no harm in joining Joseph on a dinner date and she was determined to enjoy herself.

Despite the fact that the taverna was busy, Joseph managed to obtain excellent service. He plied Thalia with wine, whilst drinking sparingly himself. After her third glass she had giggled and accused him of trying to make her drunk, which he had denied vehemently whilst topping up her glass again.

It was nearly midnight when Joseph finally paid the bill and they began to walk along the cobbled streets towards the main gate. Halfway there Joseph stopped in consternation.

'I forgot your flowers!'

'What do you mean?'

'I bought a bunch of flowers for you and meant to bring them to your house.' He took her hand and turned her in the opposite direction. 'We'll drop by and get them. We can go out by the other gate.'

Unresisting Thalia accompanied him and they clattered their way down the cobbles until they reached the warehouse. Joseph unlocked the door and ushered Thalia inside. He switched on the light and directed her towards the stairs.

'You can go up if you like or wait here. I need to wrap them up. I left them in the sink to keep them fresh.'

Thalia led the way up the wooden stairs and looked around Joseph's room curiously. 'I've never been up here,' she said.

'I like it,' Joseph answered as he took the flowers and wrapped them in piece of paper. 'Sit down. Would you like some coffee?'

'No, it's late, I really must go home, Joseph.'

'Whatever you say.'

Without argument Joseph led the way back down to the warehouse, carrying the flowers in the crook of his arm. He slipped his hand into Thalia's as they reached the Athanasiou Gate. Thalia yawned and Joseph squeezed her fingers. 'Soon be home.'

At her door Joseph hesitated. 'Could I come in just for a moment? I really need the bathroom.'

'Of course.' Thalia pointed out the room to him. 'Would you like a coffee?'

'That would be great,' called back Joseph as he sprinkled the powder into a flower, flushed the unused toilet, rinsed his hands and emerged.

He entered the kitchen and handed the bunch to her. 'Smell this one. I've finally found out which one has been scenting everywhere out since I bought them.'

He thrust the flower beneath her nose and she dutifully bent her head and inhaled.

'They're beautiful, thank you.'

'Are they all scented? I just asked the florist to select whatever was on offer.'

As Joseph had hoped Thalia sniffed at the bouquet again. She gave a little giggle. 'I feel quite light headed. I must have had too much wine.'

Joseph shook his head. 'Not at all. I'll finish making the coffee. You'll soon feel better. You just sit there and continue to smell your flowers.' He pulled a chair from the kitchen table and she sat obediently.

Joseph pretended to busy himself preparing coffee whilst watching Thalia. She leant back in the chair and closed her eyes.

'I do feel strange, Joseph.'

He went over to her and took the flowers, placing them on the table. 'How do you feel?'

Thalia stretched and opened her eyes. 'I can't describe it, sort of floating, like I'm in a dream, yet I feel wide awake.'

Joseph bent and kissed her full on her lips and was gratified to feel her response. He pulled her to her feet and enfolded her in his arms, crushing her to him.

'Joseph!' She tried to wriggle free, but he held her firmly and she could feel him undoing her dress, whilst he continued to kiss her face, her hair, her neck.

Slowly he pulled the dress off her shoulders and she did not resist as he drew the straps over her arms and it fell to the floor. He continued to hold her whilst he deftly undid her bra and began to kiss her naked breasts. With his free hand he unbuttoned his shirt and shrugged himself out of it.

'Joseph, no,' Thalia managed to murmur, as his naked chest pressed against hers and he turned his attention to his trousers.

'Oh, yes, Thalia. You know you want me.' He scooped her up in his arms and opened the door to her bedroom, placed her on the bed, removing the last of his clothes rapidly and joining her. He eased her panties lower and began investigating and caressing her with his fingers whilst he continued to kiss her breasts.

Thalia was unable to resist responding to his attentions. Her body seemed totally out of her control. All she knew was she wanted a release from this wonderful, exhilarating feeling that had built up inside her and was threatening to explode any moment. When Joseph entered her she cried out and he smiled grimly. He had accomplished what he had planned to do, not only had he enjoyed making love to the girl, he knew he had taken her virginity before she married Manolis.

Lakkis thumped the table before him and almost shouted down the telephone at Dimitris. 'I can't keep her any longer. Thalia has had to return to work and I can't spend my time escorting her around, nor can I keep her locked in her room all day.'

Dimitris frowned. 'She can't come back to the boat yet. The police are still snooping around.'

Lakkis sighed. 'I'll manage the girl for a couple more days. Let me know when you've arranged other accommodation for her.' He replaced the telephone and sat deep in thought. He had enjoyed himself with the girl during the evenings, excusing his late return to his wife as pressure of work whilst Dimitris was staying at the island. He would speak to Thalia that evening and see if she would be able to arrange for some more time off work.

He was surprised when the telephone rang again almost immediately and it was his wife requesting that he came home at once.

'I can't come home now. I'm at work.'

'You have to come home, Lakkis,' she insisted. 'It's Thalia and it's very urgent. There's something wrong with her. I need you here, Lakkis.'

With a sigh Lakkis informed his office staff that he had to return to Rhodes town and he hoped to be back shortly. He hurried up to the top floor and into Sorrell's room. Hurriedly he gave her an injection and left a plate of food covered on the side. 'I can't stop,' he informed her. 'I'll try to get back later.'

Sorrell looked at him with large, terrified eyes. 'What happens if you don't get back? What about my injection?'

'You'll just have to wait until the morning. You'll live.' He closed the door and locked it without a second thought.

Lakkis was not prepared for the white faced, evidently nervous girl who was waiting at his house.

'What's wrong? Has something happened at work?'

Thalia passed a trembling hand over her forehead. 'I'm just not feeling well. I didn't go into work. I came here to be with Aunt Maria.'

Lakkis looked at his wife. 'How long has she been here?'

'She arrived just after you'd left for work.' Maria wrung her hands. 'There's something terribly wrong and she won't tell me.'

Lakkis took Thalia's chin in his hand and turned her face up towards him. 'I want to know, Thalia. I am your guardian now your father is dead. I have a right to know if you have a problem. I shall be your father-in-law in a few months. You can always trust me to help you.'

Thalia's eyes filled with tears. 'I can't tell you.'

Lakkis pushed her into the nearest chair. 'I insist that you tell me.'

Thalia shook her head. 'No.' Thalia lifted distressed eyes to her uncle's face. 'I just can't marry Manolis.'

Lakkis placed an arm round her shoulders and he felt her

stiffen beneath his touch. 'What do you mean? You can't marry Manolis. Your wedding is all arranged.'

'He wouldn't want me now.'

Lakkis frowned. 'What do you mean? Of course Manolis wants to marry you.'

'Not now,' she whispered.

Lakkis turned his niece to face him. 'What are you talking about, Thalia?'

'Something happened.' She buried her face in her hands. 'I am so ashamed.'

'You must tell me whatever it is that has happened. How can I help you if I do not know the problem?'

'I let someone – have me – last night.' She broke into a torrent of sobbing. 'I didn't mean it to happen.' It had taken all her courage to make her way to her uncle's house and now he was here with her she did not know how to tell him Joseph had seduced her.

Stunned Lakkis enfolded his niece in his arms.

'I didn't mean to do it, honestly, uncle.'

Lakkis patted her shoulder. 'Just tell me what happened.'

'I went out to dinner last night. I thought he was just being kind to me, he was so nice.'

'Who did you go to dinner with?'

'Joseph.' She spoke his name in a whisper.

'Joseph!'

'He told me how sorry he was to hear about my father and asked me to go out to dinner with him. I said no at first, then I talked to Suzanna, and she said there was no reason not to go out to dinner with anyone just because I was betrothed.'

Lakkis struck his head. It was his fault for arranging for Thalia to spend a week with the girl. No doubt she had known what Joseph would do to his niece and saw it as retribution for the indignities he had inflicted upon her.

Thalia continued in a low voice. 'He took me to a lovely restaurant in the old town and I really enjoyed being there with him. He was good company and we laughed and talked. It was quite late when we left and he said he would walk me home. We had just started on our way when he said he had forgotten the flowers he had bought me and we went to the warehouse for them and left by the Athanasiou Gate. He wrapped up the flowers and walked back to my house. When we reached there he asked if he could come in to use the bathroom. I didn't see any harm in it.'

Maria stroked her niece's hand and Lakkis poured himself a brandy, took a mouthful, then handed it to Thalia and poured another glass for himself.

'I asked him if he would like a coffee and he agreed. I had just put it on when he gave me the flowers. They were beautiful.' Thalia's voice broke again. 'They had a lovely perfume and I smelt them. Then I began to feel strange. I thought I had drunk too much wine, but I'd only had three glasses. Joseph told me to sit down and said he would make the coffee. I began to feel as though I was floating, nothing seemed real, the flowers seemed to grow larger; they seemed to be talking to me.' Thalia took a gulp of the brandy and choked. When she had finished coughing she looked at her uncle. 'I think, maybe, he gave me something. He started to kiss me, and – and – do things to me.'

Lakkis stood up. 'Tell Maria exactly what he did to you, everything.' He strode out of the room and stood outside the door to ensure he heard every word she said.

Maria rocked her niece gently. 'Where did he touch you?'

'All over. He took my clothes off!'

'Did he undress himself?'

Thalia nodded.

'And then?'

'He put me on my bed and – it happened.'

'Did you try to stop him?'

'I did at first, when he started to kiss me, then I couldn't.'

'Why couldn't you?' asked Maria sharply.

Thalia shook her head. 'I don't know. Everything seemed so wonderful. It was as if I was in a dream, as though it wasn't really happening to me.'

Maria pursed her lips. She patted Thalia gently who lifted imploring eyes to her aunt.

'Tell me it wasn't true.'

'Where were you when you woke up this morning?'

'At home. On my bed.'

'Can you remember anything more? Anything Joseph said?'

Thalia shook her head. 'I don't remember anything after Joseph – did it to me.'

Lakkis re-entered the room and Thalia realised he had heard every word.

'How did you feel when you woke up?' he asked.

'Terrible.'

'Tell me, exactly.'

Thalia frowned. 'I was cold and shivering. I felt bruised all over, but my skin felt odd, itchy. I had a shower and I felt better after I'd had some coffee, but my head still aches and I keep trembling and shaking.'

Lakkis nodded grimly and sat down beside her again. 'I want the doctor to have a look at you. There's nothing to worry about. I just want to make sure you are perfectly all right. I'll ask him to come here and Maria can talk to him, explain the situation. I'll have a word with him afterwards.'

Thalia tried to protest, but he would have none of it.

'I insist.'

'You're not cross with me, Uncle?' she asked timidly.

Lakkis shook his head. 'You were not to know. Maria, take Thalia up to the room she used when she stayed here. I'll 'phone the doctor.' He watched the two women leave the room and clenched his fists. Joseph would pay for this.

Lakkis waited impatiently until the doctor had finished his

examination and beckoned him into the living room as he came down the stairs.

'How is she?'

'Physically she's perfectly all right. No internal cuts or bruising.' The doctor looked at Lakkis with a penetrating gaze. 'Your wife implied that she had been raped. There was certainly no sign that she was taken by force.'

Lakkis waved his hand. 'She was drugged.'

The doctor raised his eyebrows. 'What makes you think that?'

'She went out to dinner with a young man. He escorted her home and said he needed the bathroom. She obviously let him in and offered him coffee. He had brought her some flowers and she said that after smelling them she began to feel strange. The symptoms she described are of someone who was drugged.'

The doctor raised his eyebrows. 'Are you a medical man?'

'No, but I know the effect drugs have on the body.'

'Mr Pavlides, if you are seriously suggesting that your niece was drugged and raped it is a matter for the police. By the medical evidence presented to me I cannot confirm that rape took place, only intercourse.' The doctor shrugged. 'As I said, physically the girl is unharmed. I have given her something to make her sleep. I imagine that when she awakes she will just feel rather embarrassed about making so much fuss.'

Lakkis regarded the doctor steadily. 'My niece does not lie. If this were a simple case of a young girl being seduced I would say no more. I know she was drugged, and the person who was responsible will very soon find they regret committing such an irresponsible act.'

The doctor frowned. 'I urge you not to act hastily. I suggest you speak to your niece again when she wakes up. She may tell you a rather different story then.'

'I doubt it. Thank you for coming – doctor.'

Lakkis added the man's title as an afterthought and slammed the door behind him. He returned to the lounge where he finished his glass of brandy and then drank the one he had poured for Thalia. Joseph would suffer.

Maria entered the lounge timidly. 'Thalia is sleeping, Lakkis. What shall we do?'

'Do? There's nothing we can do.'

'What about Manolis?'

Lakkis shook his head decidedly. 'There is no need to tell Manolis. I will talk to Thalia when she has recovered. The wedding will go ahead.'

Maria bit her lip. She was not sure that Manolis should be kept in ignorance. Suppose he found out at a later date? She dared not argue with her husband.

'You are to stay with her,' Lakkis ordered. 'When she wakes you must talk to her, see what else she can tell you about the incident. I have to get back to the hotel. I have business there to attend to.'

Lakkis entered Sorrell's room and found her prowling around like a caged animal. 'You cannot keep me a prisoner,' she immediately remonstrated. 'I demand that I am allowed out.'

Lakkis sat down on the side of the bed. 'Because of you my niece has been raped.'

'Because of me?'

'You told her she should go out to dinner with Joseph.'

Sorrell shrugged. 'I said there was no harm in going out to dinner with anyone.' Inwardly she exulted. She could see how the news had affected Lakkis and she was delighted. It served him right for the way he had treated her.

Lakkis grabbed a handful of her hair and placed his face close to hers. 'Joseph will find out what happens to people who upset me. Remember that.' He released her and pushed her away. 'You will stay in this room until I decide where it is suitable to send you.'

'Send me? What do you mean?'

Lakkis ignored her questions. 'I will bring up some more food for you. I have arrangements to make.'

'What arrangements?'

Lakkis regarded her coldly with his green cat-like eyes. 'You will find out.'

Yiorgo and Takkis sifted through their notes and Yiorgo made a cryptic list.

'We really have very little firm evidence. We know Nikos died from an overdose of heroin. Heroin was found in the chocolates on board the *'Aegean Pride'*, Dimitris Stephanotis's boat. The chocolates are supposed to belong to the American girl who has disappeared. Most drug arrests on this island have been centred on the *'Aegean Gem'*, a hotel owned by Dimitris Stephanotis. We know where the drug is being packaged. We need some direct links. I know he's involved. I also know there's something staring us in the face that we're missing.'

'I'd like to find out a good deal more about that man Dimitris. Athens still hasn't come up with any more information, have they?'

Yiorgo shook his head. 'If we could get him into custody we might be able to persuade him to talk.' He smiled grimly.

'I think we need to watch that bay, see if we can find out when that man receives delivery and who from.'

'I'd rather find out who he's delivering it to after he's finished the packaging.' Yiorgo frowned. 'I think we're going to have to ask Lambros to help us with a bit of surveillance work.'

'You can't follow anyone up that road without them knowing,' observed Takkis.

'No, but you could have someone waiting at the top who could follow him, see where he goes to make his deliveries.'

'Well that rules both of us out. He'd recognise us immediately.'

'Exactly. That's why we need to speak to Lambros.'

Lakkis drove away from the hotel in Faliraki towards the small town of Afandou. He knew the men he wanted to find and exactly what he was going to ask them to do. He drove slowly down to the beach and parked his car next to the mobile cafeteria where Stelios worked. Stelios regarded him warily as he approached.

Lakkis pretended to study the hand written menu of snacks available until the two customers before him had been served and left. 'I've a job for you and Makkis.' He leaned closer to the man and explained exactly what he had in mind.

Stelios nodded. 'You can rely on us.'

Lakkis eyed the man coldly. 'I hope so. Give me a bottle of water.'

Stelios handed over the bottle without a word. Lakkis always asked for him and his brother when he had a little bit of intimidation planned for someone who was not keeping in line and the pay would be good.

Lambros listened carefully to Yiorgo instructions. 'I suggest we use a number of different hire cars. One will pretend to be broken down a short distance from the turn off and another has stopped to help. As soon as the van emerges, one driver leaves, ostensibly to get help for the stricken motorist. Assuming the van makes for Rhodes town there is just the one main road and we can have another car waiting at Kamiros to take up the tail. It will be more difficult in the town, but there are so many hire cars around at this time of year that he's unlikely to take much notice if he keeps seeing the same one. Tourists frequently get caught up in the one way system and go round a number of times.'

Takkis frowned. 'How do we find out exactly what he has delivered? We can't very well march in and demand to examine the goods without alerting him.'

Lambros smiled. 'This week you find out where he delivers. Next week you can have men waiting at the various places to undertake a search if necessary. There is always the possibility that he does not do the delivery, but that someone collects from him. Had you considered that alternative?'

Yiorgo nodded. 'The men at the top of the turn off can cover that. Make a note of anyone who goes down. We should be able to discount hire cars, but ask them to record their details anyway.'

Lambros nodded. He had read about surveillance duties, but he had never before been asked to carry them out.

Cautiously Lakkis made his way along Mandraki harbour. Twice he strolled past Dimitris's boat before he decided there was no one watching it. Now he sat in the cabin, a glass of ouzo before him and discussed the problem that Sorrell was now presenting to him.

'I can't keep her there any longer. She's been locked in today and Thalia is unable to come down. I can't keep her a prisoner indefinitely. Sooner or later she will find a way to bring attention to herself and I don't want to have to explain to the police why she's there.'

'Take her to your house.'

'Don't be stupid, Dimitris. I can't take her to my house and keep her a prisoner there. Goodness knows what stories she would tell Maria.'

Dimitris smiled. He had a very good idea of the kind of stories the girl would be able to tell Lakkis's wife. He stroked his chin and frowned. 'Suppose she was taken down to Christos's place? She could roam around outside there. No one would see her because of the walls. Provided he keeps the gates locked there is no way she could get out and there's no one around whose attention she could attract.'

Lakkis considered the idea. 'I suppose it would be possible for a few days.'

'Don't worry. At the end of the week you can deliver her to Joseph. I shall have left Rhodes.'

'Have the police said you can go?'

'Not yet, but I'm tired of sitting here. If they do not give me permission to leave I shall take a ferry.'

Lakkis pursed his lips. 'They'll look for you.'

'They can look, but I doubt very much that they will find me,' Dimitris smiled confidently. 'I know how to disappear.'

Lakkis returned to the hotel at Faliraki and went straight up to the room occupied by Sorrell. She cringed away from him as he entered and he smiled.

'Come here and say hello to me properly.'

Sorrell neither answered nor moved.

'Come here,' barked Lakkis.

Slowly Sorrell slid off the bed and stood before him. He gripped her arm viciously. 'If you behave yourself you may find you have some new accommodation tomorrow.'

'I'm going back to the boat?'

'No. You will be going to stay with a friend of mine. He has a house in a very secluded bay far from any town or village. There will be no need to keep you locked in a room during the day as there is nowhere for you to go. Besides, if you did decide to go off on your own where would you find a supplier? Imagine how you would be feeling after twenty-four hours. It would take you far longer than that to walk to the nearest habitation. Provided you behave yourself you will be able to lounge outside as you please during the day. Regrettably you will have to be confined whenever he has to leave on business and over night.'

'How long do I have to stay there?'

Lakkis shrugged. 'A few days.'

Sorrell swallowed hard. Her mouth felt dry. 'And will he have a supply for me?'

'There is no need for you to worry about that. Christos is quite capable of administering to your needs. He will have his instructions from me. Any bad behaviour on your part and he will conveniently forget that he needs to give it to you.' Lakkis smiled, evidently relishing the threat he was making to her. 'I regret I am unable to spend any longer with you today. I have some rather urgent business that needs to be taken care of.' He released her arm and ran his hand across her breast. 'I shall have to make up for lost time tomorrow.'

Sorrell shrank away from his touch.

Lakkis addressed an envelope with Joseph's name and slipped the letter he had written inside. He smiled grimly. That should bring the young man hurrying to the city wall for a promised assignation. He passed the warehouse in the early afternoon and checked that the doors and shutters were securely fastened before he pushed the envelope beneath the door.

Lakkis parked his car in a strategic position on the road that ran parallel with the perimeter wall of the old town. He extinguished the lights and slipped down as far as possible in the passenger seat. To anyone passing he would be almost unseen and certainly unremarkable. From his position he could see Stelios and Makkis lounging against the low wall, smoking and drinking beer. They looked no different from the many other groups and couples who did the same throughout the day and early evening.

He scanned the road ahead and checked in his side mirror anxiously. There was no guarantee which direction Joseph would walk from, or even that he had returned to the warehouse and found the note. He sighed deeply. If he did not take the bait tonight he could well try and contact Thalia himself the following day and that would cause a problem. When she denied all knowledge of the proposed meeting it would definitely put Joseph on his guard.

He looked at his watch again. He had only been there for ten minutes and it already felt like hours. He stiffened. A figure was appearing in the distance and Lakkis slid from his seat in the car, raised his hand to the two men by the wall and slipped into the shadow of the trees.

Joseph was feeling extremely pleased with himself. The note

from Thalia asking him to meet her at one in the morning had been a pleasant surprise. Obviously she had enjoyed her evening the previous week and wanted to make arrangements to repeat the experience. That would teach her uncle who had betrothed her to his son. It could be even more amusing if she decided not to marry Manolis because she preferred him. He sniggered to himself as he turned off towards the perimeter wall and then frowned in annoyance when he saw the two men lower down.

Stelios and Makkis saw the signal. Both men finished their cigarettes and tossed their beer cans over the wall. Leisurely they began to walk in Joseph's general direction. As they reached him Stelios shot out his left hand and grabbed his arm, delivering a punch to Joseph's stomach with his right fist at the same time. Makkis punched him in the ribs and Joseph doubled over.

Joseph had no way of defending himself against the onslaught. He tried to cry out, but the kicking he was receiving in his ribs meant only a low groan was emitted. He was struggling to remain conscious, whilst trying ineffectually to avoid their blows. He tried to curl his body into a ball to deflect the kicks to his ribs and stomach, only to receive them in his lower back, sending pain shooting up his spine.

The men paused for breath and hauled Joseph to his feet, making him think his ordeal was finally over. Suddenly Lakkis's face was close to his own and he could feel the man's breath on his cheek.

'Now you see how I treat people who double cross me. You should not have touched her.' A fist crashed into Joseph's face and he felt the grip on his arms tighten.

'Get rid of him.'

His legs were seized and he had a feeling of falling through space. He landed heavily, the breath knocked out of his body and blackness invading his mind.

Stelios and Makkis continued on their way. Lakkis returned to his car, slipped back into the driver's seat and started the engine.

He cruised along the road until he reached his employees, leaning through the window to hand them a thick envelope. As soon as it had been taken from his hand he revved the engine and drove on towards the junction, taking the turn off that led to his house.

Joseph regained consciousness and opened his eyes; only to close them again as nausea overtook him. He lay, sweating, waiting for the feeling to pass, conscious now that his body was battered and bruised, every breath a knife-like pain. He opened his eyes again cautiously. It was still dark, the stars were bright above him, but seemed to be moving around. He closed his eyes again.

He longed to take a deep breath, but dared not risk the excruciating pain that he now knew accompanied it. He lay there, trying to remember what had happened. Two thugs had set upon him. He thought he was going to meet Thalia. He emitted a loud groan. Lakkis had arranged it. He had been waiting for him.

Joseph drifted in and out of consciousness and the next time he dared to open his eyes he saw the sky was lightening. He also saw that he was laying in the moat of the castle and with a shock he realised he had been thrown over the wall. His head still hammered as he squinted at his surroundings. He must move and get back to the warehouse. A long hot shower was needed to relieve his aching body and some painkillers would take away the worst of the effects. His mind told him to sit up, but his body refused to obey the command. Sweat began to stand out on his forehead as he struggled mentally to overcome the physical handicap, but nothing happened. He groaned from deep inside as he realised he was paralysed from below his waist and consciousness left him once again.

'Electra! Electra! Come here!'

The dog continued to stand just out of sight in the moat, barking loudly.

'Damned dog,' grumbled Panayiotis. She knew they never

went further than this point for their early morning walk. No doubt she had found a cat sitting just out of her reach.

'Electra! Come here,' he called again.

The normally obedient bitch continued to ignore him and he quickened his pace. He would have to put her lead on and drag her back or he would be late for work. He rounded the outcrop of stones and ran to the body he saw, pushing the dog out of the way. Electra immediately stopped barking on his arrival. Panayiotis felt for a pulse and to his relief it seemed strong. He looked around him in consternation. As usual there was no one else walking in the moat at this time of the morning.

'Stay,' he said firmly to Electra and she sat obediently, wagging her tail. 'Guard.'

Electra dropped down and lay beside Joseph's body. She watched with troubled eyes as her master walked as fast as possible towards the entrance to the moat.

Panayiotis arrived panting at the gateway. He was not built for rapid movement and his face was red with sweat pouring down his cheeks, despite the early hour. A taxi driver was sitting in his cab, hoping to catch an early fare, and he approached him anxiously.

'I need help. There's a body in the moat. Fallen from the walls, I should think.'

'That's a damn fool thing for anyone to do,' remarked the driver.

'Go to the hospital. He needs an ambulance.'

The driver frowned 'Why don't I take you there? You can tell them exactly where he is.'

Panayiotis shook his head. 'I can't. My dog found him and I've left her there. You go and get help. Tell them I'm about half way along and I'll be waiting for them.'

'Who's going to pay my fare?'

'I will,' shouted Panayiotis. 'Just go, will you?'

The driver smiled. 'Keep calm, or you'll be in need of an ambulance as well.' He started his cab and Panayiotis drew in a breath of relief. He mopped his face with his handkerchief and began to retrace his steps along the moat.

Electra was still lying beside Joseph and she whined softly as her master approached. 'You're a good dog,' he said, and patted her gently.

Joseph's eyes flickered open, then widened in fear as he saw the gaping jaws of the dog only a few inches from his face. A tongue rasped down his cheek and he closed his eyes again. He was going to be attacked by a stray dog and there was nothing he could do to prevent the animal from molesting him.

'Give over, Electra. He doesn't want a wash from you.'

The man's voice seemed to come from far away and Joseph opened his eyes again. Standing over him was a portly man, who was mopping his face to clear it of the sweat that had once more accumulated and was running down his cheeks.

'Help,' whispered Joseph, weakly.

'I've already sent for it. You just lay there until the ambulance comes.' Panayiotis checked his watch. He was going to be late for work, that was obvious, but how long would he have to wait before the ambulance arrived? He lowered himself down next to Joseph. He was not at all sure what he could or should do for the young man, but felt he should stay with him. There was no obvious sign of bleeding, but by the look of his legs, twisted into unnatural positions, he had broken bones and to move him could make his injuries considerably worse. He had no water with him; then he remembered an injured person, probably needing surgery, should not have anything to drink beforehand. He resigned himself to waiting, wishing heartily that he did not have a dog that he exercised each morning in the moat.

The ambulance men, when they finally arrived, were efficient. They rapidly assessed Joseph's obvious injuries, placed him in a neck brace and loaded him onto the ambulance.

'Can you give us some details, please, sir? His name and how the accident happened.'

Panayiotis shook his head. 'I can't tell you anything at all about him. I was walking my dog, same as usual, and she began to bark. I thought she was after a cat, but she wouldn't come back to me when I called, so I came round to see what was wrong. I checked he had a pulse and then rushed back and asked a taxi driver to go to the hospital for help. I thought I ought to stay with him until you arrived.'

The ambulance man frowned. 'You just found him?'

'That's what I told you.' Panayiotis sighed. 'Can I go now? I'm already late for work.'

'Can I have your name and address, please? Just in case anyone asks.'

Panayiotis sighed even more deeply. 'Yes, of course.' He rattled it off and watched to ensure it was written down correctly.

'Is he going to live?' he asked timidly.

'I should think so. It looks like bruises and broken bones to me, but the doctors will sort him out. No need for you to worry. He was very lucky you came along when you did.'

Panayiotis nodded. 'Can I go now?'

Kyriakos and Spiro stood by the car, chatting desultorily. This was just about the most boring duty they had ever been asked to undertake. They had waited there all morning and not a single car had taken the turn off, nor had one come up, although tourists had passed frequently along the road. No fishing boat had put to sea, but half a dozen labourers in the fields could be seen packing produce into boxes.

Kyriakos lit another cigarette and kicked the butts at his feet beneath the car. 'They probably only deliver to the town one day a week, and I'll lay a bet that day was yesterday.'

Spiro shrugged. 'They probably deliver it at night anyway.'

Kyriakos sniggered. 'Thank goodness we drew the day duty then. It wouldn't be much fun up here at night.'

'It's not exactly 'fun' now.' He bent his head towards the open bonnet as he saw a car approaching.

'Look on the bright side. It could be raining.' Kyriakos straightened up as the car passed them by without a second glance.

Their onerous duty continued well into the afternoon. Two hire cars turned down the side road and could be seen negotiating the bends cautiously. From their vantage point the men could see the building where Christos worked and they watched as both cars used the patch of wasteland in front of the building to turn and begin the climb up the winding hill road.

They noted the registration numbers and the name of the car hire firm and wrote against each one '*did not stop*' and the time. Kyriakos looked at his watch.

'How much longer?'

'Two hours.'

'I've a good mind to have a sleep.'

Spiro shook his head. 'You can't do that. Something's bound to happen if you shut your eyes.'

'Could be a good thing, then. I suggest we bring a pack of cards tomorrow.'

An engine could be heard before a car came into sight and both men looked beneath the bonnet of their own car. The vehicle could be heard to slow and to the men's delight and surprise turned off down the narrow side road. Kyriakos read off the number plate and Spiro entered it onto the list. They watched the driver negotiating the mountain road with confidence, reaching the lower ground and drawing up abruptly outside Christos's house.

'Bingo,' murmured Kyriakos.

'Maybe.' Spiro was sceptical.

'You drive slowly towards Kamiros and I'll go on down the main road just before he returns. If he doesn't pass me I'll come back and wait here. You go on to Kamiros and let Manolis know.'

Spiro nodded and lowered the bonnet, whilst Kyriakos continued to watch the car and building far below.

'Here he comes,' he said finally. 'I didn't see him put anything into his car. Maybe it was just a social call.'

Spiro sighed. 'If he doesn't pass me I'll assume he's gone towards Apolakia, probably to cut across to Gennadi and you're following.'

Kyriakos nodded. At least they were going to do something after hours of inactivity.

It had taken Lakkis almost half an hour of arguing with Christos until the man finally agreed that Sorrell could be moved to the small house where he spent the day.

'You must keep the perimeter fence and the gates to the beach locked all the time. Make sure you keep an eye on her. No pilfering of supplies.'

Christos had argued that he could not do his job and be watching a girl at the same time. 'I need to concentrate. I have to measure exactly.'

'Lock yourself into the kitchen – or lock her outside.'

'Suppose she manages to get out and take a boat, or tries to swim round the headland?'

'You make sure there are no oars left in the boats. If she swims round the headland there is nowhere she could climb ashore, she would have to come back. I doubt if she can swim that strongly anyway. Tell her there are treacherous currents and she'll be washed up on the rocks. Any trouble and tell her that she won't get her shots when she needs them. Keep her waiting half an hour and she'll do whatever you say.'

'What about the farmers? She might approach one of them and ask their help.'

Lakkis sighed in exasperation.

'Make sure she's locked in the house if they come down for anything. Tell her they know she's here and will be keeping an eye on her to report back to me. Don't worry, Christos. She's too frightened of me to try anything.'

Finally Christos had agreed and Lakkis had assured him he would be well remunerated for his services. 'After all,' he added, as a final inducement, 'it's Dimitris's orders.'

Kyriakos returned and greeted Spiro anxiously. 'Did he go towards Kamiros?'

Spiro nodded. 'I let him overtake me by the taverna and used their telephone to alert Manolis. It shouldn't have been difficult for him to follow a green saloon.'

Kyriakos consulted his watch. 'Another couple of hours and then we should be relieved.' He scratched his chin. 'We won't be able to pretend to have a broken down car tomorrow. If the owner of that car comes again he'll be suspicious.'

Spiro shrugged. 'That will be up to Lambros.'

The men continued to watch and wait; the workers in the fields stacked their tools into the small, stone store houses, climbed into their trucks and made their way to their homes. At precisely six o'clock Antionius drew up and thankfully Kyriakos and Spiro returned to Rhodes town to meet with Lambros. At seven Christos locked his house, climbed into the van and drove up the winding road. He turned towards Kamiros and then took the road to Embonas. On reaching the small town he parked the van, locked it, and entered his house. Antionius hung around for a further half an hour, then decided his presence was becoming obvious, as there was no taverna where he could sit and pass the time and no small shops that he could browse. He drove back to Rhodes town, hoping that Lambros would approve his actions.

The destination of the green saloon car excited Yiorgo. 'I knew there had to be a connection that we were missing.'

Takkis looked at him. 'You mean the harbour master's brother?'

Yiorgo nodded. 'Somehow Christos receives the drugs and does the packaging. We don't yet know how he distributes them, but there has to be a connection between him and the *'Aegean Gem'*. Why else should Lakkis Pavlides visit him?'

Takkis shrugged. 'A social call?'

'It's possible, but unlikely. If it were social he would surely visit him during the evening at his house. I think it might be interesting if we obtained a search warrant for the *'Aegean Gem'* and also for *The Grapevine*.

'I'll ask Lambros. It will be too late tonight, but we should be able to have them by noon tomorrow.'

'How about visiting *The Grapevine* for a quick drink?' suggested Yiorgo.

Takkis nodded. 'If you want.'

'There's just a chance the bar tender there will let something slip.'

Together they wandered through the narrow streets until they reached the square where the taverna was situated. Alecos was moving swiftly between the crowded tables.

Yiorgo shrugged. 'Not much chance of talking to him at the moment. Shall we go and eat and come back later?'

Takkis agreed, and they wandered through the square to a taverna round the corner that served meals.

'I'll be glad to get back to home cooking,' observed Takkis. 'I'd like to be at home with my wife eating her moussaka instead of this tourist rubbish.' He dug his fork into the dish in disgust. 'This has probably been sitting here all day and heated up.'

Yiorgo helped himself liberally to salad and saganaki. 'You should eat vegetarian. They can't reheat this.'

Takkis snorted. 'Don't you believe it!'

They lingered over their meal, hoping that by the time they had finished, *The Grapevine* would have quietened down. At ten o'clock they called for their bill and took a circuitous route to arrive back at the taverna. Alecos greeted them with a scowl.

'I was just about to close up.'

'Really? It's early to close.'

'I've had a busy day.'

'Yes, we were going to call in earlier, but when we passed by you were full.'

'Just locals wanting the gossip.'

Yiorgo raised his eyebrows. 'Must have been interesting to pull in so many.'

Alecos shrugged. 'You know what small communities are like. They wanted to know if I knew anything about Joseph.'

'The man who took your job and your girl?'

Alecos nodded. 'Fell over the castle wall.'

'Really?' Takkis could not keep the surprise from his voice. 'How did that happen?'

Alecos shrugged. 'I've no idea. They found him this morning. I expect he was drunk. What can I get you?'

'We'll just have a beer.'

Alecos placed them on their table and continued to clear and mop the others, dumping empty glasses on the bar ready for washing. He yawned as he worked and Yiorgo raised his eyebrows at Takkis. If Joseph had not been drunk when he had fallen, did this young man have anything to do with the accident?

'If you're tired why don't you leave this until the morning?' suggested Takkis.

'I can't. I've got to open up the warehouse tomorrow morning. Lakkis dragged me out of bed this morning to go up there; then he expects me to come back and run the taverna until the early hours.'

'Bit unreasonable of him.'

'Someone's got to do it.'

'What did you say that warehouse stores? Organic flour? Surely those who want it could be contacted and asked to come just one morning a week whilst Joseph's out of action.'

'It doesn't work like that,' Alecos replied sulkily. 'Have you finished?'

Takkis placed the money on the table. 'Yes, we'll not keep you any longer.'

'Strange that Lambros didn't tell us about Joseph's accident,' remarked Yiorgo as they walked away.

'Probably didn't think it was relevant to our enquiries.'

Yiorgo shrugged. 'I'd like to know the circumstances of the accident. It might be worth our while to pay him a visit tomorrow. Enquire after his well-being.'

'If Lambros is suspicious he'll have had an officer take his statement.'

'I'd still like to find out for myself.'

Lambros was surprised when the two detectives asked after Joseph. 'He's in hospital. I've got a man stationed by his bed, but he's been sedated. No identification on him to help us. According to the doctor he broke his pelvis and both legs in the fall. He's covered in bruises, but,' Lambros shrugged, 'they could have been caused as he tumbled down. We'll have to give him a couple of days to recover sufficiently from the anaesthetic and regain full consciousness. He can't be expected to give us any information until then.'

'Do you think it likely that he fell over on his own?' asked Yiorgo.

Lambros shook his head. 'He was some distance from the foot of the wall. If he'd fallen he should have been at the base, or reasonably close.'

'Meaning?'

'I think he was thrown.'

Yiorgo raised his eyebrows. 'Who would have cause to throw him over the wall?'

'Alecos,' suggested Takkis.

Lambros looked at both men in surprise. 'Do you mean Alecos at *The Grapevine*? Why on earth would he want to throw him over?'

Yiorgo perched on the edge of the desk. 'Alecos told us Joseph had fallen over the castle wall, said the locals had been in gossiping. Also, according to Alecos, this man Joseph took his job and his girl. Reason enough to want to get even with him, I would have thought.'

'Reason enough to rough him up,' agreed Lambros, 'but hardly good enough for attempted murder. Besides, it would take two men to throw him.' Lambros dismissed the subject. 'I've arranged for Manolis and Babbis to watch the turn off today. They'll be on scooters. Spiro will wait at Kamiros. Same arrangements as before.'

Yiorgo nodded. 'I thought we might pay another visit to Mr Stephanotis today.'

'What more do you hope to get from him?'

'I thought we might talk about fingerprints,' Yiorgo smiled to himself. 'I would like him to explain how his fingerprints match those of a dead man.'

Manolis surveyed the bay through his binoculars. 'Our friend has arrived. His van is there.'

Babbis leant against a tree. 'Let's hope there's a bit more movement today than they had yesterday. There's a limit to the number of times cars can break down here, or tourists stop to take photographs.'

'They could disguise us as birds and put us up in the trees.'

Babbis snorted. 'How are we supposed to follow anyone then? Fly?'

Manolis smiled to himself. He had forgotten Babbis had no sense of humour. 'We might be in luck,' he lowered the binoculars. 'There's movement down there. He's just placed a box in the front of the van and gone back inside the house.' He raised the glasses to his eyes again. 'Here he comes with another one. He's put that inside as well. Now he's locking the door and getting into the cab.'

Babbis got astride the scooter. 'Let me know when he's half way and I'll go down to the next scenic point and pretend to be taking a photograph.'

Manolis nodded. He had lost sight of the van as it ground its way slowly up the hillside. It appeared again after a short while and had a collection of boxes in the open back. 'I think he's collecting whatever they've been gathering from the fields. It must mean he's taking them in to a market.'

The van took a considerable time to complete its journey up to the main road, and it was the sound of the labouring engine that alerted Babbis to its proximity.

'I'm off,' he announced, and kicked the scooter into life.

Manolis placed his binoculars into the seat of his scooter and held up the camera, as if taking a photograph. He seemed to be holding the pose for ever before Christos appeared at the turning, halting and judging his time carefully before he crossed the on-coming stream of traffic and began to drive towards Kamiros.

Manolis mounted the scooter, and as soon as an opportune break in the traffic occurred, followed. It was easy to catch up with Christos's van, and Manolis memorised the registration number. He stayed behind him until he felt certain he was not going to take a side turning, then overtook and rode on to Kamiros.

Spiro was waiting at the taverna on the main road and Manolis ignored him, taking a seat at an empty table further down and ordering coffee. Whilst he waited for the drink to be brought to him he took out a cigarette and patted his pockets, finally rising and approaching Spiro and asking if he had a light.

'He's on his way. *ROK 5754*. Load of boxes in the back, so he might start delivering anywhere on the way.'

Spiro nodded, left the money on the table for his beer and went towards his car. From the glove compartment he took out a map and pretended to be consulting it, whilst waiting for Christos's van to pass. To his surprise the van turned in and the taverna owner greeted him with a smile.

Christos immediately went to the rear of the van and let down the tailgate. He hauled off two boxes of tomatoes and carried them round to the rear of the taverna. A box of lettuce and another of cucumbers followed.

Spiro groaned to himself. If this was going to happen all the way to Rhodes town he was going to have a problem following without being noticed. He could obviously not stop everywhere that Christos made a delivery. With his map in his hand, he returned to the table where Manolis was sipping at his coffee.

'I'll keep tabs on him to Kalavarda. You find a 'phone and say we want someone to take over at the turn off to Fanes. He may go straight through, of course. You go back and tell Babbis to ride up to Soroni; I'll go on to Theologos. You meet up with me there and we'll see what's happening.' He raised his voice as Christos jumped back into his cab. 'Thanks for your help.'

Spiro found trailing Christos a nightmare. He seemed to stop at every small taverna and off-load a few boxes each time. Spiro pretended to take photographs, he bought postcards, cigarettes, a lighter, guide book, asked for directions and gazed in shop windows, each time Christos stopped and he was relieved when they reached the turn off to Fanes and he recognised the driver of the hire car sitting by the signpost pretending to consult a map. Christos turned off and Spiro continued along the main road, sure that his colleague was now trying to be as unnoticeable amongst the tourists as he had been.

He slowed when he reached Soroni, drawing in beside Babbis and explained the situation to him.

'I'm going on to Theologos,' he announced. 'I'll meet Manolis there and tell him to go on to Kalomonas and you go to Paradisi. If we keep on hopping over ourselves the chances are that he won't spot us.'

'Has he taken anything from the front of the van?' asked Babbis.

'Not that I've seen. It's all been farm produce from the back.'

'What a way to spend a morning,' groaned Babbis. 'I'd rather be in the office.'

Spiro grinned. 'I wouldn't. This is almost like a holiday, dashing around on a scooter in the sunshine.'

Christos continued through the small villages, stopping at the tavernas until by the time he passed through Kremasti the back of his lorry was empty. Spiro breathed a sigh of relief. Now the man would either go to deliver the boxes he had placed in the cab or return to the bay. He followed at a safe distance as Christos took the road to Pastida and through Kakari to join up with the main road leading to Faliraki. The tourist traffic was much heavier now and it was most unlikely that Christos would realise that anyone was tailing him.

He pulled into the drive for the *'Aegean Gem'* and Spiro drove on, parking a short distance down the road. Swiftly he left the car and began to walk down the drive towards the hotel entrance, hoping he would be taken for a guest. Christos's van was parked at the side, but there was no sign of the man.

Spiro stood in an agony of indecision. Dare he risk looking through the window of the cab to see if the boxes were still there? If he were spotted he could hardly pass as a hotel guest who had lost his way. Deciding he would take a chance he hurried forward until he was abreast of the window. There on the floor were the two boxes. He retreated back to the main drive, now he would have to find an excuse to hang around. On the right hand side next to the drive entrance was a tourist kiosk and he made his way over to it gratefully.

He flicked the postcard holders round, pretending to study them, moving out of the way as a tourist tried to do the same, and looking at the headlines on the newspapers instead. He was just beginning to wonder how much longer he would be able to stay there when he saw Christos return to the van, get in and slam the door. Spiro immediately returned to his car and was ready to follow wherever he was led next.

The green van wound its way slowly through the congested area until it reached the main road leading to Rhodes town and Spiro sighed with relief. He had no way of contacting the other men who had taken part in the surveillance and ask one of them to meet him and take over. He drove steadily, allowing the van to always be ahead of him by two or three vehicles and followed it into the outskirts of the town up to the Athanasiou Gate of the medieval town. Christos spoke to the attendant and the barrier was lifted, whilst Spiro hurriedly found a place to park his car. He knew he would have little trouble in finding the van as no vehicle was allowed, or able, to drive very far into the city during the day.

Spiro hurried down the cobbled road, turning through the double arches and dodging the wandering tourists as he went. As he emerged from the second arch he saw Christos in the act of parking the van directly in front of him. He sauntered past without giving him a second glance, stopping at the small general store on the opposite side of the road. The woman sitting outside called across to Christos.

'He's not there.'

'I know,' he called back. 'I've got the keys. Just got to drop something off for him.'

Spiro again pretended to examine the dusty postcards hanging up outside and watched as Christos unlocked the side door to the warehouse, removed the two boxes from the passenger side of the van and hurried inside with them. Spiro waited no longer. He almost ran back to the barrier and ducked into the pay phone that stood at the side of the road.

Lambros listened to his request and agreed to have a scooter at the gate as soon as possible. 'I'll send Babbis. Try to delay him until you see him arrive.'

Spiro groaned. How was he supposed to stop the man from driving off? He stood outside the phone booth until he saw the van waiting at the barrier, then he walked across.

'Excuse me, but I think you have a flat tyre.'

Christos frowned. The road he had just traversed was bumpy in the extreme but he had noticed nothing amiss.

'Which side?'

'That side,' said Spiro, waving his hand airily.

'You can't stop there,' the attendant said, and already there was a car hooting behind him impatient to leave.

With a frown of annoyance, Christos drew away and parked on the taxi rank. He cut the engine and jumped down from his cab to inspect his tyres.

'I can't see anything wrong.'

Spiro inspected them slowly and critically, taking his time as he walked round the van and ending up standing in front of the engine. 'I'm sorry, must have been the road you were on. I didn't know you could drive into the old town.'

'You can't unless you're delivering.'

'Oh, I see. That's a shame. I'd like to have tried my hand at some of those corners.'

Christos returned to his cab and waved at Spiro to move from the front of the van. Spiro seemed not to understand and Christos shouted from the window. 'Move out of my way. I want to get on.'

'Oh, sorry. Didn't realise.' Spiro waved his hand apologetically and moved to one side, wishing Babbis would appear. All he could do was watch Christos drive towards the roundabout and hope he would take the road to Faliraki.

Babbis appeared some five minutes later and grunted at Spiro. 'I'd only just finished my report when they said you wanted me out again. Where is he?'

'I hope he's on his way back to the '*Aegean Gem*'. He's just unlocked the warehouse here and deposited the boxes. With luck he's going to return the keys.'

'You'd better let Lambros know, maybe get someone else down there to take over from me for when he leaves.' Babbis revved the engine of the scooter and swung out into the traffic on the main road.

Spiro retrieved his hire car and made for the police station, reporting quickly to Lambros his conversation with Babbis.

Lambros nodded. 'I'll send Manolis down. You can fill in your report now. The others have finished theirs. No doubt Yiorgo and Takkis will want to see them as soon as they return.'

Spiro sighed. He was sick of looking at picture postcards, but even that would be preferable to writing up his report of the day's travelling.

Babbis had no difficulty in catching up with Christos's van and kept it in sight all the way to the *'Aegean Gem'*. He waited outside the drive, watching the van for any sign of movement, until Manolis arrived.

The two men stood together, hoping they looked like any other tourists. Manolis lit a cigarette. 'Did he see you following him?'

'I don't think so. I don't think he's noticed anyone all day.'

Manolis flexed his legs. 'I shan't be sorry to get off this scooter. I'm too tall for one of these.'

Babbis touched his arm. 'Here he comes.'

They watched as Christos threw three expensive looking suitcases into the back of the van; then opened the door to the passenger seat. He removed the handles on both sides of the door and placed them beneath the driving seat. Lakkis appeared leading a girl by the arm, and helped her into the van; she looked sulky and bad-tempered. Lakkis slammed the passenger door shut and raised his hand to Christos as he drove off.

This time Christos took the road to Kalytheis, by-passed Pastida, and met up with the main road just before Paradisi. The traffic on the secondary road had been light and Manolis had held back, but once on the main road he was able to ride at a steady pace and kept the van in sight until it turned down the road to the bay. He drew up and removed his binoculars from beneath the seat, waiting for the van to reach the small house down on the shore.

Christos climbed out and locked his door behind him; he closed and padlocked the wire and metal gate behind him before removing the suitcases from the back. Having unlocked the door he carried them through into the house and returned to the van where he re-fixed the handle to the passenger door and helped the girl out. She stood and looked around, then turned and began to speak rapidly to Christos, waving her hands and arms. Christos stood and waited until she calmed, then took her elbow and steered her through the door, closing it behind them.

Manolis smiled to himself. No doubt she had been promised a fun packed night in a first class hotel. What a shock she had received!

Sorrell looked around the sparsely furnished room. 'You expect me to stay here!'

Christos looked at her sadly. 'I'm sorry I can't offer you anything better.' He waved her to a chair and sat down opposite. 'To be quite honest with you, I don't want you here. It's not convenient for you or me.'

'Then take me to a hotel.'

Christos shook his head. 'I can't do that. I've had instructions from Mr Lakkis and I have to do as he says. First of all, let me make everything quite clear to you. During the day I shall be working and you are free to lie outside in the sun. Unfortunately you are unable to use the beach, but it isn't very pleasant. The pebbles are more like boulders and there are submerged rocks in the water. There is a perimeter fence and I shall keep the gates locked. If you become a nuisance to me I shall be forced to lock you inside the house all the time.'

Sorrell frowned. 'You mean I'm a prisoner down here?'

Christos shook his head. 'I don't like that word. Call yourself a restricted guest. You may have noticed as we drove here how far we are from any town. There would be little point in you trying to walk back up the hill thinking you could get back to the main road. If any of the farmers saw you they would immediately bring you back here. I also understand you need a little something on a regular basis and if you left here it is most unlikely that you would be able to procure it.'

Sorrell listened to him in a sulky silence. 'How long do I have to stay here?'

'Just a few days. Mr Lakkis had no choice. He thought you would prefer to be here, where you can move around in relative freedom, than locked in a hotel room.'

'I don't see why I have to be locked in anywhere.'

'That is Mr Dimitris's orders.' Christos shrugged. 'I am simply carrying out my instructions. I have to keep you locked in.'

A look of alarm crossed Sorrell's face. 'What about my shot?'

'I will give you sufficient before I leave for the night. There's a bit of food in the fridge, so you can make yourself a meal. Please,' Christos leaned forward. 'I have a very sick wife. I am dependent on this job with Mr Lakkis. If you will just do as I have said there will be no trouble for me and I promise you it will only be for a short while.'

'What's wrong with your wife?'

'She had a very bad accident some years ago. She is badly crippled and suffers a lot of pain.'

'So who looks after her whilst you're here?'

'My mother-in-law. You see, if I can trust you, it will make life easier for both of us. I shall be able to work as normal and you will be able to wander around outside as you please. If I find that you are a nuisance I shall have to keep you locked in this room.'

'Are you threatening me?'

Christos shook his head. 'No. I am simply telling you how it has to be.'

Yiorgo and Takkis arrived at the *'Aegean Pride'*, knocking at the door leading below decks until Dimitris opened it. He stood blocking the doorway.

'Yes?' he asked abruptly.

'May we come aboard for a short while? We have had some results from our fingerprint department that we would like to discuss with you.'

Dimitris shrugged. 'If you must. Will I then be allowed to leave this harbour?'

'We are doing our best to ensure you will be inconvenienced no longer than necessary,' replied Yiorgo disarmingly. He sat down at the saloon table and placed a folder on the table in front of him.

'As you know, we requested that you and your staff gave us your fingerprints for the process of elimination. Athens found those of Anders and Frida on their files. They could find nothing under the name of Dimitris Stephanotis.' Yiorgo regarded the man before him steadily.

'That is because I do not have a criminal record.' Dimitris smiled triumphantly.

Yiorgo nodded. 'Quite so. The only information known about Dimitris Stephanotis is that he was sent to Leros when he was aged fifteen.'

Dimitris shrugged. 'A coincidence of name.'

'A coincidence indeed. Two male children born on the same date on the island of Karpathos and having the same name? But putting coincidence aside, the fingerprints we took from you were found to belong to Christos Drakonisis, a young man from Santorini, who is registered as deceased. I wonder if you would care to explain that to us, sir?'

Dimitris face paled and his eyes shifted nervously from one man to the other. 'There must have been a mistake.'

Yiorgo shook his head. 'There was no mistake. You see, the prints found on the syringe were also those of Christos Drakonisis, in other words, your fingerprints.'

Dimitris did not answer. His head was reeling. After all these years without anyone before questioning his identity!

'I think you should accompany us to the police station. You

will be able to contact your lawyer and have him present when you make your statement.'

'You mean you are arresting me?' Dimitris could not believe his ears.

'Let's say that you are helping us with our enquiries. I am sure you will be able to give us satisfactory answers to a number of questions and then we will have no need to pursue the matter further. Shall we go?' Yiorgo rose and picked up the folder.

'I can't go now.'

'Why not?'

'I have to attend to business matters.'

'I regret that we have to insist. Your business matters will have to wait a short while.'

'And if I refuse to accompany you?'

'In that case we would be forced to arrest you.'

'On what grounds?' Dimitris challenged them.

'Obstruction of justice. We have a car waiting.'

'I need to speak to my crew.'

Yiorgo nodded. 'By all means. If you would like to call them.'

Dimitris gave him a venomous look and called loudly for Anders who appeared promptly. 'Telephone Lakkis and tell him I have gone ashore for a short while to assist the police in their enquiries. Whilst I am away I expect you to look after the cruiser as I have instructed you.'

'Yes, sir.' No flicker of emotion crossed Anders's face as he watched Dimitris leave the saloon accompanied by the two policemen.

Anders watched them walk along the harbour arm. Once he was certain they were not returning he took a screwdriver from his tool box and proceeded to unscrew the hand rail that ran the short distance of the companion way. From the hollow interior he emptied the rolls of notes, packets of drugs and a crumpled passport into a pile on the floor. He sat back on his heels and looked at the small fortune before him. Should he obey his employer's instructions and burn everything?

Frida stood at the top of the companionway and looked at him quizzically. 'Well?'

'What do you think?'

'I think we should wait awhile. He could be back in half an hour and he won't be very pleased to see you've carried out his instructions so promptly.'

'Suppose the police come back with a warrant and start to take the boat apart?'

'Why should they – and even if they do we deny all knowledge. There's nothing to connect us in any way.' Frida gave a sly smile. 'If he doesn't come back and they don't find it he won't be able to prove you burnt it. Put it back, Anders.'

Dimitris was ushered into a small side room and asked to take a seat. Yiorgo and Takkis sat opposite and Takkis smiled at him.

'I'm sure this won't take very long, Mr Stephanotis. We just want to tie up a few loose ends in our enquiries.'

'I demand to have a lawyer present.'

'That is your right and if you would like to give me his name and address I will telephone and ask him to come immediately.'

'That's impossible. He's in Athens.'

'In that case I suggest we bring you a telephone and you call him yourself. It would probably be advisable to ask him for the name of a local gentleman who could act for you.'

'I only trust him with my affairs.' Dimitris folded his arms and sat back.

'Quite so, but it could save considerable inconvenience if you used someone based on Rhodes.'

'What do you mean?'

'The very earliest your lawyer could be here would be late this afternoon. There would be no time for you to speak to him before we go off duty. That would necessitate placing you in a cell for the night, and I'm sure you would prefer to avoid that indignity.'

'You said you were not charging me with anything. That I was only helping with your enquiries. You can't put me in a cell for the night.'

'We would consider it was for your own safety.'

'My safety! I'm not in any danger.'

'But you could be. We would rather look after you and ensure that no harm befall you.'

'That is a trumped up excuse.'

'Is it, sir?' Takkis looked at Dimitris and raised his eyebrows. 'What makes you so sure?'

Dimitris rubbed a hand over his forehead. 'I should like to telephone Mr Pavlides. I will ask him for the name of his lawyer.'

'That's a sensible idea.' Takkis smiled. 'I'll get you the telephone.'

'Lakkis, I need the best lawyer on Rhodes. No, I can't discuss it over the telephone. It's nothing to do with the hotels. It's personal. I am at the police station now. No, they won't let me leave until I've made a statement. Just get a lawyer down here as soon as possible.' Dimitris slammed down the telephone and glared at Yiorgo and Takkis.

Takkis unplugged the telephone. 'We'll leave you until your lawyer arrives. Would you like some refreshment?'

Dimitris shook his head. This would need thinking about.

Dimitris was left for almost two hours to think before Lakkis arrived with a solicitor. Access to Dimitris was denied to him and he left the police station a worried man. Mr Spinades looked puzzled.

'Can someone please tell me why I am here? I do not know Mr Stephanotis and I have no idea what he is charged with.'

Takkis and Yiorgo escorted him to the room where Dimitris was waiting without saying a word. On unlocking the door, Takkis ushered the solicitor inside.

Mr Spinades looked from one man to the other and then threw his briefcase on the table. 'If I am acting on behalf of Mr Stephanotis I am entitled to privacy during our discussions.'

'Naturally. Please let us know when Mr Stephanotis is ready to answer our questions.'

Yiorgo and Takkis withdrew. Yiorgo let out his breath. 'Now we shall see what we shall see! Let's go and find Lambros and see what those surveillance reports say.'

Mr Spinades shook Dimitris by the hand and sat down opposite his client. 'I regret that I do not know why you are here. I suggest you give me an outline of the circumstances. I will make some notes and then I will no doubt have some questions to put to you.'

Dimitris shrugged. 'I was asked to give my fingerprints. I did so and according to the police they match with a dead man. There is obviously some mistake. I was asked to come down here and help with their enquiries.'

Piriklis Spinades held up his hand. 'Please. Let us start at the beginning. Why were you asked to give your fingerprints?'

Dimitris sighed. 'Nikos Pavlides, the harbour master died after visiting my boat for a meal. Unbeknown to me he had taken some chocolates from a box belonging to a young lady who was travelling with me. Also unknown to me these chocolates had been laced with heroin and appear to have been the cause of his demise. The young lady has since disappeared. She left a syringe in a bedside drawer that the police took away. They then asked for my crew and myself to provide them with fingerprints for the process of elimination.'

Piriklis nodded. 'And this young lady? Can you give me her name?'

'Susanna Hirsch, an American. We met in Athens over a year ago. She had a desire to travel to the islands and I offered her passage.'

'You had no idea she was using drugs?'

'I explained to the police. I am sure they will allow you to read a copy of my statement.'

'Of course. You are certain you do not know where Miss Hirsch is now?'

Dimitris spread his hands. 'I would have told the police if I knew. I was ashore and she decided to leave. I have no idea where she went and she is irrelevant to my problem. I would like you to ask the police to release me at once.'

'I'm sure they will do so once this little matter of the fingerprints has been cleared up. I suggest that we ask them to bring in your original prints and also those they say belong to someone else. You will then give another sample and it will be quite obvious that they do not match and there has been some confusion.' Piriklis sat back. The solution was so simple.

Dimitris rubbed his hand across his face. 'I am not prepared to give them any more prints. They have made a mistake and they must release me immediately.'

Piriklis frowned. 'Mr Stephanotis, it is extremely unlikely they would release you on my request. It would be far better to prove they are wrong.'

Dimitris compressed his lips. 'As my lawyer it is up to you to convince them.'

Piriklis sighed. 'I am unable to accuse them of making a mistake unless I can prove the error.'

'Then offer them some money. I will pay. I will also double your fee if you are successful.'

'Very well.' Piriklis stood up and knocked on the door. 'I will try.'

He returned to the main office where Yiorgo and Takkis were waiting.

'I have spoken to Mr Stephanotis and he is convinced there was a mistake made whilst trying to match his fingerprints. He has authorized me to make you an offer.'

Yiorgo raised his eyebrows. 'Has he? If we have made a mistake why should he be trying to bribe us?'

Piriklis shrugged. 'I know only what Mr Stephanotis has told me. I suggested his prints were taken again and compared a second time, but he is unwilling to comply with my suggestion.'

'And why do you think he is unwilling?' asked Takkis.

Piriklis did not answer.

'I can tell you why,' Takkis continued. 'We can take his prints a hundred times and they will still be those of Christos Drakonisis. According to police records a young man was found floating in the sea off the coast of Santorini some twenty or so years ago. His body had been in the water a considerable amount of time and he was completely unrecognisable. It was assumed by his relatives and the police that the body was Christos Drakonisis as he had a shark's tooth on a leather thong around his neck. At the same time, a young man, Dimitris Stephanotis, who was destined for the island of Leros disappeared without a trace. The two events were never connected in any way at the time.'

'You are quite certain of this?'

Takkis nodded. 'We are interested in Mr Stephanotis for a number of reasons, but first we would like the matter of his identity cleared up.'

'May I ask what the other reasons are?'

'At this stage I would rather not divulge them. It could be detrimental to Mr Stephanotis. Obviously if we decided to bring any charges against him we would inform both of you of every detail.'

Piriklis frowned. 'Maybe I'd better speak to Mr Stephanotis again.'

Dimitris looked hopefully at Piriklis who shook his head. 'I think we need to discuss your problem a little further.'

Dimitris banged his hands on the table. 'There is nothing to discuss. I told you to make them an offer.'

'I did so, and it was refused. There appears to be some confusion over your identity and they are insisting it is cleared up before they can release you.'

Dimitris closed his eyes. What had happened all those years ago? He would have to make the story plausible. He did not want to be subsequently arrested for murder.

'I lived on Santorini. A ship docked and a young man slipped ashore, how I do not know. I was hanging around the harbour and he asked me for directions. He was obviously a little simple and finally asked me to show him the way. I agreed. He told me he was being sent to Leros, but I didn't believe him. We went into a taverna for a meal and he suddenly went berserk. He began to beat the elderly couple who owned the place. I tried to pull him off, but he was too strong for me. Finally he raided their till and ran off down the road. I followed him with the idea of retrieving the money and returning it to the couple.

He ran down the path towards the beach and continued on round the headland. It was very rocky, and he started to jump from rock to rock until he finally slipped and hit his head. I didn't know what to do. I sat there for a long time. I kept expecting him to wake up; then I realised he was dead. It dawned on me that I might be accused of killing him for the money he had taken.

Finally I went through his pockets. He was destined for Leros as he had told me, so I thought no one would miss him. I took his identity papers and placed the shark's tooth that I always wore around his neck. When it was dark I went back to my room and collected some clothes. The next morning I took the first ferry away from the island and when I finally reached Athens I decided I would become Dimitris Stephanotis.'

Piriklis listened intently and made notes as Dimitris spoke. 'I see. How old were you when this – incident – took place?'

Dimitris shrugged. 'Sixteen, maybe seventeen.'

'Did you go back to the taverna to see how the couple were and return their money?'

Dimitris shook his head. 'I did not dare. They would have called the police and had me arrested. I was quite innocent,' he declared.

'I see – and what about your parents? Did you tell them you were leaving?'

'I had no parents. By then they were both dead and I was alone in the world. No one was going to miss me either.' Dimitris sat back with a smile. The story sounded plausible, he had only twisted the truth a little.

'Why didn't you tell the police this in the first place?'

Dimitris shrugged. 'I didn't think they would believe me.'

Piriklis looked at Dimitris sceptically. 'I'm not sure that I do,' he remarked coldly. 'Maybe we could go over some of the points again.'

Sorrell examined the small house after Christos had left. Apart from the living room, there was a back room that held a bed and the kitchen. The toilet was in the yard and she had been left a bucket. She shuddered. There was no way she was prepared to stay here, even for one night. She looked around the kitchen. Lifting a cloth on the side she revealed a small scale with the merest traces of brown powder adhering to the pan. Painstakingly she mopped up the grains with her finger, held it before her nose and inhaled deeply. That was a bonus. She examined the kitchen more thoroughly; if Christos had been weighing up some of the drug he must have a further supply hidden somewhere. Her eyes alighted on a small locked cupboard.

No doubt Christos had taken the key with him. Sorrell looked around frantically. There must be some way she could open it. She examined the two drawers in the kitchen finding they held only a small amount of cheap cutlery. She needed something that would not bend or break to force the lock. The only item that had any substance was a saucepan. If she could manage to insert the handle and use enough force the lock should snap.

She tried in vain to push the handle into the crack, finally giving up. There had to be a way. She looked around the kitchen again and picked up a knife. The blade slipped easily between the door and the side of the cupboard, but as soon as she exerted any pressure it snapped and she sat back on her heels sighing with frustration. Maybe she would be able to find something suitable outside, but Christos had locked the kitchen door before driving away.

Enraged, Sorrell hurled the saucepan at the kitchen window and stared in surprise as the glass cracked. She wrapped the cloth that had covered the scales around her hand, lifted the saucepan and hit the window pane with as much force as she could muster. Still using the cloth to protect her hand she pulled away the jagged pieces of glass, throwing them outside to the ground. The window would be just about large enough to climb through and it was only a short drop to the ground.

Cautiously she poked her head through the opening and clicked her tongue in annoyance. Unless she could rely on landing on her feet she was going to be badly cut by the glass that was strewn below. She needed to think.

Once outside there would be no certainty she would be able to get back through the window unless she could find something to stand on. If she was forced to spend the night out in the yard she might at least be reasonably comfortable. She knew that once the effect of her latest dose began to wear off she would be cold and shivering.

'Push the bedding out through the window,' she told herself. That way she would be protected from the broken glass and have something to cover herself with if necessary.

She dragged the pillow and blanket from the bed, throwing the blanket over as much of the glass as possible and dropped the pillow on top. She wondered idly what Christos's reaction would be in the morning if he found her outside and the property damaged. She ran a trembling hand over her head. She did not want to be found outside – she wanted to get back in, raid the locked cupboard and escape. As an afterthought she collected the empty bucket and dropped it outside to the ground. It might just give her enough elevation to climb back through the window.

Deciding to take a chance Sorrell pulled the chair over to the broken window and stood on the seat. Cautiously she leaned back until her head and arms were outside. Her groping fingers found the projecting frame of the window and she wriggled into a sitting position on the sill. Carefully she pulled up her feet until they were also resting on the sill. Trusting that the wooden frame was not rotten and would hold her weight she pulled herself upright. Taking a deep breath she released her grip and jumped, landing on her knees.

Regaining her feet she looked at the two outhouse doors. One she knew was the toilet, she just hoped the other would not be locked and would hold a suitable implement for her to break into the cupboard.

She turned the handle and to her relief it opened, dragging on the ground where a hinge had rusted and broken. As Sorrell's eyes became accustomed to the dark interior she could make out a number of forks and spades and her heart sank. They would be useless. She pulled them to one side, letting them fall noisily to the ground. Behind them was an old wooden ladder, leaning lopsidedly where one leg was rotting away. There was nothing there that would help her to break the lock.

She leaned against the door jamb and felt close to tears. She was convinced there was a supply of heroin in the cupboard and she wanted it. The more she thought about it the more desperate she became.

Her legs trembling she decided to use the toilet before attempting to climb back through the window into the kitchen. She was relieved to see a light switch on the wall and grateful that the bulb worked.

She shuddered. The toilet was disgusting. The pan was stained and there was a flimsy scrap of paper left on the roll that stood on the dirty floor. A cardboard box in the corner caught her attention and she looked inside hoping a fresh toilet roll would be stored there.

In the bottom of the box there was a miscellaneous collection, scraps of wire, screws, nails, an old padlock, a couple of screwdrivers, a hammer and a pair of pliers. Sorrell's heart leapt. She had found what she needed.

Standing on the upturned bucket she found it relatively easy to climb back through the window, although hampered by the screwdrivers and hammer that she had clutched in one hand. Back in the kitchen she attacked the locked cupboard vigorously and within seconds she had splintered the lock. She gasped when she saw the amount of heroin that was stored in there. Taking advantage of an open bag she scooped out a small amount and made a line on the kitchen table and sniffed happily.

She stretched. That felt so much better. She certainly knew she had enough to keep her happy until the morning. She was tempted to take some more, but a sixth sense told her it was more important to keep a modicum of clear headedness if she wished to make good her escape before Christos returned.

In the corner of the living room her three cases stood where Christos had placed them and she unfastened them quickly and examined the contents. To her consternation there was no sign of her jewellery or her passport, but she let out a sigh of relief when she saw that her black evening shoes with the diamonds firmly stuck into the heels were in their customary bag. What she needed now was a pair of sturdy sandals and also some beach shoes for her journey over the rocks. A pair of trousers would be practical and a jumper in case it turned cooler during the night, although that was unlikely.

She placed all the packets of heroin, her precious shoes, the sandals, trousers and jumper into a large beach bag, added some of the bread and a piece of cheese from the fridge and the two bottles of beer. Carefully she leaned out of the window as far as she could and lowered the bag to the ground.

In the last of the daylight she examined the locks on the gate in the perimeter fence and realised that without keys or wire cutters she could certainly not leave in the conventional way. She walked down to the wooden gates that shut off access to the beach and managed to peer through the gap in the gates studying the strip of boulder-strewn land that the sea lapped against. She bit at her lips. The wooden doors were securely padlocked and too high for her to reach the top and attempt to haul herself up. If she could find something to stand on it might be possible to climb over the gates and make her way to the beach. From there she had easy access to the road they had driven down. She had no idea how far she was from Rhodes town and she had no money to pay for a taxi, even if she could find one in such an out of the way spot. She had to make a decision and she had to make it quickly. If she was going to leave she needed to do so under the cover of darkness.

Placing her beach bag by the gates Sorrell returned to the outhouse and blocked the door open with a couple of spades to give her as much light as possible. She threw the remaining spades and forks out of the way of the door and groped for the ladder she had seen earlier. It was heavy and it took all her strength and determination to manoeuvre it over to the doorway and by the time she had it out in the yard the sweat was pouring from her body. She dragged it awkwardly over to the gates and propped it up lopsidedly. Tentatively she placed her foot on the first rung and tested it before she decided it would take her weight. She climbed unsteadily until she could look over the gates to the beach below. She studied the drop carefully. There was every chance she would break her leg or bruise herself severely as she landed on the boulders.

She stood balanced precariously on the rotten ladder. Should she take the chance? Then she remembered the bedding. If she threw that down on the rocks her fall would be cushioned to a certain extent. She climbed back down carefully and collected the blanket and pillow from below the broken window. She dropped the bedding onto the rocks below and lowered her shoulder bag before releasing her grip on the strap. Taking a deep breath she mounted two more rungs of the ladder and hoisted herself up on top of the gates. She sat astride them and took a deep breath, finally swinging her other leg over. She turned and gripped the top of the wooden gates, letting her body drop as far as possible before releasing her grip. She landed clumsily on the bedding that gave a slight protection from the boulders and knocked the breath out of her. The sea sucked greedily at the rocks in the moonlight and Sorrell realised that she was frightened.

With infinite care she inched her way forward, slipping and sliding on the stones, her feet wet and cold. Twice she lost her footing and sat down heavily. By the time she had manoeuvred around the projecting rocks and reached the small beach she was breathing heavily and perspiring freely. She removed her shorts and used them to dry her feet before donning the trousers and sandals, then left her shorts and beach shoes pushed behind a rock.

The road curved upwards from her and she knew she had a long walk before she would reach the main road. She glanced at her watch, it was twenty past eight. With a shrug of her shoulders she started the climb.

It was almost midnight when she finally reached the main road. She had stopped frequently to rest as the road seemed to go on interminably. Thankfully she sat on the verge and finished the last few drops from the second bottle of beer. A car rounded the corner on the opposite side of the road, going too fast for her to wave down. She must move to a straighter stretch of road where she could signal to the next vehicle that passed. She needed to have an excuse for being in such a deserted spot at that time of night. Another passed, and she rose to her feet hurriedly, throwing the empty beer bottle to one side.

She had no idea in which direction lay Rhodes town, but prudence told her to stay on the same side as any approaching traffic. It was easier to walk on the side of the road than the verge and she plodded doggedly along, until she saw the lights of a car approaching. She waved her hand frantically and it drew to a halt a short distance in front of her and the driver wound down the passenger window.

'What's the problem? Can I help?'

Sorrell smiled at him in relief. 'Could you give me a lift? I really need to get to Rhodes town, but anywhere would do.'

The driver frowned. 'You're miles from the town. Where's your car?'

'Broken down.'

'Where?'

Sorrell waved her hand vaguely. 'Somewhere down that road.'

'Maybe if I took you back down I could get it started for you?'

Sorrell shook her head. 'I don't think so. It hasn't actually broken down. I put it into the ditch.'

The driver gave a slight smile. 'The best I can offer you is a lift back to the taverna at Kamiros. They'll have a telephone you can use.'

'I'd be very grateful.' Sorrell opened the car door and slid into the seat. 'I feel very foolish.'

Without answering her, the driver drove past the side turning, then reversed into it and crossed to the opposite side of the main road. He drove carefully along the main road until they finally dropped down to the shore and he drew up outside a dark taverna.

'It looks as if they've closed up for the night. I suggest you knock and wake them up.'

Sorrell looked at the darkened building uncaring. She was considerably closer to the town than she had been half an hour earlier; and also knew she was travelling in the right direction.

'I can't stop. My wife will be worried as it is.'

'There's no need. I'm terribly grateful to you.' Sorrell opened the door and waited for the driver to complete his turn and drive away.

She sat down on the steps of the taverna and pulled out the bread and cheese, eating voraciously, not realising how hungry she had become. She cupped her hands and drank from a small fountain that decorated the patio, wishing she had not discarded the beer bottle so thoughtlessly. A number of cars passed as she sat there, but none going in the direction of Rhodes town. She was going to have to start to walk again, but before that she would open one of the packets and have a small boost.

Reluctantly she rose to her feet. At least the road was relatively flat, which made it easier. Looking at her watch she saw it was nearly two in the morning. The best she could hope for was a workman setting off early.

By six she was nearly at Fanes, although she did not know that. Throughout the early hours of the morning she had walked steadily, but now each step was becoming more of an effort. Her legs were aching and her feet were sore. She sat by the side of the road and ate the remains of the bread and cheese and sniffed again at the brown powder. The desire to lie down and sleep almost overcame her and it took all her remaining will power to stand and continue to walk along the dusty road until the drug gave her the usual feeling of euphoria. She had walked for no more than ten minutes when she heard the sound of an engine behind her and as the car hove into view she waved frantically.

'Please can you give me a lift? I need to get to Rhodes town urgently.'

'I can take you as far as Soroni. I'm on my way to work.'

'I'd be very grateful.' Sorrell opened the door and slipped in beside him.

'What's your rush?' he asked.

'My mother. There's been an accident. The hospital telephoned and asked me to get there as soon as I could.' Sorrell lied glibly.

'If you want to hang around the entrance to the power station I could ask one of my colleagues to give you a ride. I'm relieving him from night duty and he goes that way.'

'That would be wonderful.'

'Why didn't you telephone for a taxi?'

'I tried and no one answered.' Sorrell was tempted to close her eyes. The movement of the car making her feel drowsy.

'Here we are.' A hand shook her arm. 'Wake up. We're here.'

They had stopped outside a barrier and Sorrell forced her eyes open. 'Where are we?' Her mouth felt full of sawdust.

'Soroni.' The man opened her door.

Sorrell made no attempt to move. 'Where should I wait for your colleague?'

'Anywhere here. You'll see him come out.' He poked his head out of the window and called for the barrier to be lifted.

Sorrell held onto the open door. 'You wouldn't have a bottle of water you could let me have by any chance?'

The man opened the glove compartment and pulled out a small bottle that was half full. 'It's a bit warm, but you're welcome.'

Sorrell sank down on the grass verge and drank greedily before resting her head on her arms.

In due course a small car appeared on the other side of the barrier and Sorrell straightened up.

'Are you the girl wanting a lift?'

She nodded. 'Yes, please.'

'Get in, then. Michaelis said you wanted the hospital. Is that right?'

'Yes,' agreed Sorrell, with no knowledge of where the hospital was situated. 'But anywhere in town will do.'

'I can go past. It's no trouble.'

'Thank you.' Sorrell sank back in the seat and allowed her eyes to close again. She desperately wanted to sleep and also she did not want to have to hold a conversation. It seemed only a few minutes before they drew up before the building and she rubbed her eyes.

'Are we here?'

He nodded. 'I've dropped you at the main entrance. They'll be able to help you at the reception inside.'

Sorrell gave him a grateful smile. 'I really am indebted to you.'

'No problem.' He raised his hand and was gone.

Sorrell hesitated. She had no idea where in the town she was, or what she looked like. In the hospital they were bound to have a toilet where she could wash. She walked confidently up the path and through the double doors, ignoring the reception area and making for a door marked as a toilet. Inside she studied her reflection in the mirror. She looked terrible.

Sorrell washed her hands and face; then ran her hands through her tangled hair. That would have to do. She refilled the water bottle and took a long drink before topping it up again. She placed a small quantity of the heroin on the side of the basin and sniffed greedily. That felt better. With a bright smile on her face she approached the woman at the reception.

'Would you be able to help me, please? I have to take a message to someone in the old town and I don't know the way from here.'

'Up to the top of the hill and down the other side. You'll be at one of the gates then.'

Sorrell checked her watch. 'How long will it take me?'

The woman shrugged. 'Fifteen minutes at the outside.'

Once outside Sorrell hesitated. Should she go down to the port and find Dimitris or go to the old town and try to find Joseph? Finally she decided finding Joseph might be the better idea. There was no certainty that Dimitris would still be in the harbour, and if he were he would almost certainly send her back to Lakkis. If she went back to Lakkis she feared his treatment of her. He would be so furious that she had escaped from wherever he had imprisoned her that he might well kill her. She had no option, she would have to ask Joseph for help.

Takkis and Yiorgo had studied the reports sent in by the surveillance team and Yiorgo was elated.

'I reckon we've found the girl. She must have been down at that hotel in Faliraki all the time. We'll take that search warrant and go down to the bay first thing in the morning, turn the place over and pick her up at the same time.'

Takkis groaned. It was more than an hour's drive to the bay from the town and no doubt Yiorgo would want to be there by seven. That would mean getting up at five, and he was no lover of early rising.

Christos drove towards the bay with a feeling of apprehension. What would he find when he got there? The girl had seemed reasonably docile and compliant when he had left, but how long would that last? He had enough heroin in the place to keep her quiet, but he was worried by the situation. The local farmers had accepted him as their means of delivering their produce to the local tavernas, but they had no idea of his real occupation.

To his relief the locks on the gate were in place, but when he opened them and saw the broken window and the ladder propped up against the gates leading to the beach a hollow feeling of fear made itself felt in the pit of his stomach. He drew a deep breath and opened the door. The bread and cheese had gone from the table, so she had either eaten it or taken it with her. He looked through into the bedroom, the bedding had been removed, but her cases were still there. He hurried to check the outside toilet; then back into the kitchen. It was then that he saw the cupboard door had been forced off its hinges and was empty. He was in a good deal of trouble. Christos lifted the telephone. He would have to tell Lakkis, much as he dreaded the idea.

Lakkis was just about to leave for his drive to Faliraki when the telephone rang. He answered it swiftly, expecting Dimitris, and was surprised when it was Christos and then angry when he heard his news.

'She has to be there,' he shouted. 'She must be hiding from you.'

'I swear, Lakkis, I've looked everywhere. There's a ladder by the gates to the beach. She must have climbed over.'

'Where did she get a ladder from?'

'It must have been in the outhouse. She's also taken something important with her.'

'What? You were stupid enough to leave some there? Why didn't you take it away with you?'

Christos hung his head miserably. 'It was locked in the cupboard. I didn't think she could get to it. Oh, my God!'

'What is it? Have you found her?'

'Police,' whispered Christos. 'A police car has just pulled up.'

'Call me back later.' Lakkis replaced the receiver.

Christos opened the door with a puzzled expression on his face. 'How can I help you?'

Yiorgo showed the search warrant. 'I assume you will comply with this order?'

Christos shrugged and opened the door wider, allowing Yiorgo, Takkis and two other policemen to enter. 'Do I have a choice?'

'Not really.' Yiorgo smiled. 'I suggest we sit in the living room whilst the search is carried out. We have a few questions we would like you to answer. First of all, where is the girl?'

'What girl?'

'We know that you collected a young lady from the *'Aegean Gem'* yesterday afternoon and brought her down here. Where is she?'

'I've no idea.'

'Come, now. This is not a large house. Wherever you have hidden her we will be sure to find her. You might just as well tell us and save us the trouble.'

'I don't know anything about her.'

Yiorgo's eyes swivelled to the suitcases still standing at the side of the room. 'I think you do. You collected her luggage, then she was seen getting into your van and later entering this house down here.'

Christos sat silently. The two policemen left the bedroom and went into the kitchen. They could be heard moving everything off the shelves, opening the fridge and then moving it away from the wall. He guessed they would also want an answer to the broken window and smashed cupboard. Now he was thankful that the girl had taken the two packs he had not had time to weigh up and also made a delivery to the warehouse the previous day. The only incriminating thing the police would find was the pair of scales.

The police finally returned to the living room and shook their heads. Takkis went out to the kitchen and supervised the removal of the scales, ensuring that they were not touched as they were placed into the polythene bag and sealed securely.

'So where is the girl?' asked Yiorgo again.

'I have no idea.'

'Stop playing games with me. She has to be somewhere. You have her luggage.'

'I was asked to look after it for a few days. I don't know where she is.'

Yiorgo looked at Takkis, who shook his head. 'She's definitely not in the house.'

'Go with the men and look outside. Go to every building if necessary and see if she's hiding in one of those.' Yiorgo looked back at Christos. 'It would be so much easier and would waste less time if you told us where she is.'

'I honestly don't know.' Christos clasped his hands together.

'If we don't find her, we shall have no option but ask you to accompany us back to the station to answer further questions,' threatened Yiorgo.

Christos shrugged. 'If I knew where she was I'd tell you. She means nothing to me.'

Takkis returned and beckoned to Yiorgo. He indicated the broken window in the kitchen and then pointed to the ladder leaning against the gates to the beach. 'I reckon she climbed over those gates. There's some bedding on the other side. She probably threw it down there to cushion her fall.'

'She could be hiding out somewhere over there.' Yiorgo looked at the small rowing boat that was turned upside down on the shingle. 'Maybe under that boat. Keep an eye on it for any movement and I'll see if our friend inside has a key to the gates.'

Drained of energy, Sorrell walked slowly down the hill towards the old town. She vaguely recognised the area as one she had walked through with Frida and turned off on the path leading to the town gate. Once she was inside she immediately knew where she was, but had no idea where to go to find Joseph or the warehouse. She walked along to where the road led down the hill, one of the main shopping streets, and decided to keep to the right. The narrow road had a few gift shops; then seemed to be residential. It was an area she had not visited before.

A woman was sitting outside a gift shop and Sorrell stopped before her.

'I'm lost,' she smiled. 'I have to take a message to Joseph at the warehouse and I have no idea where it is.'

The woman frowned and called to her husband.

'Where's the warehouse?'

'What warehouse?' The man appeared, wiping his hands down his trousers.

'The one that sells organic flour,' said Sorrell.

'Oh, that one. Down the hill,' he waved his hand. 'Walk to the Athanasiou gate. It's one of the buildings on the right.'

'Thank you.'

Sorrell continued, slipping and sliding on the cobbles. She had forgotten how difficult it was to walk on them in leather-soled sandals, and was not at all certain that she was walking in the right direction. The road was deserted of inhabitants and before her she could see mounds of rubble. As she reached the piece of waste land the road veered to the left for a few yards and then she was able to turn right or left. To the right she could see the arch of a gate and hoped it was the one she wanted.

There were only three buildings on the right hand side of the road, the last of them looking like a storehouse on the ground floor. Sorrell hammered on the door and it was opened by a young man who peered at her curiously.

'What do you want?'

'Joseph.'

Alecos frowned. 'He's not here.'

'Please,' Sorrell leant against the door jamb. 'Please help me.'

Alecos looked around. The two women sitting outside their general store were looking at him curiously.

'Come in,' he said, and all but pulled her through the entrance, slamming the door behind her. 'What do you want?' he asked.

Sorrell could feel herself shaking and shivering. 'I'm a friend of Joseph's,' she tried to collect her thoughts. 'He said he would help me. I've been held prisoner and managed to escape.' She licked her dry lips. 'I've been walking all night and I'm exhausted.'

Alecos eyed her suspiciously. Was Joseph running a little business on the side? 'Who are you?'

'It doesn't matter who I am. Joseph knows me. Please,' she begged, desperately.

There was a knock on the door and Alecos looked worried. 'Get upstairs,' he ordered, 'and keep quiet.'

With trembling knees Sorrell mounted the stairs and found herself in Joseph's apartment. As her eyes grew accustomed to the dim light she could see the outline of his bed and made her way towards it. At least she would be able to lie down and hopefully sleep for a while. She kicked off her sandals and lay down thankfully.

Alecos dealt with his customer and scratched his head. What was he supposed to do about the girl? He picked up the telephone and dialled the number for the *'Aegean Gem'*. Lakkis answered with alacrity.

'I've got a girl here,' blurted out Alecos.

'What do you mean?'

Alecos drew a deep breath. 'About half an hour ago a girl knocked on the door and said she was a friend of Joseph's. She claims to have been walking all night and at the moment she's asleep upstairs on Joseph's bed.'

Lakkis was speechless. Could the girl have reached Rhodes town in such a short time?

'Are you there?' asked Alecos.

'Yes, yes, I'm here. What does she look like, this girl?'

Alecos described what he could remember of Sorrell, long dark hair, large eyes, good figure, but she had seemed frightened and exhausted.

Lakkis smiled to himself. 'Listen to me carefully, Alecos, and follow my instructions exactly.'

Yiorgo was feeling frustrated. The police had opened the suitcases and found nothing except clothes and toiletries. The out building had been thoroughly searched and also the beach. There was no sign of the girl in the vicinity.

Apart from the luggage, the only indication that she had ever been there was a pair of shorts and beach shoes stuffed out of sight behind a rock.

Yiorgo held them up and showed Christos. 'So where is she?'

'I've told you,' he spoke sulkily. 'I don't know. Maybe she went for a swim. The currents are strong round here. Maybe she couldn't get back in and went to the next bay.'

Yiorgo shrugged. 'Very well. I believe you when you say you don't know where she is, but it is very important that we find her.' He decided to elaborate on their enquiries. 'We need to speak to her to eliminate her from our enquiries into a suspicious death that occurred recently. It is fairly certain that she had no hand in it whatsoever, but we have to confirm that. Someone,' he leant weight to the word, 'is trying to prevent us from interviewing her.'

Christos face paled. 'I was only asked to look after her for a couple of days. I wasn't told why.'

'And who was it who made this request?'

'I – I don't know his name.'

'Oh, I think you do. I think it was Mr Lakkis Pavlides. Why else would he bring her out to your van at the *'Aegean Gem'*?'

'He said he had been asked to send her here.'

'And who had asked him?'

Christos shook his head. 'I'm just a van driver. I don't ask questions.'

Yiorgo shook his head sadly. 'Maybe you should. I regret we have to ask you to come to the station with us to answer a few more questions.'

'You mean you're arresting me? Why? I don't know anything about that girl.'

'It isn't just the girl, Mr Gilades, there's also a pair of scales in your kitchen that have come to our notice. We're taking those with us also. Our forensic laboratory will be asked to examine them and if I'm not mistaken there will have traces of heroin on the pan.'

Christos's face was ashen. 'You can't arrest me. My wife needs me. She's an invalid.'

'Well, provided we are satisfied with your answers you should be back with her very shortly.'

Christos looked close to tears as he picked up his jacket and was escorted out to the police car.

Alecos clattered up the stairs to where Sorrell was lying on Joseph's bed

'Get up,' he said abruptly and Sorrell opened her eyes and groaned.

'I can't.'

'Yes, you can. You can't stay here. I've spoken to Joseph and he said I was to help you. You're to come with me to my sister's house.'

Sorrell looked at him bemused. 'Why can't I stay here?'

'If you stay here the people who held you prisoner will find you. At my sister's house you'll be safe.'

'Where's Joseph?'

'He's out of town for a few days.'

Sorrell shook her head. 'How do I know I can trust you?'

Alecos sat down on the side of the bed. 'Do you have a choice? I've told you my sister will look after you, but you'll have to do as I say.'

'What do you mean?'

'You'll have to stay in the house. If you go out you could be seen. If you stay inside no one will know you're there.'

'How long will I have to stay there?'

'I don't know. Until Joseph returns, I expect. He'll look after you then.'

Slowly Sorrell swung her legs over the side of the bed. 'I can't walk very far,' she announced.

'You won't have to. She only lives a short distance away.'

Sorrell bent and replaced her sandals. When she stood her legs felt weak and her feet were so sore she could hardly place one before the other. Alecos watched as she made her way slowly down the stairs and stood in the warehouse waiting for him. Almost as an afterthought he went to the shelf where a quantity of cigarette packets sat, minus their cellophane wrappers. He placed them in a carrier bag and hung it over his arm. The loss would be attributed to Joseph and Lakkis would think he had been running a little business of his own on the side.

Cautiously he opened the door. As usual the two women were sitting opposite in their chairs and Alecos frowned. He would just have to brazen it out. He snapped the padlock on the door and took Sorrell's arm.

'This way, I'll take you. Nadia will be so pleased to see you.'

Sorrell looked at him in surprise and said nothing. She was too busy concentrating on walking.

Alecos steered her into the main road opposite, crossed two small intersections and turned left. Half way down the row of houses he stopped and knocked on a door.

'Closed,' came a sleepy voice from inside.

'Nadia, it's me. It's urgent. Open the door.'

Sorrell felt that she would collapse if she was not able to sit down soon, and the wait for the door to be opened seemed interminable. Nadia, dressed only in a grubby dressing gown, poked her head round the opening, her eyes opening wide when she saw Alecos had a girl with him.

'Let us in,' he said tersely and Nadia opened the door. 'She needs a bed,' he jerked his head towards Sorrell.

Nadia raised her eyebrows. 'She'll have to share mine.'

'Take her in and I'll explain.' Alecos released Sorrell's arm and she nearly fell over with exhaustion.

Nadia opened the door to her bedroom and pointed to the rumpled bed. 'Make yourself at home.'

Sorrell did not answer; she kicked off her sandals and fell on the soiled sheet gratefully.

Nadia folded her arms. 'What's this all about, Alecos?'

Alecos placed a finger to his lips. 'It's orders from Lakkis. You're to keep the girl here. She mustn't go out. She's on the run from the police. Here,' he pushed the carrier bag into her hands. 'Hide it somewhere safe.'

Nadia's eyes opened wide. 'She can't stay here! What about my clients?'

'You'll have to put them off for a few days. It's only until Joseph comes out of hospital. He'll look after her then.'

'If I have to put off my clients, tell Lakkis not to expect any rent money this week.'

Alecos grinned. 'If it means losing out on his rent he won't leave her here for long. I'll be back when I've closed the warehouse. Just keep her quiet and inside, and not a word about this,' he tapped the carrier bag. 'Make sure you put it somewhere safe.'

Nadia nodded and pulled her wrap closer. 'Can I get back to sleep now?'

'Look on it as a holiday.' Alecos grinned again as Nadia shut the door and locked it behind him.

Alecos returned to the warehouse and telephoned Lakkis to tell him that he had carried out his instructions

Yiorgo and Takkis supervised the detention of Christos Gilades and ensured that the scales would be sent immediately to the forensic laboratory to be tested.

Yiorgo rubbed his hands together. 'If his wife really is an invalid he might be willing to give us information in exchange for an early release.'

'What now?' asked Takkis.

'I think we visit the warehouse next. See exactly what Alecos is selling on behalf of Joseph. When we've dealt with him we can move on to *The Grapevine* and see if there's anything in there.'

Unsuspecting Alecos answered the door, expecting a customer and was taken aback when he found the police on his doorstep. 'What do you want?' he asked.

'We have a search warrant for the premises.' Yiorgo flashed it before him and placed his foot inside the door.

Alecos shook his head. 'It's not my warehouse. I'm only doing a favour whilst Joseph is off sick. I know you.' The realisation came upon him suddenly. 'You're the men who've been visiting *The Grapevine*.'

Yiorgo nodded. 'That's right. We know where your regular work is, so just let us have a look round here and there'll be no problem.'

Yiorgo and Takkis stood each side of Alecos as the policemen examined the ground floor, finding crates of organic flour and cartons of cigarettes. Sitting beneath a small table were the two boxes that Christos had delivered the previous day and Yiorgo stood in front of them protectively. The police disappeared up to Joseph's living quarters and very quickly found the false bottom in the chest containing some thousands of drachmas. They returned with the information to Yiorgo and Takkis.

'A false bottom to a chest; looks like he stored his savings in there. Nothing else,' announced the policeman quietly.

Yiorgo nodded. 'Let's take a look in these two boxes.' He stood to one side and Takkis lifted the lid. Inside, carefully packed were small transparent packets containing brown powder.

Yiorgo turned to Alecos. 'So what is it that you dispense from here?'

'Organic flour.'

'And?'

Alecos shrugged. 'Cigarettes.'

Yiorgo picked up a packet, finding there were only seven inside. 'Where are the others?' he asked.

'I smoked them,' answered Alecos. 'That's my packet.'

'What about these boxes and their contents?'

Alecos shrugged. 'I've no idea about those.'

Takkis wrote out a receipt for the boxes and Alecos was asked to check and sign that the quantities stated were correct. The money from the chest was counted and the amount written on an official form, signed by both officers.

'Shall we go?' asked Yiorgo.

'Go? Go where?' asked Alecos.

'I think it would be more suitable if you accompanied us to the police station, so that you can make your statement. Before that we will call at *The Grapevine* and see if we find anything of interest there. We have a warrant.'

'Can I make a 'phone call?' asked Alecos anxiously.

'Who to?'

'I must let Mr Lakkis know what is happening. He owns the warehouse and the taverna.'

'I think that can wait until later.' Yiorgo turned to the two policemen who had accompanied him to undertake the search. 'Put the boxes in the car and drive them back to the station. Ensure you get a receipt when you hand them over. Check that the money goes into the safe. Make arrangements for two more officers to meet us at *The Grapevine*. We'll be waiting for you.'

Sulkily Alecos locked the door to the warehouse and set off towards *The Grapevine* with Yiorgo and Takkis. He was not at all sure what was happening, but he did not feel at all comfortable as he was escorted back to the taverna. He unlocked the gates and lifted the shutter to the bar.

'That's a good idea. Let's have a beer whilst we're waiting,' said Takkis and silently Alecos went to the fridge and brought three beers to the table. He knew what they were looking for and was thankful that he had taken the packets from the warehouse and left them with his sister.

Yiorgo looked at the uncomfortable young man. 'How long have you worked here?'

'Four seasons.'

'What do you do in the winter?'

'This and that. Whatever comes along.' Alecos moistened his lips. 'Why are you searching the place?'

Yiorgo rubbed the side of his nose and looked speculatively at Alecos. 'We've heard that one or two – unsavoury things – happen here about.'

'What kind of things?'

'Well,' Yiorgo appeared to hesitate. 'There was that unfortunate accident the young man Joseph had. What can you tell us about that?'

'Nothing.' Alecos looked at them fearfully. 'I swear it was nothing to do with me. The first I knew of it was when Mr Lakkis telephoned me.'

'So Mr Lakkis told you about Joseph?'

Alecos nodded. 'He telephoned me early and said Joseph had

met with an accident and would I go up and open the warehouse. He said he would drop the spare keys in before he went down to Faliraki.'

'So Mr Lakkis came down here to give you the keys. What did he say about Mr Konstandides's accident?'

'He just said he had fallen over the castle wall.'

'And do you think that is the truth?'

Alecos shrugged. 'That's what I was told.'

'Just suppose he didn't fall, suppose someone pushed him? Who do you think might have a motive for wanting Mr Konstandides out of the way?'

Alecos shrugged again. 'I don't know.'

'I remember you telling us that he had taken your job at the warehouse and also taken your girl. That would be a motive for many people.'

Alecos's eyes were wide and fearful. 'I didn't push him. Mr Lakkis said he would be leaving at the end of the season and I could have the job then.'

'And what about your girl?'

'I've already got her back.'

'So you wouldn't have any reason to give him a push?'

'I swear I had nothing to do with it. Ask him. He'll say I was nowhere near him.'

'Where were you that particular night?'

'I spent the evening here.'

'And after you closed? What did you do then?'

'I would have gone to bed.'

'What kind of time would that have been?'

'Probably about midnight, maybe later. It would depend what time I finished clearing up.'

Yiorgo nodded sombrely. 'That would have been about the time of the accident.'

Alecos jumped to his feet. 'What are you trying to do? I keep telling you I had nothing to do with it.'

'That we will have to see. Ah, this looks like our colleagues arriving now.' Yiorgo stood up and gave his instructions to the two officers. 'If we could just have the keys to the house, please, Alecos.'

Alecos handed over a bunch of keys. 'That's the front door,' he mumbled.

It took over three hours for the police to search the premises and when they reported back to Yiorgo he was disappointed. 'Absolutely nothing! Well, I am surprised.'

Alecos had a smirk on his face. 'I knew you were wasting your time.'

Yiorgo shrugged. 'The public often think we have wasted our time, but you'd be surprised how many times something turns up, often in the most unlikely places. Now, if you would like to lock up, we'll make our way to the police station.'

'What for?'

'I did explain to you earlier. We need a statement from you regarding the sales from the warehouse.'

'I still want to telephone Mr Lakkis.'

'Later,' replied Yiorgo grimly. 'He will be informed of the proceedings in due course.'

Alecos was thoroughly frightened. He had been sitting alone in the cell for hours and he had no idea what was going to happen to him. He tried to marshal his thoughts. He had not needed to open the boxes of heroin, and he decided he would continue to deny all knowledge of their contents. There was no way the police could prove otherwise. They had not asked him about the girl and he would not volunteer the information. To do so would lead them to Nadia, and that was another thing he did not want them to know about. He just wished he could speak to Lakkis. He would tell him the best thing to do.

Christos sat with his head in his hands. How much longer would he have to sit here before the police took his statement and released him? They had to release him. He must return to his wife. His mother-in-law could not look after her indefinitely.

Dimitris was closeted with his solicitor. He sensed that Piriklis did not believe his story. The man kept asking for more details of the incident of years ago, and although Dimitris could remember exactly what had happened he was not willing to disclose the information unless it became absolutely necessary. He had spent one night in the cell, having been refused bail, and as far as he could see he would be spending the next one there also.

Lakkis was worried. He had telephoned Christos and then Alecos and received no reply from either of them. He did not know if Dimitris was still at the police station or whether he had returned to his boat. If he had been released Lakkis was sure that he would have left Rhodes as he had proposed. The prospect of Dimitris disappearing alarmed Lakkis. Without the millionaire's presence the entire blame for the operation they had been running could fall on him and he did not want to speculate on the consequences.

He was almost relieved when an unmarked police car arrived at the *'Aegean Gem'* and he was asked to accompany the two men to the police station in Rhodes town. At least he should now know what was happening. He was placed in a side room and asked to wait.

'Who shall we see first?' asked Takkis.

'Alecos, I think. I'm not convinced that he's as innocent as he claims, but we haven't got anything we can charge him with unless he likes to make any admissions.'

'Do you think Alecos had anything to do with the Joseph Konstandides incident?'

'Who knows?' Yiorgo shrugged.

'You heard what he said earlier. I doubt if he'll change his story and unless Joseph can positively identify him there's no way we can charge him with it.'

Alecos spent an hour giving his statement. As Yiorgo had surmised, the answers to his questions did not differ from those he had given earlier.

Yiorgo regarded the nervous young man gravely. 'We are going to release you, but there are conditions imposed. You are not to enter the warehouse. You can open up *The Grapevine* and continue your work there. I need hardly tell you that you will be under surveillance. If we are in any way suspicious of your activities you will be arrested and I do not expect that we will be so lenient the next time. Do you understand?'

'Yes, sir,' whispered Alecos and hurried from the police station.

Christos sat before Yiorgo and Takkis silently. He was not sure what was expected of him. Finally Yiorgo looked up from his notes.

'Would you please tell us exactly what your job entails.'

'I deliver the produce to the local tavernas.'

'And how many days a week do you do that?' asked Takkis.

Christos shrugged. 'Three, sometimes four. It depends.'

'What does it depend on?'

'Whether the fruit and vegetables are ready and how much the farmers have picked.'

'Do you always deliver to the same tavernas?'

'Usually.'

'And who employs you to make these deliveries?'

'No one employs me. It's my business. It's how I make my money.'

Yiorgo raised his eyebrows. 'So who pays you? The farmers?'

Christos nodded.

'There are, what, a dozen farmers? And you deliver three, sometimes four times a week. I would not have thought that would have provided you with enough money to run a van and cover your living expenses. What other work do you do?'

'Odds and ends. Anything that comes my way.'

'What kind of odds and ends?'

'Take messages, deliver things from one taverna to another. A bit of painting in the winter months.'

Yiorgo wrote on the pad of paper in front of him. 'And what do you use the scales for?'

'I don't.'

'Really? Why do you have them if you don't use them?'

'They're just there.'

Yiorgo looked at the man in front of him levelly. 'So what was in the boxes that you delivered to the warehouse in the old town?'

Christos shrugged. 'I don't know. I was just asked to deliver them.'

'And who asked you to make the delivery.'

'I didn't ask his name.'

'Oh, I think you know very well who asked you to deliver them and what they contained. You had been weighing up heroin, hadn't you? Each week you make up the packets and deliver them to the warehouse ready for further distribution, don't you?'

Christos's eyes swivelled nervously. 'I don't know what you're talking about.'

Yiorgo sat forwards. 'You have been under surveillance and we know you make up the packets and then deliver them. This week you visited the *'Aegean Gem'* and collected the keys to the warehouse as the usual man is in hospital. Having deposited the boxes you went back down to Faliraki to return the keys. That was when you were told to take the girl back with you, wasn't it?'

'I have no idea what you're talking about.' Christos swallowed nervously. 'I was asked to go down to the *'Aegean Gem'* to collect the girl's luggage and take her back with me for a couple of days. That's all there was to it.'

Takkis shook his head. 'There's a good deal more to it than that. I suggest you tell us the whole story. Why were you asked to take the girl?'

'I wasn't told why.'

'Wasn't it because the police were looking for her?'

Christos shrugged and did not answer.

Yiorgo sighed deeply. 'Mr Gilades, I'm afraid I find your answers most unsatisfactory. I regret that we will be charging you with being in possession of drugs, distributing drugs and kidnapping.'

Christos's face paled. 'You can't do that. What about my wife? I have to be with her. She's an invalid.'

Yiorgo spread his hands. 'The choice is yours. If you are honest with us we may be able to allow you to go home. If you were to give us further information that was of assistance to us we might even find we could drop some of the charges against you. We'll just take your fingerprints, Mr Gilades, for the records. I trust you have no objection?'

Christos looked at the detective miserably. 'They should already be on record. I've done time.'

Yiorgo raised his eyebrows. 'And what offence had you committed?'

'I needed money for drugs. I was arrested for robbery.'

'When was this?'

'I served five years. I was released three years ago. I've not committed any crime since – and I'm clean.'

Yiorgo shook his head. 'I think the possession of drugs with intent to supply is a criminal offence. Added to the other charges you could be looking at a term considerably longer than five years.'

'If I tell you what you want to know will you allow me to leave?'

'Very likely, but we will have to be convinced that you are telling us the truth and not holding back any information.'

Christos swallowed and rubbed his hand over his head. 'I do

weigh up the drugs,' he said quietly. 'It's part of my job to weigh them up and take them into the warehouse once a week.'

Yiorgo nodded. 'And where do these drugs come from?'

'I get a message to go fishing. I anchor in a certain place and at some point a boat arrives and hands me a package.'

'And where does this boat come from?'

'I honestly don't know. It's dark and I was told it was better not to be nosey.'

'Do you really expect us to believe that?'

'Truly. I don't know. I've never been told.' Christos spoke earnestly.

'All right, we'll gloss over that for the moment. You might remember a little more later on.' Yiorgo smiled at the man's discomfiture. 'What happens to these drugs after you have delivered them?'

'Again, I don't know. I presume someone else collects them. I was just told to take them to the warehouse.'

Yiorgo sighed. 'So who pays you for delivering to the warehouse?'

'Mr Lakkis.' The words were mumbled.

'Would you mind repeating that name. I'm not sure if we heard correctly.'

'Mr Lakkis.'

'Mr Lakkis who?'

'Mr Lakkis Pavlides.'

'The manager of the '*Aegean Gem*'?'

Christos nodded.

Yiorgo sat back and smiled. 'Thank you Mr Gilades.'

'May I go now?' asked Christos anxiously.

Yiorgo shook his head. 'I think we need to have a few more details before we can comply with that request.'

Christos spent a further hour answering their questions to the best of his ability and by the end of that time both Yiorgo and

Takkis were convinced he knew nothing more. They left him whilst they went outside to confer together and agreed they would release him, but he would have to appear before them again the next day.

Yiorgo sat in front of Christos and explained the conditions for his release and Christos agreed gratefully.

'Now,' Yiorgo turned to Takkis. 'Time for Mr Pavlides, I think.'

Alecos hurried to Nadia's house and knocked on her door. She was still in her dressing gown and she frowned and put her fingers to her lips when she saw him.

'The girl is still asleep.'

Alecos sat down and placed his head in his hands. 'I've just come from the police station. They came to the warehouse and searched it, then went to *The Grapevine* and searched there. Afterwards they took me into custody to make a statement.'

'What for?'

'They found some boxes in the warehouse. Luckily I hadn't had to open them and I'd brought the packets here, so I kept telling them I knew nothing about them. They can't prove anything against me, but I've got to be careful. They said they would be watching me.'

Nadia frowned. 'I had a look in her bag. She's got two large packs in there. What am I supposed to do with those?'

'Hide them. Give her just what she needs. We don't want her to go wandering off to sell it anywhere.'

Nadia nodded. 'What did Mr Lakkis say?'

'I wasn't allowed to telephone him.'

'I think you should. Use my 'phone.'

Alecos nodded and dialled the number of the *'Aegean Gem'* only to be told that Mr Lakkis had left some time ago with two men, although his car was still outside. Alecos replaced the receiver thoughtfully. It sounded as if Lakkis had been picked up by the police also.

'What about the girl?' asked Nadia.

'Make sure you keep her. Do as Lakkis said until he takes her off our hands.'

Nadia frowned. 'How am I supposed to keep her here if she decides to leave?'

Alecos smiled. 'She has a habit. If she's reliant on you for her supply she'll not go far.'

Nadia gave him a doubtful look and walked into the bedroom. Sorrell woke up abruptly as Nadia placed a hand on her shoulder, her eyes wide with fear.

'Where am I?' she asked.

'You're quite safe,' replied Nadia. 'Get up when you're ready and I'll make you something to eat.'

Sorrell nodded. She noticed sleepily that she was still dressed in her blouse and trousers despite lying on a bed. As her eyes focused she looked at the plain white walls, the frilled pink bed cover, the pink lamp and pink curtains. It was obviously a woman's room. Slowly she swung her legs over the side and winced as her feet touched the ground. Tentatively she put her weight on them and holding on to the end of the bed took a couple of experimental steps.

Feeling extremely unsafe she walked through into the living room and sat down on the sofa.

'I feel terrible,' she muttered.

Nadia placed a glass of water beside her. 'You've been asleep for hours.'

Sorrell looked from her to Alecos. 'Why am I here?'

'I brought you this morning,' Alecos reminded her and Sorrell nodded slowly. 'You turned up at Joseph's and I brought you here so you would be safe. Remember?'

Sorrell took a mouthful of the water. 'Where is Joseph?'

'He had an accident. He'll be in hospital for a few days.'

'What happened to him?'

Alecos shrugged. 'I'm not sure. He seems to have been drunk and fallen over the castle wall.'

Sorrell appeared to consider that information. 'What am I going to do?'

'You're going to stay here with me,' announced Nadia firmly. 'Apparently the police are looking for you, something to do with the harbour master's death. Mr Dimitris told them you'd left the island.'

'I had nothing to do with it.' Sorrell was adamant.

'I'm sure you didn't,' Nadia placated her. 'But if the police are looking for you it's better for you to stay here.'

'Lakkis will find me.' Sorrell looked at Nadia fearfully.

'Why should Lakkis want to find you?'

'I don't know. He kept me at his hotel for a week, then he locked me in my room and sent me off to wherever that man Christos lives. All my clothes are there.' Sorrell looked at Nadia in distress.

'You can manage without those for a few days,' retorted Nadia brusquely. 'You won't be going anywhere.'

'What do you mean?'

'You say you don't want Mr Lakkis to find you and you don't want the police to find you. The choice is yours. You can either stay here, in the house, with me, or you can go wherever you please and see who finds you first.'

Sorrell shivered. 'I need a shot,' she muttered.

'And where do you think you're going to get a supply if you go wandering off on your own?' asked Nadia. 'You stay here and do as I say and you'll have no problem at all. I'll look after you.'

Sorrell swallowed. Her mouth felt dry and she could feel the beginning of cramp in her stomach. She lifted dull eyes to Nadia. 'I've got plenty of my own.'

Nadia shook her head. 'You did have – and I'll not ask where you got it. Alecos relieved you of it, for your own good. We wouldn't want you to overdose and harm yourself. I'll give you what you need provided you do as I say and behave yourself.'

Lakkis sat in the interview room hoping that neither Yiorgo nor

Takkis realised how nervous he was. He crossed his legs and tried to smile.

'I trust this will not take very long? I do have a hotel to manage.'

Yiorgo smiled back. 'That will depend upon you, Mr Pavlides. If you are able to answer our questions to our satisfaction we should be no more than an hour or two. I understand your lawyer is with Mr Stephanotis at present. Do you wish to start without him or would you prefer to wait until he is free?'

Lakkis frowned. 'How long will he be?'

'I have no idea. We could start with the easy questions first. You're free to call a halt whenever you wish and wait for your lawyer.'

Lakkis confirmed his name, address in Rhodes town, that he had been the manager of the *'Aegean Gem'* for five years and owned the taverna known as *The Grapevine*.

'So how long have you known Mr Dimitris?' asked Yiorgo.

Lakkis shrugged. 'About seven years, I think.'

'And how long have you been the owner of *The Grapevine*?'

'Ten or eleven years.'

Yiorgo raised his eyebrows. 'So you gave up running a profitable taverna that you own to become an employee at a hotel?'

Lakkis spread his hands. '*The Grapevine* only makes a profit during the season. By the time I had paid my overheads there was very little left. It was more profitable for me to manage the hotel and have an annual salary. It made sense to employ someone else to run the taverna during the summer. It is only until my son leaves the army, then he will take it over.'

Yiorgo frowned. 'You found it difficult to make a reasonable profit, you say. How will he manage?'

'I had a family to support. When he has married, he and his wife will live there, but he will not have the same outgoings. He will not have to pay rent – it will be my wedding gift to them.'

'Is he planning to get married?'

Lakkis nodded. 'He is betrothed to my niece, Thalia Pavlides. When his army duties finish they will be married.'

'I see. The man, Alecos, who runs the taverna at the moment. What can you tell me about him?'

'He's a local man. He worked part time for me during the busiest time of the season when I ran the taverna. He proved reliable, so he was the obvious choice to run it on my behalf.'

'And he manages to make a good living?'

'He doesn't complain, but he doesn't have a wife and family to support and I allow him to lodge in the house.'

'What will he do when your son takes over? Will he still be employed by you?'

Lakkis shrugged. 'I could find him a job at the hotel if he wanted one. He may wish to move on to another taverna. I would give him a good reference. We haven't discussed it.'

Yiorgo raised his eyebrows. 'I understood from Alecos that you had promised him employment at your warehouse next season.'

'I may have mentioned it in conversation. Nothing was definitely offered to him.'

'Now, let us move on to the man, Christos. He was seen at your hotel earlier in the week. What was he doing there?'

'He delivers fruit and vegetables to us regularly.'

'What else does he deliver?'

Lakkis frowned. 'I really would not know in detail. I usually leave my head chef to deal with the food suppliers.'

'But on the last occasion you were seen talking to Christos.'

Lakkis tried to relax. 'I asked him to take the young lady back to Mr Dimitris's boat.'

Takkis nodded. 'Why was the young lady with you at the hotel? I understood she was travelling with Mr Dimitris.'

Lakkis lowered his eyes, feigning embarrassment. 'I believe Mr Dimitris had met someone else who had attracted him.'

Takkis raised his eyebrows. 'I see. So he asked you to take her off his hands?'

'He suggested she had a change of scene at the hotel for a while.'

'And what did she do whilst she was there?'

'The same as the other guests. Swam, sun-bathed.' Lakkis shrugged.

'Wasn't she lonely?'

'My niece came down to be with her. She had had a few days off work to recuperate from the shock of her father's death.'

'So why did you ask Christos to take her back to Mr Dimitris's boat?'

'Mr Dimitris asked me to arrange it.'

'Really?'

Lakkis licked his lips. 'That's what he said to me.'

Yiorgo rose and walked across the room, a worried frown on his face. 'Can you prove Mr Dimitris spoke to you regarding the return of his companion?'

'No.'

'You see,' Yiorgo turned to Lakkis, 'Mr Dimitris said he had no idea where she was.'

'I don't know why he told you that.'

'The other thing I find rather puzzling; is that Mr Gilades did not take her to Mandraki harbour. Instead he took her to a rather deserted spot on the coast where he works. Do you know the nature of his work, Mr Pavlides?'

'He delivers the local produce to the tavernas and some hotels.'

'That is one of his jobs. Now, the warehouse you have in the Old Town, the one where Alecos thinks he will be working next season. What exactly do you store there?'

'Organic flour.'

'Quite. Who buys this flour?'

'Many of the bakeries and some of the hotels who do their own baking. It has become fashionable.'

'Can you give us a list of these establishments?'

Lakkis shook his head. 'I leave all the paperwork to Joseph. You would have to examine that.'

'We intend to. We have it here. How is the young man?'

Lakkis shrugged. 'I believe he's recovering.'

'How did you hear about his accident?'

'I'm not sure. Someone told me.'

'Who was that someone?'

'I don't know. A man walking down the street, I think.'

Yiorgo looked at the man in contempt. 'I find it strange that an employee of yours should meet with an accident, a very serious accident, I might add, yet you cannot remember who told you. Have you been to visit him?'

'I've been busy.'

'Of course.' Yiorgo nodded. 'I believe you also sell cigarettes from your warehouse?'

Lakkis nodded. 'The main supplier is the other side of town. It's a more convenient place for the locals.'

'Quite so.' Yiorgo leaned forward and placed his fingertips together. 'Now, Mr Pavlides, please correct me if I am wrong. You own a taverna and a warehouse. You employ two young men to run these places on your behalf and you are a hotel manager. How can you afford to do that on your salary?'

'I'm a careful man when it comes to finance.'

'You also have a large house. How long have you lived there?'

Lakkis licked his dry lips. 'Five years, about.'

'Since you became the manager of the hotel – yes? Where did you live before that?'

'At *The Grapevine*.'

Takkis raised his eyebrows. 'I had no idea the position of hotel manager paid so well.'

Yiorgo lit a cigarette and appeared to be considering his next question. 'Can we return to this young man Christos Gilades. Who pays him for his delivery work?'

'How should I know?'

'You should know very well. Part of Mr Gilades work entails weighing up packets of heroin and subsequently delivering it.'

Lakkis looked at his shoes and did not answer.

'Who do you think pays him for that work, Mr Pavlides?'

'I don't know,' muttered Lakkis.

'I think you do know. Christos Gilades assured us that he was working for you. He delivers the drugs to your warehouse. Where do they go from there?'

'I know nothing about them.'

'I find that very hard to believe, Mr Pavlides. You pay a young man to weigh them up and deliver them to your warehouse and after that you have no knowledge of what happens to them?'

'It's nothing to do with me.'

'Then who is it to do with?'

Lakkis did not answer.

'Very well. I take your silence as an admission of guilt. We will be charging you, Mr Pavlides, with drug dealing.'

'No!' Lakkis looked up at them with frightened eyes. 'I have nothing to do with it. You can't charge me.'

Takkis shook his head sadly. 'Unfortunately we have no choice. I suggest you make suitable arrangements for the welfare of your family as you will be leaving them for a very long time.'

Lakkis licked his dry lips. 'I need to see my lawyer.'

Yiorgo pulled the telephone towards him. 'I will see if he is free yet.' Yiorgo replaced the receiver after a short conversation. 'I regret he is still with Mr Stephanotis. We'll take a short break and return later. Can I get you anything, Mr Pavlides? A beer, coffee, cigarettes, whilst you wait?'

Lakkis shook his head. He had been foolish not to request the presence of his lawyer before they started questioning him. He had been so confident that he could talk his way out of the situation by feigning ignorance.

Yiorgo raised his coffee in salutation to Takkis. 'I think we're finally getting somewhere.'

'What about this man Joseph? When will we be able to interview him?'

'I thought we'd go to the hospital tomorrow. We'll have to get clearance from the doctor to question him. Apparently he's said nothing about the assault so far.'

Piriklis paced across his office. What could he do? What should he do as a lawyer? It was his duty both to uphold the law and also to serve his client. It was even more unfortunate that he should have been asked to represent both men. He tapped his pencil against his teeth; then flung it across the room in frustration.

Elias looked at him in surprise. 'What's the problem?'

'I just don't know what to do.'

Elias sat back in his chair. 'About what? Do you want to talk it through?'

Piriklis eyed his colleague doubtfully. 'I'm not sure that I should. If I refuse to continue they may ask you to take my place.'

'I'm far too busy to take on any more work,' replied Elias firmly. He was already certain if Piriklis was pulling out from a case there was no way he would be prepared to take his place. He was a junior partner and would not have the experience or command the respect that Piriklis did in a courtroom.

Piriklis sighed. 'They're both denying all knowledge of the charges. I know they're neither of them telling me the truth. I think they're both guilty, up to their ears, but they both expect me to find some way that they can wriggle out and escape the consequences.'

'What charges?'

'Drug smuggling, receiving, distribution, assault, kidnapping, possibly murder.'

Elias whistled through his teeth. 'And you think they're guilty?'

Piriklis nodded. He walked across and closed the door firmly. 'This is confidential, of course. I was asked by Mr Pavlides to visit Mr Stephanotis in prison. Mr Stephanotis was being questioned about the disappearance of a girl and the death of Nikos Pavlides. It appears Nikos Pavlides was poisoned when he helped himself to some chocolates that were laced with heroin.'

'Was that done deliberately to cause his death?'

'Mr Stephanotis denied all knowledge of the heroin in the chocolates. He said he bought them for the girl who was travelling with him.'

'What does the girl say?'

'She's disappeared. Mr Stephanotis says she packed and left the boat whilst he was ashore and he has no idea where she is. Mr Lakkis Pavlides, who just happens to be the manager of Mr Stephanotis's hotel, says Mr Stephanotis asked him to accommodate her at the hotel for a week as she was bored with Rhodes town.'

'So if she is at the hotel she hasn't disappeared.'

'She was there. Mr Pavlides says that Mr Stephanotis asked him to send her back to his boat. Instead of putting her in a taxi, or driving her up himself, he put her in the van belonging to a delivery man. This man took her down to the bay where he works and left her there over night. When he returned the next day she had disappeared. There were a pair of shoes and shorts on the beach; her luggage was still there, but no sign of her. No one seems to have seen her since.'

'Do you think she went for a swim and drowned?'

'I don't know what to think. Mr Stephanotis says he gave no such instruction as he did not know she was at the hotel and Mr Pavlides swears he did know and told him to arrange her return with the van driver.'

'What does the van driver have to say?'

'I haven't spoken to him yet.' Piriklis ran his hand through his thinning hair. 'Then there are the fingerprints. In the course of their investigations the police took prints from the crew and Mr Stephanotis. Apparently the girl's cabin yielded nothing due to the industrious woman who does the cleaning. Mr Stephanotis's fingerprints were confirmed as those of Christos Drakonisis, a man who was thought to be dead. Mr Stephanotis told me some story that many years ago he saw a robbery and chased after the man to apprehend him. The man fell and hit his head and Mr Stephanotis swapped identities with him as he thought he would be accused of the robbery and subsequently murdering the man.'

'That's preposterous. He must think you and the police are stupid if he expects to be believed.'

'I've tried to press him for details, but he says it was too long ago to remember clearly and has no relevance to any of the present proceedings.'

'Do you believe that?'

Piriklis shook his head. 'I don't know what to believe, but I can't defend a man to the best of my ability unless he's honest with me, guilty or not.'

'And you think they're both guilty?'

'I do, but if I agree to continue with their cases I have to know everything. I could be laughed out of court by the prosecution evidence otherwise.'

Elias nodded soberly. 'In my opinion you should only represent one of them. If their stories contradict each other as you defend one you'll be accusing the other. Tell one of them to find another lawyer.'

'I'll have to work for Mr Pavlides, then. I've been his lawyer for a number of years. He recommended me to Mr Stephanotis.'

'How do you feel about Mr Pavlides? Has he been honest with you in the past?'

Piriklis shrugged. 'Who knows? I had no reason to disbelieve anything he told me. At least he didn't ask me to bribe the police as Mr Stephanotis did.'

Elias gaped. 'I thought that practice had been stamped out.'

'They say every man has his price. No doubt some of the police would have jumped at the chance to settle their debts.' Piriklis smiled wryly. 'Thanks for listening, Elias. Do me one more favour – if you're asked to represent Mr Stephanotis, refuse. We'd be arguing against each other in court and I'd have no one I could discuss the case with and clear my mind.'

Elias smiled. 'I told you, I'm far too busy to take on any more work.'

The doctor received Yiorgo and Takkis in a small side room and agreed they could speak to Joseph for a few minutes.

'You have to understand that he is badly injured. It is a miracle that he is still alive.' The doctor shrugged. 'When he eventually realises the state of his injuries he may wish that he had not survived.'

'What are you implying, doctor?'

'Well, I would say, judging by the bruising on his body, that he took a beating before his fall. He would have had to bounce down the side of a mountain to end up with that many contusions. He would have fallen straight down to the ground, there is nothing for him to hit on the way.'

'Could he have hit the wall as he fell?'

'Extremely unlikely, as you well know. The distance his body was found from the base of the wall indicates that he either jumped over or was thrown. If he jumped it was either to escape whoever was attacking him or he was attempting suicide. Personally I don't think he did either.'

'What makes you draw that conclusion?'

The doctor leaned forward. 'Assuming he was being viciously assaulted, he would not have been physically capable of evading his attackers. If he wished to commit suicide there would be better places to attempt it.'

Yiorgo nodded. 'Apart from the bruising, what is the extent of his injuries?'

'Slight concussion, obviously, although he appears to be recovering well from that. His pelvis is broken in three places, both legs and his right arm. His cheek bone is smashed, there could be damage to his eye and his nose will never look quite the same again.'

'In your opinion, were those injuries caused by the fall or were they inflicted on him beforehand?'

The doctor shrugged. 'Impossible to tell for certain. The facial damage could be from a severe beating. I would say the fractures were caused exclusively by the fall, but I could be wrong.'

'Do you think Mr Konstandides might know?'

'He might, but he is very weak at the moment, and also on morphine to help combat the physical pain he is suffering. I would ask that you be very gentle with your questioning and restrict yourselves to just a few minutes.'

Yiorgo nodded and made for the door. 'Thank you for your time. We'll speak to the officer at his bedside first. If he has gleaned any information we may not need to speak to your patient until he's a bit stronger.'

Takkis relieved Stelios from his monotonous task. He sat in the chair the policeman had occupied and studied the prone figure, swathed in bandages, before him. He wondered what the doctor had meant by his oblique reference to the injuries that could make Joseph wish he had not survived.

Stelios leaned back against the wall. 'What have I done to deserve this?' he asked. 'I'm bored out of my mind sitting here all day.'

'Luck of the draw. Has he said anything?'

Stelios shook his head. 'Nothing that makes any sense. He keeps saying 'Thalia' and has said 'Lakkis' a couple of times. I was told I wasn't to question him, so I just noted how often he said their names. Apart from that he's asked for a drink and more morphine.'

'Has he spoken to the doctor or nurses at all?'

'Only said yes and no when asked if he wanted anything.'

Yiorgo nodded. 'We're not allowed to question him for very long. Give us ten minutes and then be back here. If we feel it's necessary to keep a guard on him next week I'll ask for someone to take your place.'

Stelios smiled. 'Thanks. I'll go and get a coffee and have a smoke. I'll also buy another newspaper. I've read every word in this one.'

Yiorgo joined Takkis and raised his eyebrows. Takkis shook his head and Yiorgo nodded.

'Joseph. Joseph. Can you hear me? Open your eyes if you can hear.'

Slowly Joseph's eyelids flickered and opened. Yiorgo moved within his range of vision and smiled gently at him.

'Hello, Joseph. I'm Yiorgo. I want to talk to you for a few minutes.' Joseph closed his eyes again and Yiorgo continued. 'I know you can hear me, Joseph. You've had a very bad time and we want to help you. Can you remember anything that happened to you before you woke up in the hospital?'

Joseph opened his eyes again. 'Thalia,' he whispered.

'Who's Thalia? Is she your girl? Do you want us to take a message to her? Let her know that you're in hospital?'

'Thalia,' Joseph repeated.

'Did you see Thalia before you had your accident?'

'Meet Thalia.'

'You were on your way to meet Thalia? Is that right? Did you meet someone else first? Someone who picked a fight with you?'

'Yes.'

'Did you know them?'

'No.'

'So why would they want to pick a fight with you? Were they drunk?'

'Lakkis knows.'

'Lakkis knows what?'

'Thalia.'

'Lakkis knows why they attacked you? Was it a fight over your girl?'

'Lakkis.'

'Is this Lakkis the man you work for, at the warehouse?'

'Yes.'

Yiorgo nodded. 'We'll have a word with him.'

'No!' There was fear in Joseph's eyes as he said the word.

Yiorgo frowned. 'You're quite safe here. No one is going to attack you again. We just want to get these young thugs off the streets. Maybe Lakkis saw the attack and can identify them.'

'No,' Joseph repeated. 'Thalia.' He closed his eyes and licked at his dry lips. 'Drink.'

Takkis poured a little water from a bottle into a plastic cup, inserted a straw, and Yiorgo held it to Joseph's lips where he sucked greedily before turning his head away and closing his eyes.

'Tired.'

Takkis shrugged and Yiorgo nodded. They were wasting their time trying to get any more information out of the man.

'You sleep for a while, Joseph. Stelios will be here to keep an eye on you, to make sure that you're safe. You can talk to him if you feel like it. We'll come back when you're feeling stronger.'

Takkis looked towards the glass panel in the door and saw Stelios hovering outside. He beckoned him in and relinquished his seat to him. Yiorgo spoke quietly.

'We didn't get much. If he decides to talk to you try to lead him on and make sure you make a note of everything he says.'

Stelios nodded. He just hoped Yiorgo would remember his promise to relieve him of the onerous duty the following week.

'So,' said Takkis, 'Where do we go from here?'

'I think we should have a few words with a girl called Thalia. She may be able to throw some light on the accident.'

'And where are we going to find her?'

'Think, Takkis. Lakkis Pavlides has a niece called Thalia. I think we start by asking her.'

Takkis frowned. 'If she was with him when it happened that could account for Lakkis knowing about it before anyone else.'

Yiorgo shook his head. 'If she was there when he fell why didn't she send for an ambulance?'

'Maybe she tried,' Takkis persisted. 'Maybe she returned to her uncle's house to call the hospital and her uncle refused to let her.'

Yiorgo looked at his colleague scornfully. 'You'll be telling me next she was the one who threw him over the wall. If Thalia Pavlides was with him it would have been much quicker for her to return to her own house and use a telephone than go to her uncle's house.'

Takkis shrugged. Let Yiorgo have it his way. 'Why don't we call on her aunt first? There's a chance the girl might be staying there.'

Yiorgo considered the idea. 'There's no harm in that. Mrs Pavlides might also be able to tell us if the girl did go there on the night in question.'

Takkis smirked to himself. Yiorgo might have poured scorn on his idea, but he had obviously not discarded it out of hand.

Sorrell sat in the sheltered courtyard of Nadia's one room apartment. She was beginning to feel considerably better. It was possible to walk without causing too much pain in her feet. Nadia had prepared a meal for them both and given her a small amount of heroin after she had eaten. If she could only have a change of clothing she would feel better still. Cautiously she approached the idea.

'Is there any way I could have my cases sent to me?'

Nadia looked at her scornfully. 'And tell everyone you are here? Don't be stupid.'

'I just feel so dirty. I haven't changed my underwear for three days.'

'Give it a wash out tonight.'

'It may not be dry by tomorrow morning.'

Nadia shrugged. 'You can always go without.'

'I ought to wash my blouse and trousers as well.'

'Do so, then. You can borrow my housecoat if you're so concerned about your modesty.'

Sorrell studied the girl from beneath her lashes. She was obviously being kind in a rough and ready way. The room she lived in was dominated by the large bed with pink covers, a pink light and pink curtains, the toilet and shower were outside and an alcove served as a kitchen. During the evening she had heard someone knock at the door on a number of occasions and when Nadia had answered she had carried on a conversation in a low voice, turning the visitor away.

'What do you do, Nadia?'

Nadia gave a chuckle deep down in her throat. 'What business is it of yours?'

Sorrell shrugged. 'None. I just wondered. You've only left the house to go shopping since I arrived.'

'I'm having a little holiday whilst you're here.' Nadia frowned. 'It can't last much longer, whether you're here or not. I shall run out of money even if they do waive my rent and percentage.'

'I don't mind if you go back to work,' Sorrell assured her.

'Maybe you'd like to join me. Sooner or later you're going to have to earn your keep.'

'I shall be all right when Joseph comes out of hospital,' Sorrell assured her. 'He'll look after me.'

Nadia raised her eyebrows. Didn't the girl know she would be expected to look after her protector?

1991
August

Maria Pavlides opened the door and looked at the two policemen fearfully. 'What do you want?'

'Nothing for you to be alarmed about, Mrs Pavlides. If we could just come in for a few moments, we have a couple of questions that we would like to ask you.'

'What kind of questions?'

'Very simple ones. We should be no more than about five minutes.'

Reluctantly Maria led them into her lounge and perched on the edge of a chair. 'Where's my husband?'

'I'm afraid we have had to detain him a little longer. He's being very helpful to us.'

Maria twisted her handkerchief nervously between her fingers. 'What do you want to ask me?'

'Can you tell us anything about a young man called Joseph Konstandides?'

'Joseph?' She looked at them warily. 'Why?'

'I understand he worked at your husband's warehouse and met with an accident a few nights ago. When did you hear about it?'

Maria looked at them, puzzled. 'What accident?'

'He fell from the castle wall.'

'Oh!' Maria's hand flew to her mouth. She swallowed hard. What had Lakkis done? The young man deserved it after his treatment of Thalia, but even so... 'I read about it in the newspaper. I didn't know it was that Joseph.'

'Your husband didn't tell you?'

'No. I don't expect he knew who it was.'

'Really?' Yiorgo regarded her quizzically. 'I understand from Mr Pavlides that he was told by a man in the street.'

Maria shrugged. 'He said nothing to me.'

'Very well. Now, the young lady, Miss Pavlides, can you tell me where I can find her?'

Colour suffused Maria's normally pale face. 'She has nothing to do with it. She doesn't associate with Joseph.'

'We only need to ask her a couple of questions. I understand she works during the day, so if you could just give us the address of her place of employment we'll be able to leave you in peace.'

Maria looked at her watch. 'She will have left for the day.'

'Then we will pay her a visit at her house, unless, of course, she is planning to visit you and you will permit us to wait?'

Slowly Maria shook her head. 'I haven't seen her for a couple of weeks. I've tried to phone, but her line appears to be out of order.'

Yiorgo and Takkis stood up. 'We'll be off, then. Thank you for your help.'

'When will my husband be home?' Maria looked at them with anguished eyes.

'As soon as he has finished helping us with our enquiries,' Yiorgo assured her.

Yiorgo and Takkis began to walk back up the hill. 'What was your impression?' asked Yiorgo.

Takkis considered. 'I don't think she did know it was Joseph who had met with an accident, but the puzzling thing is why didn't her husband tell her? The other thing that struck me was her reaction when you asked about her niece. Why should she jump to the conclusion that the girl was involved?'

Yiorgo shrugged. 'Who knows! Maybe we should get a warrant to search Lakkis Pavlides house.'

'I think we'd be wasting our time. He wouldn't keep anything incriminating on the premises.'

'What about the hotel?'

Takkis shook his head. 'Even more unlikely. An employee could come across it. What better way to ensure a pay rise?'

Yiorgo stopped in his tracks and turned to Takkis. 'You may have got it!'

'What do you mean?'

'Think about it, Christos Gilades is employed by Lakkis Pavlides to deliver drugs to the warehouse, Joseph Konstandides passes them on to the dealers as required. Joseph realised who's behind the operation and asked for a pay rise. The response to his request was to be thrown over the wall.'

Takkis considered. 'It's feasible, but it still doesn't explain the disappearance of the girl.'

Yiorgo continued walking. 'I think she's a red herring that we're chasing. Hitched a lift around the islands for services rendered. Dimitris Stephanotis got tired of her and sent her off to the hotel. When Lakkis Pavlides tired of her he sent her away. She's probably left the island by now, hitched another lift, no doubt.'

'Leaving her clothes behind?'

'She probably reckons she can replace those easily enough. We didn't find her passport or any money or jewellery amongst her belongings, so she's probably carrying plenty on her. I think we can forget her.'

Takkis lit a cigarette and drew on it deeply. He was not as convinced as his superior that the missing girl was of no consequence.

'Who's there?' called Thalia as Takkis knocked on her door.

'The two detectives who called on you after the sad demise of your father,' replied Yiorgo.

Cautiously Thalia opened the door, having secured the safety chain. 'What do you want?'

'We have a couple of questions we would like to ask you. May we come in?'

Thalia nodded and released the chain. 'Please go through.'

Yiorgo noticed the pallor of the girl as she sat before them. She had obviously still not recovered from the shock of her father's death.

'I am sorry to have to trouble you again, Miss Pavlides. We called on your aunt earlier as we thought you might be there and she said your telephone was out of order.' Yiorgo looked very deliberately at the socket where the telephone line had been unplugged.

Thalia followed his look. 'I was receiving so many calls after the death of my father that I disconnected it.'

Yiorgo nodded understandingly. 'People mean to be kind, but it can be too much at such a time. You have not telephoned your aunt?'

'No. I saw her a few days ago.'

'She thought it was more like two weeks since she last saw you.'

Thalia was about to correct him when she changed her mind. If her aunt had not mentioned her visit of five days ago she must have had a reason. 'What did you want to ask me?'

'It concerns the young man Joseph Konstandides who is employed by your uncle.'

If possible Thalia's face went whiter and her eyes took on a frightened look, her reaction not lost on Takkis.

'When did you last see him?'

Thalia swallowed hard. Who had told the police? Surely not her aunt or uncle, maybe the doctor? 'I went out to dinner with him a week ago.'

'Did you often go out with him?'

'No. It was the first time.'

'And when were you going to go out with him again?'

'I wasn't.'

'You did not enjoy yourself?'

Thalia took a deep breath. 'He asked me to dinner as a way of showing his sympathy for the death of my father.'

'There is no romantic attachment?'

'None.'

Yiorgo frowned. 'You did not arrange to meet him again on another evening?'

'Definitely not.'

'You're quite sure?'

'Of course I am. Why are you asking me this? What has Joseph said?'

'Joseph, unfortunately, has said very little so far. You are aware that he is in hospital?'

Thalia shook her head. 'I had no idea.'

'Unfortunately he met with an accident and is badly injured. We spoke to him earlier today and were under the impression that he was planning to meet you when the accident occurred.'

'What happened to him?'

'He fell over the castle wall.'

'What!' Thalia's horror was not feigned, her colour drained completely and Yiorgo thought she might faint. He moved to her side and took her hand, feeling her body go rigid as he did so.

'Put your head down, Miss Pavlides. Takkis, could you fetch a glass of water?'

Thalia bent her head. She did indeed feel faint. She sipped at the water gratefully. 'How did he manage to do that?' she asked finally.

'That is what we are trying to find out. Obviously he was badly injured, broken bones, concussion, cuts and bruises. We spoke to him earlier today. He kept repeating your name and we are under the impression he was on his way to meet you when he fell.'

Thalia shook her head. 'I had no arrangement to meet with him. Maybe he was planning to meet me at work or come to my house. I had made it clear to him that I was not interested in any future meetings. I am betrothed to my cousin, Manolis.'

Yiorgo shrugged. 'No doubt he is confused, but you understand that we had to ask you.'

'Of course.'

Yiorgo and Takkis took their leave. They were both inclined to believe that Thalia Pavlides was speaking the truth, but why had her aunt claimed she had not seen her for two weeks and the girl said it was only a matter of days?

Thalia sat in the chair and buried her face in her hands. She needed to think, no, she did not want to think. She wanted an assurance from her uncle that he had played no part in Joseph's accident. She wished she had not visited them and confessed that she had been intimate with Joseph, but who else did she have to turn to now her father was dead? Tears rolled slowly down her cheeks.

The hammering on her door finally drew her to her feet and she slipped on the security chain before opening it a crack to see her aunt standing outside. Without a word Thalia unchained the door and Maria walked in.

'What have you been saying to the police?' demanded Maria.

'Nothing.'

'I saw them leave. You must have said something.'

'They asked me if I had arranged to meet Joseph. I told them I went out to dinner with him, but nothing more. You didn't tell them?' Thalia's eyes opened wide in horror.

Maria shook her head. 'I told them I hadn't seen you for two weeks. I've tried to 'phone you, but your line is dead.'

'I unplugged it,' confessed Thalia.

'Why did you do that?'

'I didn't want Joseph bothering me. I thought he might telephone.'

Maria rose and plugged the telephone back into the socket. 'He won't be bothering you, he's in hospital.'

'The police told me. They say he fell over the castle wall.'

Maria nodded grimly. 'Pity he didn't break his neck. I didn't come here to talk to you about him. The police have arrested your uncle.'

'Uncle Lakkis! Why?' Thalia dreaded the answer to her question.

'I don't know. I haven't been allowed to see him. They went down to the hotel.'

'Oh!' Thalia let out her breath in relief. 'It's probably something to do with his taxes or fire regulations I expect.'

'That would be no reason to keep him in prison.' Maria wrung her hands. 'I don't know what to do. Shall I ask Manolis to take some leave and come home, or will he and Lakkis be cross with me for making a fuss? I have all these decisions to make and you unplug your telephone!' For the first time Maria began to cry quietly.

Thalia took her aunt's hand. 'I'm sure there must be some very simple explanation. Why don't you 'phone Manolis and explain the situation to him? He could decide whether he should ask for some leave and come up to town.'

'Do you think I should? I don't want to worry him unnecessarily, but I don't know what to do for the best.' Maria's voice broke again.

'Speak to Manolis. 'Phone him now.' Thalia handed the telephone to her aunt. 'I'll make some coffee for us.'

'Don't you want to speak to him?'

Thalia shook her head. 'Not just now. I don't really feel up to it.'

Thalia returned as her aunt replaced the receiver. 'They can't contact him at present. He's away from the base on one of their manoeuvres. The commander said he would give him a message as soon as the platoon returned.'

Thalia nodded thankfully. She really did not feel that she wanted to see Manolis for a while. He would expect to put his arms around her and kiss her and at the moment she did not want to be touched by anyone.

'And now?' asked Takkis.

'A meal would be a good idea. Somewhere relatively quiet where we can talk.'

Takkis nodded. 'It's still early, nowhere should be too busy yet.'

They walked into the old town, avoiding the restaurants frequented by the tourists, until they spotted one that was virtually empty. They chose a table at the back and ordered a beer whilst they waited for their meal.

Yiorgo took out his notebook. 'This is what we know at the moment. Christos Gilades takes drugs to the warehouse. Lakkis Pavlides pays him. Lakkis Pavlides owns the warehouse. Joseph Konstandides is employed by Lakkis Pavlides to look after the warehouse and he is now in hospital, either by accident or design. Dimitris Stephanotis owns the hotel where Lakkis Pavlides is the manager. The harbour master dies of a drug overdose after an evening out. We are pretty certain he inadvertently killed himself by eating the chocolates he had taken. The chocolates came from Dimitris Stephanotis's cruiser and are said to belong to a girl who has disappeared. On the face of it that would clear Dimitris Stephanotis.'

Takkis held up his hand. 'I agree with you so far, but what about the fingerprint problem?'

'I was coming to that.' Yiorgo lit a cigarette and narrowed his eyes against the smoke as it curled up. 'I think we need to go to Santorini to see if his story checks out.'

Takkis groaned. 'Wouldn't it be simpler to ask Athens to look up the archived reports?'

Yiorgo snorted in derision. 'How long would that take them? Months. You know what a mess they are in. If you ask for a file from the previous year it throws them into a panic. No,' he shook his head, 'It will be quicker to go to Santorini ourselves. We'd probably have to go eventually anyway.'

'So when do you plan to leave?'

'We'll find out about flights or ferries tomorrow and take whatever's available. We can hold Mr Pavlides and Mr Stephanotis; charge them both with something and refuse bail. If we can get back within a week Joseph Konstandides should be in a fit state to give us some more information and, who knows, Mr Pavlides may have been forthcoming.'

'What about the others?' asked Takkis.

'Mr Gilades is frightened out of his skin. He'll do as he's told. I don't think that youngster, Alecos, knows anything, and I suggest we forget the girl. She could be anywhere.'

Yiorgo and Takkis arrived on Santorini in the early evening and took a taxi to the hotel in Fira where they had reserved a room. Yiorgo decided there was little point in approaching the police station that night and together they walked through the cobbled streets.

'Pretty place,' remarked Takkis. 'I shall be interested in seeing it in daylight. I've heard the views are spectacular.'

Yiorgo nodded. He was deep in thought. From the little he had seen of the island there seemed to be sheer cliffs down to the sea and Dimitris Stephanotis's story of chasing someone down to the beach seemed very unlikely.

The day dawned hot and airless. By the time the two men had walked from their hotel to the main square where the police station was situated they were both mopping their faces. It was a relief to enter the dark interior, where they made themselves known to the young policeman on duty.

He shook his head. 'I know nothing about it. I would have been a child at the time. Go and have a beer at one of the cafes whilst I make a few telephone calls. Come back in about half an hour and I'll let you know how I've got on.'

Yiorgo and Takkis took his advice, finding a shady taverna in the main square, where they watched the tourists and inhabitants mingling. Yiorgo managed to curb his impatience for three quarters of an hour before paying their bill and returning to the station.

The young officer greeted them with a smile. 'I've both good and bad news for you. I've located the officer who dealt with the case. He's retired now and no longer lives on Santorini. He moved over to Rhodes to be nearer his daughter after his wife died.'

Yiorgo clenched his fists. He should have thought and telephoned the island before they had made the trip. 'Would we be able to read the files on the case?'

'You can if you wish. You'll need to go to the archive office at the top of the hill. They should be able to dig them out for you.' He took his pencil and pulled a sheet of paper towards him. 'You're here. Turn left then follow the road going to the right until you see the hotel at the top of the hill. Just before you reach the hotel is the archive office. Would you like me to telephone through to say you're on your way?'

Yiorgo nodded. 'Tell them which files we want. Hopefully they can have them ready for us. I'd appreciate having the name and address of the retired officer. We can speak to him when we return to Rhodes.'

'Thank you for your help,' added Takkis as they left.

The files gave a graphic description of the injuries to the elderly couple who had been robbed, the man subsequently dying and the woman living a vegetable existence due to extensive brain damage. Records of the fingerprints taken at the taverna listed only those of Christos Drakonisis.

Yiorgo raised an eyebrow. 'Strange that only his prints should be recorded. In a taverna you'd expect to find any number of prints, from total strangers to regulars.'

'Maybe they could account for the others and only kept these as he appeared to be the culprit.'

'Sloppy,' remarked Yiorgo, and continued reading. For a further hour they continued reading and making notes, until Yiorgo declared himself satisfied. 'Back to the police station, I think. I'd like to speak to some of these people mentioned in the files. Mr and Mrs Drakonisis could be interesting; also the taverna couple had a daughter. I'd like to speak to her and hear what she has to say. I'm hoping that young officer will be able to give us their addresses.'

Takkis nodded in agreement. 'Do we tell Mr and Mrs Drakonisis that their son is alive and well, kicking his heels in jail on Rhodes?'

'I don't think so. Certainly not at the moment, anyway. I'd like to know where the taverna was situated. Did anyone see this chase that was supposed to take place?'

'That's a good point. Someone must have seen something.'

Armed with addresses and directions, accompanied by further sketch maps, Yiorgo and Takkis retraced their steps up the hill to the carpet shop that was nearly opposite the archive office. An elderly man sat in the dark interior running his beads through his fingers.

'Excuse me, Mr Drakonisis?'

The man nodded.

'Would it be possible to have a few words privately with you and your wife? It's of rather a sensitive nature.' Yiorgo had thought carefully how he would approach the couple.

'What's it about? I've got an import and export licence for the carpets.'

'You're not in any trouble, I assure you. We'd just like to ask you about something that happened some years ago.'

Mr Drakonisis regarded them suspiciously. 'You'd better come up.' He led the way from the shop, stopping to alert the shop keeper next door that he was leaving his shop unattended, and mounted the stone stairs at the side.

As he opened the door he called out to his wife. 'We've got company.'

A small, white haired woman peered round the door of the kitchen. She wiped her hands on her apron. 'I was just washing up,' she explained.

'We shouldn't have to interrupt you for very long,' Takkis smiled at her. She reminded him of his grandmother.

He took a seat in the tiny living room and waited for his eyes to become adjusted to the dimness. The room was crowded with furniture, barely room to move between each piece, and every surface held a photograph of a smiling young man. Taking up most of one wall was an enlargement of one of the photos, flowers tucked behind the corners and a shark's tooth hanging on a nail beneath. Even at a distance and in the poor light he could see the resemblance to the man they knew as Dimitris Stephanotis.

Yiorgo hesitated. He had no wish to reopen old wounds. 'Please believe me when I say I do not want to cause you any distress.' He swallowed and continued rapidly. 'I understand that you lost your son in the most tragic of circumstances some years ago.'

Mr Drakonisis nodded and his wife wiped her eyes on her apron. 'He was such a good boy,' she said.

'How long had he been missing before his body was found?'

'Three weeks.' A look of pain passed over Mr Drakonisis's face.

'Did you have the distressing job of identifying his body?'

Mr Drakonisis nodded.

'What made you sure it was him?'

'The shark's tooth.' Mr Drakonisis pointed to where it hung on the wall. 'He always wore it.'

'You weren't able to recognise him?'

'Not after all that time in the sea.'

'Can you tell me exactly where he was found?'

'Round at the headland. Wedged between the rocks.' Mr Drakonisis wiped a surreptitious tear from his eye. 'Why do you want to know?'

'Another young man went missing at approximately the same time. He has never been found. We just needed to confirm the identity of your son so we can cross him off our list.'

Mr Drakonisis regarded Yiorgo suspiciously. 'You could have done that from the police records. You didn't need to come and see us.'

'Unfortunately the records from so far back have gone missing. We would never have dreamt of troubling you otherwise. You've been very helpful. Thank you for your time.' Yiorgo rose and walked over to the enlarged photograph. 'This was your son? A fine looking young man. Such a tragedy.' Shaking his head sadly he shook hands with the couple and made for the steps.

Takkis followed him, longing to return to the open air. 'I'd like a beer,' he admitted to Yiorgo.

'So would I, but I'd like to get back down to the square first.'

They walked in silence, finally taking their seats at a secluded table and ordering refreshment.

'So what did you think?' asked Yiorgo.

'I felt sorry for them. Fancy only being able to identify your son by the token he wore round his neck. They've virtually built a shrine to him in that room. It was so claustrophobic.'

'But the photographs were quite definitely of our friend Dimitris Stephanotis. So much for his mother thinking he was a good boy.'

'So much for him saying his parents were dead.'

'So he did! I'd forgotten that. He obviously didn't want us over here sniffing around.' Yiorgo finished his beer. 'Another?'

Takkis nodded. 'No doubt we're going to have to climb to the top of that hill again. I shall need it.'

'No, we're going down first. We'll both need it on the way back up!'

They negotiated the cobbled steps, covered with donkey excrement, carefully. On reaching the small harbour they looked back up at the sheer cliffs. Yiorgo tried to decide which of the buildings was originally the taverna, but whichever one it was, it was situated a considerable way from the rocky shoreline.

'I wonder which headland the old man meant?'

Takkis looked along the line of concrete, noting the ramshackle buildings one always found on a waterfront. 'It looks like a dead end that way.'

'Then we'll go that way first. If it is a dead end we know it has to be the headland to the right of us.'

It was even hotter down in the shelter of the bay and the two men trudged along slowly. The concrete ended and a cinder track could be seen running along to the headland.

'So much for your dead end!'

They had to walk in single file on the narrow path that wound its way along the base of the cliffs. On their left the red and black cliffs rose majestically and on their right were a collection of jagged rocks of lava protruding from a deep, impenetrable, blue sea. From the brilliant sunshine the men had walked into the shade and both of them shivered at the drastic change in temperature.

'I really do not like this island,' stated Takkis.

'I wouldn't choose it for my holiday.'

They rounded a curve and reached an inlet in the cliffs where the water sucked greedily. The path was no longer in evidence and Yiorgo looked at the jumble of rocks before them.

'It should be possible to continue, but I'm not game to try. One slip and you would probably break your ankle.'

Takkis peered over his colleague's shoulder. 'If Dimitris Stephanotis is telling the truth about chasing someone over the rocks they could well have slipped.'

Yiorgo nodded. 'The problem is I don't think he is telling the truth. You lead the way back and we'll have a look the other side.'

Cautiously they returned to the concrete and walked across to where a similar cinder path led towards the headland. The path was wider and the sea a little further away from its edge. As they reached the promontory they were surprised to see the ground level off and a wide expanse of sparse grass, cinders and rock was spread before them. In the shade of the cliffs a car was parked and winding its way upwards was a wide road.

'I guess that's your route down if you have four wheels,' remarked Takkis, 'although why one would want to come down here beats me.'

'Fishing, I expect.' Yiorgo peered into the sea where the lava rocks were again in evidence but they did not have the same menacing appearance as the ones they had seen on the other side. 'From what we've seen I feel sure the body was found on the left side of the bay. Few people are likely to walk round there for fun. It could have stayed hidden for months.'

Takkis mopped his face. 'Is there anywhere down here where we can get a beer? I can't face walking back up there yet.'

Yiorgo grinned. 'We don't need to. We'll take the cable car.'

'Why didn't we do that on the way down?' grumbled Takkis.

'I wanted to see exactly what it was like to walk down. I can well believe that the local lads can run up and down at will, but if you were a stranger to the island would you try to run down that cobbled path? Those donkey droppings make it lethal for a start.'

Takkis stopped. 'Why don't we talk to those donkey men? I bet some of them have been driving those beasts up and down since they were children. Surely they would have seen a chase taking place.'

The donkey drivers laughed at Yiorgo and Takkis. No one ran down the path. One or two stalwarts ran up, but even the donkeys sometimes slipped on the cobbles on the way down, besides, if you were in a hurry, the cable car would be quicker than running.

The two men laughed with them. 'There,' declared Yiorgo, 'I won my bet. I told you no one would run down.' He slapped Takkis on the back. 'Come on, let's take the cable car.'

They found the taverna that had been owned by the elderly couple without a problem. It had become fashionable and expensive but the proprietor was unable to help them.

'I bought the place five years ago. It had been deserted until then. Apparently it used to be a taverna and the original owners had been robbed and beaten up so no one came near.' He waved his hand airily at the gaily coloured umbrellas set out on the patio overlooking the bay. 'Hence the new look. The locals never come, but the tourists like to watch the sunset. It's one of the best spots on the island.'

Yiorgo looked over the edge of the patio. The path leading down to the bay could be seen for a few yards, then it was hidden by the other houses that projected out over it. Further glimpses of it could be seen lower down, but the concrete area in the bay was completely invisible. Whatever happened down there would be unseen by anyone higher up.

He was beginning to think they had wasted their time in visiting the island. The last chance they had to find any new information lay with the daughter of the original taverna owners who worked in the local bank and Yiorgo was not feeling very hopeful.

Katerina Lemkis had the air of someone perpetually in a hurry. She looked at her watch as she entered the private room at the bank that they had been ushered into a short while earlier. She seemed puzzled that she should be expected to know the details of her father's demise.

'I really cannot help you. I was at University in Athens when the attack took place. Obviously I returned home immediately, but my father had died of his injuries. I was only concerned with my mother. For a while I thought she was improving, but I was wrong.'

'Would it be possible to speak to your mother? There's just a chance she might remember something,' suggested Yiorgo.

Katerina shook her head. 'It's out of the question. The only word she has ever uttered since the attack happened is '*Christos*'.'

'Christos?' Yiorgo was alert.

'The name of my brother. He died shortly after he was born.'

'If we showed your mother a photograph of the man who we think attacked her do you think she might be able to identify him?'

For the first time Katerina smiled. 'Impossible. She's blind.' She looked at her watch again. 'Is there anything else? I need to check my till and get home. I have my mother to see to before the children come back from school.'

'Of course. I'm sorry if we have delayed you.' Yiorgo opened the door and looked back at Takkis in despair. 'Just for a moment I thought we might be on to something there when she said the name Christos.'

Takkis shrugged. 'Short of someone coming forward and saying they witnessed everything that took place I don't think we have a hope of finding out the truth. Our only hope now is that retired police officer, Phoebus Andropolou.'

Two days later when Yiorgo and Takkis walked into the police station in Rhodes town they were greeted triumphantly by Lambros.

'I've some good news for you. Piriklis Spinades has talked Lakkis Pavlides into making a statement. We refused to let him see anyone except his solicitor, even when his wife and niece came calling we turned them away.'

'And Dimitris Stephanotis?'

'He's refusing to say a word until his solicitor arrives from Athens. Piriklis said he could not represent both men, and as Mr Pavlides was his original client he felt he should work for him.'

Yiorgo nodded with satisfaction. 'We only called in to let you know we're back on the island. We're driving down to Koskinou now. Can you phone Piriklis and ask him to meet with us this afternoon.'

Phoebus Andropolou was found sitting in his garden and he greeted the two men with pleasure. 'I don't get many visitors, and I find the hill somewhat tiring now,' he wheezed.

Yiorgo took in the wizened frame of the man and was quite surprised he could walk anywhere. 'Good job you're no longer living on Santorini, then. That island is one long hill!'

Phoebus gave a chuckle that turned into a cough. 'Never noticed it when I was younger.' He pressed his hand to his chest. 'Now, how can I help you?'

'About twenty years ago there was a robbery at a taverna at Fira. The owner died and his wife was left an invalid. We've read the report in the archives, but we'd really like to hear what your thoughts were at the time.'

Phoebus frowned. 'That's going back a bit.' He pulled a tin of tobacco from his pocket and proceeded to roll a cigarette. 'I'm not supposed to do this any more, but a man's got to have a bit of pleasure.' He drew in the acrid smoke and coughed violently, finally spitting onto the patch of grass beside his chair. 'There was never a lot of crime on the island. A few arguments over who owned a patch of land, the odd fight when people had imbibed a little too much, but nothing nasty, not until then, anyway.'

'Who reported the crime?'

'The man who lived next door. He returned from work, washed and had his meal, then went in to spend the evening playing backgammon with old Spiro. He did the same thing every night, except Sundays. Sundays he used to visit his son and daughter in law in Mesaria.' Phoebus was racked with coughing again and they waited patiently until it had subsided. 'He took one look and came up to the station and told me. I thought he'd had a drop too much. I couldn't believe what he was saying. Blood all up the walls and over the floor! Thought he was exaggerating. Sad to say he was speaking the truth. I sent him up to the hospital to get a doctor; then I began to have a look around. The remains of a meal had been knocked to the ground, broken bottles and glasses, and mixed in with everything was the blood.' He took a last lungful of smoke from the cigarette and coughed again. 'Damned things,' he commented as he dropped the butt on the ground and placed his foot on it.

'I waited until the doctor arrived, then sent Makkis, the neighbour, back up to the police station with orders to bring back reinforcements. I couldn't leave the place, but I needed help to go through everything, besides, I didn't want to spend too much time there alone. The mad man might come back. Two of my chaps came down, but before they could do anything for me the doctor asked them to carry the couple up to the hospital. I went next door with Makkis and we both had a stiff drink. I don't know who needed it more, him or me!

Anyway, to cut the story short, we found the jar Spiro used for his takings was empty and the box he kept beneath his bed had also been taken. We examined everything for fingerprints, of course, and there were plenty of them. Took us hours, then we had the tedious job of matching them up. Some were just smudges, most of them were from Spiro and his wife, but on the neck of a bottle we found a nice print that didn't belong to them.'

'Who did it belong to?'

'Christos Drakonisis. Young chap, not long out of school, and working in his father's carpet shop. I felt really bad about having to go up there to arrest him. I'd been at school with his father, we'd played football together, even gone after the same girl at one time.'

'How did you know it belonged to him?' asked Yiorgo.

'I'd had him in the station when he was about thirteen. He'd helped himself from one of the local shops, not very clever about it. The shopkeeper saw him and he was wearing the stolen jumper when we detained him. He said he had felt cold and had planned to return later to pay for it. I gave him a lecture and took his prints, wanted to frighten him more than anything.'

'Was he ever in trouble again?'

'Not that I knew.'

'So when did you go to arrest him?'

Phoebus shook his head. 'I didn't. It had taken us almost three weeks to sift through the prints and single out the one on the bottle; then we started comparing it with those we had on file. I decided I'd go up first thing in the morning; then I had a report that a body had been fished out of the rocks down by the harbour and I was needed down there. I think that was worse than when I found the old couple. Have you ever seen a body when it's been in the water for a while?' Phoebus shuddered.

Takkis nodded. 'Only once. That was enough.'

'Who was it?' asked Yiorgo.

'Christos Drakonisis.'

'Did you know it was him when you saw the body?'

Phoebus shook his head. 'What there was left of him was unrecognisable. Fish eat flesh, you know.'

'What about his clothes? Had they eaten through those?'

'He didn't have any on. I covered him over with my coat until the doctor came down and took him up to the morgue. I then had to write up a report and I couldn't face going up to arrest Christos Drakonisis that afternoon. I reckoned he'd still be there the next day. I was both right and wrong on that score.' Phoebus rolled himself another cigarette. 'Still gets to me,' he muttered, 'when I think what those fish had done. Anyway, the next morning I went up to the carpet shop. I asked for Christos and his father said he wasn't there. I asked when he would be back and he said he didn't know. The boy had taken off a few weeks previously and they'd not heard from him since.'

'Weren't they worried?' asked Takkis.

'No, he'd done it before. He'd go off and live rough for a couple of weeks, then turn up again. The first few times it happened we went out looking for him, then his father no longer used to report it. He knew he'd turn up again when he was ready.'

'So where did he go, and why?'

Phoebus shrugged. 'No idea. He said he needed to get away on his own to 'sort himself out.' We decided he was a bit odd, but harmless.'

'But now you changed your mind?'

'Certainly did. Whoever had attacked that couple had acted like a maniac. The only print we had was his and he had disappeared. I asked to have a look in his room, not that it told me much, but his mother said she couldn't see anything missing. Then I thought about the body. It was just possible he'd gone for a swim. I had to ask his father to come down to the morgue and have a look.' Phoebus's face became anguished. 'I tried my best to prepare him, he was physically sick when he saw it. The only thing he could identify was the shark's tooth he wore round his neck.'

'You didn't take fingerprints from the body?' asked Yiorgo.

Phoebus turned scornful eyes on him. 'There were no fingers to take prints from.' He lit the cigarette he had rolled earlier and was convulsed with coughing. 'I closed the case,' he said when he had recovered. 'What was the point of distressing them further? I let them think their son had gone for a swim and got stuck in the rocks. I put in a report, of course, but recommended no further action. It seemed pretty obvious the boy had robbed the couple, went for a swim, probably to remove the blood, and drowned.'

Yiorgo frowned. 'You're sure the body was that of Christos Drakonisis?'

'His father identified him.'

'Yes, but only by the talisman he wore. Anyone could have put that round his neck.'

Phoebus pursed his lips. 'What are you suggesting?'

'Recently we arrested a man and when we ran a check on his fingerprints they didn't tie up. According to the records the fingerprints belonged to a dead man, Christos Drakonisis.'

Phoebus shook his head. 'It can't be. There must be a mistake.'

'I think you had a second murder. The body you found in the sea was Dimitris Stephanotis. Christos Drakonisis had killed him as well as the old man.'

Phoebus looked at Yiorgo scornfully. 'There was no one of that name living in the town.'

'He didn't live here. A ship put in and amongst its passengers was a family who were relocating to Santorini. Only the parents were staying on the island. The young man was on the way to

Leros. He probably came ashore, ostensibly to say farewell to his parents, and unfortunately for him he met up with Christos. According to the man we have in custody it was Dimitris Stephanotis who killed the couple and Christos tried to stop him. He chased him down to the beach where he fell and hit his head on a rock. Christos was frightened he would be accused of the crime, took the man's papers and left the island.'

Phoebus frowned deeply. 'I suppose it's possible, but why weren't other fingerprints found at the taverna? And why didn't anyone from the ship report the man destined for Leros missing?'

'They probably didn't realise until the hospital authorities at Leros came on board to collect him. The ship would have docked at various islands, picking up and putting down passengers. As far as they knew he could have gone ashore anywhere.'

A further bout of coughing shook Phoebus's fragile body and Yiorgo waited until it had subsided.

'I want to press charges. We can't prove, at the moment, that he's involved in anything else, but I have a feeling that if he was out of the way one or two people might be willing to talk to us and we could get to the bottom of the drug trafficking that's taking place over here and on a couple of the other islands.'

Phoebus spread his hands. 'I can't help you. You have my report, that will have to suffice.'

Yiorgo looked at the man in concern. 'You might be called to give evidence.'

Phoebus gave him an ironic smile and shook his head. 'How long will it be before this case comes to court? A year, maybe more? You know what solicitors are like for being able to delay matters. I've been given three months at the outside.'

Yiorgo and Takkis arrived at the station in good time for their appointment with Piriklis Spinades and Yiorgo suggested that Lambros should bring them up to date with events whilst they had been away.

'What's the position with Joseph Konstandides? Has he said anything?'

Lambros shook his head. 'Says he had spent the evening in the town and was attacked by a couple of men as he walked home. Claims to have no idea who they were or why they attacked him.'

'Hmm. I'm not sure I believe that. Has he been questioned about his job at the warehouse?'

'I asked him about that myself. According to him he sold only organic flour and cigarettes. Denies all knowledge of drugs. He's not a user and says he's not a pusher. The money in the chest he swears belongs to him and he has saved it from his wages. Apart from those boxes that Christos Gilades delivered we have no evidence against him at all.'

'And he was not there when they were delivered!'

'Exactly. I asked him about previous deliveries and he said they came regularly and someone else would collect them the following day.'

'Did he know what they contained?'

'He says not. He also said a different person came each time to collect them.'

'Do you believe him?' asked Takkis.

Lambros shrugged. 'I'm not sure, but again, I have no reason to disbelieve him and I've taken off the guard by his bed. I couldn't justify his presence once we'd taken a statement.'

'No sign of that girl?'

Lambros shook his head. 'She's obviously left the island. What's going to happen about her belongings? They're still with Mr Gilades.'

'Tell him he can dispose of them. We searched them thoroughly and there was nothing. Maybe his wife could make use of them.'

'Does he still need to check in each day?'

Yiorgo shook his head. 'Make sure he knows he's under observation. Tell him he can continue to deliver the farm produce,

340

but he's not to go near the warehouse. It might be a good idea to do a spot check on his van once in a while.'

Lambros nodded and made a note. 'Dimitris Stephanotis's solicitor should be arriving tomorrow morning. Do you want to see him first and tell him what Stephanotis is being charged with?'

'We'll put him in the picture.'

Piriklis arrived promptly and shook hands with Yiorgo and Takkis. He looked more at ease than the last time they had met and took three thick files from his briefcase.

'Do you want to read this, or shall I give you a summary and you ask any questions later?'

'A summary for now. I'd like a full copy to read later.'

Piriklis passed one to each man. 'I had them copied ready for you. Now,' he leant back in his chair and placed his hands behind his head. 'Lakkis Pavlides is the owner of *The Grapevine* as you know. The man we know as Dimitris Stephanotis turned up on the island, bought a hotel, made extensive alterations and then offered the job of manager to Mr Pavlides. Mr Pavlides saw an answer to his financial problems and accepted. A couple of years later he moved out of *The Grapevine* into the house where he now lives and employed a young man to run the taverna.' Piriklis turned over the first few pages of the report. 'Now we come to the interesting bit. According to Mr Pavlides, he had only been managing the hotel for a short while when Mr Stephanotis invited him to dinner on his cruiser. Over dinner a proposition was put to him. For a consideration he was to turn a blind eye to any transactions that took place on the beach between customers and locals. Apparently he didn't ask what these transactions were, he just agreed.'

Yiorgo snorted. 'I don't believe it. The man's not a fool.'

'He said that for a certain amount of time he noticed nothing; then on one or two occasions he saw that some of the guests appeared to be under something other than the influence of alcohol.

As the season got under way there were a number of young locals on the beach, which, of course, is supposed to be private to the hotel. Apparently he spoke to Stephanotis who told him to ignore it. At the end of the season he received a bonus. Events repeated themselves the following year and then he asked Stephanotis if he would guarantee him for a loan as his sister in law was very ill and needed treatment. Stephanotis apparently was very understanding and asked to meet the family. He agreed to pay all the medical expenses.'

'What! I don't believe it. Why should he offer to do that?'

'The brother, Mr Nikos Pavlides, was the harbour master. It seems they came to a little agreement about where the port police would patrol on certain nights. I imagine Mr Pavlides was so relieved to have his wife's medical expenses covered that he would have agreed to anything.

Stephanotis paid regular visits to the hotel and on each occasion he left a little 'gift' for Lakkis Pavlides. With the bonus each year and the 'gifts' Pavlides decided he would move from *The Grapevine* and he put down a deposit on the house where he is now living. He was doing very nicely, just by turning a blind eye. Unfortunately for him it didn't stop there. Stephanotis's import business had grown and it was too risky for him to transport the goods to the delivery point, so he employed Christos Gilades to receive, weigh, pack and deliver on.'

'Under cover of delivering the farm produce! That gave him access to every hotel in the area.'

Piriklis nodded. 'Lakkis Pavlides received a salary increase, part of which was to cover Christos's wages, which he dutifully put into the bank for him each week. The system seems to have worked well for a couple of years, but then the business became too much for Christos to cope with. He complained that the increased amount he was expected to package took so much of his time that he was having difficulties with the deliveries. Pavlides dutifully passed this information on to Stephanotis and the next thing he knows he is the owner of a warehouse in the old town. Supplies of organic flour and cigarettes were ostensibly sold from there as a cover, and once a week Christos would drop off a plentiful supply of heroin. As it was required by the dealers they would drop in and purchase what they wanted to pass on to the pushers.'

'Enter Joseph Konstandides as the warehouse man.'

Piriklis nodded. 'That's the bare facts; the details are in the file.'

Yiorgo frowned. 'Not a lot to convict him on.'

'Personally,' Piriklis leaned forward, 'I don't think you have a case against him. He's been very foolish, but has not actually dealt in drugs himself. It is not against the law to accept an annual bonus or gifts.'

'I'd like to read his full statement before I make up my mind about that. We'll continue to hold him pending further enquiries.'

Piriklis shook his head. 'I really don't think you can. I shall be applying for him to be released on bail.'

Yiorgo raised his eyebrows. 'There is the little matter of the girl and the assault on Joseph Konstandides. I would certainly oppose bail until we have cleared him in our enquiries.'

'Are you charging him in connection with either event?'

Yiorgo shrugged. 'Who knows! Did you ask him to explain why the girl went with Mr Gilades or ask if he knew anything about the accident?' Yiorgo flicked the pages of the file in front of him.

Piriklis shook his head.

'Then I suggest you meet with him again and let us have further statements from him. If you still feel he has no case to answer we'll consider bail at that stage. Until then he stays behind bars and no visitors except yourself.' Yiorgo stood up. 'Thank you for your time Mr Spinades. No doubt we shall be meeting again very soon.'

Yiorgo tapped the file in front of him. 'Bed time reading. I suggest we visit Mr Konstandides and ask after his progress. This time you can do the talking.'

Joseph looked considerably better than he had on their previous visit, despite still being encased from the waist down in a plaster cast. He closed his eyes as they approached, feigning sleep.

'I'm sorry to disturb you, Mr Konstandides.' Despite Takkis's gentle touch on his shoulder Joseph winced with pain.

Reluctantly Joseph opened his eyes and acknowledged the presence of the detective. 'What do you want? I gave a statement the other day.'

Takkis nodded. 'We read that earlier. A great pity you did not recognise your attackers. We'd like to take them off the streets. I really wanted to speak to you about our earlier conversation. Do you remember any of it?'

'No.' Joseph's eyes took on a wary look.

'That's unfortunate, but I can remind you. It's just to clear up a few points for us. You were not able to say very much, but you kept asking for a girl called Thalia. You gave us the impression that you were on your way to meet her when you were attacked. Would that be correct?'

'No. I was on my way home.'

'Where had you been during the evening?'

'Round and about. Walking, watched a football match in one of the bars, had a few drinks.'

'Did you see anyone you knew?'

'No.'

Takkis looked towards Yiorgo, who nodded to him to continue.

'You also said '*Lakkis knows*' about the attack on you. Why should you say that, Mr Konstandides? Mr Pavlides is your employer, I believe. Why should he wish to attack you?'

Joseph frowned. Had he said that? 'I don't remember,' he replied honestly.

'Would Mr Pavlides have any reason to attack you?'

'No.' Joseph's mouth felt dry. Had Thalia reported his seduction of her to the police?

'You see,' Takkis spoke thoughtfully, 'If Mr Pavlides injured you he might well do the same again when you are discharged. I'm sure you wouldn't want that to happen.'

Fear showed in Joseph's eyes and Takkis pressed home his advantage. 'At the moment we happen to have Mr Pavlides at the police station on another charge. He's spoken to his solicitor and it's highly unlikely we'll be able to get a conviction. We have a lot of circumstantial evidence, but no proof, you understand. Now, if Mr Pavlides did attack you and you brought assault charges against him; that would strengthen our hand considerably. Think about it. We'll come back and see you tomorrow.'

Lukas Menetakis listened quietly to the charges Yiorgo listed against Dimitris Stephanotis, making an occasional note. Finally he rose. 'I find this quite extraordinary. I will speak with Mr Stephanotis and I'm sure he will have an explanation. For a man of his standing it is degrading to have been kept in custody, when, in all probability, there is no charge for him to answer. You could end up being sued for wrongful arrest.'

Yiorgo shrugged. 'We'll meet with you again later.'

Dimitris greeted his lawyer with relief. 'I trust you will be able to have me released in time for a decent lunch?'

'That will depend, naturally, I will do my best. I have heard the charges that are to be brought against you and now I would like to hear your side of the story.'

Dimitris repeated the story he had told Piriklis whilst Lukas listened patiently. When he had finished Lukas shook his head.

'I cannot represent you unless I know the truth, Mr Stephanotis. Would you care to start again?'

Dimitris glared at him. 'I am telling the truth. How much do you want? I can afford to pay.'

'I'm not for sale, Mr Stephanotis. If I agree to represent you I shall send you my bill at the conclusion and expect it to be honoured. Now, let's go through your statement again.'

At the end of a further hour Lukas pushed back his chair. 'I'm sorry. I cannot act for you. Your fingerprints are on the bottle and you say you may have picked it up. Why were no fingerprints found that belonged to the other young man who you accuse of the crime?'

Dimitris remained silent and drummed his fingers on the table.

'Then there is this change of identities. An innocent man would not do that. He would have immediately alerted the police and they would have apprehended the criminal.'

'I told you,' growled Dimitris. 'I didn't think they would believe me.'

'I'm inclined to agree with you.' Lukas gathered up his papers. 'I shall make arrangements to return to Athens tomorrow. If you wish to make any alterations to your statement before then please let Lambros know.'

Alarm showed on Dimitris's face for the first time. 'You can't do that. I need you to get me off this charge.'

'As I explained to you, without knowing the truth of the matter I am unable to help.'

'Suppose I pleaded extenuating circumstances?'

'And what would those be?' Lukas raised a quizzical eyebrow.

'I was inadvertently under the influence of a hallucinatory drug.'

'Really,' remarked Lukas dryly. 'I think you may have to do a little better than that.'

'Please, let me explain.' Dimitris licked his lips.

Lukas shook his head. 'I am not prepared to listen to another pack of lies.'

'This is the truth.'

Lukas looked at his watch. 'I will give you a further half an hour, no more.'

Dimitris ran a trembling hand across his forehead. This was obviously going to be his last chance to exonerate himself.

'I am Christos Drakonisis. I was an only child, born rather

late in the life of my parents. They had no understanding of the needs of a teenage boy. Every so often I had a compelling need to get away. I dreamt of leaving Fira and making a new life for myself, but where could I do that on Santorini? I began to go off into the countryside and pretend I was on my own. I was able to manage for a week or so, then I would be so hungry and dirty I would have to return. On the day in question I had been on my own for just over a week, living in a rough shelter that I'd built. I was hungry. I'd been living on vegetables, mostly lettuce and carrots that I used to collect at night from a nearby farm.

As I began to walk back to Fira I saw some mushrooms. I filled my pockets and ate them as I walked along. I knew I was pretty dirty and thought I'd go and clean myself up in the sea before I presented myself to my parents. On the way down to the shore I passed the taverna. The smell of food was too much for me and I went inside and ordered a meal. I was half way through it when the old man brought me the bill. I had no money, but I would have returned and paid later. He said I could clean the path and steps outside of donkey droppings in exchange. A red mist seemed to come down before my eyes. I picked up the bottle and hit him over the head. I can't remember anything after that.

The next thing I knew I was down by the sea. I was covered in blood and thought I must have cut myself. I walked on the cinder path round into a secluded area and took my clothes off. I couldn't see any injury on me, so I went into the sea, taking my clothes with me and washing them. I laid them out on the rocks to dry and laid in the sun myself. I don't know how long I lay there, my head didn't feel right. I suddenly realised someone was watching me and sitting in the shadow of the cliff was a boy about my age. When he saw me look at him he came over and sat beside me.

At first he began to chat, nothing out of the ordinary, then he told me he was bound for Leros. I asked him why and he smiled and didn't answer me. He put his head on my shoulder and began to stroke my leg. I tried to pull away, but he put his arms round me and tried to kiss me. I was horrified. I hit him, hard, and his head snapped back, releasing me. As I struggled to get up he caught at my leg and I hit him again. This time he fell backwards and banged his head on the rocks. He didn't move again. I sat there for a while wondering what to do, then I went through his pockets and found his papers. It seemed the answer for me. I wanted to leave Santorini and if it appeared that I had drowned no one would look for me. I undressed him, hung my shark's tooth round his neck, and pushed him into the water. I just couldn't think straight.'

'For someone who wasn't able to think properly you seemed to know exactly what you were doing,' remarked Lukas dryly.

'I think I was still being affected by the mushrooms. I got dressed; then placed his shirt and trousers over mine. His jacket was a bit tight, but wearable. I planned to sneak home and take some money for a ferry passage from my father's savings. On the way back up I passed the taverna. Something drew me towards it. I walked inside and I was petrified. For some time I just stood and looked, I knew I had something to do with it, but I couldn't remember what. I did not even dare to return to my home. I was very careful not to get any blood on myself when I went behind the counter and emptied the money jar. There was only a bit of change in there, so I went into their living quarters and found the box under the bed. I walked back up into the town and took the road to Athinios where I caught the next ferry to Piraeus. That was when I became Dimitris Stephanotis.'

Lukas looked at the man sceptically. 'You really expect me to believe that?'

'It's the truth. I didn't realise the mushrooms would give me hallucinations and when I hit the boy it was in self defence.'

Lukas sighed deeply. 'Let's go back through in detail.'

'Another visit to Mr Konstandides, I think,' said Yiorgo. 'You can question him again. We want more information about that warehouse. Hopefully when we've finished with him Mr Menetakis will be ready to meet with us again.'

Takkis nodded. He had formulated various questions in his head, but no doubt others would occur to him depending upon the answers he was given.

The detectives had to wait until the doctor had finished examining Joseph. When he emerged from the curtained off bed he signalled to the men to follow him into the passage outside.

'I understand that you have a job to do, but I think you should be aware of Mr Konstandides condition. I have not yet broken the news to him, but he is crippled for life. We shall obviously do our best, but it is doubtful he will ever walk again. The base of his spine was damaged. We are hopeful he will recover the full use of his arms and be able to use a wheelchair.'

Yiorgo scratched his ear. 'I appreciate what you're telling us, doctor, but I would like you to explain his future to him. We think he knows who attacked him. If we could persuade him to reveal a name to us we could press charges and probably get compensation for him. He's going to need a considerable amount of help when he's eventually discharged.'

The doctor shook his head. 'It's far too early to give him that information. There is always a chance that we are wrong in our assessment of the spinal injury. The recuperative powers of the body are nothing short of a miracle very often.'

Takkis frowned. 'You have no objection to us questioning him on another matter? We won't need to mention his accident.'

'If you feel it is necessary.'

Joseph looked at them warily as they approached. He had thought for hours about their previous conversation and had decided there was no way he was going to name Lakkis as being the instigator of the attack. Lakkis would immediately defend himself by claiming it was revenge for the rape of his niece and then it would be himself who was facing charges.

Takkis smiled at him. 'Feeling better?' he asked.

'No.'

'I'm sorry about that. I'm also sorry that we have to trouble you again, but we do have a few more questions we would like to ask.'

'I've told you I don't know who assaulted me,' stated Joseph firmly.

'It's not about the attack. It's about your job at the warehouse.'

'What about it?'

'Who employed you?'

'Mr Lakkis Pavlides.'

'He paid your wages directly?'

'Yes.'

'How were these paid to you? Credited to a bank account?'

'No, he gave me cash each week.'

'And what did your duties involve?'

'Answering the telephone and having the orders ready when the customers called.'

'What did the orders consist of?'

'Flour or cigarettes, sometimes both.'

'And what else, Mr Konstandides?'

'Nothing else.'

'What about the boxes that Mr Gilades used to deliver to you?'

'I told the other policeman about those. He would deliver them one day and they would be collected the next.'

'So you had no idea what was in them?'

'No idea at all.'

'I find that very hard to believe. Surely natural curiosity would have compelled you to open one?'

'It wasn't my business.'

Takkis leant forward. 'I'm going to take you into my confidence, Joseph. I probably shouldn't do this, but I think you ought to know. I told you yesterday that we have Mr Pavlides in custody. We are almost certain that he has been involved with the distribution of drugs around the island, but we're having a hard time proving it. Now if you know anything that would strengthen our case we'd be grateful to hear it. There would be no need for us to disclose where we obtained the information. We'll leave you to think about it.'

Joseph closed his eyes. This could be the ideal way to revenge himself on Lakkis, but there was Dimitris to be reckoned with.

Manolis arrived in Rhodes town, having managed to beg more compassionate leave from his commanding officer.

'I shall go to the police station,' he announced to his mother. 'I'll get to the bottom of this. It's ridiculous that father should be locked up. Whatever charge they think they have against him he should be allowed bail.'

Manolis met with the same refusal as his mother and Thalia. Furiously he told Lambros that he would be consulting his solicitor and he would be taking the whole of the police department to court for wrongful arrest. Lambros refused to be intimidated and suggested the young man spoke to Piriklis Spinades, who was acting on behalf of Lakkis Pavlides.

Manolis returned from his afternoon visit to the solicitor subdued, but still angry. He strode up and down, waving his arms and shouting at his mother. Silently Maria sat and listened to him, her eyes continually straying towards the clock. Thalia had promised to call in after work, as she had done on the last few days. Maria hoped her presence would have a calming influence on her son.

Thalia hurried down the road. It had been her night for staying late at the office. All day she had wrestled with her conscience and her feelings. Much as she abhorred the idea, she must visit Joseph and see if her uncle had been involved in his accident. She knew her aunt would be waiting for her, but the hospital was

351

only a short distance out of her way and she would stop no more than a few minutes.

She was directed to Joseph's bed and she looked down on the prostrate figure in the plaster cast. 'Joseph?'

Joseph opened his eyes and tried to smile. 'Thalia!'

'I've only come to ask you a question. Was my uncle involved in your accident?'

'You know he was. You sent me the letter arranging to meet me. You set me up.'

Thalia shook her head. 'I didn't write any letter, Joseph. I'm sorry you're hurt.'

She turned on her heel and left the ward. Once outside she leant against the wall, her hands clenched. She should never have told her aunt and uncle about her experience. She had turned to them for help and support to enable her to recover, more mentally than physically, not for revenge.

Feeling she had regained control of herself she hurried up the hill towards her aunt's house and let herself in. She stopped in the doorway when she saw Manolis. He broke off in mid tirade and seized her in his arms, surprised to find that her body went rigid beneath his touch.

'What's wrong?' he asked, puzzled by her reception of him.

'I'm just surprised to see you. Shall I make some coffee?'

Maria nodded. 'Please, dear.'

'I'll have a drink instead,' announced Manolis. He poured a large whisky. 'I need this after what I've been through today.'

Thalia slipped into the kitchen. She would make her excuses and leave as soon as she had drunk her coffee. Her aunt did not need her now Manolis was here to take charge. Her hands were shaking as she returned to the lounge and placed a cup and glass of water beside her aunt. Manolis had finished his whisky and poured a second, but to his mother's relief he had quietened down.

He smiled at Thalia. 'How are you getting on with our wedding preparations? It's only two months away.'

Thalia dropped her eyes. 'I haven't really had time to think about it, what with Pappa and now this trouble with Uncle Lakkis.'

Manolis frowned. 'You should have sent out the invitations by now. We drew up the guest list months ago, and you agreed to write them.'

Thalia still would not look at him. 'I think we ought to postpone our wedding for a little while, until Christmas, maybe?'

'Postpone it? Whatever for?'

'Until we know what is happening to your father.'

Manolis downed the last of his whisky. 'Nothing is going to happen to Pappa. I spoke to his solicitor today and he said the police have no grounds to hold him. He's expecting them to release him at any time.'

Thalia looked up timidly. 'I still think we ought to postpone it. I don't feel ready. My Pappa's death was such a shock.'

'You'll be over it by then,' Manolis assured her. He poured another whisky. 'Heart attacks happen. You have to be thankful that it didn't happen on the day. That would really have made things awkward.'

Thalia did not answer him. She sipped her coffee, wishing she had not come to visit her aunt. She wanted to go home and be able to sit and think quietly. Her aunt insisted she stayed to eat with them and it seemed an age before she could decently make her excuses and prepare to leave.

Manolis promptly insisted on escorting her home. There was no way he would brook any refusal on her part and she really had no reason to refuse his company.

Manolis took her hand in his and they walked up the hill in silence. 'What's wrong with you?' he asked.

Thalia shook her head. 'Nothing.'

'Yes there is. You've hardly said a word to me. Anyone would think you didn't want to see me!'

'I'm rather tired. I haven't been sleeping very well.'

'Shall we go for a drink?'

Thalia shook her head. 'I'd rather go straight home. I have jobs to do.'

'I could do with one.'

Thalia turned reproachful eyes towards him. 'You've had six whiskies in the last hour.'

Manolis shrugged. 'I can hold my liquor.'

'Then go for a drink when you have left me.'

Manolis continued as if he had not heard her. 'That's what you ought to do. A stiff drink before you go to bed and you'll sleep like a baby.'

'Maybe that would help your mother. I don't think she's sleeping well at the moment.'

'A glass of wine puts her to sleep! You should see what we men are able to put away when we get leave to go to the local taverna in the evenings,' boasted Manolis.

Thalia took her key from her purse. 'Thank you for walking back with me. I'll see you tomorrow, Manolis.'

Manolis grabbed her arm. 'That's no way to say goodnight to me.'

Thalia wriggled herself free. 'Not on the doorstep, Manolis.'

'I'll come in.' He pushed the door open as she unlocked it and followed her inside. 'Now,' he said, 'I'll say goodnight to you properly.'

He took her in his arms and pulled her close to him, the whisky on his breath making the bile rise in her and she turned her head away.

'Please,' she said. 'You smell of whisky.'

'You'll get used to that,' his lips sought hers and she twisted desperately to avoid the contact.

'Manolis, please, leave me alone.'

'Leave you alone? Why shouldn't I kiss you? I shall do a lot more than kiss you in a few weeks time. It won't be any good you asking me to leave you alone then.' He felt Thalia's body trembling beneath his touch and completely misunderstood her reaction. 'Can't wait? I know; I feel the same.' He pushed his hand up inside her blouse and squeezed her breast. 'I can't wait to have you.'

'No, Manolis, no, please, please, no!'

'It's too late to start saying no.' He pushed her back towards the couch, making her stumble and she fell to the floor, Manolis landing on top of her and knocking the breath from her body. He pushed up her skirt and Thalia began to flail wildly, hitting her arm against the leg of the couch and breaking her wrist watch. He caught her wrists and held them easily in one hand whilst he ripped at her underwear with the other, finally forcing her legs apart with his knees.

Thalia sobbed and gasped for breath. This hurt. This was not how it had been with Joseph. He had been gentle. She screamed and Manolis placed his free hand against her windpipe. 'Any more of that and I'll give you cause to scream.'

'You're hurting me,' sobbed Thalia.

'It only hurts the first time. You'll be ready now for our wedding night.'

Inadvertently a scream rose to her lips again and Manolis pressed on her throat. She could feel herself choking, the room was spinning round and blackness was descending upon her.

Manolis had left by the time Thalia regained consciousness. She lay still, dazed and frightened. She did not dare to move in case he was still in the house and ready to assault her again. It hurt to swallow and the smell of vomit made her want to retch. She clawed her way onto the couch and closed her eyes, tears forcing their way through her lids and trickling down her cheeks.

It was some two hours before she finally placed her feet on the ground and tentatively rose, holding onto the couch, before she dared to let go and grope her way towards the light switch. Cautiously she went from room to room, switching on every light as she did so; petrified that Manolis would be waiting in a dark corner for her. She locked and chained the doors with hands that continued to tremble before she made her way into the bathroom, removed the remainder of her clothes and stepped into the shower.

The hot water revived her, but she was horrified when she saw the dark bruises on her body, particularly around her neck. She sat on the stool in the bathroom, her head in her hands and tried to think. There was no way she could marry Manolis, and there was no way that she could refuse him. Her uncle would insist that the marriage took place. She shivered. If that was how men behaved towards their wives she did not want to marry anyone. At least Joseph had not hurt her.

Recalling Joseph made her tears flow again. He thought she had arranged for his accident to take place, but he had not told the police. He obviously did care for her. She shivered again and pulled her towelling robe closer. Her head throbbed and she rose and opened the medicine cabinet, there were some tablets somewhere. Her eye fell on her father's razor and she picked it up speculatively. She hurt so much that she would hardly notice a little more pain.

Whilst the resolve was still with her she returned to the lounge, avoided the pool of vomit left by Manolis, and sat at the writing desk. The pad of blank paper looked back at her; then she began to write.

'I, Thalia Pavlides, wish this statement to be used by the police.

My uncle, Lakkis Pavlides, sent a message to Joseph Konstandides, asking him to meet me. I knew nothing about this. I believe Lakkis Pavlides assaulted Joseph and threw him over the castle wall.

Please tell my aunt, Maria Pavlides, that I am sorry.

I was raped tonight and there is no way I can marry Manolis.

I have taken the only way out.'

Thalia signed the letter, placed it inside an envelope and addressed it to '*The Two Detectives*' at the main police station in Rhodes town. She took a deep, shuddering breath, then realised she had no way to get her missive to them. She did not feel capable of dressing and walking to the nearest post box and she could not leave the letter in the house in case Manolis should find it.

Dragging her weary body into the kitchen she looked across at her neighbour. A light was on in their bedroom, but the rest of the house was in darkness. Across the envelope she wrote '*URGENT – PLEASE DELIVER THIS FOR ME AS I AM UNABLE TO DO SO.*' Quietly she unlocked the back door, crept barefoot along the path and across the intervening patch of grass, and pushed the envelope through their letterbox. She had no idea how long it took to bleed to death when you cut your wrists, but she was certain that by the time she was discovered and the letter opened they would not be able to question her.

Yiorgo and Takkis had returned to the police station hoping to see Lukas Menetakis, but he did not appear. Instead they heard Lambros's account of Manolis Pavlides's visit to the station and his threats to sue them, which was followed by a visit from Piriklis Spinades.

'I have come to demand the release of Mr Lakkis Pavlides. He has no charges to answer.'

Yiorgo raised his eyebrows. 'Did you ask him about the girl Mr Gilades took away in his van?'

Piriklis nodded. 'Apparently Mr Stephanotis telephoned to say he wanted the girl back on board the cruiser. A short while after that he telephoned again and said it wasn't convenient after all. Mr Pavlides said he could no longer keep her at the hotel and it was Mr Stephanotis who suggested that she went down to the bay for a few days.'

'Now that's interesting,' remarked Yiorgo. 'How did Mr Stephanotis know about Mr Gilades and where he worked?'

Piriklis shrugged. 'It's a small island. Everyone knows everyone else.'

'But Mr Stephanotis does not live here. He only visits and stays on his cruiser. Make a note Takkis. We need to ask Mr Pavlides for some more details.' Yiorgo turned back to the lawyer. 'And the assault on Mr Konstandides? What did Mr Pavlides have to say about that?'

'He denies all knowledge of it. Says a passer by told him.'

'And on the word of a stranger he telephones Alecos and says he will drop the spare keys to the warehouse down to *The Grapevine* and Alecos is to run the warehouse whilst Joseph is absent.' Yiorgo shook his head. 'He made no attempt to visit the hospital and find out the extent of Mr Konstandides's injuries, and why didn't he? Because he knew exactly what had happened. No, Mr Spinades, I regret to say that Mr Lakkis will have to stay with us a little longer until we are entirely satisfied that he is as innocent as he claims.'

Despite all the arguments put forward by Piriklis Spinades, Yiorgo stood firm and the lawyer left a disappointed man. Now he would have to face that aggressive young man again and tell him he had been unsuccessful in gaining his father's release.

Mr Danilidou picked up the envelope from his doormat and looked at it curiously. Why couldn't Thalia deliver the letter herself, she worked quite close to the police station

He looked out of the window at her house and saw all the lights were on. Maybe the girl was not well.

'Anna, are you dressed?'

'Nearly.'

'Pop next door and see if there's anything wrong with Thalia. All her lights are on and she's put an envelope through our door.'

'Does she say she's not well?' Anna finished buttoning her blouse as she came down the stairs.

Efthimios shook his head. 'No, she's asked me to deliver this letter to the police station as she says she can't.'

Anna frowned. 'I'll go and give her a knock.'

It was only a matter of minutes before Anna returned. 'There's no answer. Maybe there's a fault on her electrics.'

Efthimios placed the letter in his jacket pocket. 'I'll drop it in on my way to work.'

Lambros looked at the letter curiously. He was tempted to open it, but it was obviously meant for Yiorgo and Takkis. He waited impatiently until the two men appeared and Yiorgo opened it quickly. He read the words, thrust the letter into Takkis's hands and turned to Lambros.

'Alert the medical services and send them immediately to Nikos Pavlides's house. We need a car.'

Lambros looked at him in surprise, but picked up the telephone. He placed the keys to his car on the desk. 'Take mine; remember some of the town is one way.'

Yiorgo completely ignored Lambros's warning about the one way streets. With car lights flashing and sirens sounding he raced by the most direct route to Nikos Pavlides's house. He hammered on the door and when he received no reply he turned his attention to the nearest window and broke the glass with the butt of his gun. Removing as much loose glass as he could and shielding his head with his hand, Yiorgo climbed through.

The lounge was in a mess. There was vomit hardening on the floor, blood on the couch and the remains of a pair of briefs kicked under a chair. Yiorgo went to the front door, wrapping his hand in his handkerchief to release the chain and locks. Takkis followed him into the second room and lying on her bed, still wearing her bathrobe lay Thalia. It was immediately obvious to both men that she was dead and Yiorgo turned away sadly.

After the preliminary police procedures had taken place the doctor was allowed to examine her body, and Yiorgo and Takkis took the opportunity to speak to Mrs Danilidou, who was unable to help them. She confirmed that her husband had found the letter that morning and she had knocked on the door in case the girl was feeling ill.

'If only I'd known,' she kept repeating.

'If only you had known what, Mrs Danilidou?' asked Takkis.

'That she was – was like that. I would have called you.' She wrung her hands. 'The poor, poor girl.'

Takkis telephoned the Town Hall where Mr Danilidou worked, and having assured him that his wife was perfectly all right, requested he returned home immediately. When he did so he could only confirm the story that his wife had told. They had retired early, sat in bed and read their respective books and not noticed that all the lights were on at the house next door until the morning. He had found the letter and delivered it.

Yiorgo sighed. 'I suppose we have to go to see Maria Pavlides and tell her about her niece. Not a job I relish.'

'Are you going to tell her about the letter?' asked Takkis.

'Not at this stage. I think we'll speak to Lakkis Pavlides and see what he has to say first.'

'I think we should speak to Mr Konstandides before him. If he thinks we have definite evidence against Pavlides he might be more forthcoming. It would strengthen our hand when Spinades comes demanding his client's release.'

Yiorgo nodded. 'We can leave them here to sift through and make a report. Let's face Mrs Pavlides.'

Maria looked tired and drawn as she opened the door to them. 'What do you want now?' she asked wearily.

'I'm afraid we bring some bad news. May we come in?' Yiorgo took her arm and gently steered her towards her lounge and into a chair.

'Is it Lakkis?' she asked, her eyes full of fear.

'No, rest assured he is perfectly fit and well. Is your son here with you? It could be as well if you were together at this time.'

'He's not up yet.'

'Then, with your permission, I'll go and wake him. Where is his room?'

'The one above this.' Maria's voice was a whisper.

Manolis had awakened a short time earlier. He felt terrible. He must have drunk a further half bottle of whisky when he returned home. He wished he had gone back to Thalia's and taken the girl again. Just wait until they were married. He would show her what happened when she said no to him.

'What do you want?' he called irritably as a knock came on his door.

'Police. I'd like you to come downstairs to be with your mother, Mr Pavlides.'

Manolis threw open the door. 'What have you done to my father?'

'Nothing, I assure you. Unfortunately we are the bearer of bad news and we think it advisable for you and your mother to be together whilst we tell you.'

'Is it all right if I get dressed first?'

'Of course.' Yiorgo stood and waited whilst Manolis stepped into his trousers and picked up a stained shirt.

Manolis sat on the couch beside his mother, who searched for his hand and held it tightly.

'I am so sorry that there is no easy way to tell you this. We were called to the house of your deceased brother in law this morning, and I regret to have to tell you that your niece had decided to take her own life.'

Maria's hand flew to her mouth and she let out a long wail. The colour drained from Manolis's face and returned with a rush. He appeared about to say something; then thought better of it.

'I have to ask when you last saw her.'

Maria was incapable of answering and Yiorgo looked at Manolis. 'I walked her home about nine thirty.' He would not meet Yiorgo's gaze and he twisted the large ornate ring he wore nervously.

'And how did she appear when you left her?'

Manolis shrugged. 'The same as usual.'

'She did not appear distressed in any way?'

'What are you insinuating?' Manolis clenched the hand that was not holding his mother.

'I am not insinuating anything, Mr Pavlides. I simply wondered if there was anything you noticed that could account for her action.'

'No.'

'How long did you stay at the house with her?'

'I don't know. A short while.'

'You were gone over an hour,' Maria remonstrated.

'I went for a drink on the way back,' growled Manolis. 'You keep out of this.'

'No wonder you were sick,' commented Maria.

Yiorgo appeared to ignore the remark. 'And when you left Miss Pavlides did you notice anyone hanging around her house or the area generally?'

'No.'

Yiorgo rose. 'Thank you both for your time. I am so sorry I had to be the bearer of such tragic news.'

Maria looked up at him, her eyes brimming with tears. 'How did she …?'

'We'll have to wait for the autopsy before we can confirm anything. Obviously we will be in touch with you again. My sincere condolences, Mr Pavlides. I understand you and the young lady had a wedding date set. This must be a terrible shock to you.'

Manolis did not answer and it was left to Maria to see them to the door.

At the doorway Yiorgo turned back to Manolis. 'There's just one thing, Mr Pavlides. May I have your shirt, please?'

'My shirt!'

'Yes, the one you are wearing.'

'No.'

'I am afraid I have to insist.' Yiorgo held out his hand. With a malevolent glare Manolis proceeded to unbutton his shirt and thrust it into Yiorgo's hands.

'Thank you.' Yiorgo folded it carefully inside out. 'I expect you can have it back tomorrow.'

'So why have you taken his shirt?' asked Takkis, once they were a short way up the hill.

'I noticed it had some stains on the front, looked like fairly recent vomit. I thought we ought to check it out. What did you think of that young man?'

'I wasn't taken with him – and he'd certainly been drinking pretty heavily the night before.'

'He admitted he had been for a drink and his mother said he had been sick.'

'That was more than one drink, more like a bottle! I wonder how long he did stay with the girl?'

'Why?'

'If, as she states in her letter, she had been raped, it would narrow down the time when it happened. One of her other neighbours might have seen someone suspicious.'

Yiorgo looked at Takkis. 'Assuming she was raped, which we won't know for sure until after the autopsy, I'm pretty sure she knew her attacker.'

'What makes you think that?' asked Takkis

'There was no sign of a forced entry. She must have let someone in and locked and chained the doors after they left.'

'She may have been frightened he would come back.'

'Quite likely. Don't you think it strange that a young lady, who struck me as rather fastidious, would not clear up vomit? If it was her fiancée, I would have expected that to be the first things she did after he left?'

'Maybe she didn't have time,' suggested Takkis.

'In that case her assailant and fiancée must have passed each other on the way out, yet Mr Pavlides says he saw no one.

Assuming there was a time lapse of even five minutes I would have thought we would have found a bowl and scrubbing brush at the ready.'

'She probably wanted to change out of her working clothes first.'

Yiorgo nodded slowly. 'So why was her working skirt and blouse ripped? If she had changed into something old it should have been those clothes that were damaged?'

Yiorgo and Takkis checked on procedures at Thalia's house, but the police had found nothing they could not account for and were in the process of sealing off the premises.

'The doctor wanted samples of the vomit and the blood. We also found the girl's watch, it was smashed.'

Yiorgo nodded. 'Have finger prints been taken?'

The policeman nodded. 'It appears she used an ordinary razor blade to cut her wrists. The razor was in the bathroom. We sent that back for examination also.'

'Thanks. You've done a good job. Have you got a spare bag around?'

The policeman nodded and handed one to Yiorgo who stuffed Manolis's shirt inside. 'I'd like this taken back for tests. We'll catch up with you later when you've finished compiling your report.'

'Let me have another look at that letter, Takkis. I want to make sure of the wording when we speak to Mr Konstandides.'

Takkis removed the crumpled copy of the message from his pocket and handed it to Yiorgo who read it briefly and returned it. 'Keep it safe. We may need to refer to it.'

They entered the ward where Joseph lay and requested that the curtains were drawn around his bed. Joseph eyed them with trepidation. What would they try to make him say this time?

Yiorgo looked down at the abused body. The bruising had really come out now, giving his face a yellowish green look, one eye all but closed.

'Mr Konstandides, I have some news for you.'

Joseph did not respond.

'We received some information this morning that we thought might interest you.'

Joseph still made no response.

'According to our informant, Lakkis Pavlides sent you a message purporting to come from his niece, Miss Pavlides, and arranging a meeting. Mr Pavlides attacked you and threw you over the wall, didn't he?'

Yiorgo waited for Joseph's reaction.

'Yes,' he said at last.

Yiorgo smiled broadly. 'Thank you, Mr Konstandides. Now we are finally getting to the truth of the matter maybe you would care to make a full statement?'

Yiorgo rubbed his hands together. 'Now for Lakkis Pavlides. I think we'll invite Mr Spinades to sit in on our meeting. He can see his reaction for himself.'

'Are you going to tell Pavlides where the information came from?' asked Takkis.

'I'll see. If he admits his involvement there's no need, but if he continues to deny that he had anything to do with it we could produce it. Take some more copies and get Lambros to put the original in the safe.'

'I'm still wondering why the girl has pointed the finger at her uncle. Do you think she knew all the time?'

Yiorgo shrugged. 'I doubt if we'll ever know the answer to that.'

Lakkis Pavlides could not believe what he was hearing. Who had seen him? Who knew about the letter? It could only be Joseph.

Piriklis Spinades looked at his client anxiously. The man looked close to a heart attack. 'I'd like to have a word with you in private. After we have spoken I will need some time alone with Mr Pavlides,' he requested and Yiorgo agreed.

'What is this proof that you have? If it is speculation on your part I can assure you that my client will sue you,' Piriklis warned them.

Yiorgo handed the lawyer a copy of Thalia's letter. 'I'd rather you did not disclose the unfortunate death of his niece to Mr Pavlides at this time. We visited Mr Konstandides earlier and he finally agreed to make a statement. It's being typed up at this moment. I'd like to make it clear to you, Mr Spinades, that we intend to charge Mr Lakkis Pavlides with attempted murder. There is no question of bail.'

Piriklis handed the letter back. 'You have no objection to me telling Mr Pavlides that his niece supplied the information in the first place and Mr Konstandides has confirmed the details?'

'Not at all.' Yiorgo sat back in his chair, satisfied that there was no way the lawyer would be able to extricate Lakkis Pavlides from responsibility for the crime.

Christos Gilades was faced with a dilemma. He had been told he could give the cases of clothes that belonged to Sorrell to his wife. He had searched through them for anything that might be useful and put them back into the cases in disgust. His Maria was at least two sizes larger than the girl and would never have worn such glamorous items. He had debated whether he could sell them in the market and decided against the idea. He had no wish to draw further attention to himself and he had no permit for a stall. For two days he considered the idea that had come to him and finally he telephoned Alecos at *The Grapevine* and offered to sell him the clothes for his sister.

Alecos was wary. He was not prepared to be drawn into any

deal that would rebound on him and place him at the mercy of the police. He refused Christos's suggestion to visit *The Grapevine* and fixed on a café in the new town for their meeting.

Christos arrived with a carrier bag and pushed it towards Alecos beneath the table. 'I've brought you a sample. You can keep these, whatever you decide. If you want the rest we'll come to an agreement about the price. I'm short of money now my work has dried up.'

Alecos held the bag between his feet. 'How much do you have in mind?'

Christos moistened his lips. 'Half a dozen cigarette packets.'

Alecos shook his head. 'Too much – and what makes you think I have any?'

'There should have been a good few at the warehouse.'

'The police only found the boxes you had delivered.'

Christos's eyes narrowed. 'You moved too fast for them.'

'They searched *The Grapevine* and found nothing.'

'There are other places they could look, if someone gave them a hint.'

Alecos looked at Christos venomously. He knew he was being blackmailed. 'I'll let you know tomorrow.'

Lakkis sat with his head in his hands. He had stressed to Piriklis that the attack he had arranged on Joseph had been revenge for the man's rape of his niece. How did she know it had been him? Had Joseph told her? If so he would tell Manolis to give her a good beating on their wedding night. It was not only what she deserved, but the only way to keep women in order.

Yiorgo and Takkis had been puzzled when Piriklis returned to them and explained Lakkis's reasoning behind the attack.

'Did the girl report the incident to the police?'

'Apparently not. She told her aunt and uncle.'

Yiorgo sighed. 'We're going to have to speak to Maria Pavlides and hear what she says. We'll also have to break the news to her that her husband is going to be charged. The further we get into this case the more I dislike it. We seem to have uncovered a hornet's nest.'

Manolis had obviously been drinking again when they returned to speak to Maria Pavlides. She appeared more nervous than ever and Yiorgo felt sorry for the woman.

'We would really like to speak to you alone, Mrs Pavlides.'

'I insist on staying with my mother,' announced Manolis.

Yiorgo shook his head. 'Maybe you could go to the kitchen or dining room with my colleague. He has a couple of questions he would like to ask you.'

'Please do as they ask, Manolis,' begged Maria.

'I don't want them brow-beating you.'

'I can assure you that no pressure at all will be put on your mother.' Yiorgo held open the door of the lounge and reluctantly Manolis led the way to the kitchen.

'Mrs Pavlides, I am so sorry to have to bother you at this time, but I do have to ask you a rather sensitive question regarding your niece. This is why I requested that I speak to you alone.'

Maria looked at him. 'Manolis doesn't mean to be rude,' she apologized for her son. 'It's the shock. He doesn't usually drink so much.'

'I understand. Now, Mrs Pavlides, cast your mind back over the past few weeks. Did Miss Pavlides come to you at any time and claim to have been raped?'

Maria's hand flew to her mouth. 'Manolis doesn't know,' she whispered.

'That is why I wished to speak to you alone. There is no need to cause him any further distress at this point. Can you give me the details, please?'

'Thalia arrived during the morning. She was crying and said

368

she had been out to dinner with a young man the previous evening. She kept apologizing and saying she hadn't meant it to happen, but she hadn't been able to stop him from molesting her.'

'And what did you do?'

'I telephoned to my husband at the hotel and asked him to come home immediately.'

Yiorgo nodded. 'And then?' he prompted.

'He made Thalia tell me everything that happened and insisted on having a doctor examine her.'

'What did the doctor say?'

'The doctor said she had not been raped, but she must have been, mustn't she? She wasn't the kind of girl to let a man have his way with her.'

'And what happened then?'

'I gave her the sedative the doctor had left for her. We wanted her to stay here with us for a few days, but she insisted that she returned to her own home.'

'Did Miss Pavlides tell you who she had been out to dinner with?'

'It was Joseph Konstandides. She said he had asked her out as a way of showing his sympathy for the death of her father. A fine way to show sympathy!'

'She told your husband that Mr Konstandides had raped her?'

Maria nodded. 'She didn't use that word, but that's what he'd done, even though the doctor disagreed.'

'And what was your husband's reaction?'

'He didn't say very much, but he was furious with Joseph. I think if the man had been in front of him he would have killed him with his bare hands.'

'An understandable reaction,' Yiorgo sympathised. 'Can you just give me the name of the doctor, please? I would like to have a word with him.'

'It was Dr. Iliopoulos from the hospital who came to see her. He didn't seem to believe a word she said.'

Yiorgo patted Maria's hand. 'Thank you, Mrs Pavlides.'

'When will my husband be home?' Maria looked at him anxiously.

This was a question Yiorgo had been dreading. Slowly he shook his head. 'I'm sorry to give you yet more bad news, but we are going to charge him formally with the attempted murder of Mr Konstandides.'

The colour drained from Maria's face and she would have fallen off her chair in a faint if Yiorgo had not caught her.

'Takkis,' he called loudly. 'Takkis, come here.'

Manolis entered the room before Takkis. 'What have you done to her?' he asked furiously as he placed his arms around his mother to keep her upright.

'I had to tell her that your father is to be charged with attempted murder.' Yiorgo did not take his eyes off Manolis as he gave him the information.

Manolis let go his mother and Yiorgo caught her a second time. He bunched his fists and appeared about to hit Yiorgo when Takkis stepped forward.

'I suggest you sit down, Mr Pavlides. It is most unfortunate that we had to bring you two such terrible pieces of news in one day. I think we should call a doctor out to you and ask for a sedative. Your mother certainly needs something and I'm sure you would also benefit from something to calm you down.'

'It isn't true. You've made this up. My father will sue you.'

'I regret to say, Mr Pavlides, that when we finally confronted your father with evidence of the crime he confessed. He is pleading extenuating circumstances.'

Manolis scowled and Maria moaned slightly as she regained consciousness. Yiorgo rubbed her hands, and then looked at Manolis.

'I suggest you telephone a doctor as my colleague advised. Look after your mother until he comes. I will make arrangements for her to meet with her husband tomorrow.'

'I want to see my father,' stated Manolis.

'We will arrange that at a later date. Tomorrow it will be only your mother who is able to visit him.'

Manolis rose and went over to the sideboard. 'I need a drink,' he muttered.

Yiorgo shrugged and turned back to Maria Pavlides. 'I am truly sorry, Mrs Pavlides.'

Sorrell was delighted when Nadia threw a bag of clothes at her. 'These are mine!' she exclaimed. 'Where did you find them?'

'I didn't find them. Alecos has bought them for you. You'll get them all back in good time.'

'Bought them? But they belong to me. They should be returned to me,' remonstrated Sorrell.

'Think yourself lucky. Christos was told to give them to his wife, but they wouldn't fit her, so he offered them to Alecos for me.'

'That was kind of Alecos. How am I going to repay him?'

'I'm sure he'll think of a way.'

'He hasn't got my passport, by any chance?'

'He didn't mention it.'

'Nadia, how am I going to leave this island if I can't find my passport?'

Nadia shrugged. 'Go to the Embassy and explain that you've lost it. They'll issue you with another one.'

'I can't do that. What about Lakkis – and the police?'

'Lakkis is still being held by the police.'

'Maybe Dimitris could help me?' suggested Sorrell.

Nadia snorted. 'The police are holding him as well. The cruiser has been impounded, so to go back there would be pretty foolish.'

'When will Joseph be back? Maybe he could get me a passport so I could return to the States.'

Nadia sniggered. 'Maybe, but I wouldn't count on it. Think

what a nice surprise it will be for him when he finds you're here waiting for him.'

Dr Iliopoulos spoke to Yiorgo and Takkis testily. 'They haven't finished the autopsy on the girl. Come back tomorrow.'

Yiorgo frowned in annoyance and Takkis placed his hand on his colleague's arm. 'We appreciate that you don't have the results from the autopsy yet. We just want to ask you a quick question.'

Dr Iliopoulos sighed. 'Go on, then. I really do want to get back so I can finish up at a reasonable time. My wife is expecting me to take her to the theatre tonight.'

Takkis nodded. 'This girl, Thalia Pavlides, I believe you were called to her aunt and uncle's home a few weeks ago? According to her aunt she had been raped and you disagreed.'

Dr Iliopoulos nodded. 'Lot of fuss about nothing. She'd been a bit too free with her favours the previous evening and cooked up the story. Intercourse had taken place, but she certainly hadn't been raped!'

'Thank you, doctor.' Yiorgo smiled broadly. 'We'll wait for you to call us with the results of the autopsy.'

Yiorgo and Takkis returned to the police station and closeted themselves in a side room. Yiorgo ran a hand through his hair. 'It's been quite a day. I just want to run through our procedure for tomorrow and then we'll have an evening off.'

Takkis was relieved. 'I feel totally exhausted.'

'First thing tomorrow we'll charge Lakkis Pavlides with attempted murder. He's probably going to claim that the rape of his niece constitutes extenuating circumstances.'

'Except that the doctor says she wasn't raped.'

'Exactly. Another visit to Mr Konstandides, I think. Once he knows Mr Pavlides is to be charged he may be willing to fill in a few more details regarding the event. He might remember the names of his actual attackers. We also want to have his version of the time he spent with Thalia Pavlides. Before we see him we need to speak to Menetakis and advise Stephanotis, or whatever his name really is, that he is to be charged with a double murder and grievous bodily harm. With a bit of luck Menetakis will want him tried in Athens or they may insist he returns to Santorini. Wherever they take him that will get him out of our hair. We still need to find out where he got his money from, but I hope we can pass that over to Athens as well. We're narcotics, not finance.'

Takkis sighed. 'We still don't know who's behind the drug cartel on this island.'

'Yes we do,' Yiorgo contradicted him. 'It has to be Stephanotis, but I doubt whether we'll ever be able to prove it without the co-operation of Lakkis Pavlides. Hopefully with them both out of the way it will be the end of the matter.'

'If Stephanotis is behind it on this island,' Takkis spoke thoughtfully, 'It probably means he's behind it on Kos and Samos.'

Yiorgo nodded. 'When we've finished up here we'll take a little trip over to Kos and see what we can uncover.'

'I'll be glad to get away.'

'We've still got to see what the autopsy results are for the girl.'

Takkis groaned. 'Do we have to stay and deal with that?'

'She's ended up as part of our investigation. We can't leave loose ends. If it looks like dragging on we'll hand it over to the locals. By the way, did Manolis Pavlides say where he had stopped for his drink on the way home?'

'He gave me the name of a couple of places. He thought it was most unlikely they would remember him as they were busy.'

Yiorgo nodded, satisfied. 'I have a feeling we should be able to bring that enquiry to a conclusion fairly soon.'

Takkis raised his eyebrows, but Yiorgo refused to be drawn.

Lukas Menetakis was not amused when he left the station having met with Yiorgo and Takkis. He had expected Dimitris Stephanotis to be charged with manslaughter, not murder, and he had certainly not expected that the police would want to have his accounts examined.

'That's preposterous,' he exclaimed. 'The man's a millionaire.'

Yiorgo shook his head. 'We'd like to know how he made his money. We're asking our finance department to sift through every transaction he has ever made, and believe me; they'll find everything down to the last drachma.'

'His financial transactions have no bearing on the case,' protested Lukas.

'On the murders, I agree, but when we first started our investigations we were looking for drug traffickers. All along the line Dimitris Stephanotis kept cropping up. I don't think that is a coincidence. I'll be interested to hear his explanation at a later date.' Yiorgo smiled at the discomfiture he had caused the lawyer.

Joseph saw the detectives approaching him and inwardly groaned. It was such an effort to remember what he had told them on previous occasions. They drew the curtains around his bed and Takkis stood beside him.

'We're becoming your most regular visitors,' he commented. 'Has anyone else visited you?'

'Why?'

Takkis shrugged. 'I would have thought some of your friends would have come to see you. Is there anyone you would like us to ask?'

'No. I don't need visitors.'

'Passes the time when you're in hospital.'

'What do you want?' asked Joseph testily.

'We thought you'd like to know that Mr Pavlides is being charged with attempted murder. Your statement and the girl's were just what we needed. We have just a couple of questions we'd like to ask you.'

Joseph felt relief flood through him. By the time Lakkis was released from prison he would be well away from Rhodes.

'It's about the young lady, Thalia Pavlides,' continued Takkis.

'What about her?'

'You took her out to dinner one evening, I believe.'

'Yes.'

'And what took place after you had eaten dinner?'

'I walked her home.'

Takkis nodded. 'And did you go into her house?'

Joseph closed his eyes. Thalia had accused him of raping her to the police.

'Yes,' he said finally.

'And what took place whilst you were in her house?'

'We went to bed.'

'The young lady was quite willing to accept your attentions?'

'Yes.' Joseph decided it would be Thalia's word against his, and she had been in no fit state to resist him.

'She did not protest, try to fight you off?'

'No.'

'Who removed her clothes? Did she do so herself?'

'I removed them. She didn't try to stop me.'

Takkis stroked his chin. 'So, in your opinion, did you rape her or seduce her?'

'Seduce her, I suppose.'

'There was no violence on your part?'

'There was no need. She became as anxious as I was.' Joseph gave a lop-sided smile.

'And what did she do afterwards?'

'Went to sleep.'

'Just went to sleep? She didn't say anything to you?'

'We'd had a considerable amount of wine during the evening.'

'So what time did you leave her house?'

'I don't honestly know. Somewhere between one and two, I would think.'

'Did you make any arrangements to see the young lady again?'

'I thought I received a note from her asking me to meet her.'

Takkis raised his eyebrows. 'And what did this note say?'

'She asked me to meet her on the castle walls opposite the road where she lived.'

'When did she suggest this meeting took place?'

'The night Lakkis and his thugs assaulted me.' Joseph spoke bitterly. 'She said she knew nothing about it.'

'When did she say that?' Yiorgo was suddenly alert.

'When she visited me, two days ago.'

'She came to the hospital to see you?'

'Yes. She wanted to know if her uncle had thrown me over the wall. I told her she knew he had as she had set me up by sending me a letter arranging a meeting. That was when she said she knew nothing about it.'

'What else did you talk about whilst she was here?'

'Nothing. She was only here for a couple of minutes.'

'Was that in the morning, or the afternoon?'

'The afternoon. She was in her work suit, so I expect she came straight from her office.'

'She appeared to be perfectly well when she visited you?' asked Takkis.

'I wouldn't know. She didn't stay long enough.'

Takkis sighed deeply. 'I never like to break bad news. Miss Pavlides committed suicide later that same night.'

Joseph looked at Takkis, stunned. 'Why?' he finally asked. 'She was getting married in October. You're sure it was suicide?'

'There's no doubt about that. Now, are you sure there's no one you would like to visit you?'

'Well, it appears the doctor was right. Presumably the girl realised what she'd done and thought she ought to cover her tracks,' smiled Yiorgo. 'Whilst we're here we may as well see if the doctor has his autopsy report ready for us.'

Takkis nodded. 'Then I suppose we'll have to face Maria Pavlides and her son with the details.'

'I think we'll avoid the details and just give them the bare facts.'

The doctor kept them waiting no more than a few minutes. 'Just finished getting it typed up,' he announced. 'Do you want me to go through it whilst you wait for the copies?'

Yiorgo nodded and the doctor pursed his lips.

'The poor girl was subjected to a particularly violent assault. The bruising around her throat shows that she was half throttled, she was probably unconscious whilst the actual rape took place.' He shook his head. 'I can state categorically that it was rape, the extensive bruising to her body, internal bleeding and tearing of the skin and tissues around the area of penetration are conclusive findings. Normal intercourse would not cause that kind of damage.'

'Had she vomited?'

'There is no evidence to show the vomit was hers. Her stomach contents were examined, she had eaten a meal recently, but no spirits had been consumed. The cause of death was loss of blood where she had cut her wrists.'

The doctor's secretary entered quietly and placed three copies of the file into his hands. He passed the copies to Yiorgo. 'The details, in medical jargon, of course, are all there. Let me know if you need anything explained. Now, if you will excuse me.'

Yiorgo nodded. 'I appreciate your help, doctor.'

'Next Maria Pavlides?' asked Takkis.

'No, back to the station. I want to see what forensics can tell us. On the way we'll call at that bar where Manolis Pavlides says he stopped for a drink. They might just remember him.'

The bar tender was unhelpful. He confirmed that they had been busy, but claimed he had no recollection of serving a man of Manolis's description on the night in question. He promised to ask the other bar tenders when they reported in for duty and telephone the station if he had any information.

'I can't say I'm very hopeful on that score,' said Yiorgo. 'If Manolis Pavlides did go in there he was not drunk enough to draw attention to himself.'

Once back at the police station the information from the forensic department was more interesting. The vomit was confirmed to be the remains of a meal mixed with a large quantity of whisky. The stains on the shirt belonging to Manolis matched exactly. Fingerprints had been found, mostly confirmed as belonging to Thalia Pavlides, but there was an unexplained print on the wooden leg of the couch. Forensics had added that her wristwatch had stopped at eighteen minutes before ten in the evening.

Yiorgo's eyes gleamed. 'Now we'll see what that young man has to say about the time he left her house. We'll also get his prints and if they match up with the one on the leg of the couch he's going to have some explaining to do. I'll ask Lambros if we can borrow his car. We can offer Mrs Pavlides a ride up to visit her husband and bring her son in at the same time.'

Maria saw the car draw up and for a moment she thought it was her husband returning. Her hopes were dashed when she saw it was yet another visit from the detectives. She called Manolis from his room and sulkily he agreed to answer some more questions.

'Can you tell me exactly what time you left Miss Pavlides house, please?' asked Yiorgo.

Manolis shrugged. 'About twenty to ten, I expect. It takes about ten minutes to walk there from here.' He sat looking down at his hands.

Maria interrupted. 'You left here at nine twenty. The clock was striking as you shut the door.'

Yiorgo and Takkis looked at the clock on the mantelpiece.

'It chimes every hour and half hour,' Maria informed them, 'but it's ten minutes fast. Lakkis usually adjusts it once a week. I never touch it.'

Takkis looked at his watch. There was a ten-minute discrepancy between his time and that of the mantel clock.

'Maybe I left her earlier, then.'

'Did you go inside the house?'

'Yes. Just to say goodnight to her.'

Yiorgo nodded. 'We called in at the bar where you say you stopped for a drink. The bar tender doesn't remember you, but he agreed they were busy. By your reckoning you should have been in there at about ten minutes to ten?'

'Near enough.' Manolis still looked at his hands. He twisted his large gold signet ring back and forth.

'And you arrived back here at ten thirty, your mother said?'

'I didn't look at the time.'

'How did you know it was that time, Mrs Pavlides?'

'I had just set my alarm clock.'

'So you didn't see your son when he came in?'

'No. I heard him being sick, but that was some time later.'

Manolis shot her a malevolent look.

Yiorgo closed his notebook. 'Thank you. You've both been very helpful.' He smiled at Maria, feeling genuinely sorry for her. 'We brought the car as we thought you might like a ride down to the station to visit your husband.'

'That was thoughtful of you.'

'You also, Mr Pavlides.'

Maria was allowed to visit Lakkis, but Manolis was asked to wait in a side room until he was called.

Yiorgo spoke quietly to a young police officer. 'He's not under arrest, but I want him to be here when I come back. Make sure you have a job where you can watch the door to that room.'

'Where's the doctor's report?' asked Takkis.

Lambros pointed to the pile of files on the table. 'I put them over there. By the way, there was a 'phone call for you from '*Heaven and Hell*', that's a bar on the main road.'

Yiorgo nodded. 'I know what it is. Did they say what they wanted?'

'Asked you to call back.'

Takkis brandished the file he was looking at before Yiorgo's nose. 'Look what it says there. *'Oval contusions on arms and throat, likely to have been caused by a metal object approximately fifteen millimetres long and ten wide.'* That's just about the size of that ring he's wearing.'

'That could be just what we need. Let's hope that print matches his. I'm going to 'phone that bar tender, maybe he's remembered something after all.'

Yiorgo returned from his telephone call with a pleased smile on his face. 'Apparently the other bar man remembers him. Went in about a quarter past ten and was definitely the worse for wear.'

Takkis jotted some figures on his notepad. 'According to mother he left at nine twenty. The girl's watch stopped at nine forty two. He was in a bar at about ten fifteen. That leaves approximately thirty minutes unaccounted for.'

'Right, let's take his prints.'

1991

September – October

Anders steered the cruiser carefully out of Mandraki harbour. The chain fixing the cruiser to the bollard had been removed that morning and they had clearance to sail the vessel back to Piraeus.

He turned and grinned at Frida. 'Where do you fancy?'

'The Caribbean.'

Anders nodded. 'We can easily get lost there for a while. We'll have to moor up somewhere quiet for a paint job, but there are plenty of deserted bays. Have you chosen a name?'

'How about '*Golden Lady*'?'

'She certainly is that. I'll start by unscrewing all the rails and then we'll find out just how golden she really is!'

Yiorgo and Takkis sat at the airport waiting for their flight to Athens. Takkis stretched his arms above his head.

'Thank God that is over. I don't ever want another case like that. We're supposed to deal with narcotics, not murder and suicide.'

'I did feel sorry for Maria Pavlides. She has no one now.'

'Better off without that husband and disgusting son. What finally got to me was when he tried to blame the girl for his actions. Said if she'd been sensible and given in to him he wouldn't have been rough with her. Rough! He damn near killed her. No wonder she took her own life if she thought that treatment was going to be meted out to her on a regular basis.'

Yiorgo took a long draught of his beer. 'I wonder what will happen to Joseph Konstandides? He can't spend the rest of his life in a hospital ward, but he's going to need someone to look after him.'

Takkis shrugged. 'He'll no doubt get by. I have a feeling that he's a survivor.'

Joseph sat in his wheelchair opposite Sorrell and regarded her steadily. 'So what made you come looking for me?'

Sorrell shrugged. 'It doesn't seem important now. I wanted to know why you had framed me for the murder of the hotel worker.'

Joseph threw back his head and laughed. 'You didn't really think I was going to admit to it, did you? You're more stupid than I thought.' He leaned across the table towards her. 'If you hadn't been so devious and given me a false name I would never have been picked up.'

'And you would have left me in jail for life! Thank you very much. I trusted you, Joseph. I knew you were a crook, but I thought you would play it straight with me after the way I had helped you.'

'You should have learnt by now never to trust anyone, least of all me. I'm only interested in what I can get.'

'So how much will it cost me for you to get me a passport?'

'A passport! You must be joking. I have no contacts over here.'

'You must have. You worked for Lakkis. You must know someone.'

Joseph eyed her speculatively; then grinned maliciously. 'I might be able to arrange a passport for you. It will take a considerable amount of time and you'll have to behave yourself and keep to my conditions.'

'What conditions?'

'You have to keep this hovel reasonably clean, do my washing, cook for me and earn your keep.'

Sorrell frowned. 'I can't get a job without a passport or identity card.'

'You'll work the same as Nadia. No work, no money. No money, no little supplies to help you through from day to day. The choice is yours. Go to the police and tell them you have lost your passport. They'll soon make a few enquiries and find out exactly who you are. It would be much more unpleasant in jail this time round. You didn't have a habit last time. They won't give you anything to help as you have withdrawal symptoms. They'll stand and laugh as you rip your clothes to shreds, tear your nails as you claw at the walls and beat your head against the bars in an effort to get rid of the demons.'

Sorrell paled visibly at the description he gave. 'You will help me, won't you, Joseph?'

'Provided you do as you're told. Remember, I can always go to the police and say I have just discovered who you really are.'

'You wouldn't! Please, Joseph, I don't want to go to jail.' Sorrell's lip trembled. 'I just want to go back home.'

'Then you'd better start making some money. Go outside and paint your name above the arch. You'll probably be pretty busy for a few days when word gets round that there's a new girl available.'

Alecos took stock of his situation. He was in charge. He could run *The Grapevine* however he wished, pocketing the profits whilst Lakkis Pavlides was in jail. He would make sure the houses were run for his profit also. Nadia was good for another five years at least and Suzanna for about the same, provided she kept her habit under control. Joseph no longer figured in the business now he was confined to a wheelchair. He was completely at his mercy. If he wanted he could throw him out on the streets and the girl with him. He rubbed his hands together as he totted up the figures in his little book. He was becoming a very successful businessman and when Lakkis Pavlides was finally released he would find that his employee had disappeared.

Maria Pavlides sat in the small apartment that she rented in Lindos. At first she had been at a loss to know what to do with herself. Gradually she came to terms with the fact that her husband and son were both in jail and she was free from the tyranny that had ruled her life for so many years. She could make a new beginning.

She had turned her hand to water colours to pass the time and a restaurant had agreed to hang a few for her. She had sold two so far and the money had made a difference to her meagre income. She still had the jewellery that she had found in the safe at their house, but she did not dare to sell it for fear that it was stolen. Maybe, one day, just before Lakkis was due to be released, she would turn it into cash and move to another island where he would not be able to find her.

1994

Giovanni nodded. 'I'll have a word with the bank manager on that. I have other plans for our profit. Do you want to hear them?'

Marianne waited, expecting her husband to begin to outline grandiose plans for the extension of their self-catering holiday business.

'I want to take you away for a few days. You've earned it.' He leant forward seriously. 'I can't afford to take you over to America to see your mother, but I thought we could have a few days away, on our own. Where would you like to go?'

Marianne looked at him in surprise. 'I'd not considered going anywhere.'

'We don't have any bookings for the last week of the season. We could actually have a last minute holiday and behave like holiday makers.'

'Maybe we could go to Ierapetra?'

'Do you want to go there?'

'Well,' Marianne considered, 'I've heard it's very popular.'

'We could drive down there on a nice weekend. I was thinking of somewhere a little further afield. How do you fancy Rhodes?'

'Why Rhodes?'

'If we do hit a spell of bad weather there is plenty to see and do over there. I know how you enjoy going around the historical sites. The medieval city is supposed to be unique.'

'What about John? He won't be interested in wandering around.'

'John will stay with Ourania. I've already spoken to her and she's quite happy to look after him for a few days. He'll be at school, so she'll be free to run the shop during the day and Yannis says he will do it in the evening.'

'You've got it all worked out, haven't you?' Marianne smiled. 'Suppose I had said I didn't want to go away?'

Giovanni ran a finger down her spine and she shivered. 'I could try exerting my charms to persuade you.' He kissed her neck and Marianne pushed him away.

'It's eleven in the morning, Giovanni!'

'What difference does the time of day make?'

Marianne pretended to consider as he took her hand, pulling her gently towards him.

Marianne and Giovanni found the medieval town on Rhodes enchanting. Marianne had insisted they visit the Palace of the Grand Masters and all the museums. 'We can go to the beach in Crete, but we can't see this every day. I couldn't bear to go back home knowing I had missed so much history.'

Giovanni indulged her, although he was more interested in studying the menus at the various tavernas and checking their prices. 'What do you want to do today?'

'Why don't we walk around inside the town this morning? This afternoon I'd like to do the wall walk, provided it isn't too hot. We've been so lucky with the weather.'

'It shouldn't take that long. We could go for a swim afterwards, or go this morning and return in time to do the walk? We've already walked in the old town.' Giovanni squinted up at the sun.

'No, I want to see the residential parts. I've seen enough jewellers' shops to last me for ever.'

'And you still can't see anything you'd like me to buy for you.' Giovanni squeezed her hand.

Marianne shook her head. 'I have the only piece of jewellery I want.'

Giovanni consulted his map of the old town. 'That should lead us to another gate; the Athanasiou.'

Leisurely they strolled down the cobbled streets, ignoring the map and taking to side turnings as they took their fancy, until they finally entered a small, neglected square. Giovanni pulled the map from his pocket and studied it carefully.

'If we cut up through that street there I think we should come out by the gate. There's really nothing to see here.'

Marianne giggled. 'That depends what you're looking for. I think we've found the red light district!'

Giovanni held her hand tighter, but Marianne insisted on dawdling along the narrow road, reading the names of the girls that were scrawled on the walls in red paint. 'Anna, Elena, Natasha – since when has that been a Greek name?'

'They're probably not all Greek girls.'

'I wonder what they're like?' mused Marianne. 'If you stood next to them in a shop, would you know?'

'There's one in her doorway,' whispered Giovanni. 'You can see for yourself.'

Marianne slowed and took in the girl who was lounging against the stone wall of her doorway. There was something familiar about her. As they drew level with the doorway they could read the name *'Suzi'* painted above and a man could be seen sitting in the courtyard in a wheelchair. He looked out at them. Giovanni stiffened perceptibly whilst Marianne drew in her breath sharply.

'Giovanni…'

'Walk on,' he ordered his wife.

As they passed, the woman glared at Marianne with hatred in her eyes and spat after their retreating backs.

By the time they turned the corner, Marianne was shaking and Giovanni put his arms around her.

'It was them, wasn't it?' she asked.

If you have enjoyed reading *Joseph*, you will be pleased to know that the next book in the continuing saga – *Christabelle* – is planned for publication in November 2009.

See overleaf for a 'taster' of what is to come.

For up-to-date information, have a look at the author's website:

www.beryldarby.co.uk

1994 – 1996

Christabelle studied herself critically in the full length mirror. As long as she could remember she had heard people compliment her mother on having such a beautiful daughter. She was just eighteen, well proportioned and with long shapely legs. She held her hair up on her head. That certainly gave her a sophisticated appearance. She spent some minutes fixing it in place before looking again at the magazine that lay open on her bed. She copied the pose of the model, shoulders back, hips thrust forward and her head tilted to the right, her left arm extended above her head and slightly to the side as if she were leaning against a column.

She turned the pages until she came to the next advertisement, sat down at her dressing table, rested her chin on her hand, and stared intently into the mirror. For the next hour she amused herself by experimenting with her hair in different styles. It was a shame that so many of the models were blonde or were wearing their hair straight. It made it difficult for her to compare her own looks with theirs. Finally bored she flipped through the magazine to see if there were any articles that would interest her, anything to delay starting her homework that she needed to hand in the following day.

Unable to put off her school work any longer she pulled the books towards her. Provided she handed in something she really did not care what kind of a grade she received. Her only interests were travel and fashion. She looked at the questions that were meaningless to her. She would telephone Dolores. If she couched her questions and remarks carefully she could usually rely on her friend giving her the answers that she needed.

Picking up her papers she went down to the lounge, grimacing as she saw her mother leaning back on the sofa, Henry stroking her leg whilst he alternately whispered in her ear and kissed her neck.

'I need to use the phone.'

Anna frowned in annoyance at her daughter's intrusion and pushed Henry away from her. She had just been about to suggest that they retired to her room where they would be more comfortable and Henry could carry out his whispered suggestions.

Christabelle turned her back on them and dialled Dolores number. 'Hi, Dol, how you doing? Isn't that homework the pits! What did you make of it?'

For half an hour Christabelle monopolised the telephone, making notes as Dolores unwittingly gave her the information she had been seeking, finally replacing the receiver with a pleased smile on her face. She collected her papers together and without a word to her mother left the room, closing the door firmly behind her. She was thankful there was the bathroom between her room and her mother's bedroom so she would not have to hear them when they would undoubtedly mount the stairs to complete the activities they had started on the sofa.

Christabelle sipped her orange juice thoughtfully. She would have to have a portfolio of photographs taken and she was not at all sure how much that would cost her. If she did not have sufficient in her savings account it would be no good asking her mother for a loan or some extra money. Anna always pleaded poverty.

She debated whether to take Dolores into her confidence. It was possible that she would lend her some money. She would promise to repay it by giving her the money she earned at the supermarket stocking shelves at the weekend.

'I do wish you would knock before you come bursting into the lounge,' Anna complained as she saw her daughter sitting at the kitchen bar.

Christabelle ignored her.

'It's bad manners, you know. Henry was most embarrassed.'

Christabelle slipped off the stool at the eating bar. 'I think I should be the one to be embarrassed. You and Henry were behaving disgustingly as usual.'

'We were not. We were just having a little cuddle.'

'With his hand up your skirt! Dirty little man.'

'He's not. He's a very nice man. He's taking me out for dinner tonight.' Anna smiled contentedly. 'I'm going to wear that new dress he bought me last week.'

'Really. Well, I hope you enjoy yourselves and behave better in a restaurant than you do when you're at home.'

'We may come back afterwards, so please knock if you want to come into the lounge and use the phone.'

'I'll do no such thing. I live here. I should be able to walk freely into the lounge whenever I wish. Tell Henry to keep his hands to himself then he'll have no need to be embarrassed.' Christabelle picked up her jacket and her bag of books and slammed the kitchen door behind her.

Christabelle opened the folder of photographs and studied them critically. Brajowski had done a good job. Each one did justice to her undeniable beauty and perfect figure. She shuddered involuntarily as she pored over those of her naked and in risqué poses. How she had hated the way he had touched her as he had altered her position, his hands had lingered unnecessarily on her breasts and legs and it had taken all her will power not to scream and run from the studio.

For a while she sat lost in thought, then a secretive smile crept over her face. She would get her revenge for the indignities she had suffered. First she would decide on the number of copies she wanted. A second visit to the studio would give her the opportunity to check on her idea and when she collected the extra prints she would be prepared to carry her plan through. What a shock he would get! She giggled to herself at the unintentional pun as she sorted the photographs, selecting only those where she was fully clothed to show her mother.

Anna looked at them cursorily. 'You certainly photograph well. I'll look at them properly later. I'm meeting Kurt for dinner and I really should get showered and changed or I shall be late.'

'Kurt?' she asked.

Anna smiled happily. 'He's so good looking. I'm sure you're going to like him.'

Christabelle raised her eyebrows. 'Really? What's happened to Henry?'

'Oh, I got tired of Henry. Kurt is so delightful. His family came over here from Germany after the war. His father was in the army, of course, but he's really a carpenter. He has his own business. Kurt had the opportunity to go into it with him, but he says he's no good with his hands.' Anna gave a little giggle. 'His family live in San Francisco and he's promised to take me there.'

Christabelle bit at her lips in frustration and annoyance. Why did her mother never have time for her? 'I really wanted to talk to you about them.'

'Surely we can talk later, dear? What's so urgent about a few photographs?'

Christabelle took a deep breath. 'I plan to send them off to modelling agencies.'

Anna raised her eyebrows. 'What makes you think you're attractive enough to be a model?'

'You've just said I photograph well. I know I look as good as any of the models in the magazines. It's just a question of showing them to the right people.'

'And how are you going to meet the right people? What on earth do you want to be a model for anyway?'

'I want to travel. I want to see America and go over to Europe.'

'You could be an air hostess and do that.'

'I'd never see anywhere. No sooner have you arrived than you have to get the plane ready for a return journey. I want to be free to travel around wherever I fancy.'

'You'll probably change your mind over the next couple of years.' Anna rose and handed the photographs back to her daughter.

'I'm not waiting a couple of years. I want to start now.'

Anna frowned. 'You haven't finished high school yet. You can't possibly think about a modelling career until you've completed your education.'

Christabelle drew herself up to her full height. 'I intend to start as soon as possible. If I wait until I've finished college I shall be too old. You need to start young if you are to get to the top and I'm already eighteen.'

Anna smiled deprecatingly. 'You think you will become a top model?'

'I intend to be the most famous model in the world, not just America,' stated Christabelle, a determined set to her mouth.

'Very ambitious of you. I'll talk to Kurt about your idea and see what he thinks.'

'This has nothing to do with Kurt.'

'Oh, it could do. He is such a delightful character. I think I may have met the one man who would make an ideal daddy for you.'

Christabelle's lips curled in disgust. 'How many times have you said that to me about your different boyfriends? I've had more prospective 'daddies' than I can count.'

'Kurt is different. Now, I really must go and have my shower or I shall be very late.'

Christabelle looked mutinously at her mother as she left the room. There was no way she was going to stop her from achieving her ambition. She collected up the photographs and returned to her bedroom. She needed the reprints and a contract; then would be the time to deal with her mother and Kurt also if the need arose.

to be continued...

Beryl Darby

YANNIS

A continuing saga

First book

The compelling story of Yannis, who comes from the village of Plaka on the island of Crete. He attends school in the town of Aghios Nikolaos and gains a scholarship to the Gymnasium in Heraklion.

Whilst in Heraklion, he is diagnosed with leprosy, shattering his dreams of becoming an archaeologist. He is admitted to the local hospital for treatment and subsequently transferred to the hospital in Athens. The conditions in the hospital are appalling: overcrowding, lack of amenities, poor food, and only basic medication. The inmates finally rebel, resulting in their exile to Spinalonga, a leper colony just across the water from Yannis's home village.

The book tells the heart-rending account of his life on the small island, his struggle for survival, his loves and losses, along with that of his family on the mainland from 1918 to 1979.

Second book

In this, the second book in a continuing saga, Anna is left to care
for her invalid mother and her sister's children when the Germans
invade Crete. A battalion of Italian soldiers is billeted in the village
to prevent a seat of resistance being formed on Spinalonga, the
leper village opposite the village.

There are resistance workers in the area.

How will she protect strong-willed Marisa from the Italian
soldiers, and impulsive Yannis from joining the resistance?

Unwillingly she becomes involved with the resistance and has
to draw on all her resources and ingenuity to fool the Italians,
finally risking her life to save the man she loves.

Beryl Darby

GIOVANNI

The third book in a continuing saga of a Cretan family

Third book

Yannis has become a successful businessman with a number of hotels. He has taken his resourceful nephew, Giovanni, into partnership. Giovanni is full of ideas to improve the business. He has only one failing – he is susceptible to a pretty face.

His younger brother, Joseph, is resentful of Giovanni's success and determined to avenge himself. With the help of a beautiful woman, he schemes and plans to bring about his brother's disgrace. His final act of revenge has dire results for all involved.

Marianne, Annita's granddaughter, visits Athens with her friend and meets relatives who were previously unknown to her. Elizabeth finds the city romantic in many ways. Later they both visit Crete, which has unexpected consequences for Marianne.

Yannis's loyalty to his extended family saves all of them from shame and humiliation.